Dawn
of the
Sister

B J MEARS

The Dream Loft

First published in Great Britain in 2016 by The Dream Loft
www.thedreamloft.co.uk

Graphic design by The Dream Loft.

ISBN 13: 978-0-9956264-0-9
ISBN 10: 0-9956264-0-5

For Mum and Dad

*

Special thanks:
To Joy for your support and encouragement,
to my ever-diligent editor, Edward Field,
and to all the friends who have
helped along the way.

'For now we see through a glass, darkly; but then face to face: now I know in part; but then shall I know even as also I am known.'

1 Corinthians 13 v 12 (King James Bible)

'Victory at all costs, victory in spite of terror, victory however long and hard the road may be; for without victory, there is no survival.'

Winston Churchill

Contents

Glossary of Terms

Brimstone Chasm: a setting and specific power of the contrap (a portal into a Hell-like realm).

contrap: a ghost machine with ten settings, each corresponding to an individual power or ability, powered by ghosts trapped within its realms.

contrapassi: jackal-headed, armoured giants (singular: contrapasso) of the *Brimstone Chasm*.

cloak/cloaked/cloaking: the ability of ghosts to become invisible upon demand (this uses energy and cannot be sustained for extended periods).

Flight: a setting and specific power of the contrap (giving one the power of flight).

Forager: surveillance software created by Melissa Watts.

Future Eye: a setting and specific power of the contrap (through which one can view the ghosts' conclusions about the future).

gallows iron: iron nails drawn from gallows or from coffins, or any other iron associated with death. Gallows iron has the ability to send ghosts on to another place.

GAUNT machine: (Guided Analytic Utility Necro Transducer) a machine that retrieves ghosts from the under realms and inserts them into the living bodies of selected victims to create *gloved* ghosts (gloves). During the process the victim's body takes on the dominant form of the ghost and is left with a faint blue glow to the skin.

GCHQ: the UK Government Communications Head-quarters.

Ghost Portal: a setting and specific power of the contrap (a portal into a ghostly realm).

Ghost Squad: Tyler's selected team of ghost spies.

gloves: ghosts paired and joined (gloved) with living people.

GPS: Global Positioning System.

Heart: a setting and specific power of the contrap (switching to the heart symbol turns the contrap into its ghost form).

Hell birds: huge, dangerous birds of the *Brimstone Chasm*.

JIC: Joint Intelligence Committee

langseax: (long seax) an angular, single-bladed Saxon longsword, the seax being the weapon from which the term Saxon derived.

liliths: winged she-demons of the *Brimstone Chasm*.

murder holes: holes set into the ceiling behind a portcullis in European medieval castles through which boiling fluids and burning wood could be dropped on attackers.

NVF: originally revealed as *New Vision Frontiers*, the NVF is an underground neo-Nazi organisation, the Nazi Victorious Federation.

Past Eye: a setting and specific power of the contrap (through which the past can be viewed).

Present Eye: a setting and specific power of the contrap (through which the present can be viewed).

reveries: ghosts who have hung around their grave sites for so long they have become zombie-like. Prolonged proximity to reveries results in a zombie-like condition for the living, and ultimately leads to suicide.

Safeguarding Skull: a setting and specific power of the contrap (prolonging life, promoting healing and preventing death).

SOCO: Scene Of Crime Officers (UK's forensics police).

TAAN: The Activists Against Nazism.

Tower of Doom: a setting and specific power of the contrap, and the tower within the *Brimstone Chasm* (a device measuring one's progress and a means of locational guidance).

the oppressor: an ancient evil spirit/fallen angel who has appeared throughout history in the guise of men (Hitler amongst them).

Tree of Knowledge: a setting and specific power of the contrap (ghosts within the contrap answer questions).

wilco: military call sign meaning 'received' and 'I will comply'.

Agents & Code Names

Freddy Carter:	*Pratt*
Lucy Denby (Mojo):	*Pointer*
Melissa Watts:	*Cog*
Tyler May:	*Ghost*

(*Weaver, Klaus* and *Chapman* are known only by their code names)

Tyler's Notes

Rules of the Contrap

1. *Never use the contrap for too long. The ghosts within only have so much power and it could shut down when you need it the most.*
2. *Always use the balancing spell after releasing or collecting ghosts. Failure to do so may have catastrophic consequences!*

THE CONTRAP

BACK

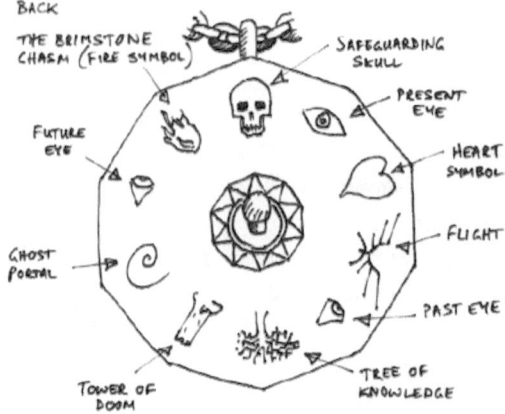

THE BRIMSTONE
CHASM (FIRE SYMBOL)

SAFEGUARDING
SKULL

PRESENT
EYE

FUTURE
EYE

HEART
SYMBOL

FLIGHT

GHOST
PORTAL

PAST EYE

TOWER OF
DOOM

TREE OF
KNOWLEDGE

SYMBOLS

- SAFEGUARDING SKULL — SAVES FROM DEATH
- PRESENT EYE — LOOK THROUGH WALLS, ETC (TELESCOPIC).
- HEART SYMBOL
- FLIGHT — MAKES YOU FLY!
- PAST EYE — LOOK INTO THE PAST!
- TREE OF KNOWLEDGE — ASK IT A QUESTION & IT ANSWERS
- TOWER OF DOOM — ACHIEVEMENT INDICATOR
- GHOST PORTAL — IT'S A GHOST PORTAL!
- FUTURE EYE — LOOK INTO THE FUTURE
- FIRE SYMBOL — ?   THE BRIMSTONE CHASM

FRONT

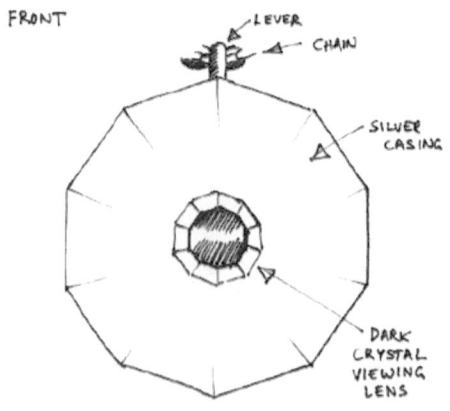

LEVER

CHAIN

SILVER
CASING

DARK
CRYSTAL
VIEWING
LENS

Contraption: (noun) a machine or device that appears strange or unnecessarily complicated, and often badly made or unsafe.

synonyms: device, gadget, apparatus, machine, appliance, mechanism, implement, utensil, invention, contrivance.

Etymology unknown. Perhaps from contrive + trap + -tion, contrivance + adaption, **cantrip (Scots dialect), a wilful piece of trickery.**

The world is at war.
South America has become
the NVF underground stronghold.

Reports substantiating rumours of
the NVF's ongoing murder of Jewish
populations and other non-Aryan
ethnicities are reaching the West.

The threat of nuclear war is ever
present and ghosts are rife across
the globe. The stronger ones can
move small objects in the physical
world. Most are able to carry
gallows blades: thin, light blades
of iron associated with death.
All ghosts have the power to
become invisible to the living.

Prologue

The two girls stole into the stark graveyard to walk with purpose between its tilting gravestones. The crunch of their boots on the late frost of the grass stirred shrill birdsong from the shade of the encompassing trees. Tyler May and Melissa Watts stood over the freshly dug soil heap of Weaver's grave and glanced around. They waited and watched in the chilled, earth-tainted air for several minutes before calling.

"Lucy? Lucy, are you here?" Tyler's breath fogged the air. A solitary raven flapped free of a grove, its raucous *caw* the only reply, and she felt the resuming stillness like the cold against her prickling skin. "There are ghosts in this place. Hidden ghosts."

"Nice try, but we have to face it: She's not here." Melissa turned away. "We should go."

Tyler cocked her head at a movement near the perimeter and stalled Melissa with a hand. In the shadows of an ancient yew, a phantom lingered. Tyler squinted in the sunlight struggling to discern translucent features.

Are you one of the good guys, or something else?

"Mojo? Is that you?" She stepped closer. "Lucy?"

The ghost of Lucy Denby, the sharp-shooting, knife-throwing Goth agent, ambled from the shade. Her confident but nonetheless *dead* eyes speared Tyler.

"I thought you might look for me here," she said. "I would have come to you eventually, I guess."

"Lucy, I'm sorry."

"Sorry I saved all those people from the bomb, or sorry I'm dead? Or do you mean sorry that you and Klaus are still alive?"

She's got even worse!

Tyler rolled her eyes and exhaled a long breath.

"I'm grateful you saved us. I'm sorry you died. It's not the way I wanted it."

"Yeah, well, we don't get to choose the way it is. We just get to play our part. And I'm all played out. From here on in, it's just you and Mel. Oh, and Klaus. We mustn't forget Klaus."

"It doesn't have to be like that, Mojo. We brought someone to see you." Tyler turned towards the gates and called out. "We found her."

Uncloaking into visibility the ghost of a handsome, sharply dressed, young agent entered through the gates. Weaver approached Lucy and the two embraced. Pulling away, he held her by the shoulders and smiled.

"You're back."

Lucy glanced down at her ghost body. "In black."

Melissa interrupted their reunion.

"There's something I have to say, Lucy. It's been bugging me for a while. I once called you an arrogant, stuck-up, spoilt blood-sucker. It was behind your back and it was unfair. I'm sorry. I was wrong."

"I know," smirked Lucy, watching Melissa squirm.

"What? You knew I said that?"

Lucy nodded.

"You learn a lot of things when you die."

An Excellent
Question

Harrow's End, 6 Nash Lane, Bromley, London

Morning light streamed across the kitchen table where Tyler sat cradling the contrap, a ghost machine so complex that it almost defied description. She stroked a finger across its silver casing. With its switch set to the *Ghost Portal* she could see the ghosts inside, the murky rolling landscape of memory mist and the Distant City on the horizon. She also saw the planet-like orb, floating over everything. She glared venomously back at this vast, black eye through the crystal lens.

"You want to spy? Spy on this!"

She snatched the contrap's chain from around her neck and hurried out to the rear garden, slamming the back door of her reclusive Victorian home on her way.

Behind the brick-built garage a pile of grey walling stones waited, one of which was large and flat. She dragged this out and dumped the contrap onto its surface, returning a moment later with another of the stones, one the size of a small loaf of bread. She glanced around.

Good. Alone.

She poised the stone ready to smash the contrap, summoning courage as the ghost of a plump, aged Russian woman named Izabella appeared before her. The ghost's puckered face bored into her peripheral vision.

"That would be unwise." Izabella's flowery, tent-like dress, once tattered and torn by trials in the *Brimstone Chasm*, was now unblemished having returned to an older and stronger state of memory. She studied Tyler through cataract-clouded eyes.

Glaring, Tyler delayed the blow, the hammer-stone barely ten centimetres from its target.

"Why? What would happen?"

Izabella pursed her lips as the wrinkles of her face deepened.

"In truth, I do not know. And that is why you must desist."

"The dark planet of the *Ghost Portal* sky – the enormous eye – it's the *Black Sun*. It *has* to be! That means it's to do with the oppressor and it keeps appearing in there each time the contrap switches itself. I have to destroy it. It's evil! You told me so yourself! Some other force is controlling the contrap. It's taking over and I can't let that happen." She quietened. "I can't let it win."

"I understand, and you *will* destroy the contrap – I've

sworn to help you do so – but not today." Izabella waved at the stones dismissively. "*This* is not the way. It could unleash immeasurable horrors: doom, death and destruction, pain and torment, the running and the screaming and the like." She waved again, shrugging off the idea. "You *are* aware the oppressor wishes to merge the realms? I fear you might hand him his goal on a platter."

Tyler let the hammer-stone fall harmlessly to the ground, her ferocity ebbing.

"Then how *can* I do it?"

Izabella stared at the contrap.

"That, my dear girl, is an excellent question."

*

Thames House, MI5 London HQ

My name is Tyler May. I am nineteen and I'm a ghost haunter. Yes, you heard correctly. Haunter, not hunter. I haunt ghosts by utilising their powers: to fly, look into the past, spy through walls, and communicate with ghosts of the under realms. I know that sounds crazy. It is crazy. And, at times, terrifying.

The contrap – the ghost machine I use when I'm ghost haunting – has ten symbols, each giving the wearer a different ability when selected with the machine's little switch. The contrap was once taken from me by a ghoul who fished it out of the Thames. I took it back with the use of a can of Mace, but while it was out of my hands the gloved ghost of Josef Mengele used it to set an ancient evil spirit free, kicking off world war three in the process. It's...

...complicated.

Tyler switched off her phone's voice recorder app.

Melissa, the blonde intellectual and IT *super-brain*, sat on a canteen chair next to her and sipped tea.

"What you doing?"

"It's a voice diary. Apparently I need to get my thoughts in order. I'm going to make a big list of everything that's happened."

"Why?"

"It's hard to explain but I've had this feeling I'm missing something, had it for a long time. You know? Anyway, Dr. Moores says I have to do it for my own sanity."

"Your shrink gave you *homework*?"

Glowering, Tyler nodded.

Melissa frowned.

"I don't understand. We have the contrap. We have the gallows ring and we know how to use it to control the reveries. We have a crack assassin ghost who can take out anything at thirty paces with a gallows blade. We have an entire ghost army – not to mention TAAN's six thousand street warriors – just waiting for the word to march. We have the backing of the *company*. What can we possibly be missing?"

Tyler recalled the featureless black eye, an unquantifiable, sinister entity observing her from within the contrap.

If it is behind the contrap's recent odd behaviour, Melissa's list is nowhere near long enough. Exactly what lurks on the other side of the Ghost Portal? *The oppressor's spies are everywhere, I'm sure. The list of surviving gloves has grown to eight, and they're only the ones we know of.*

She changed the subject.

"You're in an annoyingly chipper mood today. Is Freddy staying over?"

"Hmmm." Melissa smiled wistfully. "Do you think Klaus will ever propose?"

"I don't know but, if he does, our kids are going to have perfect teeth. Anyway, I'm recording some stuff in the hope I'll spot something. Figured it couldn't do any harm. Want to help?"

"Not really. I'm working on a new version of Forager and I'm in the middle of a research project. You know how it is – have to keep my head in the zone."

"Fine."

Melissa forked salad into her mouth as Tyler continued to record and detail her run-in with Mengele five years previously on the bank of the Thames. She backtracked to voice a note about the gloves.

Shortly after I found the contrap, ghosts appeared. Yes, they appeared to me in the machine, but others also glimpsed them elsewhere. In an hour, their status went from mythical to scientific fact, and now it's common for the general populous to notice them around.

More sinister was a new phenomenon that pre-empted the arrival of the phantoms in our world – gloved ghosts – ghosts recovered from the other side, paired with and housed in, the bodies of innocent living victims.

A neo-Nazi, Leopold Bagshot-McGuire, was respons-ible. He headed up a team that created the GAUNT machine and did the unthinkable. They brought back Nazi war criminals. The gloved ghosts take on a physical form in mortal flesh. The kidnapped children Bagshot used are hidden and trapped inside this form, dominated by the ghost. They call it the 'dominant force'.

She listed the current gloves at large. Those she knew of.

Angel (the ghosts of Josef Mengele and Adolf Hitler, AKA the oppressor) – gloved with Steven Lewis
The ghost of Adolf Eichmann – gloved with Harry McGrath
The ghost of Reinhard Heydrich – gloved with Susan Ellis
The ghost of Otto Keller – victim unknown
The ghost of Elisabeth Schneider – victim unknown
The ghost of Walter Ebner – victim unknown
The ghost of Wilhelm Huber – victim unknown
The ghost of Friedrich Lange – victim unknown

There is an oddity: Their skin is iridescent. We have yet to establish why. They try to hide their glow using makeup and wearing gloves, hats and scarfs, but darkness reveals their true nature, the peculiarity impossible to conceal; their hands, their faces, any skin not clothed, glows a pale shade of blue.

We traced and acquired artefacts for each of the original six gloved ghosts. Sneaked and spied. Snooped and stole.

Himmler obliterated Hitler's glasses outside Westminster Cathedral. Now Hitler's the only one we need an artefact for. To use the contrap's magnetic draw on Angel, I'll need Mengele's artefact and one for Hitler or it won't work. I know the draw can work. I used it firstly on Hitler before he escaped the portal, and later on Goebbels. I carry the artefacts in my bag.

Where I go, they go.

It turns out Hitler's ghost is also a spirit they call the oppressor. He wants to merge the under realms. We can only speculate at the chaos this would inflict on our world.

One of the gloves, Reinhard Heydrich, we refer to as Lord of the Reveries. There's a good reason for that. Reveries are ghosts who have hung around their own graves for too long. Albert says this leaves them depressed to a point of oblivion. Soul hungry, they will drain the will of any spirit, living or other, who ventures near. Bad news: Heydrich has a ring of gallows iron that controls reveries.

Good news: so does Mel.

The contrap is the link to the under realms and has two portals. The oppressor will do anything to get his hands on it. I hope to destroy it before that happens.

The Ghost Portal *can be viewed or entered through the contrap's crystal. It is a realm of the dead.*

I know.

I've been there.

In the Ghost Portal there's a place called the Shivering Pool, a phantom pool of water unlike any other. It will suck your will dry like a reverie and drown you in its apathetic depths. Most that enter never emerge. They are lost forever.

Do not drink its waters.

There's a second realm, also. The Brimstone Chasm *is a bad place.*

I've been there, too.

It smoulders. Everything in there smoulders. Cruel monsters rule its lands. They torture spirits who are no longer fully ghost. Entering the Chasm changes a spirit into a half-ghost state. A ghost with a semi-translucent, yet physical body. One that can suffer hunger, thirst and pain.

Like I said, the Brimstone Chasm *is a bad place.*

I put Bagshot and Himmler into the Portal. Later we discovered Mordecai chains and I took Himmler, Goebbels and Bagshot from the portal and threw them, chained, into the Chasm, leaving them in the tower's oubliette. Back then we didn't know about gallows iron and its ability to send a ghost on. Whatever that means.

Staring blindly into space, she recalled her venture into the Chasm. The endless daily suffering of the starving half-ghosts toiling in the contrapassi death camps. The boiling day. The freezing night. The *second death*, a perpetual cycle of murder and re-emergence that allowed such a torturous existence.

The torturers, giant beasts twice as tall as men, are covered in shaggy fur and have the heads of jackals. The contrapassi wear brazen armour and sport a variety of weapons: machine guns, whips, scimitars, clubs and more.

Solace came in two forms alone.

When in the Chasm I had miraculous wings of flame. I don't know why, but they appeared each time I found hope. The wings helped.

The Tower of Doom *was the second respite: a relatively safe and stable retreat from the outside horrors, with a table enchanted to provide food and drink in a high chamber. The tower was considerably better than its name suggests.*

She clicked the recorder off and glanced at Melissa's plate.

"Give me steak any day."

"You can keep your steak. I happen to like salad."

Tyler turned her nose up.

"I want to destroy the contrap. I'm going to trace the owners of the contrap right back as far as I can.

Hopefully I'll learn something useful."

Mel looked up.

"Good idea. What do you have so far?"

Tyler took out her notebook and turned to the page where she had begun to create a timeline of the contrap's previous owners. Melissa leaned closer.

Circa 1650   *Eucrates Onuris IV*

↓

Ramla

↓

Hemmings

(Zebedee's great uncle, unwitting owner)

↓

Circa 1880   *Zebedee Lieberman*

↓

~~*Circa 1900*~~   *Orealia Stephensen (Anna)*

DOD: 27th **March 1891**   ↓

Myah Dorf (Orealia's sister)

↓

Ivan Kremensky (father of)

↓

Circa 1945   *Izabella Olga Kremensky*

(& Valentina Kremensky)

Beneath this initial chart Tyler had left a gap of several lines. Below this were listed the names of the more recent owners.

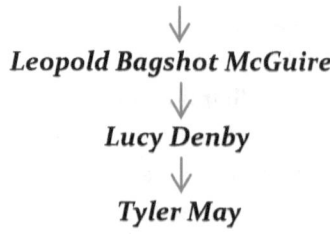

Leopold Bagshot McGuire

Lucy Denby

Tyler May

"There's this gap between Izabella and Bagshot. That period of the contrap's past is a mystery. Same thing before Eucrates Onuris IV. We don't know who had it then, where it came from or who made it. I figured if I could find out how it was created I might learn how to destroy it."

"It would be easier to work out who had it after Izabella."

"I know."

"My guess is that Josef Mengele acquired it somehow and used it to help him hide out after the war. That's why he could use it when he fished it out of the Thames. Have you asked Izabella? Maybe she knows who had it after her. Maybe she gave it to someone, or bequeathed it in her will."

*

Harrow's End, 6 Nash Lane, Bromley

Izabella Olga Kremensky had left no will. Nor did she have any heir to whom she may have left her worldly possessions. Tyler booted her laptop and reread Izabella's obituary while Albert Goodwin, the ghost of a chimney sweep's boy, watched from across the living room. Albert always watched over Tyler. That was his unofficial job, an unspoken arrangement that suited Tyler fine.

Izabella Olga Kremensky, previously of Harrogate, daughter of the late Ivan Kremensky, died recently during a sightseeing tour of Germany. Izabella, who enjoyed the early years of her life in London, emigrated to her ancestral homeland of Russia some years ago, where she continued to prosper. The University of London wishes to express its belated thanks to Izabella for her generously bequeathed library of more than four thousand books. The executor of the will would hear from any claimants with ancestral relations to Izabella, who leaves no apparent heir to her significant remaining fortune.

"Izabella, are you there?"

Izabella appeared, hunched in the doorway. She shuffled closer.

"What do you want?"

"What happened to the contrap when you died?"

Izabella peered out of the Victorian bay window at the road and fields beyond.

"I don't know."

"It says here you died during a sightseeing tour of Germany. Where exactly did you die, if you don't mind me asking?"

"As it happens I do mind. I don't want to talk about it." Izabella huffed and turned away.

"What? What is it?" pressed Tyler.

"I said I don't want to talk about it."

"But it could be important." Tyler watched Izabella's rounded shoulders heave. "Why won't you talk to me?"

"I have to go."

When Izabella had waddled away, cloaking into

invisibility, Tyler asked Albert.

"Find Zebedee, will you?"

Albert left, reappearing moments later in the room with Zebedee in tow.

"How may I assist, Miss May?" Zebedee doffed his top hat.

"It's Izabella. She won't talk about her death. All I asked was where it happened and she clammed right up. You have a way with her. See what you can find out."

"Why do you wish to know about her death?"

"I'm researching the past owners of the contrap and there's a gap after her name. I want to know what happened to it next. It could be important."

"Right you are. I'll be back in a jiffy." Zebedee cloaked.

"How long *is* a jiffy?"

*

The next day Zebedee reported back to Tyler, a weary look on his face.

"Did you find out? What did she say?"

Zebedee stroked his beard.

"She's a sullen old trout, but I had her talking in the end. She's ashamed. That's why she doesn't want to talk about her death."

"Why?"

"You know she was on a sightseeing tour of Germany when it happened?"

"Yes."

"That isn't the exact truth. In 1948 she left Russia on a quest, of sorts. Her aim was to collect as many ghosts into the contrap as possible, to make it more powerful, you understand. Her tour *did* begin in Germany, as her obituary suggests, but it was inaccurate. She didn't die in

Germany but in Poland."

"Poland? But why would she go to... Wait a minute. Nineteen forty-eight, that's three years after World War Two ended." Tyler recalled countless ghostly faces within the *Ghost Portal*, all of them victims of Nazi concentration camps, and everything fell into place. "She collected ghosts from death camps?"

"Yes, though now she is appalled by her actions."

"What happened?"

Wilson's Old & New

Zebedee lit his pipe and smoked while pacing.

"Do you *really* wish to know? It's quite an ugly story."

"Zebedee..."

"All right." He raised a submissive palm. "I'll tell you. After the war Auschwitz-Birkenau, the Nazi death camp, was opened to the public as a museum of the holocaust. It was an obvious choice for Izabella's grim quest. She visited the site during the day as part of a tour and noted the rooms full of artefacts left behind by the Nazis. These artefacts were the possessions of the dead, you understand; shoes, clothes, photographs, thousands of them, all just waiting for Izabella to use with the contrap. She revisited that night when the place was closed. She used the contrap to help her break in and visited room after room of artefacts where she summoned thousands of ghosts, collecting them in the *Ghost Portal*. A despicable act, I know! But there we are. She was leaving when–"

Izabella uncloaked, ashen-faced.

"I was leaving when somebody who must have been tailing me struck me over the head. I dropped dead. My murderer took the contrap and reaped my ghost, too."

"Who was it?" asked Tyler.

"I didn't see. My murderer was careful and once I was in the *Ghost Portal* I hid myself in the Distant City."

*

Thames House, MI5 London HQ

Melissa strode briskly at Tyler's side.

"No, you're wrong. It *could* have been Mengele."

"But after the war Mengele fled to Argentina," said Tyler.

"That was not until 1949. I checked. In 1948 when Izabella was killed, Mengele was still hiding out in Germany. He'd changed his name and the allies thought he was dead. Who's to say he didn't follow Izabella across the border for a jaunt in Poland? You ask me, it all makes perfect sense. That's where he gained his reputation during the war as the Angel of Death. He must have known Auschwitz like the back of his hand. Izabella made it easy for him when she went there. He took the contrap and he kept it until he died."

They reached their new office, pausing at the door sign.

DWM

Agents knew these initials stood for Denby, Watts

and May, the founding members of the Department of Investigation in Response to Paranormal Threat. Watts and May entered, nodding to Chapman, the head of the Joint Intelligence Committee, as they passed him to find seats.

"Sir."

"Sir."

"Is Denby joining us today?" asked Chapman.

"Presumably she's here already, Sir." Tyler sat as Lucy uncloaked in the seat next to her.

"Reporting for duty, Sir." Lucy saluted playfully.

"Good to have you back, Denby, alive *or* dead. I have what we've all been waiting for. News on Angel."

Tyler straightened in her chair. Chapman swept images across a presentation touchscreen – various CCTV angles of Angel at Heathrow Airport – and continued. "This is him yesterday morning entering the country under the name Roger Blight."

"Angel was *here*?" Tyler failed to conceal her fury.

"Relax. He was, but he left before we knew anything about it. These images were flagged up during a routine system trawl, through facial recognition. I'm sorry we missed him but that's the way it is. What's of interest to me is what he did before leaving the country, the reason for his visit."

"What do we know?" asked Tyler.

"Not much. I had analysts work through the night tracking his route through every available security camera." Chapman dragged a transport map of Great Britain onto the screen and zoomed into southern England. "This is his journey." A dotted red line expanded from Heathrow, London along the M3 heading south-west. "He was here for less than a day before flying out heavily disguised and under another identity, Uriah Johnson, which is why we missed him. He took a plane to New York where he vanished." The red line turned at Dorchester and inched back towards London.

"Why New York?" asked Lucy.

"We don't know. MI6 are looking into it for us."

"Why Dorchester?" asked Melissa.

"That's what I want you three to find out. Whatever the story, it must be highly important for Angel to risk the journey himself. What we *do* have is plenty of CCTV. Analysis shows he spent most of his time there visiting a bookshop." Chapman positioned an image of Angel in a trilby and a black trench coat, crossing the street towards the entrance of *Wilson's Old & New*.

"Maybe he wanted to buy a book," said Lucy.

"The shop mainly deals in second hand books, rare editions and collectables. If it's a cover, I want to know what for. The proprietor is one James Nathaniel Wilson, a widower aged fifty-eight. He's traded books his entire life. Drop everything else. Get over there and see what you can dig up."

*

Tyler spent a good part of the drive to Dorchester deep in thought while Melissa sped past slower traffic. She recorded more of her story.

The Hope Bringer. That's what my ghost friends have taken to calling me, though I don't see it myself. I'm nothing special.

Just one girl.

They know things, things they won't talk about. Things they can't talk about. And the contrap is full of them. There's an entire city of ghosts in there. In the

Ghost Portal. *It's known as the Distant City, but Zebedee calls it Memoria Gravitas. The whole place is made of an ever-shifting memory mist.*

She stopped recording when she hit upon a recollection: a conversation she'd had with Albert years ago when she was trying to learn what the contrap was. Albert had searched for someone in the *Ghost Portal* who knew about the contrap and he had mentioned a witch, and what *was* the contrap, if not a product of witchcraft?

"I asked around, yeah. Not many on this side knows much about no device. But there was this one old maid. Said she'd seen somefing like it before. Back when she were alive, she said. Seems she were a witch, ya' see. She were helpin' another old girl. They were tryin' t' trap a ghost. They had this thing, this device, and the idea was to get the ghost to go into it so they could use its power for themselves. But somefing went wrong and the old maid got sucked into the device instead. Says she's been dead ever since."

"So the device can trap the spirits of living people as well as ghosts?"

"I s'pose. That's what the old maid told me anyways. From what she said, it's easier that way. Ya' see, to trap a ghost, ya' first gotta find one. An' that ain't always so easy."

Tyler had thought about this for a moment.

"Do you think she was tricked by the other witch? Perhaps it wasn't a mistake. Perhaps nothing really went wrong."

"Who knows, Missy?"

In the back seat Albert remained cloaked, but she knew he was there with Lucy.

"Albert, do you remember speaking to an old witch in the *Ghost Portal*? It must have been around five years ago."

Albert slowly materialised.

"Yeah, I fink so."

"Could she have owned the contrap? Was *that* what she was talking about?"

"Maybe."

"Can you describe her? Think you could find her again?"

"I can try, Missy. I'll 'ave t' go back in the portal, o'course. The old girl must be somewhere in the Distant City."

"Great. Pull over Mel."

"What? No. We're on the motorway."

"Use the hard shoulder. This won't take a minute."

Melissa sighed and circumvented traffic to pull over. Tyler and Albert left the car as vehicles hurtled by and she aimed the contrap's crystal at him.

"Be quick Albert. I need you. Phasmatis licentia."

*

Dorchester

Tyler studied the shop front from across the road. Wilson's Old & New fronted the city street with an age-old façade. Its name, rendered in flaking, maroon paint from a bygone era, complemented the piles of dusty books and the scattering of oddities behind its windows. In one corner an antique china doll lolled sadly against a battered sunburst guitar while, opposite, a rust-worn typewriter whispered echoes of past lives. Tyler sensed countless ghosts lingering and would normally have avoided such a place.

Lucy uncloaked next to her and Melissa.

"Seems quiet enough. No sign of James Nathaniel Wilson."

"You mean the shop's unattended?"

"It appears so."

"That's odd."

"Maybe he's popped out for something."

"I'm not sure. I sensed death."

"Okay. Harrow and Blithe should be here any minute. Let's go."

Tyler took a deep breath and crossed the street. Pushing open the glass-panelled door she paused as the antiquated entrance bell jingled, the dry smell of dust and decaying paper pungent in her nostrils.

"Hello? Mr Wilson?"

Silence.

"Mr Wilson, are you there?" She walked into the shop, a shiver of fear quickening her senses. To her left a counter ran out from the wall to section off part of the space for the keeper. To her right, tall bookshelves formed rows like a giant's ribs, each crammed to the top with books.

Where's Wilson?

A sudden regret made her draw the contrap from her shirt. She switched from the *Safeguarding Skull* to the *Ghost Portal*.

"Albert, are you there?"

Beyond the crystal, the grey memory mist danced in lazy swirls. Albert had gone.

Probably halfway to the Distant City by now.

She switched back to the *Safeguarding Skull* and

tucked the contrap away as Lucy drifted deeper into the shop, her chunky boots floating a foot above the ground. Sunlight from the windows hazed dust particles in the air. Tyler nosed through a scatter of books on the desk. Amongst them a first edition of Dickens' *A Christmas Carol* caught her eye. Beneath it she discovered a first edition of Sir Arthur Conan Doyle's *Hound of the Baskervilles*, its cover red with gold text. She picked it up. "Some of these must be worth a fortune."

"Wait! I feel something." Lucy closed on the counter where a purchase ledger lay open next to a paint-chipped, manual till. "There is death here."

"You sure you're not smelling your own armpits?" asked Melissa.

Lucy curled her lip into a fake smile.

Tyler lifted a half-empty cup of coffee from the surface.

"Cold."

Melissa skirted the desk and froze.

"I think I found Wilson." She looked away from the figure on the floor behind the desk. "They broke his neck."

Tyler joined her to view the body and stooped to check for a pulse. Laying haphazardly on his side, James Wilson, grey haired and dressed in elbow-patched tweed and loafers was bearded, pale and as dead as he could be. Tyler took her phone from her jacket pocket but before she could speed-dial Chapman, it buzzed.

"Ghost, airport security just raised a red flag. Blight is back and he's heading your way. If he returns to the shop he'll arrive in around ten minutes. Prepare to take him down. Tasers only. Capture and secure–"

"No. This time I'm taking no chances. I'm putting

him into the Chasm at the first opportunity."

"Ghost, don't make me regret enlisting you."

"Sir, Wilson's dead. The NVF got to him first."

"That's unfortunate. Listen, stay put. Angel appears to be alone and we have him under close surveillance. I'm sending backup. I think we have him this time. Capture and contain. Got that?"

"But, Sir, the last time–" The line died. Cursing, she shoved her phone back into her pocket. "Angel's on his way."

"Seriously? Here?" Melissa swore.

"We're to sit tight. First chance I get, he's in the Chasm."

"Why's he coming back?"

"Who knows?"

Melissa studied the open ledger.

"Nothing of help in here. No mention of Roger Blight or any other pertinent name. Not in the last few weeks, anyway."

"Why come all this way from Argentina, or wherever he was, to this pokey bookshop?"

"It's not just books," said Melissa. "There are other bits and pieces."

Lucy drew closer to Tyler.

"I was joking when I said it before, but maybe I was right. It's not so ridiculous to think he wanted a book of some sort, one on magic or the under realms." Lucy peered around at the walls adorned with framed antique maps and etchings. "For all we know Angel commissioned Streicher to find Astral Theorem and *that* turned out to be a very important book. What if there are others? This Wilson guy may have found something."

"Surely he wouldn't risk that journey just to commission a search."

"So, what?" asked Melissa. "His first visit was to collect the goods? If so, his current journey makes no sense."

"He left something, or he wants more."

"There's no time for this." Tyler flipped the sign on the door to *Closed*. "In less than ten minutes Angel's going to walk through that door and we must be ready."

Ruth Cobbler

Melissa paled and watched the street through the shop front.

"I get it, but what's the plan?"

"We lie in wait and surprise Angel once he's in the shop. One of us has to Tase him. While he's immobilised I'll use the contrap."

"Chapman wouldn't like that."

"Chapman's not here."

"We don't have any Mordecai chains," said Lucy.

"It doesn't matter. It's still better to put him in the Chasm, chained or not and, without a Hitler artefact, a Taser is our only option to immobilise and disarm."

"Okay," said Lucy.

"Not okay. When Mr Chapman learns we've lost Angel to the Chasm we'll be kicked out of the company."

Tyler glared at Melissa.

"I don't care. With the oppressor gone, it would be game over. We win."

"You're forgetting all the other gloved innocents out there. Who's going to rescue *them?*" Melissa shook her head and turned away to rummage around in the shop.

"What are you doing?" demanded Tyler.

"We only have a few minutes. I'm looking for clues. Why did Angel come here and why's he returning? There *has* to be something here he wants."

Lucy shrugged.

"You can't fault the logic of Superbrain."

"Watch the street, Mojo." Tyler searched bookshelves and books stacked on the floor.

Zebedee Lieberman uncloaked amid the dusty shadows towards the back of the shop.

"Miss May, there's a second room hidden behind the last bookcase."

Tyler followed Zebedee down a narrow gap between the shelves and the rear wall to a door. Pulling on forensics gloves she opened it and peered in. Wilson's back office was a scattered mess of papers and more books.

"Someone searched here already."

Hardbacks were piled high on several desks near a chunky PC and printer, while smaller bookshelves lined the other walls. She took out the contrap and was about to set it to the *Tower of Doom* when she changed her mind and switched instead to the *Ghost Portal*, checking for Albert one last time.

"Albert? Albert, come back."

To her surprise, his soot-stained face emerged through the fog of the crystal.

"There you are. Good. I need you out here. Phasmatis–"

As he drew nearer, a second figure appeared at his side.

"I found 'er, Missy. I found the ol' gal."

The woman at his side hobbled closer as the mist around her cleared. In skirts of russet, a grubby white apron and matching bonnet, her form stooped with age. Deep crevasses accentuated the features of her haggard face as she narrowed her eyes at Tyler through the crystal.

"Is it you, Mary?" the old ghost mumbled with a strong Scottish accent.

"Who's Mary?" asked Tyler.

"Mary, of course! My sister! Is she there?"

"No."

"Oh. Then, name youself, y' wee scunner." The ghost leant forward, opening her better eye wide to stare like a wizened cyclops. Tyler noticed the woman's bad eye was strangely white and lacking a pupil. She decided not to ask what a scunner might be.

"My name's Tyler May. Who are you?"

"Ruth. I thought y' might 'a' been Mary. I do so wish tae speak with her. All these years. It's been so long."

"Listen, Ruth, I don't have much time–"

Ruth wagged a decrepitly bent finger at Tyler. "You *must* find her!" Her favoured eye roved about furtively. "Find Mary Cobbler! Bring her t' me!"

Melissa continued to search the bookshop while Lucy stood guard. Tyler wondered how long she had before Angel arrived.

"Why?"

33

"Because I would talk with her, scunner!"

"*I* need to talk to *you*, but I'm running out of time and you're really not helping."

"Why would y' want tae talk t' me? I'm nought but a harmless, old spinster." Ruth said, batting what remained of her ancient eyelashes.

"I don't think that's all you are. I think, once, you were a witch. You know about the contrap, don't you? Did you own it at some point before you died?"

Ruth dropped her mawkish demeanour, narrowing her eyes again.

"Do you mean the cantrip?"

Tyler's phone buzzed. Swearing, she slid it from her pocket.

"Sir?"

"Angel's nearing the shop. Harrow and Blithe are in position outside. Capture and contain. Do we understand each other, Ghost?"

"Yes, Sir, but–"

"Do it." Chapman ended the call.

Tyler looked back into the crystal.

"I have to go. Stay there. I'll be back." She switched to the *Safeguarding Skull* and re-joined Melissa and Lucy in the shop.

"Mojo, the sign!"

Lucy flipped the sign back to *Open* and cloaked as Angel, in his trilby and coat, rounded a corner further down the street outside.

"Hide!" said Tyler, turning into the small space between the last bookcase and the office door. She crouched, realising her mistake. She had left the contrap's lead box in her bag on the counter top. If the contrap was not concealed in its box Angel would sense it. She stepped closer to the counter but paused to check before breaking cover. A tiny crack between book tops and the next shelf up allowed her a glimpse of the door. Angel entered, jingling the bell.

Too late, he's here!

Slowly she edged towards the end of the bookcase, switching the contrap to the *Brimstone Chasm* and turning its lever full circle until it clicked back into its original position. Soft footsteps sounded from further down the shop.

"Vorago expositus," she whispered as Lucy uncloaked at her side. The *Brimstone Chasm* opened, releasing a waft of sulphuric gas as the crystal boiled with hot, orange light.

"Where's Mel?" whispered Tyler

"Trembling in the next aisle."

"Tell her to move. Now!"

Lucy cloaked.

More footsteps sounded as Tyler stepped out with the contrap poised, but the shop door closed with another ringing of the bell. Outside, Angel fled.

Slipping her Taser from its holster, Tyler bolted after him with Lucy close behind.

Across the road, two of Tyler's other agents – a bulky man named Blithe and a shorter, balding man named Harrow – fought through a gaggle of pedestrians to give chase.

Angel rushed down a side road of Georgian houses. Tyler followed, emerging on West Street surrounded by pedestrians. She tore past a tea shop, a stone church and a black and white timber framed pub, tracking Angel's black trilby up ahead. She grabbed a comms ear-piece from her pocket and tucked it into her ear.

"Harrow, Blithe, where are you?"

"Behind you. We lost the mark and turned back to search."

"Cog?"

"Behind Harrow and Blithe. Sorry. Looks like you and Pointer are our best bet."

Lucy levelled with Tyler and held out a translucent hand.

"In case I meet any bad ghosts."

Tyler slid a gallows blade from her jacket and passed it.

"Not Angel."

"I promise." Lucy snatched the blade and sped on, not bothering to cloak. Screams punctuated her route as she flew through bodies of the crowd.

A clutch of people outside a bank blocked Tyler's view as she crossed the road. She glimpsed Angel's hand reaching up to remove his hat. Now all she could see of him was his head, like all the other heads amidst a melee of visitors outside an old church building hosting a Tutankhamun exhibition. He ducked inside.

Lucy reached the entrance as two Nazi grey coat ghosts materialised, gallows blades outstretched. More screams echoed as pedestrians and visitors scattered. Lucy weighed her two adversaries and smirked.

"Come on then, boys." She backed away as Tyler sprinted to catch up. While Lucy sparred, Tyler slipped past to enter the exhibition, her Taser at the ready. Inside she studied each visitor in turn, the place milling with tourists and students.

"Blithe, Cog, he's in the Tutankhamun exhibition. Watch the front. Harrow, check for a back exit."

"Wilco."

"Wilco."

"Wilco."

Lucy joined her, and Tyler pocketed the extra blades won from the grey coats.

"They won't be bothering us again."

After fifteen minutes the girls conceded.

"We've lost him." Tyler checked for a back door and found every way locked. Leaving the hall she made a final sweep, finding only Melissa.

"Thanks, Mel. Where *were* you?"

Melissa bit her lip.

"I'm sorry. I was nervous. And then Mojo popped up next to me and I nearly died. I was getting ready to Tase him when he ran."

Harrow and Blithe arrived, failure etched on their faces.

"Search the area," said Tyler. They nodded and left. "The shop's unattended. Mel, get back there. I'm going to locate Angel with the *Past Eye*, try to track him down."

Melissa returned to guard the shop while Tyler set the contrap to the *Past Eye* and rewound to a point where the crystal lens showed Angel, hat in hand, ducking into the exhibition. Ignoring the strange looks from pedestrians and exhibition visitors, she entered. The crystal showed Angel walking swiftly through the exhibition interior, past displays of Egyptian artwork and artefacts, and a reconstructed chamber of gilded grave goods. Striding to the back of the building he turned in behind a display board, opened a door and walked through. Tyler took the contrap away from her eye to try the door handle.

Locked, like the last time I tried it. Great. So someone helped him get away and now he's long gone.

She raised Blithe.

"Do me a favour and have the entire area cordoned. Distribute Angel's mug to all officers."

"Wilco."

She considered continuing her hunt with the *Past Eye* but knew how that would turn out. With every painstaking minute of tracking with the contrap, Angel would widen the gap, making his capture less and less likely. Instead, she decided to return to the bookshop, hoping to find what he had come for.

*

Lucy floated near the bay windows. "He's quick. I'll give him that. Someone helped him escape. No one disappears like that. No one living, anyway. Not even a glove."

Fuming, Tyler called Chapman.

"He gave us the slip, Sir."

"So I hear."

"Last seen leaving the back door of the Tutankhamun exhibition on West Street."

A quietness leaked in like a rising flood as Chapman digested the details.

"I'll have local authorities alerted. Maybe we can get lucky. What about Harrow and Blithe?"

"Harrow's dredging the streets. I sent Blithe to cordon the zone."

"Good. Make a thorough search of the bookshop. He was visiting for a reason. Get me answers, Ghost."

"Yes, Sir."

Tyler took her bag from the counter and threw herself into the chair next to Wilson's corpse.

"I suppose we should search him, too."

"Tutankhamun," said Melissa. "Do you think there's

an artefact there that he's after?"

"Who knows? Go back with Lucy, see exactly what they have there. A big exhibition like that, they're going to have decent cameras. Learn what you can."

Melissa glanced at the corpse. "You don't mind..."

Tyler sighed. "Go ahead. Some of my best friends are dead."

With Melissa and Lucy gone Tyler had the shop to herself.

Slipping on a fresh pair of gloves, she took a camera from her bag and photographed the body from every possible angle. She stooped to fold back Wilson's jacket and wriggle his wallet free before searching his other pockets.

A fountain pen, a handkerchief and a fob bearing five keys.

Walking to the door she glanced up and down the street.

All quiet.

Several pedestrians paced the pavements but none were heading towards the shop. She flipped the sign to *Closed* and, taking the keys, locked the door and left. She passed cars parked on the road, clicking Wilson's car remote at three second intervals as she went. Five cars down, a grey Ford Escort flashed its lights in response. She opened the driver's door and climbed in.

The glove box held a pair of black leather driving gloves and the car's manual in a folded wallet. She checked the sun visors and beneath the seats.

Nothing.

Exiting, she popped the boot, uninspired by a crate of car products: polish, oil, cleaning cloths, de-icer and a travel fire extinguisher. She closed the boot and locked the car.

Back in the shop she sat at Wilson's counter and stared at the other four keys. One was certainly a house key. She called Chapman.

"Sir, anything in Wilson's residence?"

"Nothing yet. I have agents searching it this minute. Nothing conclusive but possible signs of a break-in."

"Okay. Keep me posted."

"Of course."

She pocketed her phone and looked at the remaining three keys. She knew one fitted the shop's front door. Testing another she found it worked the back office door. She checked fruitlessly for a rear exit and studied the remaining enigmatic key.

What are you for?

Frustrated, she took out the contrap and set it back to the *Ghost Portal*. Beyond the mist in the crystal Albert and Ruth waited.

"Oh, the wee scunner's back," muttered Ruth, her roving eye fixing upon Tyler.

"You mentioned something called a cantrip. What is that?"

"Why should I tell *you?*"

Tyler thought for a moment. "Because I might be able to find Mary for you."

"Do you propose a trade?" asked Ruth, rolling every R.

"Precisely. Do we have a deal?"

"You do swear t' find m'sister and bring her t'me?"

"No, but I swear I'll try."

Ruth shrugged. "I s'pose that be close enough. A cantrip is a device. A rather special one."

"It's a ghost machine, isn't it?"

"Aye, it's an engine driven by the power of the ghosts within. A cantrip does many wonderful things. Yet you have a cantrip in your hands! I am within your cantrip and you speak from the mortal side of the dark glass. So why ask what you already know?"

Tyler considered admitting that she wanted to learn how to destroy the contrap but thought better of it.

Can I trust you, Ruth Cobbler?

"Cobbler. That's *not* a Scottish name, is it? But you *are* Scottish, at least, your accent is."

"So I am, as Scottish as may be! Yet nae, the name isnae. My sister and I left Scotland when..." Ruth's eye searched the skies. "When the need arose."

"When the need arose? What do you mean?" Ruth gave no answer. "Something happened, didn't it? Did someone learn about your cantrip? You were exposed and had to run. It would have been called witchcraft. Let me guess, they burned witches alive back in your day. You had to escape and change your names."

"T'is nae concern of yours! Why do you pester me so?"

"How did you come by the cantrip, the thing I call the contrap? Did you and Mary take it from someone?" Ruth avoided Tyler's gaze. "Why conceal it? The contrap's been passed from hand to hand for generations. That would be the norm. Either someone gave it to you, or you took it from someone. But no..."

Ruth muttered, shook her head and let her good eye wander.

"You're squirming like an eel on a hook. Something else happened." Tyler's eyes widened with sudden comprehension. "You made it. You and Mary created the contrap!"

"Enough! Seek her where her bones rest. Find Mary or git oot o' ma face!" Ruth turned away, quickly swallowed by the portal's fog. Tyler shouted after her.

"I'm not done with you, Ruth Cobbler!"

Witches

Tyler glared into the crystal.

"Tail her, Albert. Don't lose her."

"Right you are, Missy." With a wave of his cap Albert vanished into the mist after Ruth.

Tyler set the contrap to the *Tower of Doom* and stood in the middle of the bookshop hoping that, if something here might help her, the tower would guide her to it. She knew that if she approached it, the tower would rise. If she walked in the wrong direction, the tower would tumble.

Facing the shop door and with an eye on the tower, she took a decisive step towards the exit. Within the crystal, stones crumbled. She turned towards the counter that concealed Wilson's body, surprised when the tower fell lower still. Facing the line of bookcases the tower continued its ruinous decline.

When she took a step towards the back of the shop tiny stones flew up to the tower's pinnacle, adding to its walls. She walked slowly, pausing to sweep the contrap around as she neared the door to Wilson's back office. Aimed at the last alcove of books, the tower crumbled. She entered the office, the tower rising steadily, leading her to one of Wilson's desks against the back wall, scattered with books and papers. A little careful adjustment to the contrap's positioning helped target a smaller area. She opened drawers and rifled through letters and stationery.

Nothing of interest.

Closing the drawers, she grabbed papers from the desk one after the other, all of them invoices for purchased books. Beneath these were piled three books of varying sizes. She laid them out on the desk and passed the contrap in front of each in turn, stopping when the tower rebuilt. She lifted the book the contrap had chosen, a heavy, cracked and worn tome bound in pale hide. If the front had ever born an inscription it had worn away long ago, but she read the title on its fragile spine.

The Witch Trials of Middle England

The bell jingled. A male voice called from the shop entrance.

"Hello?"

Tyler replaced the book and walked into the shop. Freddy Carter, codenamed Pratt, stood in the doorway with Tyler's German boyfriend and fellow agent, Klaus, close behind.

"Come in." She hurried to embrace Klaus, flashing a hesitant smile. "I didn't know Chapman was sending you."

"He's finally transferred us to DWM. We're officially all yours."

"Great. I wish I could give you better news about your first assignment but this is already a mess. We had a chance to take Angel but we screwed up. We don't know how he gave us the slip. Mel and Mojo are checking the building where he was last seen. You can help me search this place, find whatever he was after. It's here somewhere. There's a dead guy behind the desk. Maybe start with him. I checked his pockets already."

"The shop owner?"

"Name's Wilson. Dead when we arrived."

Klaus took a coin from his pocket and tossed it.

"Heads," said Freddy.

Klaus slapped the coin onto the back of his hand. "Tails. You search the dead guy. Check every nook. I'll start over here." Klaus searched a stack of books in the corner between the till and the window while Freddy grimaced and headed over to the body.

"Any idea what we're looking for?"

"No. Hoping we'll know it when we see it." Tyler re-entered the back office and stuffed *The Witch Trials of Middle England* into her bag. For half an hour she searched Wilson's boxes, books, filing cabinet and desk drawers. Finding nothing else of interest she left the office.

Lucy uncloaked nearby.

"No luck with the CCTV."

Melissa returned, met Tyler's gaze and shook her head.

"Nothing. Angel walked through the crowds passing several cameras. They caught him entering but he didn't come out."

"Perhaps he's still in there, hiding."

"I tracked him with the *Past Eye*. He definitely went through a door towards the rear of the building."

"I left Harrow watching the place, so we'll know if he shows up."

"Fine. What about the exhibits?"

"Plenty there that might interest him. There's a reconstruction of the tomb's antechamber. The artefacts are real, mostly burial objects like golden statues, chests, stools, a throne. I didn't see any iron, only gold."

"Could he have used one of the chests like a spirit trap to escape?"

"I don't think so. The gloves are physical beings, not just ghosts, and all the objects are covered by cameras. If Angel had gone anywhere near we would have seen." Melissa passed a CD in a clear case to Tyler. "Here, a copy of the last week's CCTV data including today."

"Thanks. Make yourself useful and join the search."

Melissa picked a book case and began examining books one at a time.

Tyler glanced around the shop. Everyone was busy. She returned to the back office. Sitting at Wilson's desk, she opened *Witch Trials of Middle England*, and read.

The contents page gave her a brief overview of the book, consisting of eleven section headings.

Introduction
A Threat to Christendom

Beneath each section heading were listed numerous chapters detailing historic accounts, court records, the changing laws and views and perceptions, and individual cases of witch trials and their outcomes. She immediately turned to the index – this in itself fifteen pages long – and scanned through until she came to the C listings. She slowed, checking each item, stopping when she found the familiar name.

Dismissing the first reference, she quickly turned to page four hundred and eight, speed-reading to locate the names. She backtracked to the start of the account and read.

The Cobbler Sisters
Much Wenlock features little in the history of medieval witchcraft, yet a little-documented, early enigmatic account recorded in July of the year 1462 is of some interest and contains several intriguing suggestions and unanswered questions.

The account involves two sisters, Mary and Ruth Cobbler, accused of witchcraft in the quiet and unassuming Shropshire village. Anne Tully, the wife of a baker, along with a miller named Thomas Lytcott reported to the prior, the then manorial lord, telling that the sisters consorted with the Devil in the form of a black cat named Lucifer, kept and rewarded by Mary and Ruth with drops of their own blood. The accusers also told of the sisters' joint participation in the killing by sorcery of three local men who had recently died of otherwise unexplained causes.

In this first instance the case never came to trial as Tully, Lytcott and the prior each vanished mysteriously soon after the accusations, never to be seen again. So, too, disappeared the priory's written records of the case.

Lucy uncloaked next to Tyler, startling her with a whisper in her ear.

"So, when are you going to tell Mel about this book? The tower led you to it, right?"

"Shush. I'm not telling anyone about it. It's nothing to do with Angel."

"Why read it, then?"

"Because I want to destroy the contrap and this book could help. You think I should tell the others so that Chapman can take the contrap away from me and kick me off the team?"

"You don't know that's what he would do."

"I don't know that's *not* what he'd do, either."

"Hmmm. I think you should tell Mel, at least."

"I'm not telling anyone. Go away. I'm busy." Tyler returned to the book.

For several years the Cobbler sisters continued to live in Much Wenlock under frequent suspicion by the remaining villagers, a population in steady decline, until 1468 when Ruth died, also of causes unknown.

Mary Cobbler was again accused of witchcraft in the summer of 1473, this time swiftly placed in the stone prison to await trial. During the following days villagers lined up to bear witnesses against her, detailing numerous events in which Mary reportedly cast spells damning individuals by name, used potions to manipulate and poison, dug graveyards to procure finger bones for use in spells, and summoned pestilence upon livestock and crops by diabolical means. Mary eventually confessed and was condemned to be hanged at the Edge Top with her cat.

Tyler added the dates to her notes.

The book went on to make general observations and statements about the case relating to the laws and judicial system of the age before the next account began. Tyler closed it, checked her watch and shoved the book into her bag.

She Googled 'Dorchester to Much Wenlock' on her phone. The route map told her the one hundred and eighty miles journey north would take three hours and thirty-five minutes.

It's gone four. If I leave now I'll be there around dusk.

Shouldering her bag she walked through the shop.

"Stay here and keep searching until you find whatever we're looking for. I'll be back soon."

Melissa looked up from her pile of books.

"Where are you going?"

"I don't have time to explain." Tyler paused at the door. "Zebedee?"

Zebedee uncloaked nearby.

"Keep an eye on Melissa."

*

Sitting in her car, Tyler Googled the number for Much Wenlock's parish council and phoned. A receptionist answered politely.

"Hello, I need access to the fifteenth century parish records of Much Wenlock. Where would they be kept, please?"

"We have no records that old here. They would be in the Shropshire archives in Shrewsbury."

"They're not accessible online?"

"Some are. Not all. You can call the office there for more information. Would you like their number?"

"Thank you." Tyler scribbled down the number in her notebook, thanked the receptionist again and ended the call. She called the new number.

"Shropshire Council, how may I help you?"

"Hello. I need access to the fifteenth century parish records of Much Wenlock. Do you have them there?"

"I'm afraid there aren't generally many records kept of that age, but yes, if written records exist for fifteenth century Much Wenlock, they'll be here."

"And where is here?"

"Shirehall, Shrewsbury."

Tyler scribbled down the address and drove.

*

At seven thirty p.m. she pulled up outside Shirehall, its substantial six floors of offices closed, their lights out. Parking around the back, she stole out to a rear entrance and checked for security cameras. There were none. She took her lock picking tools out from her coat pocket and picked the door lock. Inside she pocketed the tools and closed the door behind her, guilt tugging at her mind. She knew she should probably be with her agents focusing on the recent developments in Dorchester, not chasing a whim and a gut feeling about the Cobbler sisters, but at least this way both bases were covered.

Shirehall was a substantial, modern, concrete and glass building with six floors, each with many rooms and corridors. It took Tyler half an hour of prowling by torchlight to find the section where the old records were kept. She searched through boxes of documents and took scrolls from their shelves, fighting her compulsion to abandon the hunt and reorder the entire collection to correct filing errors. A further two hours of sifting left her weary and having second thoughts.

Am I wasting my time here? If I don't find anything in the next hour I'll drive back, tell them I was following a hunch that didn't pay off.

She took a break and descended to the ground floor where she purchased crisps, chocolate and coffee from a vending machine. Halfway up the stairs on her way back to the records rooms she realised the tower might lead her straight to the documents she needed. She set the contrap to the tower and within five minutes narrowed her search to a single box of papers, dragging this out from a high shelf and setting it on a desk. She worked her way through each document in turn until a name shook her from the monotony. Unfolding the flattened scroll, she battled her way through the flouncy, faded Old English text, bypassing any words that were un-recognisable, but understanding enough to make sense of it. The first part of the initial line doubled as the document's title.

This is the Last Will and Testament of Mary Cobbler of Abbot's Wood, Much Wenlock, Shrewsbury. I give to my sister, Ruth Cobbler, all my worldly possessions and wealth, such as it is, my portion of the cott part-owned, in which I have lived, all coin and jewellery, clothing and surviving livestock. I will for my mortal remains to be interred within Abbot's Wood, nearby the aforementioned cott.

Proved at Much Wenlock Court 1^(st) July 1459 before Prior Roger Barry, witnessed by Mary Cobbler, clerk Geoffrey Dun and Agnes Snow here signed.

She consulted her notebook, checking the date and adding notes. In 1459 both sisters still lived. Beneath a fold in the old document she discovered an addition to the main text. With much scrutiny of the scrawling handwriting she discerned enough to know it was an inventory of Mary's belongings added soon after her hanging, dated August 12^(th) 1473, the receivers of which were apparently in debate due to Mary's lack of surviving beneficiaries.

The house and smallholding of Copse Hill
2 goats in goodly health
4 fattened pigs
6 red hens
Bed linen - 2 fine sheets and a quilt of eiderdown
3 goodly chairs of oak
1 bed of solid build
A purse of coin - 4 pounds, 15 shillings and six pence

1 golden neck chain
6 rings of silver
2 silver medallions set with gemstones
3 iron cooking pots, well used
1 horn cup
1 wooden spoon
1 iron fork
1 set of bellows, well worn
2 wooden bowls

Tyler reread a line as a shiver traversed her spine.

Two silver medallions set with gemstones? Two *contraps?*

Much Wenlock

The night encroached as she drove into the village of Much Wenlock. Passing streets scattered with medieval, timber-framed, black and white houses she used her satnav to traverse the town centre, winding to the outskirts where the ruined abbey towered into the murky heavens. She pulled over to stretch her legs and walked around the remaining high cloister arches where, centuries ago, the chants of monks had echoed. Ghosts were close. Their presence chilled her marrow. She walked back to the car as rain fell.

Lucy appeared in the passenger seat, an eyebrow raised.

"What are *you* up to?"

"Mojo, I wish you would warn me before you do that! Go and haunt someone else."

"You want to tell me why we're two hundred miles from where we should be?"

Rain dashed like shards of pitch to deepen the night. It pelted the car with an incessant drumming, misting the air. Tyler could barely see past the bonnet. She tried not to think about what might be out there stalking her.

"I wondered if you'd follow me."

"Yeah, yeah, I saw you looking for stuff and reading things but I didn't bother."

"I'm here to see the ghost of a witch called Mary Cobbler. She lived in the woods nearby over five hundred years ago. I think the contrap had a sister and at the point of her death Mary owned both of them."

"What's this got to do with Angel?"

"Nothing. Like I said, it's about me destroying the contrap. Well, it *was*. Now it's about an entirely different matter. I know I need to get back to Wilson's but I have to see if Mary Cobbler is here first. It's the only way to know for sure."

"So you're looking for a witch's grave."

"Yes."

"You know they used to pin a witch's body to the bottom of the grave to stop the witch from rising from the dead. It's an ancient custom dating back at least as far as the Bronze Age. They found bog bodies pinned, face down, to the bottom of the marsh with willow stakes. It's also where we get the legends about vampires being staked through the heart, from later graves, you know, medieval ones. They would also bind up the witch's jaw, or wedge a stone in her mouth to stop her corpse from uttering the spell that would reanimate her. Or they'd simply dump a massive stone on top of the body to prevent the witch from rising."

"You know a lot about dead witches."

"I used to read about stuff like that."

"That figures."

Tyler started the car and studied the satnav.

"There's still a patch of woodlands a short way north of the abbey. There's a fair chance that's where Mary was buried. If not, her grave can't be far away. That's my best bet for finding her ghost."

She drove for several minutes and pulled up alongside a stretch of forest. She switched off the engine but left the headlamps on, illuminating the trees.

"No blades. I don't want to scare her off."

Leaving the car she climbed a slippery bank and walked into the woods where the rain fell in large droplets from the canopy above and a damp, leafy decay soaked the air. She drew the contrap from her shirt and set it to the *Ghost Portal*.

If I'm right, I might need another artefact of Mary's to summon the witch's ghost. But what?

When she thought she was deep enough into the woods she turned in a small clearing, watching, the rain spilling with a patter on the forest floor around her.

"Mary! Mary Cobbler, are you there?"

She repeated the words, calling as loudly as she dared. The rain drummed. She walked on, willing Mary to make an appearance with each step. Reaching a patch of level ground she noticed the low remnant of an ancient wall overgrown with ivy, moss and last summer's ferns. Her torchlight traced the outline of a decayed building broken by trees, shrubs and fallen branches, and the rubble of a fireplace, also smothered by dead creepers.

Here the vegetation receded to edge a clearing devoid of life. The reek of decay floated to her in a stagnant atmosphere and a small voice in her head whispered.

This was their house! This was the house where the sisters lived!

Tyler placed the contrap against a stone of the ruined wall.

"Mary Cobbler, I summon you out! Come to me! Show yourself! Come out, now. I must to speak with you."

When Mary did not appear, Tyler tried again, this time using the summoning spell Izabella had used in the *Brimstone Chasm*, wondering if that would work.

"Fero tuli latum, phasmatis licentia hac, Mary Cobbler."

Immediately the rain ceased and a wind mounted to scatter damp leaves and swirl them from the ground in torrents. They flew past Tyler like fleeing birds as, amid the gloom of the trees ahead, a pale and haggard figure arose.

Tyler shivered, sensing evil. All around the ghost a foul, reeking miasma thickened, its green and milky fronds meandering like vaporous tentacles.

"Wait, spirit, and tell me your name." Tyler gagged at the stench and stepped back.

The pale ghost delayed its languid approach.

"Choose, dowk heid. Do you wish t' see me or no?" The ghost's accent matched Ruth's.

"You *must* be Mary Cobbler, Ruth's sister."

"I am she. *Why* do you summon me forth?"

"I had to. I need your help. I have a cantrip and I need you to tell me how to destroy it. You created them, didn't you?" Tyler studied Mary, hoping to predict her response while Mary gazed back with mild interest. "You and your sister, you made one each. And if you created them you must know how to destroy them."

"Have you spoken with m' sister? Be she–" The greenish mist probed closer.

"What? Still in the cantrip where you put her? Yes. Only, now it's mine. Some very bad people want to take it from me and if there's a second cantrip they'll be after that too. Did you make two of them?"

Mary's face split with a sly smile, her eyes deepening to black pits as her fog enveloped its target. Tyler's head throbbed with a deepening pain as a distant ringing swelled in her ears. She steadied herself against a tree, nausea pervading her innards.

"Be you afeared?" the crone hissed.

"Tell me, did you and Ruth make one each?" Tyler sensed the pain emanating from the witch. "Stop it! What are you doing?" She dropped to her knees, grasping her head. The noise in her ears intensified as she struggled to her feet, determined to close on Mary. She stepped nearer as fear shadowed Mary's face. The witch vanished with a sound like burning oil.

Tyler stumbled back to the wall, held the contrap against it and took aim, shouting over the din in her head.

"Phasmatis licentia!" She drew the contrap's lever clockwise.

Mary uncloaked as the invisible force dragged her essence closer. In a bolt of iridescent light she shot through the crystal and into the *Ghost Portal*.

Tyler slumped to the ground, passing out amid the thinning fumes.

*

Lucy stooped over Tyler's fallen form, wondering if she

would ever come round.

"Tyler! Wake up, Tyler. We have to go." Again Lucy forced herself to focus energy into a physical form, slapping Tyler a third time across the face. The phone in Tyler's pocket continued to buzz. "Tyler, you're needed. Get up!" With one concerted effort she struck Tyler's cheek with an audible *crack*. Tyler roused, wincing from a thunderous headache, the lingering ringing in her ears and now a stinging cheek.

"What? What is it?"

"Answer your phone. Someone keeps calling, probably Chapman, and you need to balance the contrap!"

Tyler shook herself.

"Right. Compenso pondera." She answered the call. "Hello?"

"Ghost, where are you?"

"Uh, chasing a hunch, Sir."

"Get to the bookshop at once. While you've been away Angel returned with backup and took down the night watch. Blithe's dead. Harrow's also been shot but I'm told he'll live. He called it in before passing out. Angel visited a hidden room. We think he took something. We need the *Past Eye*."

*

In Wilson's Old and New, Tyler viewed the scene. Bullet holes in the bay windows radiated fractures like hammered ice. Blood-soaked carpet showed the place where Blithe had fallen and bled out. Melissa walked with her, gawping at the scene through thick-rimmed glasses. Around the interior, forensics officers in white paper jumpsuits, masks and polythene boot covers worked.

Chapman glared at the hapless agents before him.

"We didn't even see the door. It was hidden behind the desk," said Melissa, leading Tyler through the shop.

A desk in the back office had been wrenched away from the wall and overturned. Where Tyler had previously unearthed the book on witch trials, a safe door in the exposed wall yawned open, the secret chamber beyond lit by portable halogen lamps.

Perhaps the tower was truly leading me to the safe room!

"This is how we found it," said Chapman, his eyes darkly ringed behind his glasses. "Josef Mengele's prints are all over it."

Tyler focused the *Past Eye* on the shop entrance and turned the little lever around the contrap's edge. Within the crystal, time rewound. In a matter of seconds she passed the point when Angel and his men forced their way into the shop. She stopped the contrap's replay and levered slowly back in the opposite direction until the image in the crystal played at real time. She watched. Blithe dozed near the till. Angel and his men approached the shop, shot Blithe through the windows and stamped open the locked door. Harrow came running, drawing his gun too late. A bullet entered his shoulder and he dropped, a blood patch growing across the white of his shirt from a second wound in his chest.

Angel strode past the bookshelves to the back office and gestured for his men to drag away the desk. Reading a note from his coat pocket, he unlocked the safe door, opened it and ducked inside.

Observing through the contrap, Tyler tailed him beneath the low doorway into an unlit room, glad when Angel found the light switch. The light revealed an entirely different aspect of Wilson's shop. Here lay ancient works, great tomes of parchment, dusty scrolls, maps and even clay tablets, each worthy of a museum display case. Ignoring these valuable and collectable pieces, Angel walked to a strongbox in the corner of the room and, taking a key from his pocket, unlocked and opened the safe. He emptied it, scattering priceless volumes and parchments across the floor, stopping when he found a white envelope. This he opened with a slice from a gallows blade, slipping the document out as a smile of gratification spread across his face.

Tyler hurried closer, passing through Angel's trace image to glimpse the folded page and read its faded title, handwritten in an official, highly embellished calligraphy.

The Last Will & Testament of Douglas Anthony de Winter

Dropping the envelope, Angel slid the will into his inside coat pocket and left the shop, his men tailing behind.

Tyler lowered the contrap.

"It's not a book. It's a will. Someone called Douglas Anthony de Winter. He commissioned Wilson to source the will."

"Why would he want someone's will?" asked Melissa.

Chapman tapped a speed-dial number on his iPhone and held it to his ear.

"Yes. Dredge the system for one Douglas Anthony de Winter. Priority one." He ended the call while Tyler fixed her earpiece in place. "Get after him. Track him as far as the contrap allows."

"He has quite a head start on me. Sir, there's–"

"Because you were off chasing a hunch. Now make it right!"

"Yes, Sir." Tyler scowled. Dragging the contrap's lever gently anticlockwise, she watched through the crystal for the point when Angel had left the shop, and followed him out into the lamp-lit street.

"Arm yourselves. Watch my back."

Around her, the Ghost Squad uncloaked. Bringing traffic to a halt they spread out in a line across the road, walking through cars and passengers, sending pedestrians running. Lucy took a fistfull of gallows blades from Tyler and passed them out to Agent Weaver, a bookish schoolgirl ghost named Kylie wearing round glasses and a purple coat, Izabella, Zebedee, Marcus the mute boy, the Roman slave girl Claudia, the pauper Isla, Bronwyn, the infantryman John, the Saxon warrior Wulfric, the hulking slave Yakubu, the Romanian gypsy twins Kinga and Danuta, and the Jewish resistance fighters, Judith and Leon.

Tyler glanced at them, a team of murdered ghosts. With the possible exception of Wulfric. She realised she had yet to hear his story. The Ghost Squad marched with determined faces.

You want a fight, Angel? Bring it on!

She tracked him and his men down the street and watched them board a black Lexus. She relayed the number plate to Chapman. Angel's driver started the car and she hurried to reach it in time to watch through the window. The car drove away.

Tyler tweaked the contrap's lever to view it again, this time slowing the trace.

Angel sat in the rear of the Lexus and took the will from his coat, unfolding it to read. Briefly she saw the text before the car pulled away whisking the will out of view. She reversed the trace and replayed it again.

While Tyler changed position in the road to see better, the Ghost Squad encircled her protectively to ward away traffic.

Replaying the trace several times she read the will a few lines at a time. It was long and uninteresting except for a paragraph late on in the document. At last she managed to pause the contrap's delicate lever, freezing the image within the crystal.

To Archibald de Winter I leave one item only, a rare and ancient jewel that requires description for purposes of clarification. The piece is set on a silver chain, its body cast in several sections of silver forming a decahedron and centred with a polished black crystal. On the reverse face are inscribed a series of small, intricate symbols around a central switch. The construction in its entirety is several inches across and blackened as though from fire, though I find no amount of polish can remove this residue.

The crystal flashed to black as the contrap switched itself to the *Ghost Portal* and the eye of the Black Sun confronted her.

No use trying to track Angel with the contrap playing up like this. It's hard enough at the best of times.

She released the contrap's lever and it rotated, clicking back to its twelve o'clock position. Switching to the *Safeguarding Skull* she reported to Chapman.

"Sir?"

"I'm listening, Ghost."

"We need the report on Archibald de Winter asap. There's a second contrap and Angel is tracking it down."

We Who
Dwell Within

Thames House, MI5 HQ
Seated in the Department of Investigation in Response to
Paranormal Threat office, Tyler took out her notebook
and turned to the list charting the contrap's previous
owners. She added the sisters with their dates and also
added Josef Mengele, writing a question mark after his
name.

Circa 1468   *Ruth (or Mary) Cobbler*
                              ↓
Circa 1473   *Mary Cobbler*

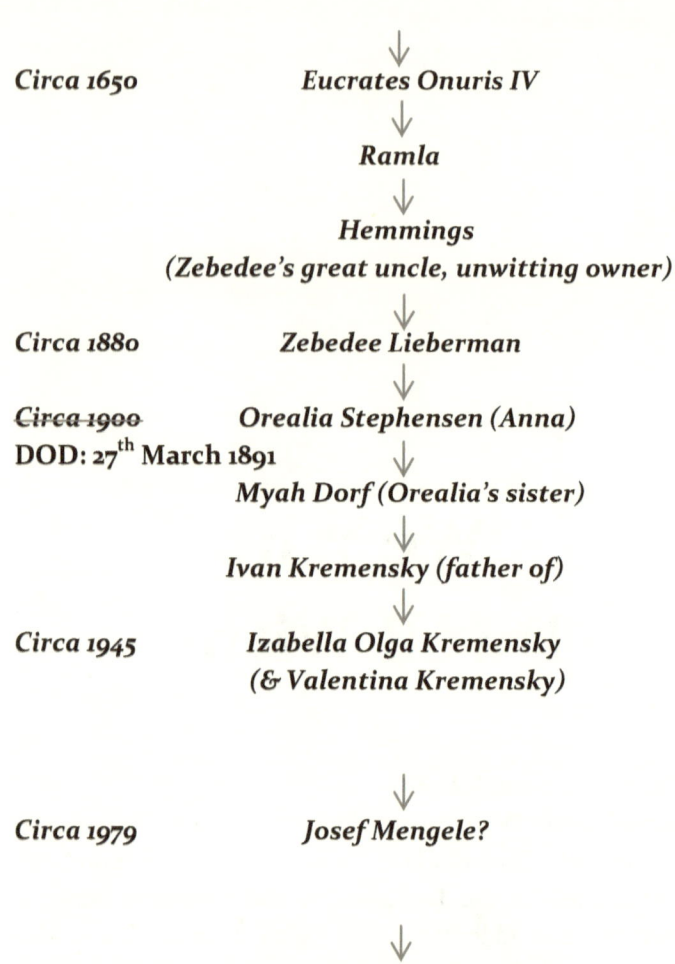

Circa 1650   **Eucrates Onuris IV**

↓

Ramla

↓

Hemmings
(Zebedee's great uncle, unwitting owner)

↓

Circa 1880   **Zebedee Lieberman**

↓

~~*Circa 1900*~~   **Orealia Stephensen (Anna)**
DOD: 27th March 1891

↓

Myah Dorf (Orealia's sister)

↓

Ivan Kremensky (father of)

↓

Circa 1945   **Izabella Olga Kremensky**
(& Valentina Kremensky)

↓

Circa 1979   **Josef Mengele?**

↓

Leopold Bagshot McGuire

↓

Lucy Denby

↓

Tyler May

The list now covered two pages with several spaces where owners were unknown, most notably the gap between

Mary Cobbler and Eucrates Onuris IV, which spanned almost two hundred years. Turning to a new sheet, she wrote a title and began a second list, adding dates she had memorised from the de Winter will.

History of the Dark Sister

Circa 1468   **Ruth (or Mary) Cobbler**
↓

↓

Circa 1594   **Douglas Anthony de Winter**
↓
Circa 1636   **Archibald de Winter**
↓

She stared at the contrap. Following a whim she switched to the *Tree of Knowledge* and asked "Who owned the dark contrap after Archibald de Winter?" Her words formed, condensing into ink within the smoky crystal before vanishing. A moment later, letters floated back into view as though scribed by an invisible quill.

The one who owned the dark contrap after Archibald de Winter is no more

The words dispelled.

"I guessed that much, but who was it? What was their name?"

After an abnormally long pause the answer

materialised.

The one who owned the dark contrap after Archibald de Winter is no more

"Great. Thanks. How can I destroy the contraps safely so that the ghosts are set free and the evil powers stopped?" More fluid letters drifted into place.

Find the scrolls of Onuris

Tyler's eyes widened in surprise.
A serious answer? Surely not!
Quickened with hope, she asked another question.
"Where are the scrolls of Onuris?"

Lost

Her heart sank.
"Really helpful. Thanks." She considered what else she could ask, hoping to beg another morsel of information. "Why must I find the scrolls of Onuris?"

You must read the scrolls of Onuris

"Why?"

Because

"I mean, why must I read the scrolls of Onuris?"

If we knew that

The words faded

you wouldn't need to read the scrolls of Onuris

"What was Onuris trying to do?"

He was trying to destroy the contraps

"Who are you? Who am I speaking to?"
The *Tree of Knowledge* took so long to answer that Tyler thought it had stopped working.

We who dwell within

Another question flew from her lips. "Where is Angel?"
Again the liquid words formed.

He is visiting Sotherby's in London

"Why is he there?"
Lines appeared and disappeared in quick succession.

I don't know
Missy
Don't trust the Tree of Knowledge
Got to go

"Albert? Is that you?" The writing ceased. "Who are you? Tell me!" At length more words appeared.

We who dwell within

"That was you, wasn't it, Albert?"

We who dwell within

Tyler phoned for a priority police cordon of the Sotherby's address and surrounding block.

"Have the police lock down Sotherby's London head office immediately. Armed officers only. No one's to enter or leave until further notice."

Melissa burst through the door.

"Chapman's back and he's steaming. Wants a meeting immediately."

"Good. So do I." Tyler set the contrap to the *Safeguarding Skull*, tucked it into her shirt and headed out with Melissa to the incident room.

Chapman and the other DWM agents were already gathered. Around the edges of the room, the Ghost Squad waited. Lucy and Weaver appeared near Chapman.

"Close the door. Where's Albert?"

"He's in the *Ghost Portal*, Sir, but Angel is at Sotherby's head office right now. I have to get over there."

"How do you know he's at Sotherby's?"

"The *Tree of Knowledge*. I know it can't be trusted but something about it was different this time. At the very least we should check the place out to be sure."

Lucy rolled a ghost throwing knife through the tips of her fingers. "We've nothing to lose."

Chapman huffed. "I think it's about time you explained yourself, Ghost. Where were you while your agents were attacked and what's this about a second contrap?"

"I was researching, Sir. Over five hundred years ago, two sisters each made a contrap. Somehow Angel has found out there's a second one, one that is blackened. He's trying to locate it. That's why he's gone to Sotherby's. There must be some trace of the other contrap there, a clue to its location."

"Mr Chapman, the oppressor must not be allowed to take possession of the contraps. One would be disastrous, but if he were to have the power of the two..."

"Point taken, Izabella. And why is Albert in the *Ghost Portal*?"

"Hmmm. I sent him in to find someone who knows about the contrap's creation and he located one of the sisters who made them. I went to Much Wenlock to find the other sister. That was my hunch. I was hoping to learn more but she's evil and she nearly killed me. I had to put her into the portal."

"Was that wise?" asked Melissa.

"Probably not but I didn't have time to think. There's something else. The *Tree of Knowledge* also told me I need to find the scrolls of Onuris."

Chapman rubbed at his temples.

"Remind me. Who's Onuris?"

"Eucrates Onuris IV," said Zebedee. "He once owned Tyler's contrap. He may have known things that could help us."

"I think I've already seen a fragment of one of the scrolls." Tyler opened her notebook and showed Chapman the page where she had copied Klaus' translation of the fragment. "I took it from Angel's office, the Hobson & Crane Industries office in Buenos Aires. The original was Latin. It's what helped me work out that the *Heart* symbol turns the contrap into its ghost form."

Chapman read the passage aloud.

"Regarding my investigations into the contraption, I believe I have found a way (solution). Upon the meeting of the four symbols (or when the four symbols come together), the pacts (could mean oaths or arrangements/agreements) will reverse (turn in on themselves, or inverse) and spirit will be released. Where the heart is concerned, one can only muse (deliberate). Perhaps this was selected as a substitute image because the more accurate (truthful) device was already engaged (in use). On another matter, today, I learned of a myth that told of the spirits succumbing to the lordship of he who wears a ring of gallows iron. Have you ever heard such a thing? A ring of gallows iron worn and wielded by my namesake, nonetheless! It is surely make-believe." Chapman paused to meet Tyler's eyes. "It's gibberish. And you think there is more to learn from these scrolls?"

"Yes, but they're lost."

Chapman shook his head and sat back in his leather chair. "We have Angel wandering about our country like he owns the place, apparently untouchable. The contrap has a dark sister, location unknown. The world is in chaos due to the NVF's warmongering – our agents have never before been spread so thinly – and we've yet to touch upon the real reason I called this meeting."

Jade, one of Chapman's old team, cleared her throat.

"Sir, if I may?"

Chapman jutted his chin. "Go ahead."

"The CCTV report shows a discreet team of agents aiding Angel's movements. They're highly skilled and organised. If we study their movements long enough we should be able to predict and countermove the next time he shows."

"No. We don't have the time or manpower. Arrest every last one of them and bring them in for questioning. Do it quickly. Perkins and Jenner, you too. Without his little team he'll be ours. I want to know the second we pick up on his trail again."

Jade scribbled notes on her clipboard.

"The rest of you will have to split up. Tyler, follow up on these scrolls and the other contrap. Neither can be allowed to fall into Angel's hands. You'd better choose a companion."

"I have Albert and the Ghost Squad."

Chapman's gaze lingered on Tyler before moving on.

"Melissa, take Klaus and Freddy. Get onto this dark matter lead."

Tyler frowned.

"What dark matter lead?"

"The reason for the meeting. While you've been busy ghost hunting, Melissa has done some research of her own. You'll recall the NVF's interest in dark matter and Zebedee's speculation about the under realms?"

Tyler nodded.

"Melissa?" Chapman handed over.

"Thank you, Sir. Analysis on the NVF Greenland Ice Stations backs up Zebedee's theory, but it wasn't the only source of data. NECRO 904 was exchanging information with multiple laboratories across the globe. One big scientific collaboration. But one particular lab appears to have been the centre of all the activity. It's tucked away on a remote Hawaiian island. The problem is, as of forty-eight hours ago, all communication from the IP ceased. I can't hack it because it's been taken offline."

"Hawaii? You're kidding."

"No. If we're to learn anything more about how the

NVF plan to merge the realms, it will be there. Don't worry. We'll not have time to surf."

The Queen
of Gravitas

Chapman took Tyler aside as the other agents left the room.

"Tyler, I'm worried about you. I'm prioritising a full psychological evaluation before you do anything else. Dr Moores awaits you in her room."

Great. Wasting time with my shrink when I should be chasing down the dark sister. Just what I need.

"Sir, I can assure you I'm perfectly fine."

"No, you're not."

*

Dr Emily Moores, smartly dressed in a trouser suit and with brown hair tied high in a bun, sat cross-legged on her chair. Her perfectly manicured and red-lacquered nails tapped lightly on the clipboard resting across her lap. Makeup was an art form she had mastered well, but

Moores had never held a gun. She had never fled through a battlefield amid explosions with threats on all sides and the only ghosts *she* had experienced were those of Tyler's squad.

Tyler examined her own hands, scarred and calloused from merciless training sessions and special operations. Her nails, trimmed to the quick, were chipped and worn.

"Come in, Tyler. Take a seat."

"Thank you." *Not*.

"Mr Chapman is very concerned about your current mental state."

"Apparently."

"You've been through an awful lot over the last few years: extreme physical and mental stress, the loss of loved ones, you've witness hideous atrocities and wholesale slaughter first-hand, not to mention the horrors of what you refer to as the Chasm."

"I guess."

"How do *you* think you're holding up?"

"Pretty well, all things considered."

Moores watched, an irritating picture of contentment.

"Do you dream?"

"I have nightmares, if that's what you mean."

"Yes?"

"Reoccurring ones about the oppressor."

"Go on."

"In my dreams he's often a fallen angel, a burned and charred ruin of a once-beautiful being. He's almost seductive, charming, but not in a good way."

"Do you relive things in your dreams that have happened?"

"Sometimes."

"For example?"

Tyler exhaled a long resigned breath.

"I see Mengele on the rooftop of a car park. He offers me chocolate and jokes about *the child within*. He means the child victim with whom he was gloved, you understand? I glimpse the oppressor in the form of Hitler's ghost leaving the contrap submerged beneath the Thames and watch as he joins with Mengele's gloved body.

"I feel the oppressor's breath close against my skin and hear him ranting about how he'll annihilate the Jews and the blacks, every *abomination*. His words, not mine. Reveries close in, hungry for my soul.

"The Chasm opens before me, preparing to consume me. It is ravenous. The ground moves like it's alive and I fear what lies beneath. Then he's back, stabbing soldiers to create his Legion of the Black Sun, and there's blood. *So much* blood." She stared into Moores' dilated pupils. "But, you know, other than *that,* I'm hunky-dory."

"You seem pretty angry with everyone, angry with Mr Chapman and me, with your associates."

"I'm angry with Angel but *he's* not here."

"So you understand you are projecting?"

"Is there a point to all this?"

"I'm afraid so. Mr Chapman has demanded an all clear on your mental health before you continue with your duties."

"My duties..."

"Yes?"

Tyler fell quiet.

"Do you feel guilty?"

"What difference does it make?"

"Lucy was killed while protecting you and the other

79

agents. It would be perfectly normal to feel guilt, however irrational."

"Then you can tell Chapman I'm *perfectly normal*."

Dr Moores allowed herself a wry smile.

"Do you feel physically well?"

"Yes, perfectly so. Perfectly, normally physically well. Thank you." Tyler decided not to mention the throbbing and itching from the cuts on her fingers where stitches were yet to be removed from her last mission, the cold ache from her old thigh wound and the constant ringing in her ears caused by the explosion that vaporised Lucy. Other than these irritations and a hundred other battle-bruises, she *was* well enough.

"That's good." Moores measured Tyler head to feet with a practiced glance and penned a note on her board. "And you've passed your medical?"

"Yes. I've killed people and that has left the deepest scars, scars that will not heal."

"So you carry guilt about that, too."

"Of course!"

"A lot of guilt?"

"More than you can imagine. I feel as though I've done something so fundamentally wrong that, whatever happens, my life is over whether I succeed or fail. Whether I'm punished for it or rewarded."

"Do you regret killing?" When no answer was forthcoming Moores altered the question. "Would you do things differently had you the chance?"

"Yes." Tyler turned away. "No. It was them or me. That was the choice they gave me."

"I'm glad you understand that. Knowing that it was *their* fault they died may be the starting point for forgiving yourself and moving on."

"*Moving on?*"

You think, one day, I'll be able to leave this all behind and move on? You poor, deluded woman.

Moores jotted more notes.

"Listen, I'm going to give you the all-clear on condition that you speak with Reverend Jacobs again. You have issues that he may help with where I cannot. He usually breaks for lunch at half-twelve. If you hurry you may catch him. I think a talk with him could be good for you."

"But I'm not that religious."

"Neither is Reverend Jacobs."

*

Reverend Jacobs' office was a small but neatly kept room at the back of the church. Despite her lack of religious inclination, Tyler had always considered him a gentleman, winsome and wise. Tall, and lively with smiling eyes, greying hair and the beginnings of a stoop, he showed her in and positioned a chair across from his own, gesturing for her to sit.

"It's been a while since we last spoke, Miss May."

"Yes. I've been busy."

"Hmmm. So I hear. Tell me, what troubles you?"

"I won't lie. Dr Moores sent me. I'm here under duress."

"Ah, I see." Jacobs smiled sagely. "A box-ticking exercise."

Tyler nodded uncomfortably.

"Please relax and consider the box ticked. You can leave whenever you like, but I *am* interested to know how you are."

Tyler smirked.

"I'm okay, all things considered."

"And what about your mission? How's that going?"

The question left her momentarily confused. Her latest mission – the destruction of the contraps – was unauthorised and would never *be* authorised.

Best not talk about that.

"You mean work?" she asked instead.

"Yes, your personal battle with Angel, the oppressor, the NVF."

"Could be better. It's problematic." She did not want to get into specifics as that would no doubt lengthen the meeting considerably. She fought to think of a subject she actually wanted to talk about and stumbled upon a matter that had puzzled her for a while. "Albert and the other ghosts call me the Hope Bringer, but I don't understand why. It's... It feels like a weight I bear."

"The Hope Bringer? Interesting. Sounds positive."

"Yes, but what is hope? An abstract concept? An idyllic dream? A useless, intangible belief that fate will somehow deal you a better hand?" Tyler stared at her palms, feeling the weight of the Reverend's expectant gaze. She shook her head. "I'm nothing special."

"Hope can be a notion. It can be a belief, but it has nothing to do with fate. Believe me, hope can make all the difference. Not out there, but in here." Jacob's tapped his head. "And what happens in here affects the choices you make out there."

"I guess, but I'm just the same as everyone else."

"The same as your friend Lucy?"

"Well, no. Nobody's quite the same as Lucy, but you know what I mean."

"You forget, we are all created as individuals. Everyone is different and we each bring our gifts to the altar. Tell me about *your* gifts. What do *you* have that no one else has?"

Tyler's thoughts turned to the contrap.

"I mean with your personality. Tell me something positive about yourself."

Tyler stared at the floor, the wall, at the reverend's interlaced fingers, freckled with years. Nothing came to mind.

"He gave you a righteous heart, Tyler. From what I know, you have a passion for doing the right thing, the correct thing, everything in its place, even in the details." The reverend switched to a different line of thought so seamlessly that Tyler wondered how he connected the two. "I have a theory about why this happened the first time. Why this war's happening again. It's all about the Jews returning to Jerusalem. Would you care to hear it?"

She frowned.

"Another time, perhaps. I have a lot on my plate right now."

"Of course, of course. As I say, it's only a theory, but I think it may interest you. Feel free to visit. I'll always make time for you." He stood, signalling the end of their talk.

Approaching the door, she turned.

"Reverend, do you think it's wrong of me to use the contrap against the oppressor? After all, even *I* believe it's evil."

"I'm not interested in judging anyone although, as I understand it, it does mean you are breaking some fundamentally moral rules. But we should never exclude the possibility that God could be working his purposes even in the darkest of circumstances. What does that discerning heart of yours tell you?"

*

Tyler peered into the *Ghost Portal*. Albert stood peering out from the other side of the lens, hands on hips. With him, Ruth Cobbler watched agitatedly, her good eye roving.

"Missy, we got a problem."

"What? Where's Mary Cobbler? Did you see her? I swear I put her in there."

"Oh, we saw 'er all right, saw 'er streak through the Distant City like a dose o'salts."

"What do you mean?"

"She's trouble, that one. She's taken over the eastern quarter."

"Taken over?"

"Made 'erself queen an' she's drawing every bad'un to her aid. The city's in uproar. She's callin' 'erself the Witch Queen of Gravitas an'er numbers are growin' by the minute."

In silence, Tyler absorbed the news. The thought of the entire population of the *Ghost Portal* turning bad was unbearable.

"What have I done?"

"You weren't to know, Missy. It ain't your fault."

Izabella and Zebedee uncloaked across from Tyler's office desk.

"It is as I feared," said Izabella. "This is serious. If the witch is not stopped, her growing power could unbalance the contrap. In essence, she could wield it from within."

"Is that possible?" asked Tyler.

The wrinkles of Izabella's face deepened. "I expect so, if she knows enough magic. There's only one thing to do. You'll have to send in the Ghost Squad and Albert's army to quell the uprising. You can't afford to have the contrap turn against you."

Albert nodded.

"Send'em in, Missy. Send'em in as soon as ya'can!"

Sentient Lenses

Zebedee Lieberman locked eyes with Tyler across her desk. He seemed somehow thinner than usual, wirier if that were possible, and Tyler marvelled at the pristine nature of his attire: his spidery frame, trousers stretching to the ground like a pair of drainpipes, black dress coat and tie, the white wings of his shirt collar protruding beneath his beard. Taking his pipe from his mouth, he cleared his throat.

"I'm afraid I bring more bad news, Miss May, though it will take some explaining. Perhaps you should send the troops into Memoria Gravitas before I begin."

"Can't it wait? I have to get to Sotherby's."

"No, it can't," said Izabella.

Mr Chapman knocked and entered the DWM office.

"Angel has slipped away again. We were too late locking down the building. Thought you should know."

"Thank you, Sir. I'll get over there ASAP."

"See that you do." Chapman stalked from the room.

Tyler stared at the closed door.

I can't be everywhere at once.

Angel was gone. She couldn't help that now. She sent the Ghost Squad and Albert's ghost army into the *Ghost Portal*, a lengthy process that left her feeling drained. That left only Zebedee and Izabella remaining with her should she require help. When she was finished she invited Zebedee to continue and, while he talked, made herself a mug of hot chocolate and took a seat, sipping and wondering if her day could get any worse.

"I'm very busy. What's so important?"

Zebedee drew his pocket watch from his waistcoat, opened it and let it dangle on its chain in front of Tyler.

"You are aware that this has never worked, not since I became a ghost?"

"Yes."

"Take a closer look."

Tyler leaned in to study the watch, surprised to see the second hand ticking with mechanical regularity.

"It's working again. So?"

"It means the balance of the realms is shifting."

Tyler closed her eyes and let her head rest against the back of the chair. "Here we go."

"I'm sorry, Miss May. We are losing the fight. I don't know how, but the oppressor is turning the tide. Obviously the witch uprising within the portal is not helping, but we know he has pursued a means to unbalance the realms using dark matter, hoping to merge them."

Izabella nudged his arm with her elbow. "It's time, Zebedee. Get on with it."

"With what?" asked Tyler.

Zebedee tucked his watch away.

"When I said nobody knows what this dark matter is – what this substance is between the plural curtains separating the realms – I wasn't being strictly honest. *I* know."

"So why wait until now to fess up?"

"Because I'm not supposed to know. No one is. I only stumbled upon the beings when searching for ghosts and the other spirits mentioned in my book, Ghost Haunting. I'm telling you now because, all of a sudden, it has become crucially relevant." Zebedee pulled a pair of Victorian welding goggles from a pocket of his tailcoat.

"I was experimenting with glasses of various compounds, hoping to develop a new lens that would reveal hidden ghosts. I was getting nowhere until one day I added a little strontium to the mix. When I looked through the strontium lenses with the right lighting I saw vague shapes that were previously absent. I knew I was on to something. I tried numerous different arrangements of layers, various compounds." Zebedee studied the wielding goggles in his hands. "The last combination of layers I tried showed a vastly improved view of the beings, but they were so bright I was blinded for a week. The lenses created a negative polarised view. I saw the dark matter beings clearly for the first time when I inserted the lenses into these welder's goggles to protect my eyes from the incredible glare. The sentients are numerous. They are everywhere. I studied them, trying to learn what they were and their purpose. My observations suggest they are incapable of thought, but they feel.

"Of course nothing much actually works in the under realms – my pocket chronometer for instance – but this morning I heard it ticking. It's a sign. I fear the shifting balance has crossed a line, one quite sinister. The varying laws of the realms are shifting with the oppressor's increasing power over the sentients."

"Are the sentients good or bad?" asked Tyler.

"Neither. They simply hold things in balance. Or, at least, they did."

"I'm not sure I understand. How does knowing any of this help us?"

"It doesn't really, although along with my watch, the goggles have also started working again. It means I can track the transforming sentients. There are positive sentients and negative sentients. As they change, so does the balance." Zebedee donned the goggles, their black glasses catching the light. He gazed around studying beings beyond her sight. "This is a warning, Tyler. I've travelled far and wide in my study. The negative sentients are becoming too numerous."

*

Within the *Ghost Portal,* Albert and the rest of the squad gathered, surrounded by his army as memory mist drifted in a haze. In the expanse beneath the rolling Black Sun, the lights of Memoria Gravitas twinkled and gleamed. Albert watched the city's endlessly shifting form. Kylie Marsh, captain of the squad, stood close by.

"So, what's the plan, Albert?"

"I don't 'ave one."

"We're going to need one if we're to stand a chance of defeating the witch."

"Agreed. We 'ave the army and then there's the rest

of the city dwellers. We need to reach them before the witch does and tell'em what's goin' on."

"Right. We should send out everyone we have to gather the city dwellers together, inform them what's happening and warn them about the witch. Shame we don't have any Mordecai chains."

"For sure," said Albert. "Let's go."

Albert and Kylie set off across the unstable morass of memory mist, the others following in a crowd.

*

Crow's Nest (MI6 black site airfield and communications centre)
15:00 hours

Melissa, Freddy and Klaus crossed the hanger of Crow's Nest to board the plane, to the uninitiated, a modest private jet. They stowed their baggage and buckled into their seats. A hostess brought drinks and returned to the cabin, leaving the agents to talk.

"So, what's the plan?" asked Freddy, nursing a light beer.

"You think I've had time to formulate a plan?" Melissa took out her laptop and set it up on the small, fixed table in front of her.

Klaus grinned briefly.

"Just as well we have a fifteen hour flight to kill."

*

Sotherby's London Headquarters

Tyler parked on New Bond Street amid the confusion of police vehicles on the road outside and ducked under blue and white cordoning tape that read POLICE LINE DO NOT CROSS. She climbed grand steps set between black framed, arched windows and black railings, to enter through the grey stone building's impressive arched doorway. She flashed her badge at the officer standing guard.

Inside the auction house she passed more policemen watching those unfortunates trapped moments after her call came through.

She set the contrap to the *Past Eye* and levered back the trace image to a point earlier in the day, ignoring strange looks from the prisoners. She located Angel after searching through the building for half an hour, and watched the trace play out.

Angel walked through the entrance hall as though he owned the place. She tracked his progress, listening when he approached an unsuspecting receptionist.

"You will bring to me a copy of the auction catalogue from the sold auction lot archive dated nineteen sixty-seven. You will do it quickly." He pulled a handgun from his pocket and held it discreetly, where she alone could see it.

"You will have to wait here while I go and search the archives."

"No. I will accompany you. Do not think about alerting anyone."

The receptionist nodded and led him deeper into the building. Tyler followed them into a long room lined with filing cabinets. The receptionist selected a cabinet, opened a drawer and searched. She took out a catalogue and passed it to Angel.

He flipped through its pages.

"Isn't that *nice!*" He pocketed the catalogue. "Stay there or I'll kill you."

Trembling, the woman nodded again and watched

Angel leave.

Tyler monitored Angel's trace image as he left the building, noting the riotous arrival of a dozen police cars as he turned into another street. He hailed a taxi and climbed in. The car pulled swiftly away from the curb, honking impatiently at vehicles in its path.

Tyler also took a taxi, pausing the contrap's lever until her ride pulled out in Angel's wake. Two hundred metres down the road she saw Angel toss an item from his window, and she had her driver pull over. She left her taxi to retrieve the discarded item from the pavement, puzzled to find it was the lot catalogue.

Rifling through its pages she stopped at a torn remnant of a missing leaf close in to the spine. The page numbers jumped from sixteen to nineteen. She looked again at the images of the auction lots, each one an antique collectable document. Some were a hundred or so years old. Others dated back as far as the fifteenth century. She noticed older parchment scrolls and even papyrus lots, their writings faded.

Unsure if she should return to the auction house or continue what felt like an impossible pursuit, she peered from the catalogue to the road where Angel had made his escape hours earlier. A glance into the contrap's crystal ended her indecision as the ominous Black Sun rolled in to fill her view. She switched to the *Safeguarding skull*, tucked the contrap into her shirt and climbed back into the cab.

"Sotheby's, please."

*

Tyler searched faces until she hit upon the receptionist sitting at a table with several co-workers.

"You're the one he spoke to."

"Yes."

"Come with me." Tyler flashed her badge and the receptionist left the table. "What's your name?" Tyler led the way towards the archive store.

"Rose Jenkins."

"Rose, I'm going to need another copy of the lot catalogue that the man stole from you. Can you get one for me?"

"No."

"Why not?"

"Because we only keep one print copy for archive purposes. We have numerous catalogues. We don't have the space for multiple back issues. The one in your hand is the only one."

Tyler swore. "There must be another record somewhere. I have to know what was on this missing page."

"There's a digital copy."

Tyler handed the catalogue over. "Please hurry."

"This way." Rose strode to an office where she sat at a computer terminal and navigated through virtual windows to a lot database. Locating the catalogue file, she clicked to open a PDF and forwarded through to page seventeen.

"Here we are, pages seventeen and eighteen." She gave Tyler her chair.

Tyler examined the pages Angel had kept, surprised to see nothing that appeared to be old.

No scrolls, no velum or papyrus. What's so special about these lots?

Page seventeen had only two lots, both listed as seventeenth century, hand-written letters of an intimate nature. Page eighteen showed three items, each one an obscure Victorian Christmas card. Tyler raised her eyebrows at the illustrations: a dead robin, a mouse riding a lobster, and an ugly child sitting in an enormous teapot.

Merry Christmas.

She dismissed the cards and returned to the letters. Both were legible, more-so once she had zoomed in. The first contained nothing pertinent as far as she could tell but halfway through the second she slowed to read more carefully.

It is for this reason I feel you would benefit far more than I from this box of jewellery. Please accept it as a token of gratitude for all you have done for my sister. I am afraid many of the pieces are of little value, though you may find one or two true gems. Alas, the wishing stone with all its characters does not work, but I do hope it brings you good luck. The box itself is carved from the finest Mahogany. I trust you will enjoy it and perhaps think of me when you polish it.

Once again, thank you! I pray I may have the good fortune to sit with you again before too long.

Yours truly,
Archi

Archi's fawning letter was addressed to Miss Meriel Renard and dated first of June sixteen forty-nine. Tyler took out her notebook and added the name and date to her new diagram, scribbling a question mark by it.

History of the Dark Sister

	↓
Circa 1594	*Douglas Anthony de Winter*
	↓
Circa 1636	*Archibald de Winter*
	↓
Circa 1649	*Meriel Renard?*

"Can you print this off?"

"Yes, no problem."

"Thank you, Rose. You've been very helpful." Tyler phoned Perkins.

"Hello, Tyler."

"Hi, Perkins. I need everything you can find on one Miss Meriel Renard. She was alive in sixteen forty-nine." Tyler found the address at the top of the letter. "Address eleven Goswell Road, Clarkenwell, Islington, London. Got that?"

Rest in Pieces

Tyler arrived home late evening and shoved a ready meal into the microwave. The fact that her team was split and heading in different directions left her unsettled. The embarrassing failure to catch Angel, the emergence of the dark sister and the lost scrolls of Onuris made her restless. She paced the kitchen floor, waiting for the beeps. Her mobile buzzed in her pocket and she dragged it out to answer the call, glancing at the caller ID.

"Perkins."

"I'm sending the data now. Should be with you any second."

"Is there a will?"

"I thought you'd ask that. I took the liberty of

acquiring a copy and reading it."

"And?"

"Meriel Renard died of smallpox in sixteen fifty-four. She left a silvered jewel, sounding uncannily similar to your contrap, to a friend named Tobias Larkin."

Tyler jotted down the name and the date on a memo pad by the kettle as the microwave issued four beeps.

"Good work. I need you to trace Tobias, specifically his will."

"I don't think he ever made one."

"Why do you say that?"

"Tobias Larkin died of the plague when he was thirty-six. I looked him up."

"You're joking. The plague?"

"No joke. The Great Plague of London in sixteen sixty-five, to be precise."

"That complicates things."

"Yes, though I was able to track down his burial. If he was wearing the dark sister when he died it could well have been put into the grave with his body. People didn't want to go anywhere near the plague victims for obvious reasons. They were rarely plundered. Anyway, it's all in my report."

"Thanks, Perkins."

Tyler carried her meal into the lounge. She set up her laptop and opened Perkins' email and its attachment. She speed-read the entire report and focused on the details about the plague death.

Tobias Larkin was buried in a plague pit less than an hour's drive from her door. Tyler bolted down a few mouthfuls of her microwave meal and grabbed her coat. At the car, her mobile buzzed.

Perkins again.

"Are you watching the news?"

"No, I'm heading–"

"Six archaeologists, each murdered in different locations this afternoon: Paul Fenton, drowned in the Thames; Michael Bayfield, car crash fatality; Jenny Loughery, a mugging gone wrong; Geoffrey Putts, supposed suicide; Emma Bletchley; an apparent drug overdose; and Jacob Marlstone, suspected heart attack. They've all worked on the recent Crossrail dig, a detail reported by the press. The police have yet to comment."

"Tobias Larkin's plague pit? I was just heading there."

"Well don't, at least, not alone. Listen, I can leave Jade and Jenner chasing Angel's agents but no one else is available. I'll meet you there in forty minutes."

"Okay."

"And, Tyler, bring your gun."

*

23:10 hours

The night was dry, moonless and black outside Tyler's car window. She watched the road. The excavation nestled close by beneath a covering of scaffold and corrugated iron, amid a rambling building site. She checked the Glock Lucy had left her as the blinding white headlights of a car swung into view and approached. The car stopped and Perkins lumbered out, lurching in the shadows to jut his formidable chin at her. She left her car and joined him at the edge of the pit, ducking beneath police tape to pick the heavy padlock that held the chain link gates closed. Perkins was twenty or so years Tyler's elder but a sound officer who, ungrudgingly, gave her the respect her early-advancement demanded. Rather than resent, it seemed to Tyler that he had decided to use his superior experience in the field to genuinely aid her, needing little prompting to offer advice while being careful not to tread on her toes. He stood a head taller than her, his scalp bristling with closely trimmed blond hair. His eyes, although too small and close-set for Tyler's liking, glimmered with a candid intelligence as he observed his surroundings.

"Seems the Old Bill *have* made the connection."

"I guess so. Do you think the dark sister's here?"

"I don't know but I intend to find out. Were there any others on the dig?" Tyler finished with the lock and eased it clear of the bolt. She opened the gate wide enough for them both to slip through. Across the site, water dripped from the scaffold, run off from the recent rain.

"Only one other archaeologist, Professor Neil Jackson, currently missing. The police are seeking him in connection with the other killings, thinking he's either the killer or he's dead, too."

"You don't say."

Perkins jutted his chin again.

"Here, give me a hand." Tyler used him for support as she descended a slippery bank to a lower platform of the dig. The damp, musty smell of mud and ancient decay was stronger here. With a further drop down a concrete face she reached the lowest level where the skeletons of plague victims littered the dirt, piled one on top of another, head to foot.

Their torches illuminated the bones like floodlights on a sea of drowned men.

Squelching through the mire around the pit, Tyler circled the remains with little expectation. Either the dark sister was still buried beneath the surface in the thick brown dirt, or someone had already found it. She presumed it was the latter but her compulsion demanded she check the entire dig.

When she had searched and was convinced it was not among the surface mud and bones, she drew out her contrap and switched to the *Tower of Doom*. With one eye on the tower she walked further from the remains. Within the crystal, small stones slowly lifted to the tower's half-built rubble walls.

"It's not here. Professor Jackson must have it."

"If he's still alive. Anything else you can try with that thing?"

Tyler gazed at the slippery mass of ribs, vertebrae, skulls, jaws, scapulae and long bones; a plethora of the highest quality artefacts with which to summon the ghosts of those dead.

"Yes." Casting around, she checked to be sure they were alone before kneeling at the side of the closest skeleton. She set the contrap to the *Ghost Portal* and placed it on top of the skull, waiting. The ghost of a middle-aged man in a frilled shirt, a long coat with many buttons and enormous cuffs, and wearing a tricorn hat, arose like a plume of cloud from the ground. Peering around, he fixed upon Tyler.

"Why do you summon me thus, Maid?"

"I'm no maid. I seek a jewel the same as this." Tyler gestured to the contrap perched atop the ghost's grizzled cranium. "Have you seen another like it?"

"I have not. Now kindly return me to my rest!"

"Very well." Tyler reclaimed the contrap and the ghost vanished back into the mire. She tried a fragmented skull while, above, Perkins prowled the site perimeter, gun poised. The ghost of an old woman in a shawl gathered from the grave, piercing Tyler with narrowed eyes. The woman's hair was straggled and loose, her dun coloured dress reaching to the ground.

"Sorry to bother you, but I'm seeking a jewel like this one." Again she gestured. "It was taken from this grave. Have you seen it?"

The old woman shook her head slowly while maintaining a sorrowful glare.

"Can you not speak?"

Again the ghost shook her head, now pointing to her stump of a tongue as she let her mouth yawn open.

"They cut out your tongue?"

The ghost nodded.

"I'm sorry. All right, I'll let you return. Rest in peace."

The woman gave one final nod and Tyler lifted the contrap from the broken skull. Like a scuttled ship, the woman sank back into the mire.

Tyler spoke to eleven ghosts, each time resting the contrap on the slick domes of skulls, cranial fragments or, where the skulls were badly shattered and scattered amongst other bones, using jaw bones. None could help until the ghost of a young girl coalesced over her skeleton, skirts and hair blowing in a wind that Tyler did not feel.

"Yes, I saw a jewel almost the same. I watched him take a muddy little box from the grave. From the box he took the jewel. He didn't put it in the tray with the other finds. He wiped it clean and tucked it into his pocket."

"Who? Can you describe him?"

The girl shrugged. "He has a beard and wears a strange hat of striped wool. They call him the professor."

"Thank you." Tyler smiled at the girl ghost, removed

the contrap and climbed out of the excavation to join Perkins. As the girl vanished, Tyler set the contrap to the *Tree of Knowledge* and spoke into the crystal, hoping that Albert would be able to help her again.

"Where is Professor Neil Jackson?"

She was amazed when an instant response floated into view.

Professor Neil Jackson flees for his life

"But *where* is he?"

London, 223 Waterloo Road
221 Waterloo Road
219 Waterloo Road

Like a possessed stopwatch the contrap lens continued to display descending addresses one after the other.

"Okay, I get the picture. How do I know I can trust you?"

You don't

The words dissolved away as more took their place.

Never trust the **Tree of Knowledge**

"Great, thanks."

You'd better hurry
Missy
He won't be there long

"Thanks, Albert!" Tyler switched to the *Safeguarding Skull* and headed for her car as Perkins strode behind. "We're done here. The professor's running for his life on Waterloo Road. He's heading for the station!"

*

The grand white stone entrance to Waterloo Station bustled with businessmen and women, students and late night revellers. The clock set into the windowed arch showed just gone midnight.

Tyler switched to the *Past Eye* and drew the contrap's lever clockwise to review the last half hour. She watched for anyone rushing and knew she had found the professor when a bearded man in a parka and a blue and red striped bobble hat tore by. Jackson was a fifty-something with a pronounced nose and furtive eyes. Among the pedestrians behind, three men pursued.

With Perkins tailing, Tyler tracked Professor Jackson as he sprinted up the station's entrance steps and followed, shouldering through the crowds around the arch. Inside, the floor opened onto a wide concourse roofed with black ironwork and glass where people hurried like ants in a hill. She studied the potential routes: shop entrances, washrooms, restaurants, cafés, departure and arrival gates, escalators and stairs, everywhere gleaming with glass, polished steel and iron. Armed police, their presence a result of the continuing terrorist attacks, held stations at all exits.

The professor dashed behind a queue of people at the ticket office and lost his pursuers for a few precious moments in which he managed to reach an escalator. Tearing the hat from his head, he stuffed it into his coat pocket and walked casually upwards as the escalator trundled. Below, the three pursuers separated to search shops, cafés and the departure gates.

Tyler found Perkins and grabbed his arm.

"He was here around twenty minutes ago. A bearded man with greying hair, medium build and a navy-blue parka. We have to find him before they do. Check the platforms. If he's still here, he'll be waiting for a train."

Perkins stared at her, desperation in his eyes.

"I've called it in but it could take forever for CCTV to track him down. Too many platforms. Too many people. You have to find another way or we'll lose him."

Tyler switched to the *Tree of Knowledge*, muttering under breath.

"Come on, come on..." The contrap rotated, clicking into position. "Where is Professor Jackson?" She waited for what seemed an age while her words drifted away and an answer floated into view.

Professor Jackson is standing on a platform in Waterloo Station

"Which platform?"

Platform

Before the number could form, the crystal flashed black and Tyler was left peering into the *Ghost Portal*. Again she switched to the *Tree of Knowledge* but once more the contrap clicked back to the *Ghost Portal* and the monstrous Black Sun.

"It's not working. We've no choice. Search every platform!"

Perkins dashed away as Tyler sped towards the departure gates where queues of people blocked her path.

Frantically, she studied the departures board for the most imminent and brandished her badge of office whilst shoving a way through, shouting.

"Security services! Make way!"

A ripple of fear permeated the lines and they dispersed with increasing speed as she neared the barrier. She ducked beneath the barrier, ignoring the cries of a dozy station guard who had failed to comprehend the badge she frantically waved. Dodging baggage, she brushed past travellers and sprinted to the first platform on her mental list. She ran the length, seeking Jackson as a train pulled in and passengers boarded. The second platform was the same; a crush of passengers waiting to leave, none of them Jackson. She had no idea where Perkins was and realised her comms ear piece was back at home. Grabbing her mobile she called him but received no answer.

Three platforms later she spied the professor on an adjacent platform. He stood, grasping an open newspaper, nervously scanning the platform entrance for threats. She considered calling to him across the tracks, showing her badge and ordering him to wait, but knew he would flee. Out of options, she hurried to the stairs of platform nineteen where she slowed to approach with stealth.

Her heart leapt as the sound of an incoming engine caused her to turn. Jackson's train pulled into the station.

Tyler ran.

Platform 19

The doors of the train opened as Tyler reached her platform exit and conductors waved new passengers aboard. She assessed the distance she would need to sprint before even reaching the beginning of platform nineteen and knew she could be too late. The trains sometimes stayed only a minute or so. Abandoning her prior plan, she crossed to the edge of her platform and leapt down onto the tracks. A thirty seconds' dash took her to the driver's cab where she slapped her badge against the side window.

"NATIONAL SECURITY! OPEN THE DOOR!"

She froze. On the other side of the window a man held a gun to the driver's head, his command muffled by the glass.

"DRIVE!"

The driver engaged the engine and Tyler stepped onto the footplate, clinging to the handrails as the train rolled into motion. She ducked aside as the agent blasted three shots at her, blowing the glass.

Perkins, where are you?

The train gathered momentum and Tyler climbed precariously onto the roof, gripping sparse handholds. She gauged she would have around ten seconds before the engine reached speeds too fast for her to cling on. With the contrap switching to the *Ghost Portal* of its own accord she dared not use it to fly.

The nearest window beyond the driver's cab was several metres away. With increasing desperation she crawled to it and slid her gun from her shoulder holster. Leaning out as far as she dared, she peered into the carriage, saw the way was clear and fired through the glass. The window fractured into a thousand jewels but held fast until she swung down, feet first, to kick it in. The entire pane folded and fell into the train, leaving a hole for her to drop through.

The train gained speed.

Further down the carriage, movement caught her eye. Through the adjoining windows she glimpsed a fight. She sped to the end of the carriage to see more clearly. In the next car the agents wrestled with Jackson. One of them clobbered him around the head with the butt of a gun and another shoved a revolver's muzzle into his mouth to bring him under control. Jackson stilled, his fear-widened eyes flicking from one agent to another.

As soon as the automatic doors opened, Tyler stepped through with her gun trained on the agent threatening

Jackson. The other two instantly turned their guns on her.

"Well, well, if it isn't the one and only Tyler May, come to join the party. The boss *will* be pleased when we present him with *both* of the silver trinkets." The agent's face was familiar: long black hair, a doughy, pale complexion, and a dimpled chin. A trilby shadowed his eyes, and Tyler knew she had seen him leaving Wilson's with Angel through the *Past Eye*.

Dough Face yanked at the chain hidden beneath Jackson's sweater until the dark sister fell free from the neckline.

"Three guns to one, Tyler. Unfortunate odds for you."

"The odds have never been in my favour. It hasn't stopped me so far."

"Shoot her," Dough Face commanded, as another voice fell from the far end of the carriage.

"LOWER YOUR WEAPONS." An armed transport officer levelled his machine gun on the gathering. "ALL OF YOU!"

Dough Face nodded to an agent who turned his gun on the officer.

"Oops," said Tyler. "Seems the odds have changed. NATIONAL SECURITY. YOU THREE ARE UNDER ARREST."

The officer took several tentative steps closer as the noise of a helicopter grew. Dough Face muttered into the lapel of his coat beyond Tyler's hearing. She noticed the miniscule comms mic pinned there.

"Then you have ID," said the officer.

"I do," said Tyler, glimpsing the shadow of the helicopter through the side windows as it overtook the train. She risked a glance up ahead at the curving tracks where the craft landed to straddle the lines. Two men fled the cockpit, running for cover. She swore and grabbed the closest seat, bracing for impact. As the engine brakes squealed, she heard Dough Face one last time.

"Farewell, Tyler May."

*

The traffic officer opened fire as the impact of the crash threw passengers sideways. The carriage left the tracks in the slipstream of the derailed locomotive. Glass burst upon the air in a multitude of explosions. Mangled metal shredded flesh as bodies slammed into seats, walls, doors, and the ceiling. Ahead of her carriage the scattered remains of the helicopter rained, burning around the flaming engine that slowed and groaned to a rest.

Blood leaked into her left eye from a gash on her temple and her right arm hurt so much that she feared it was broken. She tested it.

No, just twisted and badly bruised.

A pain shot up her shoulder like a burning knife every time she bent her elbow. She staggered upright, limping on the wall of the overturned carriage. Through dust and smoke she searched. Professor Jackson and the NVF agents were gone. She took out her phone to call Chapman but it was dead, its screen smashed and its casing bent. She looted a working phone from an unconscious passenger and dialled.

"They have it." She scanned around for a reference point but saw nothing useful, the backs of houses and graffiti covered concrete sidings. Blood oozed down her face and across her mouth. Her head throbbed with a faint-threatening nausea. She could barely speak. "Train crash. Waterloo. Twelve fifteen to Reading. Cordon and search. Three agents. Professor Neil Jackson. The dark sister."

A new pain silenced her, pulsing at the base of her neck. She dropped the phone and collapsed.

*

The twenty-five metre yacht coasted at an easy pace slicing the crystalline, blue Pacific. Elysium's black glass, white decks and hull, gleamed in the sunlight as MI6 field agent Akana eased back on the throttle. A hundred metres from port, stony slopes plummeted into the sea forming a rocky shoreline upon which little grew. Akana gestured towards it.

"Lehua Isle, the most remote of the Hawaiian Islands. A horseshoe off the shore of Niihau, formed from the remains of a volcanic crater. You'll see it soon. Keep your eyes on the edge of the cove. We're passing the northern coast of Kauai." Akana lifted his baseball cap to wipe sweat from his brow. A local, born and bred, he wore a Hawaiian shirt of blue Hibiscus flowers over his bronzed skin, his jet black hair slicked back beneath his cap.

Klaus followed the coast through field glasses as the small island came into view. Lehua was little more than a long curving bay rising to a craggy peak, its slopes all but barren of grass. In the hook of the bay an odd-looking structure lodged, spanning from the beach into the sea. Three pairs of supporting stilts plunged into the beach, stretching from the sand to the waves, the construction resembled a gargantuan insect that had landed and taken root, its wings of solar glass folded across its rounded back. Other than the oversized legs, the laboratory block shared an uncanny similarity with those Klaus, Melissa and Freddy had witnessed in Greenland.

"It looks kind of temporary," said Klaus. "Like it could raise its legs and float away at the push of a button."

"But that's it, all right." Melissa read the company logo emblazoned along the laboratory's side in square, chunky letters above a suspended metal walkway. "Aloha Research; the nerve centre of the NVF laboratory network. Can you get us closer, Akana? We have to get in, somehow."

Akana steered the yacht nearer and let the engines idle. "I can take you in for a closer look but you'll have to use the dingy if you want to beach. It's too shallow for the yacht, and I've done my homework: This place never sleeps. Whatever they're doing in there, they do it day in, day out."

"We'll wait until dark." Klaus focused in on the lab through his glasses. "Akana can drop us on the other side of the island tonight."

*

The army rumbled to a halt, Saxons leaning on their spears and Vikings on their axes. Slaves and Victorian chimney sweeps brandished smouldering branches impregnated with fire-fog taken from the Chasm, while the Roman soldiers carried short swords, pila and tall standards.

At the army's head, Albert paused to observe the ever-shifting buildings of the Distant City. Before him sprawled an eclectic mix of constructions: tower blocks of concrete, thatched wattle and daub roundhouses, grand Roman villas, black and white Tudor cottages, stone houses from many eras, brick terraces and all kinds of homes including several caves. The closest, a Viking longhouse, drifted slowly past the front ranks as though sliding on a bed of ice while, behind it, the curved towers of a castle grew taller with each second. High-rises hummed with their gentle transformation as cuboid flats swapped places, rising and falling, and migrating left and right in a bewildering dance. Between each of these dwellings, the memory mist rolled and floated in dense drifts. Where a building grew, the mist closed in to form the new growth. Where one decreased, or changed position altogether, the mist dissolved like desert sand on a ceaseless wind, only to reassemble elsewhere.

Somewhere beyond this strange urban edge, the Witch Queen sat enthroned, expanding her hordes.

Albert turned to his diverse assortment of warriors.

"Wait 'ere while I scout ahead. Kylie, Marcus, with me."

The three ghosts left the army and slipped silently into the city, passing the drifting longhouse and skirting the castle moat, that undulated as though alive. Albert scrutinised each of the castle's narrow slits but saw no movement within. Each of the buildings appeared deserted and, after several minutes of investigation, they found the temporal streets and alleyways empty.

"We'll 'ave to try one of these 'ouses," said Albert. "See if we can't find someone inside." He approached a stone cottage, sneaking to a side window where he peered in, whispering to Kylie and Marcus.

"Too dark. I can't see nuffink."

He crept around further to try the back door. It opened at his touch and he spied through the slim gap, expecting a stream of abuse for disturbing the occupants. No torrent came. Pushing the door wider, he stepped into the inner gloom, sensing this, too, was vacant.

"'Ello? Anyone at 'ome?"

On they searched, pressing deeper into the city until they reached a low-built, squalid hovel. Before it, a small garden of flowering plants waltzed. From the doorway a hooded ghost watched the trio approach, his eyes in deep shadow.

Albert called to him.

"Hey, Mister, where is everyone?"

The hooded ghost shuffled in his doorway.

"Gone. Chains, so many chains," the man lamented.

"Gone where?"

Stooping, the man hobbled out from the entrance to limp closer. Leaving the hovel's shade, his appearance became more apparent. His face was withered and wrinkled. His hands, protruding from the long drooping sleeves of his rust brown robes, were emaciated and claw-like, the knuckles swollen and rheumatic.

"Gone with the witch. One way or t'other they's gone. She didn't want me. No, she didn't want old Josiah. She just laughed and said I was good for nothin'."

"What do you mean, one way or the other?" asked Kylie, stepping closer.

"Either they went willingly to join her legions or she took 'em by force, see? They came marauding in the night, like thieves with chains!" Josiah repeated the word chains many times and babbled indiscernibly until Albert clenched his shoulders, glaring at him.

"Where are they?"

"Where did she take them?" demanded Kylie.

Josiah's focus sharpened as he peered briefly from Albert to Kylie and back again. Turning, he raised a crooked finger to point further into the city where a tower pierced the horizon, menacing high over its surroundings.

"There."

"That's new," said Kylie.

Albert released Josiah, who staggered and sat upon a rock near his swirling garden.

"Marcus, go back and fetch the army. Bring them 'ere, all right?"

With a nod Marcus turned and left, dodging through the foggy paths and streets.

*

The water shimmered differently at night. Beneath Elysium's lamps it seemed menacing to Melissa, its gentle surge deceptive.

Dressed all in black with assault boots, combats and a high-necked jumper, Melissa watched the sea lap against the dingy as Klaus descended the yacht's fixed ladder to board ahead of her and wondered what horrors lurked beneath the surface. Freddy embraced her on the pristine deck one last time.

"Good luck. I'll be here, waiting."

Melissa nodded, clasped the gleaming chrome ladder top and lowered herself towards the dingy.

"Take my hand. You'll be fine." Klaus guided her aboard and took up the oars as she tentatively lowered herself onto a plank seat. "It's not far."

Across the water the rising arête of Lehua loomed, a grey hump against the night sky.

Klaus rowed, closing the gap between them and the volcanic shore. This side of the isle offered no beach, but a plethora of steep crags snagged its length. Klaus aimed for a crevice between two outcrops and drove the boat in hard until it buffeted against rock. He swung a grappling hook, releasing the rope to fly up onto the dry slope. Tugging it back until the hook bit firmly into the hill, he tied off the dingy and helped Melissa climb out and onto the island.

115

He threw a pack over his shoulders and scrambled ashore to begin the climb. In his night-ops gear he appeared as a fleeting shadow against the low growing scrub of the incline. Behind Melissa on the yacht, Freddy watched through night vision goggles. She glanced back with an unsettling feeling that this could be her last mission.

*

Albert found a rickety ladder and, bracing it against the hovel wall, climbed to the roof. He crawled to the apex for a better look at the witch's tower. A ring of tall windows beneath the tower's conical roof glowed with light.

That's where she is. From that 'igh chamber of the tower she can keep watch over the entire city.

Far below, the haphazard misty streets phosphoresced with an odd, murky green hue, broken here and there by stronger, flickering ghost lights. Albert imagined they were the camp fires of the witch's numerous hordes.

Whatever spell she cast over the city's population must 'a' been formidable.

He descended and reported to Kylie.

"A green mist. How peculiar."

"It's the witch's doing. It 'as to be."

"Do you think she knows we're here?"

"I expect so. I bet she 'as spies everywhere. Wait. Where's Josiah?"

"He was over there by the garden just a minute ago."

"Well, 'e ain't now." Albert checked the hovel and, finding it empty, called. "Josiah?" Greeted by silence he kicked the door jamb. "He's a spy! What did I tell ya'?"

"We'll have to be more careful. I guess she knows

we're coming now."

"Guess so. 'Ow could I be so stupid?"

"Don't blame yourself, Albert. You weren't to know. I don't suppose we stand much chance of a surprise attack anyway, not when we're trailing your entire army through the city."

A spark kindled in Albert's eyes. "You're right. We'll split 'em up, send 'em different ways. We'll be far 'arder to detect in smaller groups and there's no open ground in the city in any case, nowhere we could march in force. We'll fight better in gangs."

Kylie pushed her glasses further up her nose. "Guerrilla tactics."

Albert stared at her. "Huh?"

"Never mind. I agree."

The army trudged into view between a line of brick houses and a mead hall. Albert assembled them in the shadow of an enormous tower block, safe from the witch's view. To address them better he mounted a ghost haystack that seemed, for the time being, stable enough, although it turned in a slow spin, for which he compensated every few seconds by taking a small step to his right.

"Listen up. We're too vulnerable marching in one great lump. We 'ave to split up an' get closer to the tower. That's where the queen is. That's our goal, all right?" Soldiers nodded. Albert designated seventy-two smaller groups referring to them as numbered gangs. He gave each gang a direction to take and sent them on their way to navigate the murky streets.

"Now go! Find as many ghosts as you can! Warn them the witch and sign them up!"

"What about the Ghost Squad?" asked Kylie, as the

last of the gangs departed into the mist.

"Don't worry about the squad. I got a special job for you lot."

Aloha

Klaus traced the line of the ridge for two hundred metres before breaching its crest. Crouching, he observed the laboratory through his night vision glasses and signalled for Melissa to wait.

Below on the narrow beach, lights glimmered from the laboratory's windows.

"All clear." He waved her on and descended the volcanic slope, staying low and watching for movement around the laboratory. Those manning its interior were little more than silhouettes behind the semi-mirrored windows.

Lucy and Weaver uncloaked close by, their translucent forms blending with the scrub and jagged rock of the isle.

"Are you guys *going* to arm us or not?"

Klaus slid four gallows blades from a side pocket of his combats and passed them.

"Be quick."

Exchanging a nod, Lucy and Weaver cloaked and drifted down to the laboratory to investigate. Passing a rank of windows and enjoying their invisibility to the living, they spied on working scientists.

Beneath the platform at Lucy's feet, dark waves rolled in to drag sand in a cyclic surge of froth and roar. She recalled the pleasurable lap of the surf washing over the flesh of her feet and ankles, the touch of warm sand like brown sugar beneath her toes.

Never again. These and a thousand other taken-for-granted simple pleasures were beyond reach.

A movement further down the metal walkway alerted her.

"There!" whispered Weaver, pointing.

A ghost guard hovered nearer in the moon shadow of the giant bug's wings.

Lucy turned and raised her blades, knowing she would soon be detected if she failed to take him down. She flew at the grey coat, glimpsing a military band on his upper arm emblazoned with the Black Sun. Sidestepping to dodge his attack, she drove a blade up between his ribs and watched his essence dissolve like foam on a wave. The roar of the surf drowned his short-lived scream as those beyond the glass laboured, obliviously.

Lucy and Weaver skirted the edge of the building, following the walkway with its long handrail, useless to them, and rounded to the other side where a second grey coat patrolled. Inching closer, Lucy stole up as he scrutinised the shore. A small motion below the ridge caught his attention. He took ghost binoculars from around his neck and studied the slope where Klaus and Melissa crouched.

From ten paces Lucy launched a blade that struck cleanly between the guard's shoulder blades. The guard collapsed like a tumbled sandcastle, his form crumbling through the grid of the walkway and blowing on the ethereal wind.

"Nice shot." Weaver nodded and they continued.

At the lab entrance on the beach side, steel steps rose from the dark sand and pumice pebbles to double doors of steel and dark glass. Lucy checked for other guards once more before handing her blades to Weaver.

"Wait here. I won't be long." Noting the sophisticated key-card locking system, she gave Weaver a brief parting kiss and entered. The doors chilled her form as she passed through into a small antechamber where rubberised suits, an offensive shade of orange, hung above a rack of transparent facemasks and breathing apparatus. A second set of doors brought her into a lab buzzing like a hive with its orderly throng of workers.

She floated, mesmerised at one end of a complex control room of blinking lights and digital displays. A bank of monitors covered one wall where several scientists sat in swivel chairs by a vast console of sliders, switches and dials. Various camera angles showed other technicians in protective gear performing the minor tasks of ongoing experiments.

Okay, let's see what you've got.

Further into the building she found the opportunity she was looking for. A bottle bearing chemical hazard symbols stood close to the edge of a shelf. Beneath, two technicians worked.

Lucy left the building and collected her blades from Weaver.

*

Two pairs of gallows blades fluttered up the slope towards Melissa. She released a small involuntary sound and pointed. Klaus turned.

"Don't worry. It's Lucy and Weaver."

They watched the blades approach and the two ghosts uncloaked. Lucy reported.

"Key-card entrance. Hazard suits in an unattended antechamber. Nothing could be simpler. You'll just need a few seconds to slip in while they're distracted, but I have an idea for that."

*

Lucy peered through the glass. Inside the laboratory, the scientists and technicians were fully absorbed in their work. On the corner of the walkway outside she beckoned to Melissa and Klaus who waited, crouching low to the ground.

All clear.

They dashed the remaining dozen metres and climbed the steps to hug the lab's wall. Klaus risked a glance around through the double doors. He crossed to Lucy and signalled.

Ready.

Lucy and Weaver cloaked, passing through the wall and into the lab. Lucy revisited the isolation chamber with the three technicians, where she had noticed the shelf with the bottle bearing the chemical hazard symbols. Weaver followed. The technicians talked.

"Did you hear? I'm being transferred. I won't be here for the big moment."

The jar was heavy but mere centimetres from the edge of the shelf. Summoning every ounce of strength in her essence, Lucy focused on the bottle and shoved.

"Where are they sending you?"

It inched closer to the edge. The techs continued their work, unaware. Again Lucy pushed, this time with Weaver's help.

"I'm waiting to hear. I don't mind as long as it isn't Ground Zero."

Another inch closer. Another joint push took the bottle further out, its base protruding.

One final shove should do it.

"Huh. Yeah, that's seriously off my tourist map, too."

The bottle dropped, exploding with a volatile, chemical shower and splintering glass. Fumes issued from every splash as a rubber suited tech slammed his hand onto a large red button set on the wall.

*

A laboratory siren startled Melissa. She took a device the size of a calculator from her pack and swapped places with Klaus. He whispered.

"What does that thing do?"

Melissa slid an extension of the device into the key-card lock and powered up. Almost immediately the door lock clicked open.

"It reads the thirty-two bit key that identifies these doors. The microcontroller then plays back the key. Simple." Melissa withdrew the key element and tucked the microcontroller away. "We're in."

They opened the doors and hurried through. In the antechamber they watched through the second set of doors as scientists, engrossed by the emergency at the other end of the building, rushed to help. Many left the room and those remaining gathered to watch the drama play out on monitors, enraptured. This was the most exciting thing that had happened in weeks.

Melissa and Klaus pulled on rubber suits and helped each other with masks and breathing apparatus. Only when fully covered did they dare ease open the other doors and creep in behind the backs of the monitor watchers. They crossed the control room briskly and entered a passage to bury themselves deep in the complex.

*

Memory mist curled in the path ahead, small whirlpools pirouetting, melting, shrinking, growing, merging. From the corner of a rubble wall Albert spied through them to the hazy shapes beyond, where a group of ghosts gathered. Among their number, grey coats patrolled, their MP40s held obliquely, pointing to the treacherous ground. Albert grunted, disheartened. Each and every enemy Tyler had ever put into the portal was here now to stand against him.

Marvellous.

Around him the remaining members of the Ghost Squad squatted, hidden behind the ramshackle ruins of a long-abandoned abbey. Kylie crept to his side.

"What do you think? Prisoners? A search party?"

"Searching for what?"

"Enemies. Vulnerable citizens. Us, maybe."

"They're armed. I've counted five guns so far. Could be more."

"We can take them. They don't know we're here."

"Not yet." Albert scrutinised the slowly moving forms for a leader. "We'll 'ave to split up if we're gonna stand a real chance. Attack from both sides. Choose your team.

I'll take the rest round the back. We'll fight every ghost between here and the queen if we 'ave to."

*

Klaus opened the door to an empty laboratory chamber.

"Quick. In here."

Melissa ran in with Klaus close behind. He closed the door and scanned the room while Melissa searched.

"What do you need?"

"A networked terminal, if possible. Anything with a USB or Ethernet port."

She stopped and swore, noticing the camera pointing at them from the corner of the room.

"We're being watched. Let's hope they don't have audio. Pretend to be working. Take readings. Measure temperatures or something."

Klaus walked to a glass tank and stuck his arms in through the long rubber sleeves that were integral to the unit. He stared through at a batch of copper-coloured hexagons nested among a mass of cables and tubes, and gave one a prod with his finger.

"What *is* this stuff?"

Melissa searched a lab cart and a wall-mounted unit flashing with LED's and dials.

"Super-cooled Germanium crystals, probably. Be careful what you touch."

"Now you tell me. There's a USB port on the side of this thing. No terminal though."

"It doesn't matter as long as it's networked." She took her phone and a USB connector from her pack, plugged them in to the laboratory system, and tapped commands on the phone's touch screen. "Two minutes and we're leaving."

A monitor on the wall opposite blinked to life as a

compressed American voice crackled from a concealed speaker.

"Unit 14, requesting statistics report."

Klaus turned his head slowly to stare at Melissa, his masked eyes pleading.

Emerging from a fear induced paralysis she snatched a clipboard and pen from the cart and bent to examine the wall unit with all its dials, lights and displays. "One minute." She scribbled readings on a sheet and joined Klaus to study more dials at the base of the isolation tank while sweat beaded on her brow. She jotted more figures before reporting.

"Core temperature ninety-six pK. Dilation forty-five. Atomic detection point zero two three nine four. Interference point zero zero seven. Output eighty-two."

"Good job, fourteen." On the monitor an orange suited researcher waved before the screen turned static and blacked out.

Melissa trembled. On her phone's screen a system message blinked.

DOWNLOAD COMPLETED

She tugged the phone and cable free of the port and headed for the door.

"Let's go. I have a *really* bad feeling about this."

*

Albert led his team through the ruins and around the side of an old barn that spun in lazy circles like an enormous top. A block of flats drifted by, temporarily blocking his view of the enemy party, but before it departed a field of medieval tents appeared, each coloured red and gold and emblazoned with a heraldic crest of lions and stars. It floated in from the obscurity of another road and Albert and his team were able to dash from tent to tent while keeping watch on their quarry. As they dodged closer the entire section of city revolved, disorienting them. The low wall of a cottage offered a more stable respite. They ran to it and Albert peered from its far end. Beyond the enemy, the tower loomed into view.

Now a mere ten metres of war-zone rubble lay between him and his foes. He nodded to Wulfric, who swung his axe high to alert Kylie.

*

Kylie signalled to her team and broke cover for the enemy line, raising a branch club in her hand.

"CHARGE!"

Behind her the others burst out from hiding as Albert and his ghosts screamed into the fight. Kylie smirked as unsuspecting grey coats stumbled in shock. They raised their machine guns but Wulfric's axe smashed the first to the ground before a bullet left the barrel.

Kinga grabbed the gun and brought it around to mow down an enemy rank while Kylie clubbed a second gun free. Yakubu reached the line and bulldozed half a dozen ghosts driving in with his bare shoulders. The Ghost Squad rallied to surround the entire group and collect the weapons of the fallen as bullet-riddled ghosts on both sides recovered and staggered to their feet, the wounds in their translucent flesh inevitably returning to states of older memory.

"Guess you can't kill what's already dead." Kylie levelled a salvaged MP40 at the captives.

"Ghost bullets, ghost death. Nothing permanent." Albert shrugged. "Not in this realm, but it'll slow anyone down who tries to escape. Find ropes. Tie up these troublemakers."

"Shame we don't have any gallows blades."

Albert shoved a gun muzzle under the chin of the nearest grey coat, leaning close to scowl in the soldier's face. "You're gonna tell me everyfin' ya'know about the witch's tower or fings are gonna get bad for you."

*

Lucy and Weaver caught up with Melissa and Klaus as they strode back through the main corridor, passing laboratory chambers either side. The ghosts uncloaked.

"Oh, good. It's you. We need one last distraction to get past everyone in the control room."

"Do you have what we came for?" asked Weaver.

Melissa nodded. "And we don't need to return."

Lucy darted ahead of the others, cloaking into thin air long before she reached the control room. She positioned herself four feet from the floor in front of the wall of monitors and uncloaked in front of a host of stunned scientists.

"Aloha, boys."

Behind them, Melissa and Klaus fled.

Prophets

Zebedee Lieberman perched on the edge of Tyler's hospital bed. He peered through the black sentient glass of his goggles, turning to her when she stirred. He slipped them off.

"Miss May, I'm sorry to disturb you."

"Angel has the dark sister."

"Quite possibly. The negative sentients are in rapid ascent. I fear we have little time before the balance tips and the realms merge."

"Will the dark sister make the difference? If the realms have yet to merge perhaps we still have chance. Perhaps the agents haven't reached Angel."

Tyler set the contrap to the *Ghost Portal* and with one

eye squinted into the crystal.

"The portal seems all right to me. It looks normal."

"That's a good sign."

Drifting through a wall, Izabella entered the recovery room.

"You need to get up, girl! Get out of bed. Much to do and so little time. Now pull yourself together."

Tyler's phone buzzed and she answered it.

"Melissa?"

"Hi. We're on our way home. I've made a cursory study of the laboratory data we took and it's not good. It appears they're tracking the progress of the dark matter balance."

"Zebedee is doing a similar thing." Tyler glanced at Zebedee as he gazed around the room through his goggles as though studying a kaleidoscope of extraordinary butterflies. "Weird, but similar."

"If their data's correct, I think the oppressor is achieving his goal. Something is happening – something big – and it's about to get a lot worse. They've been collating a whole lot of ongoing research and charting a general trend. The figures are dropping lower daily and fast approaching something they're referring to as Zero Minus One."

"What's that?"

"A pivotal point. A major downward shift. Something *very bad*. And they're predicting it will happen within the next twenty-four hours."

"The merging of the realms?"

On the end of the line Melissa fell silent before answering.

"I think so."

Tyler's mind spun with fears. *Hell spilling onto Earth.*

Too late. The end.

"Angel is about to receive the dark sister. NVF agents are taking it to him as we speak. Would that be enough bad energy to make the difference?"

"Most likely. We have to stop it happening or all Hell is going to invade planet Earth."

"But I don't know where the dark sister or Angel is, and the Ghost Squad is in the *Portal* along with Albert and his army."

"You have to try something. Ask the *Tree of Knowledge*, try anything. Lucy heard some researchers talking. They mentioned not wanting to be anywhere near Ground Zero."

"Ground Zero?"

"The point at which the realms will merge."

"You mean an actual location on Earth?"

"Exactly."

"Where?"

"From my brief analysis I'm guessing somewhere in the Middle East. I need more time to be sure, but my preliminary results came up with a likely venue: Jerusalem. It kind of makes sense when you look at where they chose to place their laboratory HQ. Hawaii is about as far away from Jerusalem as you can get. When the Chasm erupts into our world the scientists will be safe on the other side of the planet, safe for a while anyway. Maybe they think they can control it, or that Angel will give them protection from the Chasm."

"Yeah, well, they haven't been there."

*

Tyler hammered a fist on the green door of the Burgess Park residence, a thousand thoughts buzzing. In the recesses of her mind, hourglass sands streamed into oblivion, fire-fog on a brimstone wind.

Jewish ghosts, always Jewish ghosts. Why? And why did Marcus come to me that day, years ago? Why find me to tell me his harrowing tale? Why the Jews? Why Hitler? Why persecute the Jews in the first place? Why not the Koreans, the Palestinians or the Egyptians or any other ethnicity? What did the Jews ever do to deserve it, beyond thriving? The more she considered the question the more peculiar it became. *Ghosts, the supernatural, a fallen demon bringing a global plague of war and suffering.*

AND ALWAYS THE JEWS.

Perhaps I'm in the right place after all!

Day off or no day off, she needed to speak urgently with Reverend Jacobs. He took his time answering the door and viewed her over the golden rims of his reading glasses.

"Miss May. To what do I owe the pleasure?"

"Not pleasure. Business." She climbed the worn steps to push past into the house, stopping in the hallway near a beautifully polished wooden staircase with a curling handrail. Too distracted to take in the tasteful Pre-Raphaelite prints in gilded frames adorning the duck egg blue walls, the elegant hall stand and the glossy parquet floor beneath her feet, her gaze bored into the Reverend's mildly surprised eyes.

"You mentioned something about a theory, a theory about Jerusalem. I'm listening."

The Reverend smiled fleetingly and gestured for her to enter his study. "Then you'd better come in. This could take a while. It's complicated."

"I don't have time for complicated. Give me the abridged version."

"Would you like tea or coffee, perhaps?"

"No time."

"How well do you know your Old Testament?"

"Not well at all."

"Hmmm. This is going to be tricky."

"Try me."

The Reverend removed his glasses, replacing them with a pair of bifocals through which he fixed upon Tyler. He pulled up a green leather Chesterfield and sat to one side of his desk, surrounded by wall to wall book-lined shelves. Impatiently, Tyler took the chair opposite.

"My theory involves certain prophecies recorded in the books of Ezekiel and Zechariah and passages from Romans. Give me a second and I'll fetch my concordance." Jacobs began to rise, but stopped when Tyler cleared her throat. "Right, yes of course. No time for that." He returned to his seat and with a quick movement flattened a wisp of grey hair that protruded from behind his ear.

"The Old Testament prophecies foretell the coming of Christ – *a Messiah will come, mounted on a donkey* – a death suggestive of the crucifixion – details remarkably characteristic of the biblical account of Jesus. It also speaks of the second coming of Christ. It's all very apocalyptic."

"Why doesn't that surprise me?"

"In any case, these scriptures I'm referring to describe events that will take place – that *must* take place – before the return of the Messiah. My theory pivots upon these events."

"Okay."

"Firstly, the Jews must return to their land. In the context of the scriptures that land can only be interpreted as Jerusalem. Secondly, the Jews must return to the Lord

– it's my belief that this refers to the non-Messianic Jews coming to an acceptance of Christ as their Messiah. But never mind the details. The long and short of it is *all* these things have to happen before the destruction of the demonic can take place – ahead of Judgement Day, if you like. These things precede the Devil's doom. Only then can the New Heaven and the New Earth be ushered into being."

"Okay, but I'm still not sure what your theory is."

"I have a theory. Throughout history the Jews have been driven from the place they call home, though their claim to Jerusalem is disputed by other nations. They've been rounded up and murdered en masse more times than any other people on the planet. Their crime? They are Jewish, God's *chosen people*. Wherever they go, they are hated. Does that not strike you as odd? Unbalanced? And what better way to prevent the Jews from returning to Jerusalem than to annihilate every one of them? So you see, the Final Solution of the Third Reich was just one more attempt by demonic powers to prevent the Jews' return to their homeland, thereby preventing the judgement of the demonic."

"You're talking about the oppressor?"

"If you believe the oppressor is some kind of demon, I am indeed."

"I don't know that I believe, but it doesn't matter anyway. Whatever I think, everything points to Jerusalem."

"Excuse me?"

"Nothing. Thanks. I'd better go. I've a plane to catch."

A woman called from the next room.

"Simon? Simon, you'll want to see this!" Mrs Jacobs

shocked face appeared in the doorway.

Hurrying to the lounge, the Reverend's jaw lowered to a full gawk. Tyler watched the TV from the doorway as jerky news footage of Jerusalem played a nightmare scene of earthquakes and unnatural lightning strikes. Buildings crumbled while others burned. Pedestrians screamed and children ran, crying. The camera tilted to take in the sky where an alarming shade of red glowed beyond gathering thunderclouds. The view lowered to a perspiring reporter, dark patches leaching from the armpits of his shirt.

"Along with this accumulation of disasters, record temperatures of up to fifty-seven degrees are causing experts to ask *why?*" The footage cut to a whirlwind of flames towering above the gilded dome of a shrine. "And that's not the end of Jerusalem's problems. Here you can see the so-called *pillar of fire*, still hovering menacingly over the Dome of the Rock."

An anchorwoman cut in over the roar of the flames.

"Can you tell us when that began?"

The reporter put a finger to his ear.

"Yes, Kate, the pillar appeared around eight o'clock Jerusalem time and has been burning for over three hours. But there's another story we recorded just a few moments ago from a local man who witnessed yet another strange occurrence."

The video feed cut to an Israeli standing in front of the blighted city, his grubby robes hanging loose. He gabbled in Hebrew before pausing to seek the right words and gesturing to his chest.

"Man wolf. A man-wolf in armour." He pointed to an area off camera before fleeing.

Tyler had no doubt about what the man had seen.

She met the Reverend's gaze.

"It's begun."

*

Albert's grey coat captives gave up little information. The Witch Queen lived in the tower, spending day and night in the high chamber with the long windows and green light. Those ghosts who refused to swear her unholy oath and join ranks were incarcerated in a windowless prison of her making, buried deep beneath the tower's foundations and hidden beyond a labyrinth of endlessly turning stone passageways. All prisoners were bound in chains conjured by her with a muttered spell and the flick of her withered wrist.

All this Albert pictured as he climbed the corner of a tenement block that rose from the fog below.

Nothing of use. No detail of the tower's weakness. No chink in the witch's armour. Only descriptions of her ruthless power over those who resisted.

He climbed to get a better view of the tower. If he and the Ghost Squad were to fulfil their mission he would need to find a good way in, a way that could lead them to the high chamber in secret.

Reaching the top of the block he sat astride the brick wall that edged its flat roof and studied the witch's tower, the lights from its long windows and its spiked, conical roof. Hundreds of feet beneath its widening base, an encampment stretched for miles. There dwelt her army, a sprawling mass of tents, horses, campfires and ghosts, too numerous to count. He mumbled to himself.

"Well, Missy, it ain't lookin' good."

A footstep caused him to turn. There on the rooftop lurked six *hunters*. There was no other word for them.

Albert caught a whiff of their grime, sweat, oil,

leather and iron. They were armed, one with a loaded crossbow, one with a Luger, another with a whip, yet another with an MP40 and two with daggers. Still more weapons protruded from their belts, a hatchet, long knives and a spiked mace. One carried a sword slung across his back, another a bow and quiver of arrows. Each hunter hailed from a different era, one hooded, one cloaked, one clad in chain mail, one in a leather jerkin, one in a tabard and the last wearing battered plate armour. All were tall and robust; killers specially selected for a task: to hunt him down.

The tallest hunter grinned wolfishly.

Albert turned away and flung himself from the parapet to dive for the fog far below. His move gained him a few valuable seconds as the hunters gave chase, launching after him in a cascade of plummeting brutes, hungry for the blood of a ghost. Without gallows blades they could not finish him but in that split second on the rooftop he had glimpsed a thirst for pain and torture in their eyes and he knew of the torment he would suffer in their hands long before they dragged his wrecked form in chains before their queen.

They plunged headlong in a downward race, tearing by the brick and windows of the block in a rush of wind. Albert neared the fog of the street below and bent his course to veer up and right, dashing by a rippling mass of memory mist.

The effort of flying in the *Ghost Portal* was costly. Drained and unable to maintain his speed, he searched desperately for a place to hide.

A tunnel, a cave, a castle, a maze, anything!

A barn caught his eye and he rushed in and thundered into a hay stack, burrowing deeply.

*

Tyler packed in a hurry. Her repeated attempts to ask the *Tree of Knowledge* for help had ended in the usual frustrating answers telling her nothing and several times the contrap switched and the Black Sun glared. Either Albert was otherwise engaged or the *Tree's* ethereal link to his consciousness had been somehow severed.

Perhaps the balance is affecting that, too. Who knows?

But her last attempt had squeezed one morsel from the *Tree*.

The scrolls of Onuris are lost beneath the altar stone

The altar stone? What altar stone? Again the *Tree* left her confused and irritated, only repeating the same answer.

She checked the *Ghost Portal* hoping to find Albert and the others returning victoriously from the city, disappointment searing when she came face to face with Travis, who picked his nose, muttered in French at her questions and blundered drunkenly off into the fog.

Clenching her jaw and feeling like no kind of Hope Bringer, she loaded her bags into her car, locked up Harrow's End, and drove to the Crow's Nest to rendezvous with Klaus, Melissa and Freddy.

Zero Minus One

Ahead of Perkins, Tyler boarded the eighty-two million pound C-130 Hercules to take in all forty feet of its cargo hold. With a range of two thousand, three hundred and sixty miles the aircraft would manage a one-way flight to Jerusalem without needing to refuel. She stowed her pack and occupied one of the inward-facing personnel seats, strapping herself into the harness across both shoulders. Beneath the seat nestled her parachute, which she had meticulously folded and packed herself.

Perkins took a seat near Tyler, leaving a space between. The hold had room enough for sixty-four airborne troops, so no need to bunch up. Perkins had paled at the news he was to fly and parachute with Tyler as her personal body guard. He abhorred flying and said nothing, but it was clear on his face. The nausea he suffered when airborne rendered him next to useless as a soldier-spy. Tyler flashed him an uncertain half-smile as he stoically prepared for take-off.

Up near the cockpit the loadmaster busied himself with pre-flight checks.

Across the aisle, Melissa watched nervously from her seat as the craft's four turboprop engines fired up with a rumble that travelled through them and added to the palpable tension.

"What's with the pillar of fire? And why the Dome of the Rock?" asked Tyler.

Melissa glanced at Klaus as he boarded, at Lucy chewing ghost gum, at Freddy checking his pack, anywhere but at Tyler.

"Remember, secure texts only from here on in." Klaus checked his pack. The others nodded.

Melissa answered Tyler. "I don't know. The Dome of the Rock is a mysterious and highly religious site. It's built over a stone outcrop known as Temple Mount and in Arabic, Haram al-Sharif, which translates as the Noble Sanctuary. Supposedly it's on the most holy part of the second Jewish temple, the one destroyed during the Roman siege of seventy CE, but it's a holy site for Muslims, Jews and Christians alike and, by the way, a bone of contention for all."

Lucy crossed her arms and hovered closer to Tyler.

"Why don't you just ask *Google* over there how we can stop the oppressor and save us all a lot of time and misery?"

Melissa glared at Lucy.

"I saw the pillar of fire on the news and everything

else going on in Jerusalem and did my research, okay?"

Lucy shrugged.

"Pray continue, *Google*."

"Stop calling me that."

"Can we get back to the pillar of fire? What else do you know about the location?"

"Yes, sorry. The Jews believe the rock is the mount where Abraham went to sacrifice his son Isaac. It's the original Mount Zion. It's also the Islamic site believed to be where Muhammad ascended to Heaven. The point is, each of these religions has its own reason for believing the place particularly holy. It's currently in the hands of the Muslims but since the fire thing happened they've evacuated the entire site."

"Wait, back up a minute. You said something about Abraham and a sacrifice?"

"Yes, it where he took his son Isaac to sacrifice him to God. You must know the story. Abraham acts in obedience to God, even though it's his own son he's about to kill, but at the last moment a ram turns up and is sacrificed instead."

"So is there an altar stone beneath the dome, one that might be referred to as *the* altar stone?"

"Yes. Why?"

Tyler explained what the *Tree of Knowledge* had said about the scrolls of Onuris, concluding, "It's obviously at the centre of what's going on."

"I figured the same thing, that it's the place. You know, Ground Zero, the epicentre of the merging realms."

"And that's all that's under the dome? A rock?"

Melissa glanced from Tyler to Lucy and back again, fear sparking in her eyes. She shook her head forebodingly.

"Beneath the rock is a cavern, partly natural, partly man-made. It's known as the Well of Souls."

"Here we go. More mumbo-jumbo."

Melissa's rage overflowed. "Shut up, Lucy, or I swear, I'll shove a gallows blade right up your–"

"Shutting up."

"The name comes from an Islamic medieval legend that says the spirits of the dead can be heard there, awaiting judgement day. No one actually knows what lies beneath the cavern as no archaeological excavation has ever been allowed. But both the Jewish and Muslim traditions relate to what's believed to be underneath. One is the belief that the Ark of the Covenant is hidden there. The earliest account is found in the Talmud. It suggests the stone marks the centre of the world and serves as some kind of cover for the Abyss, whatever that is. A cover, like a cap stone."

"And why am I only hearing about this now?" asked Tyler.

"It's only just become pertinent."

"*Pertinent*? That's one word for it. You did catch the report about the contrapassi sighting?"

"Yes," said Melissa.

Tyler's inner voice whispered. She tried to hear but the sound was too faint, too distant beneath the drone of the idling engines and her other competing thoughts. Forcing everything else from her mind, she listened more acutely, homing in on the small words until they surfaced.

Seek the scrolls of Onuris. What lies beneath the Dome of the Rock? Where lie the scrolls of Onuris?

"We have to go there and seal the well before the under realms flood the world."

Lucy took a seat next to Tyler, not bothering to

buckle-in.

What's the worst that can happen?

"*If* we can get there in time."

Melissa nodded. "I agree, but how are we going to do that?"

Klaus closed the hatch and strapped himself in as the plane taxied out of the hanger. Tyler watched the world go by through one of the plane's small windows.

"I haven't a clue."

*

Stone-like, Albert listened for sounds of the enemy: footfalls, a heavy breath, a snippet of muttered conversation. A scuffling reached him beneath the hay as a hunter entered the barn to pause a few yards from his hiding place.

"He's in here somewhere. I can smell 'im."

Albert tried to picture the barn interior he had glimpsed before burying himself. A long wooden ladder, an upper platform piled with barrels and sacks. On the straw-strewn ground floor a larger stack of hay slumped against one end of the gables and a heap of full sacks dominated the centre. Here a second hunter paced.

"Morville, get up there and search the barrels. Sprigg, Dobbs, take the hay. I'll check the sacks."

Albert heard them stomping across the floor. A moment later a spear tip pierced the packed hay, grazing his left earlobe. He yelped and thrashed his way out. For a moment he stood gazing around at the search party as they each turned his way. He darted between the closest pair and launched himself through a window as they lashed at him with sword and mace. A shot resounded as a bullet whistled past his neck. Albert hurtled through the air to a massing block of memory-mist-concrete where doors appeared and vanished among roving walls and sliding walkways, and he entered through the narrowing gap of a collapsing window.

Inside he sprinted down a passage as doorways coalesced at his sides, his hollow footsteps resonating. Behind him the hunters howled and raged.

Hard, grey concrete greeted him wherever he turned. A newly formed door gave him access to a barren chamber. No exit. He turned back and tried another, this one opening onto a lobby, featureless except for seven shrinking doors. He threw himself at the first, heaved it open and staggered through, finding only a void.

Too late.

He fell.

A lift shaft? A well? A pit? A trap? It did not matter. He was drained of energy and could no longer fly. He welcomed the darkness that thickened all around as he plummeted deeper. The darkness would hide him, would engulf him like a limitless black blanket.

The darkness was good.

*

Tyler watched ground lights twinkling in the night far below as the shoreline came into view through her window. Tracer rounds flashed across the sky, joyless fireworks of death. The Gaza Strip lit up with a military firestorm as nearby explosions shook the plane. The pilot's voice crackled above the engine's drone.

"Oxygen masks on. We're heading high. Too hot down here."

Tyler unbuckled her seat harness and fitted her mask, drawing an invigorating rush of pure oxygen that made her pupils dilate. The others did the same as she unfolded a map of Jerusalem awkwardly beyond the pack strapped to her front. A back-heavy descent could end in disaster, so any gear other than the parachute had to be carried on the front.

"The old city's on the verge of collapse. Allied forces hold the centre for now but keep clear of the northern wall. The Russians breached it a few hours ago and the streets are awash with troops. Once you're down, head for the Dome of the Rock. You should be able to find it easily enough."

"Yeah, a mile high pillar of fire is pretty hard to miss," said Lucy.

"The Morocco Gate's right here." Klaus pointed to a location on the map. "It's the visitors' gate. Could be our best chance for access."

"Guards?" asked Melissa as Perkins snapped a full magazine into his DPS-15.

"Probably, but the city's in such a mess we don't know. Our intel is vague and unreliable at best. Chapman lined up a rendezvous with an agent who works in the complex, someone who knows their way around, codename Jara, but she's currently unresponsive. I get the feeling she's fled or already dead. We'll soon know which. We're supposed to rendezvous at the gate, zero two hundred hours." Tyler checked her G-shock watch. "Twenty-five and counting. Our countersign is *mountain*. Jara's is *valley*."

"So basically be prepared for anything," said Lucy.

The pilot spoke again.

"Approaching eighteen thousand feet. Entering Israeli airspace in five, four, three, two, one." A red light by the hatch indicated the impending drop zone.

Tyler watched through her window as the tower of flame came into view, a streak of swirling fire stretching

145

from the dome to the firmament like a burning tornado.

"Green light in five. Check your gear. Goggles and helmets on." Klaus tightened a strap on his chute harness and lowered his goggles into place. The others followed his lead, Melissa shaking so badly that she failed to clip her straps together. Tyler took over, holding her gaze, fixing her harness and goggles. She passed Melissa her helmet complete with hinged night vision goggles.

"Look at me. Take a breath. We're going to make it through this."

Melissa nodded as the red light started flashing.

"I thought you were the one with the panic attacks."

Tyler smiled. "We each bring our gifts to the altar."

"Pardon?"

"Nothing. Come on. We don't have long." They clambered down the fuselage in the blinking glow of the red light.

The loadmaster triggered the hydraulic cargo ramp allowing a shriek of wind to tear at them as the ramp slowly lowered, a colossal jaw descending from a whale-like mouth preparing to spit them out.

"Mel, you first." Klaus eased her towards the ramp while she clutched Freddy's hand.

"Why me?"

"Don't worry. We'll be right behind you."

Melissa nodded, too anxious to pursue an answer. Lucy appeared.

"I'll go with her."

Mellissa flashed a nervous smile, hesitating as the red light turned green.

A sudden barrage of explosions lit the air. A second blast followed quickly, shaking the plane. Through the trembling floor they felt the wrench as part of a wing dashed to pieces, splintering into the night. The Hercules banked and lurched into a nosedive as warning lights along the cargo hold blinked manically and a new droning increased, dissonant and high; the craft's death cry.

"GO, GO, GO!" Lucy screamed over the din. She grabbed two gallows blades from Tyler and stepped out ahead of Melissa amid a bitter torrent of rushing air, fighting to hold her position. "Jump, Mel. I'll be with you all the way!"

Melissa inched cautiously closer to the edge. Drawing a deep breath, she closed her eyes and stepped out of the injured plane to dive, screaming, towards the ground. Behind her, Tyler, Klaus and Freddy followed. Melissa called over the hurricane in her ears.

"Lucy!"

Tumbling violently in the ferocious air she lost sight of the others. The Hercules flashed in and out of her spinning view. She screamed.

With Lucy nowhere to be seen, Melissa plummeted alone. She spread her arms and legs attempting to stabilise. The lights below grew larger and she steadied her freefall position fighting for control.

Grinning, Lucy caught up with her.

"See? Piece of cake!" she yelled over the torrent.

"Yes. Falling's the easy bit!" The cold wind chewed at Melissa's face even through her mask.

Lucy cupped her hands around her mouth. "You'll need to open your canopy soon. Not far to go now."

"Thanks. What *would* I do without you?"

"Die, probably. Check your altimeter."

*

Tyler leapt from the plane a second after Melissa and

levelled out into a half-decent freefall stance. Behind her the plane dropped, its damaged wing pivoting downwards into a spin. She watched in horror as a stocky member of her team exited and the Hercules rolled, swatting him dead. Perkins, the loadmaster or Klaus. She couldn't be sure which. She had no idea what happened to Freddy.

Not Klaus. Please don't let it be Klaus!

A pang of guilt struck her for wishing Perkins or the loadmaster dead instead. Turning away she searched the heavens for Melissa and, spying her below, streamlined to dive closer.

*

Melissa scowled before glancing at the chunky altimeter strapped to her wrist. Freefalling at one hundred and fifteen miles per hour, she passed three thousand feet. She yanked on her canopy release and grasped her harness straps as the silk billowed open, a sudden black expanse violently arresting her fall. She studied the closing ground below, urgently seeking a safe spot to land. Amid the flashes of gunfire and missile strikes from the city's edge, she glimpsed the rambling, narrow streets and flat-tops of pale Jerusalem stone. A flurry of bullets dashed through her canopy tearing it along one edge and she veered to her left, fighting to counterbalance the chute. Battling to target a fast approaching road, she lost control and dropped, rolled painfully on frosted cobbles, stopping when a wall impacted her ribs and face, mashing her mask into her cheekbone.

A jolt of hot pain lit up her brain, momentarily bleaching her vision. Her focus gradually returned as a night shadow descended overhead.

Tyler alighted close by, quickly removing her headgear, unclipping her chute and rolling it into a ball, which she dropped, along with her helmet and goggles, over a wall into a small courtyard.

Merry Christmas. Sorry there's no dead robin on a card.

She found the helmet vision-restricting and cumbersome and hated wearing night vision goggles. She could see well enough at night without them and so all they really did was prevent her from using the contrap. Checking the street and drawing her gun, she crossed to Melissa.

Along the road, house doors dripped with red paint, each one marred with a hastily sprayed Star of David, marking their occupants for death. She didn't mention the death she had witnessed in the air after baling out. Didn't think about it. *Couldn't* think about it. Her breath fogged as she whispered.

"So much for record temperatures. It's freezing. You okay?"

Melissa winced, peeling off her mask, goggles and helmet.

"Could be better. I guess it's the Chasm taking effect. Remember? Baking during the day and freezing at night. You jumped. Why didn't you fly?"

"I'm saving the contrap's power and, anyway, one random switch from this thing and I'd plummet like a stone. It's safely in its lead box."

"Of course."

Tyler unclasped Melissa's chute and balled it. She ditched it over another wall and hauled Melissa to her feet. Ahead, the pillar of fire blazed over the city.

"This way."

Gunfire and missile strikes pummelled the night and a long, sudden shadow swept across the cobbles at the end of the road.

"What was that?" Melissa's eyes darted frantically.

"I don't know but, it was big." Tyler took the contrap from its lead box and hung it around her neck. Tucking it into her jumpsuit she led the way.

Whatever made the shadow is somewhere ahead, perhaps stalking the next street.

The report of the contrapasso sighting flared in her mind as she stole closer to the junction, edging boundary walls. Footfalls from the other end of the street warned her. Two men with machine guns crossed a road and disappeared behind buildings.

She turned back towards the pillar of fire, nearing the end of the road. A damp smell hit her, a pungent, animal stench. At the junction she hugged the corner wall to peer around, fully expecting to find a towering contrapasso ready with a gun, but the next street was empty. Sighing with relief, she crossed and headed into a new road, this one narrower than the last. She passed beneath an arch of pale stone. Market stalls edging the way lay abandoned, their goods displayed for no one. Acoustic guitars, bongs, pipes, shirts, sandals, headscarves and rugs hung from walls, tiled awnings and canopies. Fruit, spices, leather bags and colourful necklaces remained in boxes and on vacant stalls. An overturned rack of scattered bangles glittered in the wavering light of the distant sky fire.

Close behind, Melissa slid on the ground, releasing a small shriek.

"What is that?" She righted herself, grabbing hold of Tyler for stability. Tyler took a Maglite from her belt and aimed its beam at the ground. A crimson trail of bloody footprints glistened; clawed impressions, three times the size of a man's. As they watched, the bloody prints crystallised with ice.

"There's only one thing that could have made these prints." Tyler tilted the torch to illuminate the trail which bent into another road running from the previous junction.

Lucy uncloaked, glancing at the frozen blood before turning to Tyler.

"You should have bought a bigger gun."

The Gate

Tyler prodded the corpse as it lay slumped against an unpainted door. Blood dripped from an ugly tear in the man's neck to pool and run from the stone doorstep. A second wound stretched from his temple to his jaw. A third began at his shoulder and ended at his midriff, partly concealed by the shredded, bloody fabric of his robe. From his stuffed pockets dangled gold and silver jewellery.

"Must have lingered too long, helping himself. Still warm. Two, maybe three minutes ago. A contrapasso did this." Tyler wondered how many of the giant shaggy beasts had so far entered the mortal realm. She hurried on, closer to the towering flames in the sky. At the next turning a tall figure startled her. She skidded to a halt as Melissa pummelled into her back and they fell sprawling on icy cobbles.

Klaus stooped to help them up.

"Anyone seen Pratt?"

"Klaus! Thank God! Not yet."

Perkins or the loadmaster, then.

Tyler scrambled to her feet, heart pounding and they crept the length of another sloping market street, hugging walls while scanning ahead for threats. They climbed ancient steps and traversed narrow passageways while always ahead the tall fire blazed. Klaus stopped to examine a confusion of bloody prints on the flagstones. He holstered his P99 in preference of the assault rifle he had carried across his back.

"Not far now. The Western Wall is on the other side of these buildings. Wait here. I want to check the way's clear."

Tyler took the contrap from the neck of her jumpsuit.

"Allow me." She switched to the *Present Eye* and scanned through walls and buildings following the route around and back to a series of large arches that sided the plaza of the Western Wall. She backtracked to a dim movement around the next corner. A fine adjustment of the contrap's lever showed her the two loitering creatures more clearly: hulking, hairy, bestial, humanoid giants with the heads of jackals, their mammoth feet ending in rapier claws. These were the worst kind, machine guns gripped in their oversized, leathery hands. Glimpsing the twin lightning bolt insignias of their brazen breastplates, she stopped abruptly and tucked the contrap away. "Not that way. Contrapassi."

"We'll have to go over, then." Klaus sloughed off his

pack and pulled out a rope and a folding grappling hook. He swung and launched the grapple up and over the closest wall between them and the plaza. Testing the grapple's hold, he offered the rope to Melissa before helping her up.

Melissa climbed to the top and stuck her head over a wall. Glancing back she hissed down to the others.

"All clear."

Tyler heaved herself up the rope and over the top, closer to the heat and roar of the pillar of fire. She noticed the fire did not actually touch the Dome of the Rock but stopped, swirling to a point of hot light a short leap above while the top of the fire vanished into heavy, revolving clouds up high in the heavens. Just how far the fire stretched beyond was anyone's guess.

The girls waited while Klaus made short work of the climb. He joined them and they watched the blaze. From here they could see the highest parts of the Temple Mount complex beyond the massive wall of enormous, pale stone blocks.

"That's the Western Wall. It's all that remains of the old Jewish temple, though it's just a retaining wall really. The ground level on the other side is much higher."

"Thanks for the update, Google."

At the base of the pillar of fire the golden Dome of the Rock shimmered.

Klaus lead them through more passageways, stairs and courtyards, kicking down every locked door that stood between him and his path. One particularly stubborn door refused to fold. Again he turned to his pack for a charge but Tyler drew out the contrap and in a few seconds picked the lock and opened the door.

Klaus pressed on, eventually exiting on a flat rooftop

courtyard cluttered with air conditioning pipes, vents and hatches. Descending a set of steel steps to a lower walkway, he paused to peer over another rooftop wall at the plaza below. Securing the grapple, he dropped the rope over the side and mounted the wall to begin a short descent between arches. A further nine stone steps led onto the plaza itself. Here, an unnaturally dense fog steamed from the frozen stone pavement, boiling up to cloud the air. Melissa ventured near, immediately wiping her face.

"Ow! This stuff stings!" She stepped back from the densest patch.

"It's fire-fog." Tyler reached out to the vaporous cloud, rubbing it between finger and thumb. It felt simultaneously hot and cold and not like a gas at all but, rather, a fine greasy substance. She quickly withdrew, brushing it from her hand with the sleeve of her jacket. "Great. It didn't really hurt in the Chasm, but here..."

Izabella uncloaked nearby, closely followed by Zebedee.

"Different realm; different rules. Beware! The Chasm will not be the same when merged with the mortal realm. The world is changing. We are changing."

"Changing? How?" asked Melissa. "Perhaps the mortal realm will still have an influence. You know, ease things."

Izabella shook her head, fixing her glazed stare on Melissa.

"I wish I could believe it so, but the Chasm's perils will only be amplified in your realm. Of course, I do not know for sure, but I imagine the second death will be a thing of the past. The Chasm will now afford no such luxury. A death in this divergent realm will be just that: a death. Even now I feel it. My spirit has begun to alter. I fear, before too long, we ghosts will become the half-ghosts we were in the Chasm, though every bit as vulnerable as you."

Tyler recalled the Chasm's *second death*. She had witnessed first-hand the killing of her ghost friends. A while later – a few hours or a day or two – the killed ghost would reappear enabling the contrapassi or the Chasm to torture, punish and kill all over again in a perpetual cycle.

"But what will happen to a half-ghost if they die?" asked Tyler. "Where will they go?"

"Child, I do not have all the answers."

Zebedee, having studied the tumultuous sky around the pillar of flame through his goggles all this time, gave a cry.

"I see them! They're coming!" He pointed at the sky around the swirling fire.

"What? The sentients?" asked Tyler.

"The negative sentients, they're streaming down in their thousands and millions. Tyler, whatever you're going to do, do it fast!"

A movement in a nearby arch drew attention. Freddy walked out to greet them, his gun in hand. "You took your sweet time."

Melissa ran to him.

"Are you okay?"

"I'm fine. Are you?"

"I landed badly but I'm all right."

Tyler walked over.

"Listen, there's at least one contrapasso roaming the streets, maybe more. Who knows? I have to enter the dome. Find the Well of Souls. See what's going on. There's no need for everyone to go, but someone should guard the entrance so we know we'll have a clear escape route."

"Agreed," said Klaus.

"I'll do it," said Freddy, holstering his handgun and taking a compact assault rifle from his shoulder. "By the way, stay out of the mist. It hurts."

"Yeah, we know." Tyler scanned the plaza, her apprehension mounting.

"Anyone seen Perkins?" asked Klaus.

"I think Perkins may be dead. He or the loadmaster was hit by the plane. I couldn't tell which."

Klaus acknowledged the news with a grim nod and peered across the foggy plaza to a covered walkway raised on stilts that ended ten metres up on the wall. He broke the wounded silence.

"That's our way in."

"So who's going in?" Fear dilated Melissa's pupils.

"You, Pointer and me," said Tyler.

"Can't I wait with Freddy? I mean Agent Pratt."

Tyler shook her head. "I don't know what I'll find in there. I need you and Pointer with me, Zebedee and Izabella, too."

Melissa gave a jittery nod. "Yes, of course. No problem." She drew her Taser.

Lucy rolled her eyes as a tremor shook the ground.

"What was that?"

"Probably another earthquake," said Klaus. "They've been hitting with increasing regularity over the last twenty-four hours."

Tyler took the lead, skirting the Western Wall and following the walkway supports around to the entrance. Turning the corner through a gap in a picket fence, she levelled her gun at the empty wooden ramp that led up towards the Morocco Gate. At the end of the passage she used the contrap and looked through the wall to the enclosure. Beyond, the precinct ranged with ancient flagstones, temple ruins, shrines, courtyards, steps and paths. Between her and the pillar of flame stretched a stone-lined lawn, scattered with trees that obscured the golden dome. Lowering her aim she focused close on the other side of the wall where a body lay, slumped and motionless. Tyler drew the contrap's lever clockwise to close in on the lifeless eyes above the veil of the woman's burqa.

"I think I've found Jara." She focused to her right, glimpsing a mosque and rows of ancient pillar remains before turning to study the Dome of the Rock through the trees. There, a Palestinian man stood guard, watching the fire lit courtyard, a machine gun cradled in his arms. She observed his movements, waiting as he glanced around. "Zebedee, can you distract the guard?"

Zebedee uncloaked to doff his hat.

"T'would be my pleasure, Miss May." He vanished and a moment later Tyler saw the guard leave his station to search the shadows further on in the complex, drawn by Zebedee's lure. Beckoning for Klaus to help, Tyler darted through the gate to half carry, half drag, the woman's body onto the walkway. Tyler checked for a pulse. Finding none, she searched the woman's burqa and pulled out a purse from which she took a slip of paper bearing a single word.

"Valley. Its Jara, all right."

Klaus made a brief examination of the corpse.

"Her neck's broken."

Zebedee uncloaked to point towards the gate with his cane.

"Something hairy this way comes."

Once more the ground trembled.

Tyler used the *Present Eye* again, refocusing on the dome's decorative arches and entrance. As the guard returned to his post a giant shape loomed out from behind a building further on and lurched up the steps to the dome. The guard screamed and ran. The contrapasso lashed with his whip, ensnared the guard's leg and dragged him away. With a metallic screech it drew a mammoth scimitar and ended the terrified man's life with one swipe.

Other guards relinquished their posts around the dome to flee.

The contrapasso left the body bleeding out in the open courtyard to stomp away in search of more victims. When she was sure the creature had gone, Tyler took a cautious step out into the open.

"Wait!" whispered Freddy. He pointed through the entrance and across the enclosure where a translucent figure ambled into the light of the fire. "Who's that?"

"There's another." Lucy pointed at a second ghost as others drifted from the fringes. "Reveries. I should have guessed."

From all around, the mournful, life-draining zombie ghosts closed in to gather at the foot of the golden dome and its towering flames.

"And their lord is somewhere close by." Slowly, Tyler retreated, hiding with the others behind the side of the gate. "Mel, you have the ring, right?"

"Yes." Melissa gawped, petrified.

"Great. Use it!"

"Right. Yes. Okay. Gallows iron... We need to clear an area free of gallows iron."

Everyone stepped back leaving Melissa alone on an area of flagstones. She glanced at each of them, horrified. "Okay. Next... Er... Chalk!" She dug in her pocket for her chalk and, hands shaking, dropped it. The chalk hit the stones, snapping in two. She stooped, grabbed a piece and sketched a wobbly circle around herself. This seemed to calm her and she stood, steadying herself with a deep breath. She closed her eyes to recall the magical list of names.

Tentatively at first, she sounded them, having memorised them from Abraham Eleazar's strange manuscript. "Namtar, Anzu, Pazuzu, Ninurta, Asag..." She recited faster until the names flowed, and quickly completed the list.

"What now?" asked Klaus.

"Now she commands the reveries," said Tyler.

More reveries appeared from the gloom of the night to gather around Melissa, gawking, their lifeless eyes vacant.

"Go!" commanded Melissa, pointing towards the dome and the other ghosts. "Clear a path to the fire!"

Her reveries turned, reaching out towards their enemy counterparts and shuffled away through the arch and into the enclosure. The enemy reveries glared and snarled, some drifting in to strengthen their wall of defence, others leaving the wall to meet the oncoming threat.

"Great," said Tyler. "Keep them busy, Mel. I'm going Nazi hunting. Anyone care to join me?"

*

Albert woke. The Hallowed Light glowed from his inner being to illuminate his bleak surroundings; the forgotten, abandoned, dead-end of a concrete lift shaft. He felt the cold damp ground beneath his cheek and pain throbbing at his temples. Peering up through a veil of mist, he saw his light glinting on the many doorways that stretched above into obscurity. He shivered, rubbed at his numb arms and searched for injuries. He was alone, at least. The six hunters were gone. He had lost them.

For now.

He felt odd. Hungrier than usual. And he ached like a bruised mortal.

That's weird. Last time I felt like this I were stuck up that...

Oh.

This *ain't good.*

Climbing to his feet, he tried to drift off from the ground, meaning to float up and out of the shaft, but gravity retained him firmly. He tried again, thinking himself perhaps too tired from the exertion of his escape and yet still he remained earthbound.

*

Tyler, Klaus and Lucy crossed a path in the enclosure to enter a grove of trees, checking for stray reveries, contrapassi and the iridescent blue of the gloves. Close by, Reinhard Heydrich, Lord of the Reveries, concealed himself while manipulating his gormless army with his ring of gallows iron.

Tyler led the way, flitting from tree to tree. Reaching the platform of ruined pillars, she crouched behind one of the stumps as Klaus joined her.

Lucy uncloaked several feet away in the open.

"What are you doing?" whispered Tyler. "You'll get us killed!"

Lucy glanced down at herself, shocked to find herself visible.

"Er, I didn't do that!" She raced to hide behind another of the stumps.

Tyler glared across and gestured with a small flick of her hand.

What gives?

Behind her ruined pillar, Lucy shook her head, bewildered.

Tyler scanned for signs of Heydrich and caught a movement across the complex amid a grove of trees. Between clumps of foliage, a ghost had drifted.

"Over there. He's hiding in the trees on the other side, probably surrounded by reveries." Following her hunch, she slipped closer tracing a treeline and crossing a corner of open courtyard to dart between more trees. This grove ended at the corner of the dome's platform but, several metres on, another strand of trees bordered the platform's far edge.

"That's where I saw something," she whispered as Klaus and Lucy drew level. "Why have you uncloaked?"

"I haven't. I mean, I didn't. I just lost the ability to remain invisible. The balance must have altered. Look at me. I'm barely transparent anymore." Lucy waved a semi-solid hand before her eyes.

"All right. We'll have to work with it. There they are." Tyler gestured towards the trees and a confusion of ghostly forms. Beyond them, a faint blue sheen betrayed Heydrich's position.

She drew out the contrap and set it to the *Brimstone Chasm*, rotating the lever full circle until it clicked back into its original place.

"Vorago expositus." A hot shimmer of Chasm light illuminated the nearby trees and their faces, and a brimstone stench fowled the air.

Across the enclosure Heydrich fled, his blue iridescence flashing between trees as he ran. Reveries rambled out from the shade to lurch at Tyler, Klaus and Lucy as they flourished gallows blades. Tyler gasped.

"The reveries! They're half-ghost, too!"

"Good," snarled Lucy. "Easier to kill." She thrust at a lumbering reverie, slashing at its outstretched hands and sending it into oblivion as another ambled into its place. More of the half-ghosts lurched through the trees to crowd in on Tyler, their gangling hands and fingers grasping for the contrap in her hand.

"Phasmatis licentia!" The contrap's crystal devoured spirits, spitting blue lightning as their essence morphed into fog and light. Three reveries fell to the ground, their dead, semi-transparent bodies collapsing. Tyler stared.

"That's a first."

Others rushed in to surround them. With a gallows blade in each hand, Klaus thrust, swiftly killing two. Lucy sent a blade spinning to lodge in the chest of another while Tyler dispatched the grizzled ghost of an Arabian warrior who dared to attack. On all sides reveries fell and Heydrich sped from the trees and crossed the platform, heading for a row of arches that lead out of the enclosure.

Tyler dodged the last reverie to give chase, leaping corpses and threading between trees. Behind her, Klaus and Lucy finished off the last of the ghosts and followed.

Heydrich escaped beneath an arch and vanished from sight even before Tyler reached the platform. She sprinted closer to the arch but slowed as a shadow enveloped the row. The shadow seeped across the courtyard as a monstrous contrapasso arose on the other side. It swept a leg over the arches and lumbered in to block her path. In one hand it swung a huge, gnarled club thundering down at Tyler. She dived to the side and scrambled away as Klaus slid to a halt, releasing a blast of machinegun fire. The monster swayed, roaring its fury and drew a whip from its belt. The lash found Klaus, wrapping his middle and the contrapassi yanked it to cast him aside.

Tyler aimed the contrap.

"Phasmatis Licentia!"

The contrapasso paused as though confused before releasing a deep, reverberating laugh that fell from his mouth like a landslide. The crystal sucked at the air as the contrapasso's spirit slowly morphed into light. It flew into the contrap only to reappear in a stream of coalescing plasma before her, but closer than before.

Interesting. In the few moments since I last used the contrap everything's changed. The merge is complete!

"Nice try, girly," it growled, swinging its club around to knock her sideways. She skidded, tumbling across the ground, coming to a halt winded, battered and bruised. Above her the contrapasso guffawed, turning to stomp away.

Lucy sprinted after the contrapasso, mounted a wall near the arches and balanced its length. Climbing the arch, she launched herself into the air and landed on the monster's shoulders. Before it could react, she gripped a gallows blade in two hands and slammed it down, burying the tip deep into the base of its hackles. The contrapasso reeled, groaned and dropped face down like a felled tree.

"You're not so tough." Lucy tussled the monster's mane, rolled off and wiped her blade clean on its fur. "You want to go after him?"

Tyler turned to take in the scene behind her.

Melissa's reveries had forged a way through the lines to the dome and were holding the others at bay. Beyond them, Melissa watched, hands on hips.

"No, we'd better get back to plan A. If Heydrich wants to keep us out of the dome, it's imperative we get in."

*

Tyler crossed the enclosure to leap up the steps of the dome's platform in the warm glow of the coiling fire. Either side, Melissa's reveries fought to maintain the open pathway. Leaving the reveries to their groping battle, Tyler passed swiftly through.

Inside, a chilling blue glow cast everything in stark relief: the frosted carpet, the gold-embellished pillars and the decorated palisade encompassing an outcrop of rock. Tyler flattened her body against the nearest pillar feeling its coolness as Melissa, Lucy, Klaus, Zebedee and Izabella entered behind.

A strange mix of shadows danced against icicles tapering from the ornate arches edging the shrine.

"It's coming from over there." Melissa pointed across the enclosure where the azure light streamed and pulsed.

Tyler scanned around using the *Present Eye* and, finding the place otherwise deserted, skirted the stone outcrop and its barrier.

"That's the rock," said Melissa. "The altar stone. The peak of the mount."

The rock stretched for fifteen metres and bore the scars from thousands of years of human focus, pockmarked with pits, incised lines and holes where ancient pilgrims had removed small blocks to take as holy relics.

Ignoring the rock, Tyler circled to the origin of the

light. To one side, the floor gave way to a set of carved stone steps that dropped through a cavernous mouth into a chamber beneath. There in the floor of the cave, an open void revolved, spewing the icy light, its edges broiling with fire-fog.

Lucy drew level with Tyler.

"That's either a subterranean geyser about to erupt or the Well of Souls is open for business." She twirled a gallows blade skilfully between her fingers. "Anyone fancy a dip?"

Well of Souls

An acrid vapour rose from the Well of Souls as Tyler and her team descended the steps to stand at its edge.

"I've seen pictures of this place, I mean of what it used to look like, and this hole's new," said Melissa.

Tyler sniffed the air. "Brimstone. This is where the Chasm is merging." Below a fringe of smoking fire-fog, sonorous tunnels of wavering, cool light ran on into unseen reaches. Across from the well a single marble pillar spanned from floor to ceiling. "I have to know what's down there."

"I can tell you what's down there," said Melissa. "Death, the Chasm, Sheol, Hell. Nothing good."

"I could use your help but you don't *have* to come."

"Good, because only a crazy person would go down there."

"Dr Moores gave me the all clear."

"Yeah, but who gave *her* the all clear?" asked Lucy.

"I have to go in. Klaus, get the rope."

Klaus peered into the well.

"Are you sure?"

"The *Tree of Knowledge* said this is where the scrolls of Onuris were lost. I have to try. And if I survive that, I'll try to seal the well."

Klaus tied his rope around the pillar and tossed the coil into the well. "If *you're* going, *I'm* going."

"No. Someone has to guard the cave. It's our only way out."

"Tyler, I won't be able to protect you from up here."

Tyler stepped close to lock eyes.

"Are you suggesting I'm incapable of defending myself?"

Klaus frowned. "I wouldn't dream of it."

Smirking, she grabbed the rope and sat to dangle her legs over the well's edge. Her smirk vanished as a low groan issued from below.

"Stay here. Guard the cave. I'll be back soon." Swinging herself through the hole, she descended the rope, hand over hand, to land on the floor of a junction surrounded by the entrances of three freezing tunnels.

Lucy jumped down to join her as, above, Melissa fretted and paced.

"Okay, okay. Wait! I'm coming with you." Melissa tentatively lowered herself on the rope.

Zebedee offered Izabella his arm and helped lower her down into the hole before climbing after her.

"Which way?" Lucy considered each tunnel in turn.

"Guess we could split up."

"Don't you dare." Melissa glared. "We stick together or I'm going back."

Tyler telescoped deeper into each of the three tunnels using the *Present Eye*, pausing when she hit upon a rock-carved chamber.

She searched for anything that could contain or hide documents of any kind but the cave-like room was a barren cell. She searched another and another, each as empty as the last, until a more interesting chamber sharpened into focus through the contrap's crystal. This room was similar to the others, carved from the bedrock and mostly empty but for row upon row of excised niches covering one wall. From each niche protruded the tubular ends of numerous dusty scrolls.

She strode into the tunnel training her gun ahead.

"This way."

The air thickened with a sulphurous stench and another rank odour, one Tyler could not place. Guiding her team through a maze of passages to the scroll room, she entered to stare. The wall comprised around sixty niches, each holding a dozen or so of the scrolls, all of which were labelled. A quake shook the room, causing the scrolls to shudder and bounce.

"They're getting stronger," said Melissa, watching dust drift in the air.

Tyler ran to the niche wall, speed-reading labels and pitching unwanted scrolls onto the floor.

"What are you doing?" asked Zebedee.

"This way we'll know exactly which scrolls we've checked. Look for anything with Onuris' name." Another tremor struck. "Hurry!"

Melissa worked from the opposite end while Lucy

walked to the corner and vanished as the low rumbled sounded again. The ground shook.

A new fear sparked in Izabella's eyes. "I don't like the sound of that."

"Izabella, you said you were becoming half-ghost, like in the Chasm. Does that mean you can move stuff? Perhaps you and Zebedee could help."

Izabella nodded and grasped a handful of scrolls.

"Yes, of course!" Zebedee joined the hunt, studying each label through his monocle.

"I can feel the parchments." Izabella drew more scrolls from a niche. "The Chasm's thrall grows!"

"Mojo, come here. We need all the help we can get. There're hundreds."

"No." Lucy reappeared in the corner. "There are thousands. There's a whole other room through here."

Puzzled, Tyler approached the end of the wall. Her last step revealed a narrow doorway, hidden by the edge of the niches and a cunningly carved dog-leg in the wall. She squeezed through sideways to enter a room five times the size of the first, every inch of wall housing more scrolls piled in niches.

"Great. We're going to be here forever."

Again the floor convulsed and miniscule fragments of stone fell from the ceiling. Melissa paused.

"Whatever that is, it's getting nearer. This entire place could collapse!"

Tyler called from the larger room. "Mel, check the tunnel!"

The trembling resumed.

Melissa crossed to the open doorway, gasped and stepped back as a gargantuan creature slithered in to view. A serpentine body blocked the entrance as it wormed along the tunnel beyond the chamber. She reeled at its hideous death-stink, watching the snake's decay-encrusted, plate-like vertebrae flash by, striping across the gap. Its rippling length ground against the tunnel's sides, shaking the rock.

Tyler and the ghosts rushed in as, mouth gaping, Melissa turned. Behind her, more of the snake's desiccated sinews and bones passed.

Melissa glared at Tyler.

"Happy now?"

The snake slowed and paused at the sound of the voice. Tyler drew a finger to her lips and they waited in silence. Inches from the reeking snake, Melissa held her breath. Tyler gawked and, catching the full strength of the stink, suppressed a gag.

The scraping of sinews and bones renewed as the serpent continued its stone-grinding crawl, the vibrations shaking the chamber and juddering the scrolls. More bony stripes thundered by. Tyler waited for the snake to go and for a quietness to settle before speaking.

"At least now we know what's down here."

Lucy poked her head out of the room to look down the tunnel. "What *was* that?"

Melissa cleared her throat and tried to sound detached. "Clearly it was some kind of giant subterranean snake or worm from the Chasm."

"Clearly," said Lucy.

Tyler swore. "It's heading towards Klaus!"

Izabella turned back to the niches.

"Klaus will have to look after himself. We've work to do."

They returned to the scrolls, searching labels with greater urgency while discarding checked scrolls.

Minutes passed, the silence periodically disrupted by more of the resonant groans. A distant burst of gunfire echoed down the tunnels. The girls exchanged looks knowing Izabella was right: Klaus *would* have to take care of himself.

"He's an excellent agent," said Melissa. "I'm sure he'll be all right."

Tyler battled to focus through an all-consuming compulsion. *Abandon the search and run to Klaus!*

Exhausting the scrolls of the small room, they concentrated on those of the larger chamber, dreading the return of the snake with each passing minute until Zebedee gave a triumphant shout.

"I have them! Look, here! Onuris. Each one labelled the same. Six in all!" He drew out the last two scrolls, adding them to the bundle in his arms. "Perhaps now we can..." He turned towards the cunning doorway where a woman wearing an eye patch levelled a gun and gestured towards the Onuris scrolls.

"I'll take those, old man."

*

A broken paintbrush, a glistening puddle, a torn page of newspaper, a lolly stick, grit and grime: Albert wondered how these things ended up there. Among the detritus he found a section of ragged, oily rope and examined its length. Way too short. He tossed it aside and glanced up, speculating.

The lowest doorway entered the shaft fifteen feet above his head. He felt the cold face of the sheer, smooth shaft with a palm and decided there was only one way he was ever going to escape the pit now that he was half-ghost and incapable of levitation.

Marcus.

*

Klaus woke with a dull, throbbing ache in his head. He reached for a wound at the back of his neck but ropes dug into his wrists and held them firmly at his back. Attempting to recall how he had ended up bound and trapped in the back of a Land Rover Defender with a drop gate and a glassless, caged rear window, he drew a blank.

Outside, the pillar of fire lit the night.

A memory stirred. A loud rumble of stone – the loudest yet – and the sudden eruption of a massive skeletal, withered head, its elongated pincer-like jaws lurching up at him through the smouldering well as he stood guard. He recalled firing a volley of shots in reflex and the giant creature writhing with the sting of bullets, but they had done little to slow it. A plume of noxious spray had spewed from its jittering mouthparts and Klaus had thrown himself out of its path. The blind head wavered briefly, sniffing him out and the pincers, as long as a man, dashed him aside. It reared out to slither up the steps, leaving the well as its full length snaked by, and in a moment was gone.

Before Klaus could recover, five men carrying machine guns descended the steps led by the one-eyed woman he knew as Valda Braun, Angel's faithful assistant. As he staggered in his semi-concussed state, his vision blurring, they had overpowered him with ease and bound him

Why not simply shoot me?

Because they plan to torture me for information later, of course.

He checked for a guard or driver, finding none. Whatever Braun was up to, she was too busy to worry about him or to consider him a real threat and he understood why.

Out in the night bigger shapes menaced.

Cramped on his side, he shuffled to the rear of the vehicle to place his size twelves against the caging.

*

Albert focused all his remaining energy to picture Marcus, silently calling his name. He did not fully understand the connection they shared, but it was undeniably there; a channel, a way, a communication, a meeting of minds similar to the melding he had recently achieved with the *Tree of Knowledge* when communicating with Tyler. Was it a shared experience that had forged the link, a communal spirit or common purpose? Albert couldn't say, but he could hear Marcus thinking when the boy wanted it to happen and so it followed...

Come on, Marcus. I need you!

*

Zebedee tightened his grip on the scrolls and stepped back as the others turned. Recognising Valda Braun, Tyler reached for her gun. Braun shifted aim in an instant as her five cohorts spread out, turning their weapons on Tyler.

"Slowly. Drop it and kick it away."

Lucy stepped in front of Zebedee and Izabella as Tyler slipped her P99 free of her shoulder holster, dropped it to one side and kicked it across the floor towards Braun.

"Hands on your head." The captives complied. "You know, I've been looking forward to this reunion ever since you took my eye."

"Is that so?" Tyler recalled the moment she jammed a spear tip into Braun's eye socket. "You could have picked a nicer venue. We could have done coffee. Maybe a light lunch."

"Oh, this will do just fine. No one will ever find your remains buried down here once I blow the tunnel." Braun took on a casual tone. "And anyway, the blast will probably summon the subs and they'll leave nothing to find. If luck is on your side and they don't come, you can look forward to a long painful death by starvation, or perhaps suffocation – whichever happens first."

In a flash Lucy launched her blades. Braun batted the first away as the second thwacked, point first, into the meat of her thigh. She fired two shots at Lucy, both millimetres wide of the mark.

Tyler smirked. "Isn't it a pig, having only one eye? You lose all depth of field."

Swallowing rage, Braun addressed her men.

"Fix a charge in the tunnel. Make sure it's enough to bring the house down."

*

Klaus stamped at the cage window. It remained firm as the Land Rover bounced under his shifting weight. He stomped again and again, bashing away as the din echoed around the scarred grounds and he feared what might hear and come looking. At last a single strand of metal bent and a joint in the cage broke free. Encouraged, he shuffled closer to the break and targeted the area, stamping harder and faster. Another of the lines snapped, closely followed by a third. He hammered until his boots punched through and half of the cage window ripped away. Shimmying over, he crawled awkwardly up and out of the vehicle, snagging his jumpsuit on the broken edges and lacerating his ribs as he fell. He struck his face on the bumper on his way down and wormed to the back tyre, bracing his shoulders against the wheel arch. Pushing with his feet he slowly righted himself and walked back to the bent caging where a length of jagged metal offered a sharp edge level with his hands. Turning, he searched blindly with his bound hands, felt the edge, and began sawing at the rope.

*

Braun backed away, her gun trained on Tyler.

"I won't waste any more bullets on you. You're as good as dead anyway. And don't think you ghosts will escape, either. The Master has altered the balance. You'll find these walls every bit as impenetrable as they are for us mortals." Feeling for the gallows blade in her thigh, she yanked it free and tossed it aside. Blood oozed from the wound. "Now, place the contrap on the ground along with the scrolls."

"No."

At Tyler's side Izabella hissed below breath. "Do it, girl. She'll not miss a second time. Better to chance the subs than the bullet!"

Glaring, Tyler lifted the contrap from her neck and laid it on the floor between herself and Bates. She stepped to Zebedee who recoiled, hugging the scrolls possessively.

"Come on, old friend. Hand them over."

Forlorn, Zebedee relented and reverently passed the scrolls. Tyler deposited them alongside the contrap before glowering at Braun.

"Take them. They're all yours."

Subs

Braun waved her gun. Behind her the five men trained their machine guns.

"We'll be all right," whispered Lucy, mockingly. "Mel has a Taser."

"Silence! Into the other room." Braun strode after them into the smaller chamber. "Hands against the wall. Eyes closed. Feet apart. Blink and you're dead." Braun backed out of the room leaving Tyler and her team propped against the wall in a line. A few seconds passed before a detonation shook the ground and blasted a shower of fragmented stone through the entrance. Beyond the doorway the tunnel collapsed. A mass of dust and smoke choked the room as darkness replaced the faint, blue Chasm light.

Tyler took a Maglite from her belt to view the damage through the thinning cloud. Where the entrance had been, tonnes of fallen rock now blocked the way.

"I guess that's that. They have both contraps. We're screwed."

*

A small scuffling sound drew Albert's attention. He peered up at the faint light that filtered in at the top of the shaft as a shadow briefly obscured it. Protruding from the edge to peer back, a face followed.

"Marcus!"

Marcus bundled a rope over the edge and it fell, dangling and snaking to the floor where its excess length coiled at Albert's feet. He heard Marcus thinking.

It's secure. Climb up! Hurry!

*

Klaus rubbed at his sore wrists and made a cursory search of the Defender. *No keys.* Arming himself with a tyre iron he ran for the cover of a nearby arch as a confusion of screaming and gunfire reverberated from the dome.

Clutching a bag, Braun sprinted from the doorway, horror stricken, blood-soaked and panicking. Behind, three of her men fled across the plaza, scattering. The dome's entrance exploded, raining splintered wood and shattered stone as a formidable lilith burst forth to shriek its war cry in the night. The she-demon flexed its broad, black wings and, sweeping them down with an almighty gust, took to the air. Clutched in its talons, one of Braun's men flailed.

Klaus guessed the fifth man was already dead somewhere beneath what remained of the dome. The lilith soared and turned, targeting the escaping men with fiery eyes. Tilting its goat-horned head it yawned to spray its flames.

As her men screamed and burned, Braun reached the Defender, not stopping to wonder at the broken cage. She flung her bag through the gap as she passed, hauled open the driver's door and scrambled in. Fumbling with her keys she hurried to start the engine.

With a crunch of metal the lilith thumped heavily onto the bonnet to lock eyes with Braun through the windscreen, narrowing them as it sharpened its claws on twisted aluminium. With an ear-shattering screech it thrust its head and yawned again to spew a stream of fire that melted glass and plastic and incinerated flesh. It gave a satisfied jut of its head and reached out with a talon to hook something from the flames. Dangling from a claw, the contrap sparkled in the firelight. The lilith screeched triumphantly and, lifting off, flew high in search of other unfortunates.

Below, the front half of the Defender blazed.

Klaus checked the plaza around the dome for other creatures before venturing out from the arch.

Braun's toast.

In the rear of the Defender he found the vehicle's extinguisher and approaching the inferno, choked the flames with blasts of dry powder. The fire died, revealing Braun's carbonised remains amid snowy drifts. Klaus recoiled from the sight. The vehicle, too, was finished.

Ditching the extinguisher into the back, he walked away, but stopped when a notion prompted him to return.

*

Tyler searched fruitlessly for a gap.

Stone walls, niches and the collapsed cavern roof. A pocket of slowly depleting oxygen deep underground.

"There must be a hundred tonnes of rubble." Lucy muttered.

"Yeah, thanks for that priceless observation," said Melissa.

"Mel, it's not Mojo's fault."

"Right. Sorry."

"We might as well turn off the torches and save the batteries." Tyler switched hers off.

"Save them for what?" asked Lucy.

Tyler sat on a boulder.

"I don't know. I don't know anything anymore. I think this is it. I think we've finally lost."

"Nonsense." Zebedee tapped out his pipe against the wall and poked a fresh pinch of tobacco into the bowl. He struck a Lucifer and lit the tobacco, puffing on the pipe's mouthpiece. "What kind of talk is that? You're not dead and those of us who are, remain with you."

Lucy joined Tyler on the rock. "Nice try, Zebedee, but I think I'm with Tyler. This feels like game over."

"No." Izabella said from the shadows, her voice laboured. "Zebedee's correct! The old fool's right. The realms have merged and what did I tell you about the Chasm?"

The others looked at her blankly as Lucy spoke.

"I honestly do not have the first clue what you're talking about."

Izabella staggered and collapsed on the floor, gasping.

"What's wrong?" Tyler left her rock to stoop as blood dripped from Izabella's side.

"Quickly! She's been shot! A bullet meant for Lucy!"

"Braun?" Melissa crossed to Izabella.

"Yes," said Tyler, realising the stubborn old woman

had stoically kept quiet about her wound. "Try to relax, Izabella. We'll take a look at you."

"Leave me be, child. There's nothing you can do for me now."

Melissa knelt over her. "There has to be something. We can remove the bullet. Stem the flow."

Paling, Izabella shook her head. "Remember the Chasm..." She quietened, eyes rolling as a death-faint suffused her. "...hope."

Dropping to one knee, Zebedee took her hand.

Lucy glared in frustration, tears of rage and sorrow dampening her eyes.

"I still don't get it. Look around you, Izabella. There *is* no hope. By definition, our situation is hope-*less*." She turned away to poke around in the litter of discarded scrolls and found one of her gallows blades. Listlessly, she stooped to retrieve it.

"No," whispered Izabella. "The situation is irrelevant. *You* are hopeless. *I* am not."

"Gee, thanks."

"I'm telling you... Hope is the only way. Find hope and kindle it. Or the mortal world is doomed." Izabella closed her eyes and stilled.

A deep rumble from below threatened to further collapse the chamber. They listened as the sound softened and eventually ceased.

"She's gone." Zebedee patted Izabella's hand and laid it respectfully at her side.

Tyler rested a palm on his shoulder. "I'm sorry, Zebedee. I'm not sure what we'll do without her."

Melissa turned off her torch.

The bedrock groaned again. "Do you think the subs will come for us?"

In mournful darkness, they waited.

*

Klaus edged the dome platform and hurried up the steps to the ruined entrance. Above him, the pillar of fire continued its burning spin. Across the expanse of the dome's enclosure another of the subterranean monsters breached the surface, its pincers groping for prey. Beyond the city horizon, the sky lightened with the approach of dawn.

He entered, noting the expansive cracks in the walls and marble pillars. *This place could collapse anytime.*

At the barrier surrounding the rock he slowed as the ground beneath his feet juddered. He looked over the barrier at a void where the rock used to be. Below, shattered rock lay in a pit. The rumbling began again and the rubble below moved. Slowly at first but then churning faster like a whirlpool, the pit erupted outwards casting gravel, stones and boulders aside and from the centre arose another of the giant snakes, its pincers gnashing.

*

In the oppressive darkness the floor shook and Tyler hoped.

She hoped that Klaus had survived and would somehow rescue them all.

She hoped the subs would never come.

She hoped for...

A warm light bathed the walls as a peculiar hot sensation bubbled between her shoulder blades, prickling her skin. She had felt it once before during her venture into the Brimstone Chasm, and knew it could mean only one thing.

Wings!

Fire flared from her shoulders, flooding the icy chamber with warmth and light. Melissa, Lucy and Zebedee retreated, gawping.

"I guess Izabella was right." Tyler flexed the wings, bathing her friends in a welcome gust of heat.

Melissa stood. "This changes everything."

"Really? How?" asked Lucy. "Unless you mean for the worse."

"Why for the worse?" asked Tyler.

"Duh. Because fire burns oxygen."

"Oh."

"Don't worry. I have an idea."

Lucy shot Melissa a sideways glance. "I hope it's better than your last–"

"Shut up. Just, for once, will you please *shut up*?"

"What idea?" asked Tyler.

"We need to make as much noise as possible."

"But that will draw in the subs!" Lucy glared.

Melissa nodded. "Precisely."

*

Klaus watched as a ground fissure radiated from the hole. Another cracked from the opposing side, followed by a third, a fourth and a fifth, each one diverging outwards to fracture the walls of the building. He quickly retraced his steps while the dome overhead splintered and cracked. Reaching the doorway he glanced back as the ceiling collapsed in a torrent of stone and dust. He fled into the night as the rest of the building imploded.

The fissures spread from the growing ground vortex, devouring everything they touched, swallowing flagstones, trees and walls. From several, black water sprang, its viscous substance oozing into streams over the ground, seeking routes to lower terrain.

Klaus ran.

*

By the light of Tyler's wings the four friends shouted and called.

They stamped at the floor and hurled rocks against the walls while bellowing noise.

Growing weary, they paused to catch breath as Melissa drew a finger to her lips.

"Shhhhush! Do you hear it?"

The ongoing drone of the bedrock deepened, shaking more dust and debris from the broken roof.

"We did it. The subs are coming!"

"But where are they coming from?" asked Tyler.

"I don't know. Listen at the walls, the floor."

They separated, each taking an area of their prison to listen, ears pressed against stone.

"Over here!" said Zebedee. "I do believe it's coming from this side."

They gathered at the opposite end of the chamber as the pervasive din of the subs heightened. More stones rumbled to the floor as across the void the roof collapsed in a further landslide and a crack split the ground, broadening with a thunderous boom from the depths below. A jumble of rubble, dirt and fire-fog churned up from the rift as a sub surfaced, its pincers gaping and grasping.

Tyler turned her wings towards the snake, cautiously backing towards it.

Sensing the fire, it recoiled with a squeal and a sound like mashing bones. Around its protruding head, thousands of bulbous grinding teeth projected to form a hard sheath that enclosed its pincers and, reeling from the flames with teeth circling, it burrowed away into an upper corner of the chamber, dripping fire-fog.

The girls gaped at the creature's bony length as it jittered through, *womping* into its new wormhole. The noise mollified and ceased, replaced shortly by a haze that issued from the hole and illuminated the eddying dust.

Zebedee brushed down his tailcoat and pointed with his cane.

"I say, it worked!" Gesturing for the others to wait, he sprang across to peer after the snake and, removing his top hat, wiped his brow with his sleeve. "All clear. Jolly good show."

"What about her?" Melissa nodded towards Izabella's body. "Shouldn't we bury her or say something, or something?"

Zebedee turned from the hole. "What would she say if she were alive right now?"

"She'd say don't you dare waste another moment on the dead while the living are at stake," said Lucy.

"And she'd be right. By Jove, that's her all right. As cantankerous and blisteringly pragmatic as ever. Onwards. Lives are *indeed* at stake!"

He took one last melancholy look at Izabella's resting form. Stooping, he took her hand and kissed it tenderly. "Farewell, old girl." Replacing his hat, he climbed, a melee of elbows and knees, up into the fire-fog laced burrow. "Onwards and upwards!"

Tyler folded her wings away and their fire gently quelled. Kneeling at Izabella's side she laid a hand on her cooling brow.

"Goodbye, Izabella. And thank you."

Steeling themselves the three girls climbed after Zebedee, scrambling up the rugged, earth-shattered tube, hunting handholds and footholds wherever possible amid the vaporous haze. The burrow twisted to an almost-horizontal angle for twenty metres before bending upwards in a near-vertical shaft. Here, progress slowed as they struggled to free-climb. They fought on, clinging to the rock face, the muscles of their arms and legs burning and, after what felt like an eternity, the angle of the shaft eased once more to an easier, hillside ascent.

The light from above brightened and a gust of air, much fresher than the fetid taint of the snake, suggested the surface was near. Several ridges later, Tyler scrambled out after Zebedee into an unearthly dawn.

On the horizon a new star burned. The Chasm's sun broiled, vast and dominating, its heat casting an altered world in lengthy shadows. Climbing to her feet Tyler surveyed the surrounding nightmarish landscape.

The dome was gone, along with the altar stone and the Temple Mount complex.

And most of Jerusalem.

The pillar of fire continued to spiral and roar over the place where the golden dome used to be. Where city streets had been, the ground now churned, swathed in the *Ghost Portal's* mist. Subs writhed, breaching like whales in an endless, nebulous ocean. Fire-fog boiled up from the banks of Sheol's black rivers to mix with the Ghost Portal's memory mist, forming a denser, clinging ether-smog. Random ghostly dwellings shifted like dunes in a desert wind, their disoriented owners wandering bleakly. Other ghosts remained fixed to the spot, bound by spectral chains. Among those remaining free, several reveries staggered aimlessly near corpses chaotically strewn around. Here and there ruined buildings of the mortal world protruded from the under-realm-soup, their smoke lines streaking the fiery sky and, beyond, dark shapes flecked the brooding clouds. In the far distance a tall tower overshadowed all, its conical peak topping a ring of long, narrow windows that shone with the Witch Queen's diabolical green light.

Dreamlike, the chorus of Nina Simone's *Feeling Good* danced into Tyler's mind.

"Tyler, are you okay?" Melissa broke the trance.

"...nauseous. I'm feeling mostly nauseous. You?"

Melissa approached to stand with Tyler, mounting a low mound of smouldering rubble that used to be a wall. The distant screech of a she-demon pierced the warming air.

"Yeah, me too."

Dawn

Across the churning ground, the battered Defender smouldered at an unnatural angle, one wheel dipping into a steaming fissure. Tyler walked to it, taking in the broken rear cage and circling to the front. She recoiled at the charred remains of the body in the driving seat and sat down to rest and think.

A broad figure emerged from the mid-distant smog as Melissa poked around in the ruins and fished out a battered assault rifle. Tyler retreated from the figure, wondering what new creature the Chasm, the Portal or Sheol had sent her way. She exhaled a deep sigh of relief when familiar chiselled features sharpened through the smog.

"Klaus!" Tyler ran to him as Melissa discarded the bent rifle.

"Have you seen Freddy?" Melissa asked.

Klaus dropped the bag he carried and embraced Tyler, releasing her as Melissa approached.

"I'm sorry. I haven't seen him. I barely escaped the collapsing dome with my life. But I've checked all the bodies around here and he's not among them."

Melissa blew out a breath in frustration and cupped her hands to call.

"Freddy!"

"No!" Klaus stayed her with a hand. "Bad idea." He retrieved his bag. "Come with me. If Freddy's alive we'll find him, but first we need to find somewhere safe."

*

Heaving himself over the shaft's edge, Albert scrambled to his feet and clamped Marcus in a bear hug, feeling his solidity. Marcus, too, had become half-ghost just as they had been in the Chasm. Albert untied the rope from the sturdy venting pipe that Marcus had used as an anchor point, coiled the rope and threw it over a shoulder.

"Thanks, Marcus."

I found some of the others.

"Where? 'Ow many?"

I'll show you. This way.

Waving for Albert to follow, Marcus ran from the shaft to enter a drifting clump of spectral buildings but, glancing around at the altered landscape, Albert stopped, giving a long, low whistle. Further on, the pillar of fire stretched from the earth to the heavens.

"Gor blimey! What 'appened?"

Oh yes, that. *The under realms merged while you were down the pit. Everything's changed.*

"So I sees." Albert glared up at a fleet of contrapassi death ships approaching through the mid-distant clouds, their plumes of smoke trailing.

We'd better go. They're closing in.

"Agreed."

He led Albert through a warzone maze of backstreets and alleys to a damaged house with a battered door hanging from a single hinge. Soot stained the wall over the boarded-up windows and a dozen bullet holes peppered its lower half. Levering the door aside, Marcus entered with Albert in tow.

Albert scanned the circle of grime-streaked faces gathered in the burned out living room: the Polish Gypsy twins Kinga and Danuta, the pauper Isla, infantryman John, Wulfric the Saxon and several other ghosts of his army whose names he could not recall.

"What 'appened? Where are the others, Kylie, Weaver and the rest? Where's my Da and Molly?"

Soberly, Wulfric shook his head. "Taken, I fear. The Witch's numbers are many."

"She came and tried to round us all up," said Kinga. "I think we were the only few to escape. Kylie and some others were captured and chained. Not with Mordecai chains, though. These chains are different. We couldn't release them. We tried, and then the Witch Queen's army dragged them off to her high tower."

His fears rising, Albert sat on the corner of a charred couch and buried his head in his hands.

Isla rose from her chair.

"We did find a stash of weapons, though! Want to see?"

*

A new sound mingled with the groan of the stirring subs.

The low rumble of an engine grew louder as a glossy black Jeep ploughed into view through the smog. Tyler drew the others aside to duck behind the crumbling walls of an unrecognisable building.

"Who is it?" Melissa squinted.

Through the vehicle's windscreen, Tyler glimpsed Angel's pale blue face beneath the rim of his trilby. He sat in the back seat, jostled and bumped by the ride over the churned ground. Other shadows in the mist closed in: the soaring shapes of liliths overhead and, behind the truck, a small army of contrapassi.

"It's Angel." Tyler judged the Jeep's trajectory. "He's heading for the pillar of fire."

"Why?" Klaus checked the magazines and rifles he had scavenged from dead guards and Braun's fallen team. He passed one to Lucy.

"Guess we're about to find out." Lucy snapped a full clip into the rifle and checked the barrel for damage and obstructions.

The Jeep slowed as it approached, stopping before the swirling flames that hovered over the ground vortex. The driver turned off the ignition and a suited man wearing dark glasses climbed out of the passenger seat. Others followed from the rear of the vehicle, each armed with an AK47. The suits scanned the encompassing devastation, levelling their guns. Their captain nodded the *all clear* to Angel as the contrapassi formed rough ranks encircling the area and Angel climbed out from the Jeep to survey his surroundings. He walked confidently across to the vortex and with a sudden leap, flung himself headlong into the fire.

Behind the ruins, Melissa gasped.

"What the...?"

"What's he doing?" Lucy frowned, training her rifle scope on the suits.

"I don't know." Tyler watched. *What does he know that we don't?* Expecting him to burn and fall into the swirling pit, she was surprised when the flames caught him. They bore him up until he was suspended mid-fire a hundred metres from the ground. He flung his arms wide and the flames began to slowly turn him. The spinning increased, speeding until his body became a hot blur amid the leaping turmoil. Yet the fire did not devour him. Rather, it added to his form, or was it that Angel grew with the heat? Tyler could not tell.

From the blur, dark fronds stretched, creeping wider with every turn and as the spinning slowed Tyler understood.

"He's transforming. I glimpsed it once before. His true form, Izabella called it."

The oppressor's new shape stabilised, lowering in the burning vortex and with a definitive rip and gust, the pillar above vanished leaving a trace of smoke to drift on the air. A strange quiet fell as all beings stilled, even the subs pausing their tunnelling.

The oppressor stood, rotating on the vortex, his charred wings outstretched. His physique had expanded into a figure larger than his former self. His clothes had burned away and instead, a polished, blackened skin, like that of a burned corpse now covered his entirety. With devilish red eyes he scanned his newly formed domain. As the contrapassi and the suits bowed down to him, a self-congratulatory smile split his face.

Tyler found his physical appearance dangerously attractive whilst loathing the notion and she knew he had once been a different kind of creature, one of intense beauty. Even now some of that diabolical allure lingered beneath his charred skin.

The oppressor is a fallen angel, Izabella had said. But what had happened to the boy, Steven Lewis, with whom the ghosts of Hitler and Mengele had been gloved? Where were Lewis and Mengele now? Trapped inside the oppressor's new form?

She noticed a detail. Around his neck hung a contrap. Not the contrap she knew but another, this one darker.

Two liliths flew down to revere their new master, alighting before him, their shapely, sensual beauty immediately enchanting him. Others joined them, dropping from the heavens and shattering the quiet with screeches. The subs churned the ground as the oppressor gave the liliths his full, adoring attention. They chorused his praises with their piercing voices.

"All hail Tribulantis, King of the Chasm!"

The contrapassi rocked on their knees, roaring their approval.

Hitler, the oppressor, Tribulantis? How many names can one guy have?

Tyler glanced behind at the blinding Chasm sun, weighing her chances. If she achieved the right angle of approach she judged the sun would mask her flight for a few seconds at least. Seizing the moment, she slid her pack from her shoulders and passed it to Melissa.

"Here. Look after this." She willed her wings back into being and launched to tear through the air like a burning arrow.

It was a crazy throw of the dice. She knew it. One last chance. And if she had paused to think it through she might never have grasped so ill-conceived a plan.

She hurtled into the gathering and shot towards the unsuspecting oppressor as shock registered on his face. She passed, snatching the dark sister from his neck. The chain broke free and she sped away, euphoria flooding her mind at her unlikely success.

She had an advantage over the gathered enemy. She was already hurtling along when they noticed her. By the time they responded, flapping and shrieking with outrage, she had gained a considerable lead.

Liliths rose in fury as, snarling, the oppressor took to the air.

Gripping the dark sister in her fist, Tyler shot away as fast as her flaming wings would carry her. She banked around a drift of phantom office blocks, hearing the roaring flames of lilith-fire but not daring to glance back, and dived beneath a ghostly bridge. Here she opened up the speed, unhindered by obstacles or the need for precision steering. The rush of her flight exhilarated her every sense and she tested her capabilities. The wings were responsive. Finely so. She had merely to think in a direction and the wings adjusted, pounding soundlessly, each feather a guttering tongue of power.

Below her a black river meandered. Tracing its course she kept low in a rolling valley for a mile or so before crossing its bank and flying over an urban, quake-wrecked district. She glimpsed chained figures standing proud of the mist amid the rubble below, motionless victims scattered haphazardly across the land.

Are those Mordecai Chains?

In other circumstances she would have descended to help.

Nearing an outcrop of more solid-looking ruins she veered right to skirt its flank and curve her path closer to investigate. The ruins appeared abandoned and large with many broken chambers, one of which had even retained its roof.

Perfect.

*

Isla collected a torch and stepped down into the cellar ahead of Albert, the beam of her light casting around to illuminate a stockpile of weapons. In one corner stacked wooden crates bore Arabic script stencilled in black paint.

"We figured that says *grenades* 'cause that's what's in 'em." Isla swept the torch along the wall illuminating a rack of rockets, a pair of rocket launchers, a variety of guns piled roughly on shelves alongside ammunition boxes and a stash of two-handed swords.

"We started to list everything. Here." She passed the list for Albert to study.

"Gather everyone in the back room. I'm calling a meeting."

*

Tyler descended, drawing her wings back to minimise air resistance. Stretching them wide she felt the air slam against their breadth, arresting her momentum and raising her as she stretched her feet to ground. She folded her wings and rushed through an entrance to hide their firelight as they diminished.

She looked around the room. It had almost survived the earthquake, drone strike, subterranean snake encounter, whatever, intact. Only one top corner was missing allowing a shaft of golden light to stripe the floor. A crack in the wall, several inches across at its widest point, meandered from the missing corner allowing her to see into the neighbouring roofless and vacant house.

All alone. Good.

She perched on the edge of a broken table to examine her prize in the stream of daylight. A close match to her lost contrap, the dark sister was the same size, shape and weight. Its surfaces, notably darker, were burnished as though burnt, and a similar crystal dominated the centre of its front. She turned it over to study its symbols.

Just like the other, a central switch gave the user a choice of ten settings and around the switch the points of an encompassing star radiated out towards each one.

The switch was currently set to a symbol so heinously infamous that Tyler shuddered at its sight: a small, but precisely engraved swastika. Following this in a clockwise direction was a spiral, an eye facing clockwise, a triangle containing an eye that peered insidiously back at her, a crescent moon, another eye facing her, a heart, a skeletal hand, an eye facing anticlockwise and lastly, a flame. Six matched those of her lost contrap.

Four did not.

She paced, wondering what each of the four did and how they might help her.

Izabella, if only you were here.

She checked several of the familiar symbols and found them just as she had expected. The *Ghost Portal* was the same although, unsurprisingly, it now only revealed her surroundings, which rendered it useless. *The realm of the Ghost Portal is here.* She might have achieved a similar effect by gazing through a murky piece of glass. Likewise, the *Brimstone Chasm* opened only to afford her the same disheartening view of the hideous new world.

I'm in the Chasm. I'm in the Portal. I'm also in Sheol and the mortal realm, all of them simultaneously.

So too, the three familiar eye symbols worked exactly

as she had expected, one showing the present, one the past, and one the associated ghosts' perception of the future. The *Heart*, no doubt, would transform the dark sister into a ghostly version of itself.

But what about the new symbols?

Her stomach flipped with nervous energy.

She switched back to the swastika and peered one-eyed into the crystal, hoping to find some revelation about the symbol's power.

Nothing.

The crystal turned smoky and dark. She tried the triangle with its staring eye.

Zip.

Switching to the crescent, she recoiled in fear as a deep shadow overtook her even before she could look into the crystal. Quickly she flicked the switch back to the *Ghost Portal*.

What was that? What happened?

She waited to see if some huge creature was close by, perhaps hovering outside the house. She dragged the dodgy table across to the hole in the roof and climbed it to peer outside. The distant airborne shapes of Hell birds, or liliths or death ships – from here she could not tell which – greeted her.

Nothing close. So what was it?

She climbed down to resume her study, cautiously switching back to the crescent symbol. Again, darkness descended. This time she waited, eyes darting around the room and flicking to the small patch of sky. When nothing happened she looked for the crystal and nearly dropped the dark sister when she noticed it and her own hand had become shadow-like, not transparent like the ghosts, but almost invisible all the same. She looked down at her body. Her skin, her clothes, everything she wore, including the dark sister and its chain, had become patches of shadow that matched her surroundings precisely. She switched back to the *Ghost Portal* just to be sure, and her body and the dark sister returned to normal. Another flick sent her appearance back into shades of night.

No, a Cloak of Night*!*

That could be useful.

Testing it further she reached out to touch the table, allowing herself a smile when it, too, all but vanished.

She tried the next foreign symbol, the skeletal hand, a second wave of nervousness unleashing in her gut. Disappointment subdued her fears when the symbol appeared to have no affect at all.

There must be a word or command that triggers it.

She took out her mobile and called Melissa's number, checking the screen when an odd tone sounded from the phone's miniature speakers.

No signal.

She swore. The satellite phone she'd brought on the mission was in her pack with Melissa.

I must return to the others. Perhaps they can help me figure this thing out. Better still, I need Ruth Cobbler, the Witch Queen's sister! Well, that's not going to happen anytime soon. I'll have to wait until nightfall before risking a flight back to the vortex.

Her gaze lingered on the crescent symbol.

Or will I?

Cloak of Night

When Tyler snatched the dark sister from the oppressor's neck she had snapped its chain. She found a lump of fallen rock and, placing the broken link upright on the stone floor, carefully hammered it home. The chain restored, she hung the dark sister around her neck and switched to *Cloak of Night*. She all but vanished as before and, stepping out from the doorway, marvelled at the way her skin and clothes morphed colour, tone and texture to match the surroundings.

She stooped to take a piece of broken windowpane from the ground alongside the house, polished it with her sleeve and propped it in the corner of the vacant window. Standing back she was astounded by her lack of reflection. She unfurled her wings, feeling them flare and stretch although in the glass they, too, were barely visible.

Pleased with her newfound ability she tucked the dark sister into her shirt and drew back her wings to lift off.

She kept low, reasoning that even with the best camouflage in the world she might still be noticed against the Chasm's brooding clouds. Flying cautiously through the pervading smog, she retraced her path around the ruinous outcrop and searched out the valley with the black river. The smog thinned to a fine mist above the dark water so she forged a trajectory low over the bank where it formed more densely.

She wound along the vale until the bridge appeared, its arching form ghosting out from the haze ahead. An hour had passed since the oppressor's transformation and, thinking he must have moved on by now, Tyler swooped beneath the bridge and veered away from the river to seek the vortex.

The oppressor and his retinue had gone. She landed close to the spiralling ground mass to investigate but, swamped by fog, risked taking off again to study the area from the sky. While she had hidden in the ruins, the under realms had continued to spill out, expanding, destroying, consuming and altering everything they touched. The buildings around Jerusalem lay in ruins, truncated by ground fissures and black streams. A mile away, wooden turrets rose from a contrapassi death camp, the tall chimneys of cremation ovens ejecting plumes of smoke and ash. Machine guns mounted in the towers looked down upon the prison grounds.

Tyler searched the area surrounding the vortex for her agents, wondering where they might have gone after she snatched the dark sister.

On her other side beneath the rising Chasm sun, an eclectic mix of dwellings clustered to form a temporal ghost village. That seemed a distinct possibility. The houses, castles, caves, mansions and flats appeared to be trying to reform a suburb of the Distant City. Further dwellings drifted in like flotsam and jetsam on the tide. The witch's tower watched over the clashing realms like a grotesque green eye on a stalk and, several miles away, another smaller, squat tower poked its battlements above the restless smog.

The Tower of Doom! *Surely they will have headed there!*

She moved to switch the dark sister to the *Present Eye* but stopped. If she did *that* she would lose her *Cloak of Night* and most likely be spotted by something deadly lingering nearby. Instead she angled her body to dive back into the safety of the low-lying smog and glided until she approached a patch of ground that appeared solid and unmoving. She recognised the ruins from where she and her agents had spied on the oppressor's transformation and, setting down, folded her wings to study the area, seeking clues.

Scuff marks in the dust confirmed her agents had fled towards the tower. Allowing her wings to dispel, she tucked her body close to a dilapidated wall, switched to the *Present Eye* and telescoped her view in to the tower.

Each click of the lever zoomed her view closer to the tower as she homed in on its roof and battlements. She gasped in dismay as the parapets sharpened into focus, equidistantly topped by a ring of six guarding liliths. Further in from the rooftop edge several contrapassi also stood sentry, their fire-blackened leader centrally enthroned. In the Chasm the liliths and contrapassi had warred, but clearly they were enemies no more, instead united by their grandmaster.

Tyler widened her view as another lilith swooped down onto the roof and approached the oppressor. The lilith paused before the throne, bowed low to the ground and presented a small offering. Tyler levered closer to get a better look. The lilith deposited the contrap, releasing its chain to coil in the oppressor's outstretched palm.

That's not good.

A bolt of panic shocked her.

If Melissa and the others are heading for the tower, they're about to walk right into the oppressor's hands!

*

Heavy with guns and blades, Klaus and Lucy led the way, edging ruins, circumventing the occasional sub and snatching quick glances at the sky.

The Chasm sun reached its zenith, burning off a margin of smog but leaving enough to blanket the land. Beyond it across the sky, like a far distant memory, the old sun battled clouds, pale, insignificant and forgotten.

The heat had risen to a sweltering high that sapped the small team of their energy and drove them to every available inch of shade. Flagging, Melissa stopped to rest in the shelter of a fir tree that had so far survived the rigors of the merge. To her side the land dropped away to a snaking stream of black water that lazed towards the horizon.

"I can't go on. I need to rest up, preferably somewhere out of this heat."

Zebedee sat on a lump of fallen masonry nearby.

"I have to admit, I'm with you there."

Lucy stood guard while Klaus climbed the lower

limbs of the tree to scan for the row of ruined houses he had seen earlier.

"It's not far, now. Just over the ridge and a short hike beyond. Catch your breath. We'll head off in two."

Overhead the new sun menaced higher, boiling with an orange-red fire.

*

Wulfric swept the parlour table clean with one arm and drew with a chunk of charcoal taken from the burned room.

"We have scouted the land. The witch's tower lies here." He sketched a rough, crumbly circle. "It grows by the hour. It is no longer a simple tower but a citadel. We're here." He marked a second cross further across the table. "This is the extent of our cluster. Ruins lie here and here. The black waters run here, here and here." He scored a network of long sweeping lines dissecting the table top. "The *Tower of Doom* sits here." He marked the tower's position, sketching its crenellations.

The infantryman, John, huffed. "This is all very well, but in a matter of hours your map will be useless. The land is constantly changing. The snakes churn the ground and the ghost houses drift and transform."

"But right now it's all we got," said Albert.

"I suppose it is." John relented and pointed to a spot on the table. "There is a small lake of black water here."

Albert pointed to a blank area on the map south of their refuge and several river lines. "What's here?"

"We do not know. This land is fog fast." Wulfric marked out other zones. "Here the wyrms abide. It is a writhing sea. Contrapassi roam this area and here they set camp." With each morsel of information the map grew in detail as he added further demarcations of the land and its perils. "Our greatest hope lies this way." He ran a finger from the cross marking their refuge, through the fog-bound netherworld and on towards the shape denoting the witch's tower. "If we can reach the tower, alive and armed, we have a chance. We may seek out a weak point in the witch's defences and attack at night when her hordes are witless, pierce their defences and free our warriors. Only then might we overthrow the tower."

Kinga smirked cynically. "You're forgetting our people are chained. With chains the like of which we have never before seen. Even if we were able to reach them we could not free them."

Wulfric slammed his fist onto the table startling the others.

"Then we must *find* a way!"

*

Klaus poked his head above the rise. A short sprint ahead lay his goal; an outcropping of ruined buildings that protruded from the smog. The area appeared to be quiet. He gave the signal, a single nod, and dashed for the ruins as Lucy, Melissa and Zebedee followed.

Klaus singled out the house that appeared the strongest and headed for it. Its front window was smashed but the walls looked intact and part of its roof remained. Thumping into the doorway, he stilled to survey the deserted street. He tried the knob and heaved open the door as his companions arrived.

"Inside!"

*

Tyler checked her mobile again.

Still no signal. The merging realms are messing with everything.

208

She pocketed her phone and switched back to *Cloak of Night*, sensing the immediate slip of familiar shadow. She summoned her wings, drawing them back with one mighty sweep that sent her up into the air. She flew higher, rising above the smog and the tops of Jerusalem's ruins and the sporadic clusters of phantom dwellings. When she was high enough to be a dot in the clouds, she soared closer to the *Tower of Doom*, scrutinizing the ground below like a hawk. Nearby, a Hell bird rode the wind, clacking, its glassy eyes fixed upon her.

*

Albert remained pensive while the half-ghosts around him exchanged concerned glances. Light spilled from a gap in the boarded-up back window to creep across the makeshift map.

"We 'ave t' find the others."

Kinga frowned. "Haven't you been listening? Kylie, Weaver – everyone – they're all in chains."

"Surely Albert meant Tyler and her agents," said Isla.

"No." Albert pulled up a chair and sat down. "I mean *the others*."

"Of course! The seraphim," said John. "They'll help us. They'll know what to do."

"It's not as simple as that, but yeah, we 'ave 't finds 'em."

"Where?" asked Danuta.

Subduing an urge to shout, Albert turned on her. "If we knew *that* there wouldn't be no problem."

"Think about it." Kinga tilted her head. "Where do they like to hang out?"

"At the gates of Sheol, but I ain't goin' back there."

"I don't mean Sheol, stupid. I mean the–"

"The Cave o' Sorrows. Of course! Wulfric?"

"I'm sorry, young master. If the Cave is here we have yet to find it."

Marcus pointed to the fog zone on the map and to the uncharted areas at the table's edges.

Albert mused. "Then we look again. We go back out there and search 'til we finds it. It's out there somewhere. It 'as t' be. We go back out there and search the fog land. We broaden the search like Marcus says, 'til we finds the Cave. Who's with me?"

Wulfric made a small hand gesture. "Aye. I'll go."

John, Isla and the twins raised their hands, closely followed by the other half-ghosts.

"Right then, that's settled. We'd better pair up and arm ourselves."

*

Around the tower, Hell birds spiralled in the thinning smog. The twisted trees, blackened by past rages of lilith-fire, encircled the hill. To one side, contrapassi hacked away at the forest with axes, clearing a path to the portcullis. On the other side of the tower liliths sprayed their flames over the trees reducing them to charred stumps.

Fearing she may already be too late, Tyler turned her study to the rooftop where the oppressor hunched like a giant bat surrounded by his acolytes. He tossed food to a clutch of Hell birds that pecked near his feet.

Since her last glance, hundreds of half-ghost grey coats had gathered to crowd the battlements, pushing ahead of them a scatter of kneeling prisoners – half-ghosts and living mortals – each one bound in chains that coiled tightly around their bodies. She searched the faces of the prisoners, relieved to find her agents absent.

She fixed upon the contrap hanging from the

oppressor's neck and considered diving for it. Doubting he would allow her to snatch one a second time, she ditched the idea. She wanted to test out her newfound camouflage before trying anything so reckless and predictable.

Instead she turned away from the tower to navigate a line back towards the vortex, hoping to locate Melissa, Lucy, Klaus and Zebedee along the way.

She flew for several minutes, passing vehicle wrecks and ruined houses and, approaching a car that had crashed into an uprooted tree, landed nearby to take a closer look as reveries ambled out of the surrounding mist. A Palestinian woman in a black headscarf sat in the driver's seat gazing blindly at the obstruction on the other side of her shattered windscreen.

Tyler folded her wings and switched the dark sister to the heart symbol, knowing that without a complete rotation of the lever, the symbol was not activated and therefore the ghosts that powered it could rest. Her *Cloak of Night* fluttered and vanished as she drew gallows blades from the bandolier beneath her jumpsuit.

She walked closer.

"Hello. Are you okay?"

The woman continued to stare straight ahead. Tyler repeated her call. Slowly, as if submerged in treacle, the woman turned her unfocused gaze to Tyler.

Tyler brandished her blades at the approaching reveries hoping to spur their retreat

"Get back!"

Wishful thinking.

They closed in, five half-ghost soul-sucking ghouls, their arms straining towards the life force of the trapped and strangely vacant woman.

Tyler took a further step towards the reveries.

"Get back or I'll finish you."

Ignored by all, Tyler had an uncanny feeling.

Am I really here? Perhaps I am invisible and the reveries are deaf.

But she *was* there and the reveries were closing in. She launched a blade, amazed when it thumped into the closest reverie, dispelling him to dust on the wind.

So the gallows blades still work in this weird merging of realms. I guess that's something.

Mournfully, the other reveries watched their dead-eyed companion evaporate and, lurching closer, they turned for Tyler.

The Citadel

Tyler felt their cold approach like a deadening of her will as they offered their gift of despair.

Izabella's disembodied voice echoed in her mind.

Despair is what the chasm realm was meant to induce. Your greatest weapon will, therefore, be hope. You must find hope in all circumstances.

The old woman's emphatic face loomed large in her memory, clouded eyes bulging, every wrinkle of her skin in perfect clarity.

Your wings, child! Use your wings!

Tyler unfurled her wings, stretching them in a broad

arc. The reveries hissed in the warmth of the glow, recoiling and dispersing into the mist. She ran to the car and opened the driver's door to reveal the woman's lower body, not trapped by the crushed metal of the car, but entombed in a sheath of shimmering ghostly chain that held her captive, mute and unmoving.

"Mordecai resolvo."

Tyler fully expected the chains to loosen and fall away, but they remained fast. She tried again.

"Mordecai resolvo!"

Nothing happening. So if these are not Mordecai chains, *what are they? And where did they come from?*

She thought again of the chained prisoners she had witnessed on the tower top and along her flight.

The oppressor? The Witch Queen?

A voice behind her made her turn.

"Ain't no good, Missy. That don't work on them chains."

*

Lucy loosed another gallows blade to spin across the dank room and *thwack* into the back of the door. Nearby, Melissa huddled on the floor still shaking from the sight that had greeted them in the empty Jewish house. Blood trailed from most rooms, each drag mark leading to the front door where the inhabitants had been removed. Dead. Presumably. In any other circumstance the symbol spayed on the battered door would have warned her, but her thoughts had been fixed upon Freddy.

Lucy retrieved her knives. "We can't just sit here. Tyler's out there somewhere."

"Yes." Klaus assessed his salvaged weapons, checking barrels were clean and discarding spent magazines. "Wish she'd made a of plan before hurtling off like that."

He finished sorting the gear and stood to watch from the smashed window of the front room. Beyond the remnants of the street a sub emerged, its oscillations shaking the foundations of the house. Hungry, it nosed downward to drill back into the ground. A shadow swept across the sun.

A Hell bird? A Lilith? Or worse?

Blazing from the mid-distance, a flash of light caught his eye.

"What was that?" The light flared again, briefly dispelling the surrounding smog. "Lucy, did you see it?"

"No. What?" Lucy joined him at the window as he pointed between ruins.

Zebedee crossed to the window. "Tyler?"

Melissa stirred from her trance of shock and apprehension.

"There. A blaze of light like Tyler's wings."

The light flashed. Lucy nodded.

"I saw it. It could be her."

Klaus collected his weapons. "Grab your gear. Hurry!"

Snatching up bags and guns, they ran from the house into the ruined street and crossed to the shade of some broken walls. They traced the fringe of a fractured building and dashed beneath an ancient arch that appeared ready to topple.

Hunkering in shadows, Klaus pointed ahead where lines of rubble converged to form a V in the landscape. "It came from over there."

Overhead, a cloud darkened to form a winged silhouette as a lilith descended upon them through the smog.

Melissa screamed.

Klaus clicked off the safety catch on his rifle and poked its muzzle over the wall to open fire. The lilith retaliated, blasting her flames through a gap in the wall between Klaus and Melissa. Lucy stood to spray bullets across the lilith's wingspan before ducking back behind the wall.

The lilith shrieked, its brain-melting cry reeling the agents. They clasped their heads until the sound diminished. Klaus and Lucy recovered to blind-fire a hail of bullets over the top as the she-demon clawed closer, the scent of human flesh in its nostrils.

Zebedee grabbed a spare gun and shot at the lilith from the end of the wall.

Klaus peered over and, glimpsing the creature's ferocious beauty, dropped his aim. Her long horns, like those of a goat, twisted elegantly up from her temples to shadow her aquiline features. Her skin gleamed beneath the sheer fabric of her robes, revealing her shapely form. She was the most alluring being he had ever seen.

Until she locked eyes with him, opened her mouth and unleashed a firestorm.

Shaking off the enchantment, Klaus took cover behind the wall and resumed battle, his bullets skimming from her bronzed curves.

"My God! What's she made of?"

Lucy shouted back over the roar of flame and gunfire. "I wish I knew!"

The creature's black-feathered wings shredded with each bullet's impact. Feeling the strikes, it swept them back for take-off, only to flounder amid the rubble and fire-fog.

"It's grounded!"

"Yeah, but it's still coming. Time to run!" Lucy leapt

out from behind the wall to offer her last covering blast of bullets while Klaus, Melissa and Zebedee retreated. A bullet slapped into the base of the lilith's neck and it dropped, sprawling in a heap and gargling blood.

"This way." Klaus led them around the body to continue their search for Tyler beneath the echo of distant gunfire. "Sounds like we're not the only ones out fighting for our lives."

*

Tyler ran to embrace Albert, sweeping him from the ground.

"We've work to do and we can't 'ang around out 'ere. Best tuck your wings away for now."

Faint smacks of gunfire silenced him.

Tyler peered through the mist in the direction of the sound. "Who's that?" As she searched, a further repeat of shots came from another direction.

"Could be some of ours. Marcus led me to a remnant. They're out searching for the Cave of Sorrows."

Tyler wondered what Chapman and the human armies were doing. How had they reacted when face to face with the merging realms? Had they fled? Or was a war raging on a distant perimeter front line? She forced herself to focus on her present situation.

"Why the Cave?"

"Not 'ere. Too dangerous." He turned away.

"Wait. What about her?" She nodded towards the car and the trapped woman.

"I found others just the same. Ain't nothin' I can do for 'em. I tried. They been touched by the oppressor or the witch."

Tyler reluctantly left the woman and the car and followed Albert back to the house with the burned room.

Once they were safely inside he explained, telling of his separation from the army, his flight from the six hunters, his rescue from the shaft and the remnant's recent expeditions. "So ya' see, if we can find the Cave we might find the seraphim."

"Mel, Mojo, Klaus and Zebedee are here somewhere. I lost them when I snatched this from the oppressor." Tyler pulled the dark sister from her shirt and told Albert all that had happened to her since their separation. She switched to *Cloak of Night* to demonstrate its shadow camouflage.

"That'll come in 'andy. What else does it do?"

She explained everything she knew about the dark sister and described what she'd seen at the *Tower of Doom*.

"So the oppressor's transformed. What about the other gloves?"

"I don't know," admitted Tyler. "I haven't seen them but they could be in the tower."

"Did you see? The witch's tower has become a citadel."

Albert led her upstairs to a room exposed by collapse. There was no need to point out the Witch Queen's domain. Far beyond the crashed car the spectral tower rose prominently. Like the threads of a spider's web, lines of fortifications radiated from its sides, each section sprawling with phantom defences. Tyler's heart sank.

"Albert, what are we going to do? What can we do against that, against the oppressor and his hordes?"

"We're gonna beat 'em, Missy, one way or another. You just see."

"If only we could get our army out of there."

"Yeah, an' if we finds the Cave of Sorrows we might

stand a chance."

"Why?"

"The seraphim. With the seraphim on board, well, that could change everyfin'."

Tyler stared at him blankly. He continued.

"You know, the seraphim. The angels."

"There are angels here, in this hellhole?"

A knowing smile spread across Albert's face. "Oh yeah. Servants of the Hallowed Light, the Masters of Howlin'. The seraphim can go anywhere."

A movement out near the crashed car stole her attention. She glimpsed Klaus and Melissa running through a thin veil of mist.

"They're right there!" She pointed and turned for the stairs. "Stay here! I won't be long." She leapt down the stairs, groping for the dark sister and, hidden beneath the *Cloak of Night*, burst out into the alley. She flexed her wings and launched herself into the low fog, skimming over the undulating ground, the ruins, rivers, trees, pits and outcrops. She landed by the car with its bound driver and scanned for her friends. Finding no one, she launched again, heading high, and immediately spotted several figures threading the mist. She chased them, overtaking them easily to set down in their path.

"Halt!"

They stopped, Klaus and Lucy raising their guns and probing the empty fog for the owner of the voice while Melissa and Zebedee searched frantically.

"Who are you?" Lucy demanded. "Show yourself or we'll shoot."

Tyler switched to the *Brimstone Chasm* to reveal herself, folding her wings as Melissa sprang forward to clutch her.

"How did you do that?"

"Follow me."

"You have the dark sister."

"Shush. This way." Seeking out the wrecked car as a reference point, Tyler headed back towards the burned house. More fog-dampened blasts of gunfire pulsed from further afield as they navigated the treacherous ground. A subterranean broke the surface ten metres ahead. Treading lightly, they skirted it to climb a rise that Tyler recognised as the ridge a few minutes from Albert's hideout. As they reached the peak a large scorpion-like creature galloped in and paused before them. A squat, arachnid face glared down at them from a stout head that, having no neck, adjoined a body covered with armoured plates. Seeing Tyler and the others, the creature rose on four hind legs, raising its four front hooves and braying like a horse. It arched its tapering, segmented tail up and over its head, threatening with a giant, spiked sting.

Lucy swore. "Out of ammo."

"Klaus?"

Klaus shook his head. "All out."

Lucy launched a rock as the creature clacked its metre-wide pincers.

The stone bounced from its head and the beast stomped in protest. Thrashing its tail, it clopped away into the fog.

"That's all we need. Giant, armoured scorpion-horses." Lucy stalked out to the spot where the creature had emerged and stooped to dab her finger in a spatter of green-blue blood on the fallen missile.

"What, on Earth, was that?" Melissa stared after it, wide-eyed.

"Who knows?" said Tyler.

Lucy rubbed the greasy fluid between her finger and thumb. "At least we know it can bleed."

A Wilful Piece
of Trickery

Albert peered out and swung the one-hinged door wide as, one after the other, Tyler, Melissa, Lucy, Klaus and Zebedee ducked inside. With a final glance around he lowered the door roughly back into place and followed.

During Tyler's absence most of the Ghost Squad remnant had returned. Several nursed new injuries but most appeared to have survived well.

No. Not survived well. *They've become* battle-hardened.

As they gathered, exchanging accounts of their sorties and various monster encounters, she studied them, a wary smile tracing her lips. *It's not much but it's a start.*

From their talk she could tell her group was not the

only one to have met a scorpion-horse.

"Any sign of the Cave or the seraphim?" she asked.

"No." Wulfric shook his head. "If the Cave is here we have yet to reach it. It is swaddled in the fog and hides its face from us."

Albert led the survivors down into the cellar to show the newcomers the glut of weapons. Tyler nodded approvingly. A small band of well-armed, organised agents could work wonders. She had seen it before.

"This is good, but what's our plan? The oppressor has occupied the *Tower of Doom*. To take it we'll need all the soldiers and firepower we can get, so first we have to break into the witch's citadel and free our army."

"Has anyone seen Freddy?" asked Melissa.

They shook their heads.

"Not since the dome," said Tyler. "I'm sorry."

Melissa glanced at the ring of gallows iron on her finger. "I have an idea."

"Yes?"

Melissa took a handkerchief from her pocket and blew her nose loudly. "The reveries are bad news, but I can control them. I think we can use them to get into the citadel. What if we were to gather a load of them and command them to surround us as we go to the citadel?"

"I get it," said Tyler. "We march right in there behind a wall of reveries. Anyone, or anything, who comes close gets zombified. Brilliant, but we still don't have any way to deal with the chains. There must be a command or something, some way to break them."

"But what?" asked Lucy.

A brief silence ensued.

"We should set a watch," said Klaus. "Change shifts every two hours. If anything sniffs us out I want to know before it enters."

"Okay. Everyone takes a turn."

"There's another problem," said Kinga. "We're all hungry."

"And thirsty," added Danuta. "Even us ghosts."

"Has anyone found food or water?" asked Tyler.

The half-ghosts shook their heads, muttering among themselves.

"Nothing much," said Kinga.

"I did." Everyone turned to Klaus. "And I found something else you'll want to see, but it means going back out there and it would be better to hold up until nightfall. We're all tired. We should rest and go under the cover of darkness."

"What did you find?" asked Tyler.

The hint of a smile curled one edge of his mouth. "You'll have to wait and see. We'll need to use your new toy to get us there and back in one piece."

"No problem."

"If you're hungry follow me." Taking a tin of steak pie filling from his pack, Klaus headed upstairs and the gathering dispersed as the expectant ghosts followed.

*

The kitchen taps were good for nothing. Tyler discovered bottled water in a back storeroom and sated her thirst. For a while everyone busied themselves, eating carefully measured rations, drinking bottled water and checking salvaged supplies and gear.

Tyler found Melissa sniffing in the corner.

"I need your help." Grabbing her by the arm and half dragging her to the burned room, Tyler called down to the cellar where Lucy worked on a comprehensive inventory of weapons and ammunition. "You too, Mojo."

Wearily, Lucy climbed the stairs to congregate with Klaus, Albert and Zebedee in the burned room. Tyler presented the back of the dark sister on the flat of her hand, in the centre of their circle.

"There are four new symbols. The crescent is the only one I can figure out. Any ideas about the other three? Obviously they could be useful in our current dilemma."

"A swastika. Why am I not surprised?" asked Lucy, chomping ghost gum. She blew a ghost bubble that burst around her lips.

"Can I see?" Melissa took the dark sister for a closer look. "When did you say the Cobbler sisters lived?"

"Mid fifteenth century. Why?"

"Remember, the swastika wasn't always the sinister symbol is has become. Before the Nazis adopted it, it had other meanings. The original Sanskrit word svasktika means *wellbeing* or *good existence*. Its meaning has also been explained as *permanent victory*. In China it's called wan. In Japan it's manji. Hakenkreuz in Germany, and tetraskelion or tetragammadion in Greece."

"Google, do we really need to know all this?" asked Lucy. "Only I have things to do." She turned back for the cellar.

"Wait. My point is when the contraps were made in fifteenth century England, this symbol was not the swastika we abhor today. It was called the fylfot and it meant good luck."

"Right," said Tyler. "That makes sense. Who wouldn't want a constant stream of good luck or permanent victory? The dark sister was set to the fylfot when I snatched it."

Lucy re-joined the circle. "Good job you took it when you did. If the oppressor gets any more victorious, it's game over."

"So you think, if I set it to the fylfot, I'll have good luck? Always be victorious?" asked Tyler.

Zebedee interjected. "To a degree." He took a long suck on his pipe and blew a series of concentric smoke rings. "But knowing the contrap as I do, I wouldn't put too much faith in it. The contrap is dangerous and tricky. I don't suppose the dark sister is any different. Their magic is dark, their origins mysterious. Remember the *Tree of Knowledge* and the uncanny collection of the contrap's previous owners trapped in the *Ghost Portal*? The enemy uses lies. Oh, he may lace the bait with truth, but beneath the surface lies abound. It's like a barrel of rotting apples. Those near the top seem juicy enough but delve deeper and you'll find a fetid stew. Be mindful or the dark sister will have you marching into battle against untenable odds thinking there is no way on Earth you could possibly lose. I very much doubt that would be the case. Perhaps I'm wrong but I think this one was created by Mary, the Witch Queen. It is, therefore, quite possibly even more diabolical than its twin." He peered around at the group and took another drag before adding, "With all my heart I wish Izabella were here to advise you."

"Me too." Tyler gazed pensively at the dark sister in Melissa's hand. "There *is* another who could advise us."

"Ruth Cobbler," said Albert.

"Yes."

"But *lawd* knows where *she* ended up. Could be anywhere by now."

Lucy popped another bubble from her mouth. "Most likely collected by the Witch Queen with all her other prisoners."

Tyler mused. *Mojo's probably right but, if Ruth can be*

found, who knows what we might learn from her about the dark sister. "We have to find her."

"I'll ask the others," said Albert. "See if anyone knows what 'appened to 'er."

"Thanks. What about the other two symbols, the skeletal hand and the eye in a triangle?"

Lucy pointed to the eye and triangle. "I've seen that one before somewhere. Doesn't it feature on an American dollar bill?"

"It's the Eye of Providence, the *All-Seeing Eye*." said Melissa. "It's supposed to represent the all-seeing eye of God."

"So what does *that* signify?" asked Tyler. "The power of omnipotence?"

"The question is, what it would it have signified back in the fifth century."

"Isn't it used by the Masons or the Illuminati or something?" asked Lucy. "They must have been around then."

"Yeah. Maybe. I don't know." Melissa shrugged restlessly and glanced outside through a gap in the boarded-up window. Somewhere out there Freddy was hiding or running, surviving or dying.

Tyler moved on. "What about the bone hand?"

"Haven't a clue." Melissa tore her gaze away from the gap and handed back the dark sister as the others shook their heads.

"Let me know if you think of something."

"What about the crescent, your *Cloak of Night*?" asked Klaus. "Can it hide more than one?"

"Let's find out." Tyler dropped the dark sister's chain around her neck and switched to the crescent, instantly merging into shadow. "It seems to affect everything I carry. Everything I touch." She rested a hand on Klaus' shoulder and a coat of shade stretched, consuming him to the tips of his fingers. She put her other hand on Melissa enveloping her, too. "How far will it go?"

Klaus laid a hand on Albert to form a human chain. Albert remained unchanged.

"Here, try touching me, Albert. Everyone."

Those still visible reached for Tyler as she stepped into the centre of their circle and each vanished as they made contact until the room appeared empty. They watched each other, amazed by the way the *Cloak of Night* shifted and morphed light into patches of shade and texture to match the damaged floor, walls and tattered, blackened curtains. Where they gathered, shadows now stood: six faint, human-shaped traces.

*

In the parlour, Wulfric honed the edges of his langseax with a whetstone. Tyler watched him work, the sword laid across his leather-clad thighs, his measured strokes gliding over the precious blade.

He paused, glancing up.

"T'was my father's and his father's before him."

"I realised I've never heard your story."

"My story?"

"The circumstances of your death. There's only one way you could've been trapped in the *Ghost Portal*. You must have been a wandering ghost caught by one of the previous owners, maybe Ruth. You were dead long before the contraps were made. To be a wanderer you must have been denied a proper grave."

"Aye, I *was* a wanderer. I shall tell you the tale. I was born the son of Wulfric, a huscarl of Wilton, a house guard and warrior, you understand. I, too, grew to become a huscarl. I took Cyneburga as my wife, a flaxen-haired beauty and a fine mother for our children. Three, we had. Two daughters and a son. Nessa, Wilburg and little Wulfric." He saddened at the sound of their names. "The Danes came like a plague. T'was only a matter of time before they reached us. In their wake they left a swathe of burning villages. When those who had fled warned of their approach, I was called away to join the shield wall and stem their flow. We battled and were routed. Those who escaped ran, some to their homes, others seeking Alfred and the fyrd, his army. Fearing for my family I returned to them."

Wulfric stilled and Tyler wondered if he would ever continue.

"You found them dead?"

"Worse. My wife was defiled before they cut her throat." His features creased with anger. "The children were taken as slaves to a Viking chieftain. Gone. All gone. Graceful Nessa, my jewel, Wilburg and my brave boy. The village was ashes. I joined the fyrd and, fighting many battles with Alfred, slew a great number of the heathen horde."

"Did you die in battle?"

"Aye, an axe blow finished me. My body lies at the bottom of a river to this day. Ne'er again did I see my wife or children. What I would give to be with them once more."

*

For the remaining few hours of the day Tyler rested the dark sister and slept, curled up on a fire-damaged couch that stank of burnt rubber.

She awoke, her nightmare climaxing as a giant scorpion horse galloped out from the fog to sting her in the heart. She sat up, perspiring, her pupils dilating. Reassuringly the room was still there. Still burnt. Still stinking. But still there, along with the rounded, sleeping shapes of others cocooned in half-light.

Only two remained awake. In brooding silence Melissa and Albert watched the outer world through slits between window boards.

Calming, Tyler switched to *Cloak of Night* and climbed the stairs to survey the shifting landscape from the roofless upper floor. Only one patch of wall remained intact to block the almost panoramic view, that of a small corner bedroom with a window overlooking a neighbouring patch of ruins.

The cooling evening air chilled her skin as a last chink of the Chasm's sun sank beneath the horizon, casting the last of the day's lengthy shadows. She viewed the citadel, which had grown so large it had gained a stability and gravity of its own. Beyond its periphery the ruined buildings of Jerusalem's refugees protruded, static islands in a shifting, vaporous sea. The *Tower of Doom* also appeared stable on its modest hill, veiled in shimmering light. The faint cries of Hell birds ebbed on the breeze as their occasional silhouettes crossed the bruised sky and its rising, silvery moon.

She reflected on all that had happened since she and her agents had bailed out of the doomed aircraft.

It's been one hell of a day and everything's changed.

Albert appeared from the stairwell to stand with her.

"You found me, even with my camouflage."

"I could find *you* anywhere, Missy. Anyway, when you use that *Cloak of Night* you don't completely disappear. There's this shadow version of ya. Easy enough to see if ya' know what to look for. Of course, it's harder in the dark"

"It's good to know its limits. What do you think of our chances?"

After a moment too long, he answered.

"Good. Our chances are good, Missy. Better now you 'ave the dark sister."

"Huh. Nice try, Albert." Tyler turned for the stairs. "We should barricade the doors and block-up the stairwell before it gets too dark. Soon it's going to get very cold."

They descended and worked with the others to close off the stairwell and blockade the front and back doors with furniture, rugs, curtains and anything else they could find. When they were done Klaus came to her in the parlour, dropping her bag on the table.

"Thought you'd want to call Chapman. I tried earlier. Got nowhere. I'm guessing the satellites are down."

"Thanks." Tyler dug out her satellite phone and tried to call. "Dead." She slung it back into her bag and checked her mobile. *Nothing.* "Looks like *he* won't be coming to our rescue any time soon."

"It's not just yours. None of the phones work." Klaus drew her into an embrace and she wrapped her arms around him, allowing her head to rest upon his chest. It felt safe. Safer. And warm.

"Do you think we could light a fire? Heat the place up a bit. It's already freezing in here."

Klaus shook his head. "I don't dare. It might draw something to us." He gestured towards a collection of packets and tins. "You should eat something. We've pooled what's left of our ration packs and Kinga found a few cans in a cupboard in the cellar. You need to keep your strength up. We should leave in an hour or so."

Merchant of Curios

Klaus removed the back door's furniture barricade, each item postponing their inevitable departure. When the way was clear they would leave, just her and Klaus. He had reassured her that he knew the way back to the house where he had stowed more of the food and a bag, but that didn't stave off the thoughts of what might find them along the way.

Do the Chasm monsters sleep in the merged realm?

She tried to think back to her time in the *Brimstone Chasm*, dredging memories of the contrapassi death camp. They had slept. She was sure of it. They had eaten and drank, roamed and murdered. But they *had* slept.

He watched her zip up her jumpsuit, concern etching

his face.

"Don't worry. It's not too far and I'll be right with you. Here." He tossed her a loaded assault rifle, grabbed one for himself and slipped another over his shoulder. The ammo pouches around his belt already bulged with spare rounds.

Tyler checked her weapon and ammunition and forced out leaden words.

"Good to go."

"Time to cloak."

Tyler switched from the fylfot to *Cloak of Night* as Klaus took her hand and they both shadowed out. He opened the door and they stood for a moment, searching the night beyond as a cold wind blustered their hair.

"Good luck," said Albert from behind. "Be quick."

"See you soon, Albert." Clenching Klaus' hand, Tyler allowed him to guide her. Crossing an open zone that spread from the ruined street, they ran to the rise. On the other side they descended to a well of fog and waited, testing to see if anything had seen them. The night sounds of the merged realms thrummed with the quiet murmur of slumbering creatures and a less distinct, discordant melody. The land itself seemed to respire with a rhyme of its own.

Every so often a faint smack of gunfire or explosions disrupted the uneasy calm. Nearby, the earth groaned as a sub lazed to the surface. Unaware of the two agents it rolled away to begin a new burrow.

Klaus squeezed Tyler's hand – *we're moving* – and climbed out of the shallow pit. He stopped dead as a pair of grey coat half-ghosts marched out of the haze ahead, their domed helmets bobbing closer. They carried MP40 rifles at the ready, the long muzzles and magazines protruding from their outlines.

Again Klaus squeezed her hand – *freeze!*

They watched the grey coats pass and mount the ridge and, when the patrol had tramped into the fog, moved on.

"Let's hope there aren't too many more around here," he whispered. "This way."

Hampered by the roving patches of Chasm and the constantly growing and retracting buildings of memory mist, Tyler tried to get a bearing. It was hard work. Each patch of Jerusalem's ruins looked the same in the dark and the icy, stinging smog veiled all.

As Klaus led the way, Tyler had the impression they were heading back in the general direction of the ground vortex. At each twist and turn, every new drifting ruin, Klaus glanced towards the witch's greenish tower, a steady, glinting marker in the night. Climbing higher ground, the *Tower of Doom* also entered their view, providing a second, albeit darker, landmark.

Klaus stopped, pointing with a shadow hand.

"There, where the land drops. See the ruined street with the arch? Third house down."

"I see it." As Tyler spoke, a tall shape lumbered from the mist between them and the row of ruins. It grew clearer as a second emerged to join it, and the far, dull clops of hooves arose. The scorpion horses walked nearer, their contrapassi riders sweeping their heads to scan the night.

"Scorp riders. Great. What next?" whispered Tyler.

Klaus silently chastised her with a finger to his lips. A further squeeze told her *wait*.

The beasts neared, following the edge of the ruined road and passed by, plodding away.

Klaus crossed their path, half dragging Tyler to the third house. Reaching the door he opened it to lead her through. She checked for threats before switching the dark sister to the *Brimstone Chasm*.

Without a word Klaus opened an interior door leading to a cellar and descended the steps. At the bottom he folded back a large Persian rug and heaved open the trapdoor beneath. In the cubbyhole below nestled the black bag Tyler had seen him carrying when he had met her near the vortex. A stockpile of tinned food surrounded the bag. Among the tins of fruit salad, beans, tomatoes and corned beef lay several cans of *Vitality*, their labels sporting an image of a spaniel.

"Dog food?"

"It's edible and nutritious. We're in no position to be picky."

"At least we'll all have glossy coats. What's in the bag?" she asked.

Klaus reached down to lift out the bag and, setting it down on the rug, unzipped it. Inside nestled six dusty parchment scrolls.

"The scrolls of Onuris?" She glared at him. "Braun stole these from us in the Well of Souls. How did *you* get them?"

"I watched Braun run for her life. She tossed the bag into the back of a Land Rover but never made it. A Lilith torched her and took the contrap."

"That was Braun?"

Klaus nodded. "I didn't know what was in the bag but I thought it could be important and took it." Easing an empty pack from his back, Klaus filled it with the food as Tyler filled hers.

"Not too much. You might need to fly." He heaved

his full bag onto his back and zipped up the one with the scrolls, passing it to her.

"Take this. It's light."

Tyler shouldered the bag and with a last glance around the house, they slipped back into the night.

*

The back door to the burned house opened slowly.

Awake and waiting inside, Melissa, Zebedee and Albert watched it swing wide. Shadows flickered and the door swiftly closed. Albert withdrew a shielding hand from his candle and raised it as Tyler and Klaus appeared in the hallway, breathless and shivering but relieved.

"You could have told me Klaus found the scrolls." Tyler aimed her accusation at Melissa while Klaus, Albert and Zebedee replaced the furniture blockade.

"Klaus said we shouldn't. We may never have recovered them and then you'd have just been angry and unstable. But you can read them whenever you're ready. We translated them after you took back the contrap and disappeared."

Tyler glared.

"I'll get to work, then."

She unzipped the bag on a chair by the parlour table and plucked out the scrolls.

Melissa pulled up a chair. "There are dates. It's a diary, of sorts."

Blanking her, Tyler sorted the scrolls into chronological order, reading the first line from each where Melissa and Klaus had translated from an archaic form of Latin into English. Albert fetched a second candle and Tyler sat down to read in the quivering light.

The following took place in the year 1623, on the fifth

day of the month of August.

Today I took a barge south, down the Golden Horn to bask in the glorious sun all the way to the brimming markets of Istanbul. Such a bazaar I have never before seen. The street food, the spices, the exotic wares – everything about the place – is enchanting to a euphoric degree. I must confess I rather overspent.

The women, oh! I shall make no further comment here except to say their beauty is surely surpassed by none the world over and the city boasts the finest from every nation. In fact, such a collection of races gather here (of each gender) as to bedazzle the eye.

Amongst my rare and magnificent purchases is a fine treasure, a silver trinket, an oddity, one of a kind with which I am most pleased. I wear it proudly about my neck even now as I scribe. I discovered it amongst a sea of intriguing artefacts on a curios stall towards the southern end. The merchant, himself a curious fellow with a withered arm and well matching his stall, seemed keen to be rid of the piece, though I wonder why. I do hope it was not stolen.

Such a wondrous day have I enjoyed that I chose to remain a while. I am bedded and boarded most comfortably here in the great city, lodged in an accommodating tavern not far from the water's edge.

Tyler glanced up from the page.

"He's quite a waffler, this Onuris guy."

"Uh-huh," agreed Melissa.

Albert leaned closer to peer at the parchment. "Anythin' useful?"

"Not yet." Using cans of soup and her gun as

paperweights, Tyler unfurled the scroll to read more.

The following took place in the year 1623, on the seventh day of the month of August.

I begin to wonder about the silver trinket. The odd symbols etched into its rear face are most perplexing and yet, upon testing the central switch, I find it does nothing. Why, then, was this switch created? Is the gem a wishing stone?

What the symbols mean I cannot fathom, although I remain entranced by the dark jewel. Without reason I have, on occasion, caught myself staring into the depths of that jewel, my mind absorbed by its beauty. A deepening notion accompanies my trance, a feeling that I am leaving our flesh and blood world to drift elsewhere.

No matter. The gem accompanies my every step, flashing in the light of the sun with gleaming resplendence. Tomorrow I leave for home.

The following took place in the year 1623, on the eighth day of the month of August.

A breakthrough today! Finding myself confined in my cabin, bound for home on board the Groene Draeck (Green Dragon), a fine Dutch trading vessel, I idled in need of stimulation. I turned once more to the jewel with its mesmerising crystal. When testing the switch, which previously had rendered no affect upon me or the jewel, I saw a wondrous sight. The crystal, dark no more, shone with a soft light and, looking more closely, I discerned a living view of a land beyond. There stood a tower beneath a brilliant moon!

Compelled, I tested, driven to seek more of the same. I switched to each symbol in turn and, in turn, peered into the crystal. A second symbol bestowed a further scene of sorts as, in the crystal, a grey vapour whirled.

Onuris' faded script was indecipherable for the remainder of the scroll. Dampness or another age old intrusion had weathered the words, though Tyler had a good idea of what it must have at one time said. She picked up Onuris' story at the top of the second scroll.

The following took place in the year 1623, on the twelfth day of the month of September.

Today I purchased return passage to Istanbul at great expense. The Dolphin is smaller and less accommodating than the last vessel (the old ship cannot sail fast enough for my liking), yet serviceable and seaworthy.

My suspicions have proven well founded. The jewel encompasses a form of diabolical doorway or passage to another place, or places, even. I mean to find the merchant with the withered hand and question him about the jewel. I fear, until I do so, I shall be possessed by curiosity!

The following took place in the year 1623, on the thirteenth day of the month of September.

The weather has turned and with it my stomach. I

yearn for dry land.
  I have learned a new fear of the silver jewel.

The following took place in the year 1623, on the fourteenth day of the month of September.

Today I saw the ghost a second time. I burn to discover the jewel's hidden secrets. The ghost is silent and staring. Behind it rolls a great orb. I feel its weight bearing down upon my soul.

The following took place in the year 1623, on the twentieth day of the month of September.

This morning The Dolphin docked at Istanbul and I gladly disembarked. I searched day-long for the merchant of curios, yet he has gone. What's more, not one single tradesman recalls his presence. I fear I must persist in my uneducated study of the jewel alone. Believing it to be magic and hoping for enlightenment I asked a local boy if he knew of a sorcerer I might visit. The boy introduced me to a whispering crone who, staring at me with small black eyes, began to reveal a source but silenced upon sight of the jewel. Tomorrow I hope for better luck.

The following took place in the year 1623, on the twenty-first day of the month of September.

Success! Continuing my quest for the sorcerer I enquired at a stall of jewellery, pots and oddments. The stallholder pointed to a narrow alley nearby, saying I should knock five times on the seventh door.

I knocked.

The Sorcerer of Istanbul

Standing guard at the rear windows, Wulfric whispered a warning.

"Contrapassi riders!"

Klaus readied a grenade as Albert extinguished the candles. Hardly daring to breathe they waited in the dark.

Beyond the barricades a creature stirred. The ground heaved out a low, mournful groan and the clip-clop of scorps arose, passed and retreated.

Albert relit the candles, their flames wavering in a draught.

Tyler read on.

An old man answered, introducing himself only as the sorcerer and I explained myself. Smiling broadly, the sorcerer invited me into his shop, a dark and dingy affair reached solely through a long passage and a hidden door, through which I glimpsed a plethora of ritualistic objects and detected a sour, dusty odour.

Trembling, I entered and looked around fascinated by myriad oddities, many so gruesome I prefer not their mention.

I was able to conceal the jewel for, overcome by an impulse whilst waiting at the door, I had tucked it into the folds of my galabia. Rather, I described it in great detail and asked the sorcerer if he recognised it. He shook his head most decisively, denying knowledge of such a contraption, and set about trying to sell me a variety of his mysterious items. I resisted, of course, until, reaching behind him and taking a small object from a cobwebbed shelf, he placed a block on the counter between us.

It was, he claimed, an Akkadian clay tablet and he promised most emphatically that all the answers I sought would be found residing within its text. The next moment he offered a warning. The tablet itself was magical and should not be destroyed without due precaution.

Hankering for sweeter air, I paid him two florins and left.

Again damage to the page blotted the ink and Tyler moved on to the last readable section of the scroll.

The tablet is cursed. I grow evermore convinced

of it. Bad luck has befallen me ever since it came to me. I plan to destroy it, though not before I destroy the evil contraption. Only one question remains:
    How to safely do so?

Onuris, I know how you feel.

An Athenian Scholar

The next scroll was extensively damaged and the few words Melissa and Klaus had been able to translate were too isolated to hold meaning. Tyler quickly ditched it and moved on to the fourth.

The following took place in the year 1628, on the second day of the month of February.

The scholar Antonius visited again today, with more news on the Akkadian text, saying his research suggests the tablet originates from ancient Babylonia and is a rare find. He has succeeded in translating a few words and phrases that I shall record here below.

...so creating a well of souls through dark glass...
...a joining that cannot be easily undone...
...harbouring the dead...
...mortal remains and a veil of moonlight...
...the four symbols...

Tyler reread the second line

A joining that cannot be easily undone? That doesn't sound promising.

It is enough to intrigue Antonius. He has promised to return soon with the entire tablet transcribed. Perhaps I will finally have the answers I have been so desperately seeking.

Ramla has recovered and I shall call upon her this night. I do believe I have fallen for her.

The following took place in the year 1628, on the third day of the month of February.

I have waited the entire day for Antonius yet he did not come. My pigeon of complaint is on the wing to Athens. Perhaps the scholar will visit tomorrow.

The following took place in the year 1628, on the fourth day of the month of February.

Still no word from Antonius. In vain, I wait.

The following took place in the year 1628, on the fifth day of the month of February.

My pigeon returned this morning without a message.

Hot blooded, I set out to find Antonius myself.

His house is empty and my temper quenched. Blood marks his threshold. I fear he is dead. The tablet is lost.

Terror seizes me!

The following took place in the year 1628, on the sixth day of the month of February.

After much brooding I decided to revisit the scholar's house, carrying with me a small, vague hope of gleaning something more. My subsequent search of the inner rooms rewarded me with a find, a partial translation of the Akkadian tablet, folded many times and stuffed between the floor stones. The parchment bears a bloody thumbprint.

The command is given so creating a well of souls through dark glass.

Thus it is done, a making that cannot be undone without dire consequences.

The pacts are drawn, the spirits bound.

A bond remains, harbouring the dead.

Their number is ten, amongst them a charm for wellbeing, the fiery pit, the mortal remains, and a veil of moonlight transpire.

...only one weakness, the four symbols...

I am astonished by the mention of the symbols. Two I recognised immediately. But why the four symbols? The details are unclear, the transcription incomplete and only one of the four symbols listed appears on the contraption in my possession. Are my suspicions compounded?   Does a second such contraption exist?

The following took place in the year 1628, on the seventeenth day of the month of April.

I now know and understand all but one of the ten symbols on the contraption.   They have aided me greatly in deepening my investigation and also in other ways. In short, I have become a wealthy man.
    The heart remains a mystery.

Tyler unrolled the fifth scroll, clamping it to the tabletop with her makeshift weights. This scroll detailed Onuris' growing romance with Ramla. She skimmed it quickly hoping for more clues relating to the sister contraps but found only one reference that could be associated.

In the cool of the evening I fly to her.

She moved on to the final scroll noting more words lost to damage. She scanned down to the next readable text.

There happened an interesting incident today. A street boy called at my house, bringing a message at sundown.

Come to the dockside at midnight tonight if you wish to purchase the sister. Bring the contraption and your gold.
    I called after the boy to ask who sent the note but

the boy was already heeling the dust halfway to Athens.

Tyler unrolled the scroll further and found a section missing where a portion of the page had been sliced out to leave a window. Delving into her bag she rummaged for her notebook. She opened it at a page where a folded piece of parchment nestled, the parchment she had taken from Angel's office some time ago.

Taking the parchment she straightened it and placed it neatly into the window. Onuris' flowing script continuing seamlessly. The date entry above the window was for the twenty-third of May, sixteen twenty-nine. Turning to her notebook she reread the familiar translated excerpt.

Regarding my investigations into the contraption, I believe I have found a way. Upon the meeting of the four symbols, the pacts will reverse and spirit will be released.

Where the heart is concerned, one can only muse. Perhaps this was selected as a substitute image because the more accurate device was already engaged.

On another matter, today I learned of a myth that told of the spirits succumbing to the lordship of he who wears a ring of gallows iron. Have you ever heard such a thing? A ring of gallows iron worn and wielded by my namesake, nonetheless! It is surely make-believe.

Beneath the parchment window one final line flourished across the page.

The sun has set and midnight approaches. To the docks I go!

Four Symbols

Tyler reclined, deliberating. Onuris' diary was tantalizingly obscure and unfinished. She had to wonder what had befallen him during his midnight excursion to the docks?

Two other questions struck her.

Does mortal remains *refer to the skeletal hand symbol on the dark sister?*

Are the four symbols *the four listed on a previous line of the scholar's translation, or are they something else?*

Onuris had been wrong about the ring of gallows iron. It was not make-believe. So what else was he wrong about?

Tyler studied the skeletal hand symbol.

"Mortal remains?"

More questions followed.

Clearly other parties were hunting the two contraps even back then. The merchant of curios had wanted rid of the contrap. Was it merely coincidence that he sported a withered hand or had the contrap somehow wounded him? The contrap or a ghost within?

She considered the sorcerer. From Onuris' account, the sorcerer genuinely seemed ignorant of the contrap's true powers or he would have at least attempted to barter for it, if not take it by other means. But then again perhaps he had. Perhaps the sorcerer had followed Onuris and later arranged the meeting at the docks.

Obviously, the scholar had delved too deeply and alerted *someone* with an interest, someone sinister, someone who had abducted or murdered him.

And then, of course, there was Onuris himself who presumably never made it back from his midnight engagement. Were his bones mouldering in the waters off a dockside somewhere near Athens? She contemplated a trip to Greece in the hope of tracking down Onuris' ghost but present circumstances would not afford it. She needed to be here. To find Ruth Cobbler. To free the captives. To fight the oppressor.

Someone has to.

Tyler turned to another note in her book.

My dearest Ramla, please keep this trinket safe until my return. If anybody comes looking for me, you must deny all knowledge of me for your own sake.

Onuris had neglected to mention his planned detour to Ramla's house before flying to the docks. He must have visited while she slept and left the contrap for safekeeping with the note. She imagined him sneaking into her room to deposit the note, gently weighting it in place with the contrap near Ramla's sleeping form.

Absorbing these details, Tyler couldn't help but feel disappointed.

"I don't understand," she said to anyone who was listening. "The *Tree of Knowledge* told me the answer would be here but it doesn't tell me anything. Not really. Not how to destroy the contraps."

"There must be *something* in there," said Melissa. "Some clue we're not getting. You *have* read it all?"

"Yes." Tyler slapped the open scroll indignantly. "There's nothing here that helps, just these couple of lines about the four symbols. I think the contraps and their magic can be destroyed by bringing the four symbols together, but it doesn't say what the four symbols are. They might not even be symbols on the contraps."

"Yes, that's pretty much what I got from it, too," confessed Melissa. "So it comes down to this. What are the four symbols and where are they?"

*

Lucy stalked into the parlour having rested for several hours.

"It's quieter out there at night. We should take advantage of it. Go now."

"Go where?" asked Tyler, preoccupied with the scrolls and their mysteries.

"To find Ruth. I'll go with Albert. We can travel quickly and secretly if it's just us two."

"But you can't cloak anymore. Do you want to take the dark sister?"

"No, don't worry. We're still half-ghost and transparent enough to hide well in all this fog. Anyway, anything unfriendly I meet is going down."

"You sure you're not going to look for Weaver?"

"Maybe. If I find him I'll bring him back, too."

Albert removed his cap to scratch his head and run his fingers through his hair. "I asked around about Ruth. No one knows what 'appened to 'er. I lost track of 'er when the army separated." Dusting ghostly soot from his cap he replaced it.

Zebedee crossed to the table. "Chances are she's in the citadel somewhere. At least, it's a good place to start."

"All right." Tyler swallowed a feeling that this might be the last time she saw either of them, but knew thinking like that would only stop her and the others from doing anything. "Go. We'll reserve Mel's reverie idea for a full assault on the citadel, *if* we ever work out how to break the spell of the chains. Find Ruth. The rest of us will guard the house and continue the search for the Cave. Be careful. Mary's a real witch, not like Silvia Bates. Her ghost nearly melted my brain just by looking at me."

Lucy and Albert gathered ammunition and a selection of weapons from the cellar store. At the door Tyler grabbed his sleeve.

"Albert–"

"I know, Missy. Be quick. I'll see you soon."

Pulling him close, she placed a kiss upon his soot-smeared forehead and a moment later he and Lucy walked into the night.

Tyler turned to Zebedee.

"There must be a few hours of darkness remaining. I guess we'd better get a search party organised. Who else is awake?"

Melissa rose from her chair, hope in her eyes. "I'll

come."

*

Belly to the ground, Weaver studied the surreal dreamscape falling from the other side of the road. There an enemy cohort guarded their prisoners. He took a quick head count.

Forty grey coats.

Around sixty ghosts from Albert's army.

Behind him fifteen ghosts, mostly Romans and Victorian Londoners, crouched in a ditch, fingers caressing their blades and cudgels. With Molly piggybacking, Mr Goodwin waited among them. Weaver gave the signal, a single fluid swipe of his hand.

Silently they hurried up the bank and crossed the road to descend upon the unsuspecting grey coats below.

Yakubu took out two troopers with a single swing of his club. Another soldier wheeled around to face the powerful African. Yakubu clobbered him with a poleaxing blow and the grey coat dropped.

Weaver grappled with another, going for the man's gun, nose to nose. The trooper snarled a German phrase that Weaver did not recognise. Weaver butted him hard in the face and wrenched the gun free as his adversary fell away, thumping into a comrade.

Weaver spun in time to shoot the first few soldiers quick enough to level their weapons. He felled half a dozen more while Yakubu claimed a machine gun and tossed it to Mr Goodwin.

Troopers further afield were less hampered. They shot at the first rank of Weaver's ghosts as Weaver and Mr Goodwin returned fire. Ghosts dropped on both sides.

The sixty prisoner ghosts rioted in response. Yakubu reached the closest of them and, taking a fistful of manacle chain in each hand, heaved. Shoulders straining, he broke iron to free souls.

*

Tyler looked over the assembled team. Klaus had agreed to head them up, aided by Wulfric. Zebedee, Melissa, Kinga and Danuta prepared to leave with them. The rest would stay behind to defend the house, taking shifts to sleep and guard.

"I don't understand," said Melissa. "I thought you were coming with us."

"There's something else I have to do," said Tyler.

"What?"

"I'm going to steal back the contrap. Whatever the four symbols are, we're going to need both contraps if we're going to destroy them. The oppressor's weaker without them, too. So there are *two* good reasons."

"But the contrap's around the oppressor's neck and the oppressor's in the tower, guarded by contrapassi and liliths and God knows what else. Do you even have a plan?"

"Don't worry, Mel. I'll start with a reconnaissance. The dark sister has rested. I'll be hidden by the *Cloak of Night*. It's dark – the *Cloak of Night* works best in the dark – and they won't expect me."

"You're gonna die!"

"No, I'm not. I promise I'll only try something if I think it's safe."

"Oh, that makes me feel *so* much better. Nothing's safe. Nothing around here, anyway."

A voice hissed from the upper floor.

"Grey coats!"

Isla ran down the stairs and into the parlour.

"Grey coats, searching the ruins."

"Where." Tyler hurried after Isla up to the bedroom window, Isla's guard post.

Isla pointed out through a slit in the broken shutters. "There."

Across a void of smog, armed grey coats systematically swarmed over a neighbouring ruin.

Tyler swore and leapt down the stairs.

"We have to move. Now!"

Ghosts rushed through the house, waking those not already roused by the commotion. They gathered belongings and began ferrying all the weapons up from the cellar. Tyler stopped in the hallway, an unwelcome realisation striking.

By the time we've gathered the weapons up from the store the grey coats will be all over us.

A rattle of gunfire somewhere outside reminded her of their proximity. The searchers had found an undesirable, hiding in the nearby ruins.

"No. There's no time. Take the weapons back. Unblock the barricades or they'll know we're here. Take everything back into the cellar and get everyone down there. Klaus, give me a hand." Tyler ran back into the parlour and viewed a tall Moroccan cabinet so wide and heavy that it had been rejected when they had made the blockades. "That'll do."

"Do what?"

"Hide the cellar door. Help me drag it out. You, too, Mel!"

While the last of the ghosts hurried down into the cellar, their arms laden with canned food, Tyler, Klaus and Melissa worked the cabinet out of the room and across the hall. They deposited it close to the door leaving enough of a gap for a person to fit through.

"Get in, Mel. Klaus and I can finish off."

"Where will you hide?"

"We'll use the dark sister. GO!"

Melissa squeezed through the gap and Tyler closed the cellar door. With help from Klaus she manoeuvred the cabinet into place, hiding the door. She turned at the sound of German voices and the approaching stomp of combat boots.

At the end of the hall, the one-hinged door flew open.

The Cleansing

Tyler switched to *Cloak of Night* as Klaus snatched her hand to become a shadow and the trooper stormed in. They dashed for the stairs unnoticed as the first of the cleansing party paused in the hall. Glancing only fleeting shadows, the trooper called back to his companions, waved them on and clomped through into the burned room, roving his gun in sync with his eyes.

Reaching the upper floor, Klaus and Tyler found a patch of dark shade beneath a jagged edge of rubble wall and reclined into it, their outlines melting away. For several minutes they listened to the cleansing below, the barking of orders, the slamming of doors, shifting of furniture and the merciless clump of heavy boots.

*

The ghosts and Melissa gathered on the cellar floor, a stillness settling over them as, above, the soldiers searched. The ghosts who had not already armed themselves did so now, tentatively watching the floorboards overhead.

Kinga glanced at Melissa.

"Where's Isla?"

*

Tyler and Klaus stilled when a long muzzle emerged from the stairwell. A trooper rose behind it and walked to the centre of the floor, stepping more casually as he sensed its emptiness. Noticing the view, he gave a crooked smile in appreciation of his newfound vantage point. Strolling to the edge he looked out at what could have been another planet and released a small, scoffing note. He shouldered his gun to pop a cigarette from a pack.

Behind him, Isla's fragile figure appeared from the stairway. Eyes wide in the moonlight, she crept nervously out and stood trembling and staring at the smoker's back.

No place to hide!

Tyler hurried to rise.

Klaus found her mouth, clamping with a hand before she could make a sound. She fought free, momentarily breaking their bond. The shadow camouflage left Klaus while Smoker, scanning the horizon, remained captivated by the landscape.

Tyler rose cautiously, soundlessly, to her feet.

Isla stood, doll-like, the tips of her fine hair trailing in the breeze.

Smoker tired of the view and paced across to the other side of the roof to look towards the spectral citadel.

Tyler stole closer to Isla, three careful steps at a time.

262

Smoker began to turn.

With a faint scuffle, Tyler dashed for Isla and grabbed her hand. Isla vanished into shade.

Smoker whipped around, snatching his gun to frown at the emptiness. The muffled din of his comrades' searching below continued. He studied the ground ahead of him, suspiciously.

He tightened his grip on the gun and eased a little more pressure on the trigger.

*

Shivering in the unlit cellar, Melissa cowered beneath floorboards snowing dust. Overhead, the soles of a trooper's boots blotted filaments of light that encroached between planks. She watched their menacing progress and gripped her gallows blade.

Around her, Kinga and the other ghosts readied their weapons, exchanging anxious glances.

A grating noise from the top of the steps turned heads. Melissa barely heard it over the thumping of her heart.

They're moving the cabinet!

John and several of the other ghosts aimed guns at the door. Danuta took a step closer to the stairs, her shoes crunching on grit. She froze.

Above, aggressive voices volleyed. The rasping of the cabinet ceased, replaced by a rapid burst of gunfire. Bullets perforated the thin boards of the under-stair wall, striping the room below with radiating shafts of half-light. Melissa braced a hand over her mouth to suppress a sob.

Kinga raised a finger to her lips.

*

On the upper floor, Smoker paused at the gunfire from

below.

Combat knife in hand, Klaus arrived at his back with a final, silent pace. Fixing a hand over Smoker's mouth, he punched the blade into the exposed neck. He released the moribund man, letting him collapse. Smoker's gun clattered to the ground.

The approaching stomp of a second trooper coming up the stairs warned Tyler. She dragged Isla over to Klaus and the corpse to camouflage them all.

The newcomer walked from the stairway, frowning at the floor.

Empty.

Except for the gun.

Tyler saw the weapon too late to reach it. Barely daring to breathe, she searched the soldier's face for his thoughts.

Where's the other guy?

And why's his gun here?

A commander called up from below.

"Alle löschen. Ausziehen!" *All clear. Move out!*

The trooper paced to the nearest edge of the house and peered over the side, returning a moment later. A metre from Tyler's nose he shrugged.

He stooped to collect the gun and with a final glance around turned for the stairs.

Tyler, Klaus and Isla listened as the cleansing party clattered out of the building and on to the next ruined street. When their sounds had died away, Tyler released Isla's hand and switched the dark sister to the fylfot. She grabbed Isla by the shoulders.

"What were you doing? Why weren't you in the cellar?"

Isla pursed her lips. "I was doing what you said.

Collecting the food and stuff. I just didn't make it back in time. I hid but then..."

"You're lucky to be alive." Tyler glanced at the dead trooper. "We'd better hide him."

*

Bullet holes riddled the cabinet and the surrounding wall. If anyone had been hiding in a cupboard under the stairs they would have died, but there was no cupboard, only a void over the cellar steps, and no one had been standing there.

Klaus and Tyler heaved the cabinet away from the door and Tyler pulled open the door. She peered down into the cellar, greeted by the upturned faces of those hiding below.

"Anyone hurt?"

Kinga shook her head and gave a thumbs up.

"It's okay. They've moved on."

"Where's Isla?" Kinga asked.

"She's with us. She's okay. Everyone out. We have a lot to do."

*

Weaver counted up the survivors, forty-three in all. Around him lay the scattered bodies of grey coats and the few ghosts he had lost.

"We can't leave them here. Drag them into the ditch. Cover our tracks."

"Molly, get down my dear." Mr Goodwin dropped Molly to the ground and helped the others drag the bodies up the slope and across the road. She wandered a few steps from the others, searching the night. Across a deep valley a hill rose and the distant sounds of battle and the flashes of gunfire and armour reached her through the fog. Molly squinted, pointing to the hill.

"Da, what's that?"

*

Albert and Lucy dashed from ruin to ruin, avoiding the drifting, unreliable phantom dwellings that roamed haphazardly between. Turning a crumbling corner they stopped short. Ahead, a grey coat clearance crew swept down the rubble road, poking gun muzzles into shattered doorways, flipping patches of fallen roofing to be sure no one was hiding beneath and smattering any hard-to-reach hiding places with bullets just to be sure.

Albert watched the crew depart.

"This way!"

He and Lucy darted across the road and up to the next knoll of ruins reaching from the mist. Albert planted his back against a wall, pausing to rub his cold, numb hands.

"This is it." Lucy scrutinised the land ahead. "Once we're past this place there's a border of dwellings and then we're into the citadel."

*

Mr Goodwin released the grey coat corpse, letting it slide into the ditch with the rest, and hurried to Molly's side.

"What is it, my dear?"

"There, on the hill. Lights."

Followed her gaze, he sensed the faint signs. He called back.

"Master Weaver, there's a battle on the hill."

Weaver joined them, nodding.

"Let's go see what all the fuss is about."

Their growing band shared out the machine guns looted from the grey coats and Weaver led them down the rolling valley side to the fogbound banks of a broad stretch of black water. Here no battle noise penetrated and fog dampened the small sounds of their passing to leave an eerie quiet.

"How are we going to cross the river?" Mr Goodwin stepped closer and surveyed the surrounding haze, Molly once more on his shoulders. Behind him the other half-ghosts gathered.

Weaver scanned the surface of the still water. "It's not a river. That's a lake."

"River or lake, we still 'ave to cross it. Could take forever to go around."

Weaver squinted, seeing no end to the lake, only black water receding into mist. "I don't know how."

Molly stared at a strand of trees further on that ran close to the bank.

"We could build a raft."

"That's a grand idea, Molly."

Weaver organised the stronger of his men to gather the largest branches they could find while others tore strips from their clothes to tie together and twist into makeshift ropes. Molly worked with the rope makers, sitting cross-legged on the freezing ground to knot strips together. Other half-ghosts combed the trees, returning with armfuls of creepers for further bindings and long, straight branches with which to steer, punt and paddle.

Clicker-clack.

Molly turned at an unfamiliar sound.

Clicker-clack. Clicker-clack.

From the black water nearby emerged a pair of probing, spindle legs. More spidery limbs followed as a creature the size of a dog and formed of death mist clawed a path onto the bank. Socketed within its skull shaped head, a single bulbous eye searched for prey.

Molly screamed.

Still Waters
Run Deep

With the dark sister resting at the *Brimstone Chasm* setting and her rucksack strapped to her back, Tyler stole out from the back door of the burned house. Pausing in the moon shadows of a fragile wall, she shouldered her assault rifle and took bearings before setting off towards the *Tower of Doom*. Between her and her goal lay a scatter of ruins, the tower top with its crenellations silhouetted by the moon, reaching higher into view.

I could use the Cloak of Night *on the journey, but what if the dark sister's ghosts tire? The power will die and I'll be revealed without warning. Better to save it for when it really counts.*

Her chances were slim, she knew that, but at least

alone she could move easily without worrying about anyone else and if threatened she could use her wings to escape without leaving anyone behind.

The night overhead weighed like a cold slab of marble. Shrugging it off, she skirted the neighbouring ruins and ventured across a rolling escarpment and on to the next.

A drift of phantom buildings floated sluggishly by. A stone barn, a battered corrugated iron shack, a thatched cottage and a taller, timber-framed Tudor house. She sprinted for the Tudor house and, finding it unlocked, slipped inside.

Back to the door, she scanned the interior.

Empty, like most of the ghost dwellings since the advent of Mary Cobbler.

Slowly the house turned in sync with its neighbours, spinning like a giant's carousel while sliding through the landscape. Tyler watched the night go by from a window, reminded of a time when she had watched from a Watford bus before the oppressor's return. Before the contrap. Before Hell had spilled its bile across the Earth.

The drift carried her towards an enclosure fenced with barbed wire and she shrank back into deeper shadows. Flaming torches on fence posts illuminated the site where contrapassi warriors trained a pack of scorpion-horses for war. The scorps shrieked and whined in torment as their masters whipped and beat them into line. One errant scorp fled in panic, dashing out from the others. Contrapassi threw ropes and hauled it to the ground where they butchered it with swords. Tyler looked away.

The drift continued past several ruins and she rested, hidden and still as her memory mist ferry buoyed her closer to the tower. It slowed before veering away.

Leaping from the phantom house she crunched onto solid land and crouched beneath the fog, listening to the approaching clop of hooves.

Parting the haze, a pair of contrapassi scorp riders loomed into view and Tyler switched to the *Cloak of Night*. She held her breath as they passed, her finger tightening on the trigger of her rifle. Their dank, animal reek fouled the air. She felt for the reassuring presence of the spare clips in the thigh pockets of her combats.

The riders searched the murk, sniffing the air, their teeth and bronze breastplates glinting in the moonlight. Beyond her they stopped, tugging on their scorps' reins.

"You smell something, Poker?" growled the larger of the two, an ugly, scar-faced brute with a whip coiled at his waist and a long, scimitar in his hand. Suspended over his head, his scorpion's sting twitched restlessly. "Cool it, Boris." Scar Face stroked the glossy plate armour of his beast's thick neck soothingly.

Poker probed the air with his long snout and leered around keenly.

"Yeah, I smell something," he whined in a higher bestial tone. He took several long sniffs, sucking in the vaporous air. "Something's here, al'right. Something stinks!" A crafty smile split his wolfish face and he twisted in his saddle to lean close, his nose wrinkling an inch from Scar Face. "It's you!"

Scar Face swung at Poker, catching him squarely on the back of the head with the flat of his blade.

"You idiot scum-worm-maggot!"

Poker guffawed despite the blow and the two coaxed their scorps on.

Tyler listened as the fog swallowed their insults and

switched back to the *Brimstone Chasm*.

*

Molly didn't stop to count the legs but there were more than six. More than eight, even. Scrambling to her feet she shrieked a warning to the others as more of the bugs crawled free of the water.

"Spiders!"

Clicker-clack. The skull bugs scurried closer, pincer-like fangs clicking.

Yakubu sprinted from the trees and, swinging a log, smashed three bugs into the air. More of them scrambled out, swarming from the lake. Yakubu swung again and again as ghosts ran to join the fight, swatting with branches, crunching the bugs and kicking them back into the water. Their spidery bodies piled on the banks and still more flooded out, clambering over their fallen siblings.

One clamped onto a slave's leg and chomped into half-ghost flesh. The ghost dropped, writhing to the ground and bugs gathered to drag his weight into the lake. Black water enveloped him and he vanished to the depths.

Mr Goodwin stared. "Where did he go?"

"They're taking him back to Sheol," said Weaver.

Legionary ghosts stabbed with their spears and swords, the bugs screeching with each thrust and jab. Among them, a stocky soldier named Quintillus made jam of the crawlers, his gladius a blur of precision. Legendary amongst his men, Quintillus' sword skills were unmatched by any in his day.

Some bugs were faster than others. Molly fled and one dashed towards her, leaping closer as she stumbled and fell.

Raising his gun, Mr Goodwin stepped between the bug and his daughter.

"Come on then, you scrawny critter!"

Clicker-clack. The bug sprang. Mr Goodwin fired. Bug guts greased the ground.

Close behind Mr Goodwin, Weaver sprayed the crawling masses with machine gun bullets. Other armed ghosts returned from the trees to join the fight and soon the banks glistened with bug gore.

A Roman slave boy shouted, pointing to a rise further on along the valley.

"Contrapassi! They come!"

A bank of mist rolled away and a crowd of contrapassi lumbered.

Quintillus dispatched five bugs with two practised strokes.

"We've been spotted. Finish the rafts and cross the lake!" shouted Weaver. "NOW!"

The bugs were all but gone. Ghosts blasted those that lingered and worked speedily to lash the last of the logs. As the contrapassi closed in, the ghosts hauled three rafts to the water's edge.

"Come on!" Weaver's glance flicked between the lake and the approaching horde.

Please, no more spiders!

The men threw the children onto the rafts before dividing themselves across the three. They pushed off the first two rafts.

"Hurry!" Weaver boarded the remaining raft with Molly, and Mr Goodwin shoved them from the bank and leapt aboard as the contrapassi entered range. The hiss of bowstrings warped the air. Arrows rained, *plapping* into the water and thumping into the banks.

273

Ghosts poled the rafts across the lake amid the lethal downpour, the adults shielding the children with their bodies. Missiles fell with increasing accuracy as the giants drew closer and the rafters reached halfway as the contrapassi descended to the trees.

The black water rippled.

Spider legs pierced the surface, like fingers groping for purchase. The bug found a raft log and clawed itself up. A legionary speared it. The bug squealed as he scraped it off against the raft's edge.

Two more bugs appeared while the passengers backed away, tipping the raft precariously.

Bugs invaded the other rafts from all sides and the killing resumed as the ghosts formed defensive rings, shooting, slashing and stabbing outward.

Behind them, contrapassi reached the water's edge to wade in. Others knelt to loose arrows.

Yakubu stomped on a bug and sent another flying with a hefty kick. He plunged his branch deep into the lake driving his raft nearer to the opposite bank. An arrow thudded into his shoulder. His legs buckled and he collapsed. Reaching back, he grasped the arrow and snapped its shaft. He staggered to his feet and took up the branch once more as Quintillus speared an invader on the tip of his sword.

The first raft nudged the bank as a second ghost fell to a spiders' bite. Again, the bugs swarmed in to bear the limp body to the depths.

Arrows flew. Bugs bit. Ghosts fell.

A ripple troubled the water's surface. He raised his gun. A gushing torrent enveloped the surface as a whale-sized mouth erupted from below.

Weaver lowered his muzzle.

"RUN!"

The great mouth rose, its skull-like face following to level its gaze at the rafters. The mouth gaped, yawning to devour as half-ghosts fled, leaping for land and scrambling ashore. With a colossal bite the beast dived for the rafts.

*

Klaus eased open the back door and stepped out, his rifle poised. Melissa stayed close as the other ghosts left the burned house.

After further map-drawing, compass bearings and heated discussions they had agreed upon a plan. Klaus and Melissa were to take a group north between the tower and the citadel, a route that followed a valley for the first few miles before rising to a jagged ruin. That jagged ruin was their reference point, a recognisable place to aim for that would afford views of the uncharted land beyond.

The ghosts had already searched widely to the east and west and with the group heading north, only the south remained unexplored. This zone was a mystery, shrouded in the densest smog from which little protruded.

Wulfric and John led the second team from the house while Melissa clasped Klaus by the arm, resisting the temptation to call Freddy's name with each step.

To the west a flotilla of death ships blackened the sky in the glow of the moon, their engines chugging embers into the night.

*

Lucy dashed across the fog to rest against the memory mist stone of a cave entrance. Ahead, the spiked fortifications of the citadel jutted, their battlements rising towards the Witch Queen's tower. Between Lucy and the outer bulwarks clustered a dense ring of other random dwellings alongside the cave.

Albert threaded through the fog to join her.

"Where now?"

"See the mansion down there?"

"Aye."

"Head for that. The building on that side will hide us from the citadel."

"Good."

"Let's go."

They ran the line of dwellings, a medieval courthouse, a Roman *mansio*, a roundhouse, a thatched cottage and a dilapidated broch. Lucy reached the mansion and hammered on the door. No reply. Flicking up the inner catch with a blade between the door and the jamb, she broke in, Albert following.

They waited briefly in the near dark interior, the witch's green light piercing the gloom in crystal shards streaming from the windows. Lucy crossed the room to look out and plan their next move as Albert joined her.

"There's a gully runnin' between them tenements, nice an' low. Looks like it ends at the citadel wall."

"Sounds like a plan. Do you need to rest?"

"Ain't no time to rest, Lucy Loo. We gotta find Ruth before things get even worse. Lawd knows what the oppressor's doin' right now."

"My thoughts entirely. We'll need your rope."

They left the mansion via another door that led them out onto a courtyard. At the end of an outbuilding they ventured into the open again and ran for the gully between the blocks. Breathless, they rested in the narrow, guttered hollow.

Hearing a voice they turned.

"Ay, aye, look what we found, Morville."

Spread across the exit stood the six hunters. One doffed his cap to Albert, replaced it and with a snide grin drew a gleaming knife.

"Yeah, Dagger, I see," said Morville, a half-ghost mail-clad knight with a longsword sheathed at his back. He speared Albert with a cruel stare. "We been looking all over for you, boy. And what's this? A *girl* with a gun?"

The other hunters laughed.

"Yeah, but you should let her go," said Albert. "She don't even know how to shoot. Ain't no fighter." His eyes flashed from the six to Lucy and back. "Put it down, Lucy. Maybe they'll let you go."

"What?" Lucy shot the word from her mouth.

Dagger angled his blade towards her.

"Lucy, huh? Such a *pretty* name."

*

Tyler crept the rest of the way through the thickest of the stinging fog with icy tears streaming her face. Crouching before the tower's dwindling forest, she wiped her eyes and spied with the dark sister's *Present Eye*.

At the front of the tower's base a heavy portcullis secured its entrance, a broad, doored arch which she knew from her previous time in the Chasm would also be locked and barred from the inside. Back then she and Albert had found the portcullis raised a foot from the ground, allowing them to slip through unimpeded. Now it rested fully closed, its spiked irons threading shafts in the cobbled ground.

From the portcullis ran a rutted track that pierced the woods, guarded either side by sword-bearing contrapassi.

She focused into the tower itself, passing through

trees and walls.   Inside, the keepers of the castle slumbered, each floor cluttered with their bodies like a sleeping anthill. Moving her view up the levels, each lit by the moon from the tower's windows, she paused to scrutinise the level below the table of plenty. There the oppressor slept, wrapped in his blackened wings, a pair of she-demons for company. Tyler levered her view in, passing through the oppressor's wings and aiming for the chest. Beneath the folded wings darkness shrouded all.

Tyler shivered and withdrew her gaze.

I guess even bad guys need to sleep.

Presuming he wore the contrap as he slept, she moved her view on to the chamber with the table of plenty, finding it laden to the brim with food and drink, and unguarded.

At least that's something.

Progressing to the rooftop she focused on first one and then a second lilith, each perched like eagles on opposing battlements and scouring the night.

Tyler set the dark sister back to the *Brimstone Chasm* and tried to formulate a plan. She judged the easiest way in would be from the roof but for that she would need to tackle the two liliths. And without raising the alarm.

The moon lingered lower in the sky and on the opposing horizon a warm glow slowly increased.

Dawn's coming. If I'm going to try something I need to do it now. There'll be more guards and more danger when the oppressor awakes.

Switching to the *Cloak of Night* she unfurled her wings and kicked off from the ground.

Boris

Weaver heaved Mr Goodwin to his feet and snatched Molly from the ground, clutching her under his arm. Other ghosts floundered at the water's edge as the great jaws crashed down to swallow the rafts. With his free hand Weaver grabbed others and pulled them, struggling, to dry ground. The lake erupted with the beast's second impact, spraying all with the deathly black water.

Its serpentine body followed into the wake as splintered logs rained down around the banks and the half-ghosts fled, slipping and groping up the slope away from the bugs, the contrapassi and the water beast.

At the top of the ridge Weaver glanced back.

Below him, a standoff ensued between the beast and

the lake-bound contrapassi. They drew bows and volleyed their arrows and skull bugs skittered on the shores.

Up ahead the ground rose and the mist cleared around the base of the battle hill. Weaver set Molly down.

"Now climb!"

*

Klaus stayed his party with a gesture. Their expedition to find the Cave of Sorrows had gone smoothly this far and he wanted no surprises. The high, jagged ruin rose before him like a beacon on a hill and a short climb took him to a point near the top from where he could survey the land.

Beyond, a long slope of broken houses dwindled into darkness. Grey coat cleansing parties swept systematically across, shocking the quiet thrum with occasional gunfire.

*

"I'm glad you like it," said Lucy. "It's the last name you're ever going to hear."

Albert watched her nervously.

"Put it down, Lucy. Put the gun down, *slowly*. They have us."

Lucy's glare flickered between Albert and the six.

A hunter wearing a tabard trained his MP40 on her.

"All right." Lucy splayed her fingers in a submissive gesture.

"Slowly," said Morville. "Like the boy says."

Lucy eased her rifle towards the ground.

"Three." She whispered to Albert. Her gun dropped lower. "Two." The muzzle rested on the ground. "One." With a lightning jerk she righted the gun to send a bullet through Tabard's chest and a second through the other

280

gunman. "GO!"

Albert turned and ran for the citadel wall, not knowing what he might do if he were to ever reach it. Behind him Lucy sprayed the contents of a magazine at the scattering hunters. She snatched the two guns from the ground and backed away. Turning, she raced to catch up with Albert.

"Albert, the rope!"

Albert slipped the rope from his shoulder and Lucy tied the end around her waist.

"Help me up!"

Taking a throwing knife in each hand she shoved a boot onto Albert's meshed hands and climbed onto his shoulders. From there she jammed the first of her blades into the mortar between stones in the wall and hauled herself higher. The next blade slid in easily and she climbed. Hand over hand she ascended as, below, the four remaining hunters saw their opportunity and regrouped.

Lucy reached the top of the wall and braced the rope for Albert's weight.

He called up as the hunters ran closer. "Ready?"

"Climb!"

Albert heaved himself up the rope and Lucy hauled from the top. The hunters launched weapons that clanged and clattered against the wall around him. They rushed to rearm as Albert mounted the top and, with Lucy, quickly dropped into the citadel.

*

Tyler climbed high to circle the tower, observing the hawk-eyed lilith guards. She had out-flown them before but that was with a head start when she'd taken them by surprise. Now she needed to judge her lead correctly before revealing herself or they would surely cremate her on the wing.

She switched from *Cloak of Night* back to the *Brimstone Chasm*. Her wings blazed into light.

The liliths locked onto her immediately, the first leaping from its parapet with a single screech of warning. The other scanned full circle cautiously before launching into the air.

Tyler darted like a swift as the two liliths gave chase, their spans dwarfing hers.

She searched the landscape far below for a place where she might lose them and settled on a forest beyond the citadel's lights. Aiming for the canopy of trees she willed her flaming wings to full speed as the closer of the pair spewed fire. Beyond range, the lilith screeched angrily as the fire stream dropped from the sky.

Tyler glanced over her shoulder.

"Come on! You can do better than that!"

The incensed lilith screamed fury and increased its pace.

Tyler swore and focused back onto the forest. The liltihs were faster than she had hoped. Building momentum, they drew great wingbeats to race for her. She needed to reach the trees before they gained on her further or they would incinerate her with ease.

Below, the shifting fringes of the citadel rolled by.

*

Albert felt Tyler's proximity in his spirit long before her fire dashed the heavens overhead like a streaming comet.

"That's Tyler!"

Two dark eagles flew by, close on her heels.

Lucy glanced skyward.

"She'd better get a shift on. She has company.

What's she doing?"

*

Tyler passed over the citadel's walls, swooping close to the witch's tower and scoping her defences.

No liliths. No contrapassi. Just ghosts. Good. Ghosts we can deal with.

She bent her path around the tower and flashed across the remaining fortifications, her followers gaining. A nearby screech scrambled her thoughts.

Wrong!

From atop the witch's tower a single lilith stretched into view and launched, joining Tyler's train of followers.

Reaching the forest fringe, she dropped into a steep dive to plummet between trees.

The liliths slowed, their wings too oversized to easily thread the woodland. They drew them in, raking the ground with their talons, steering through the gaps and ducking branches as Tyler darted on, gaining ground. She slowed to coax them deep into the woods.

The deeper the better.

In the thickest, densest patch she shot behind a broad trunk and folded her wings. She switched to *Cloak of Night*, vanishing into the shadows, and headed out of the opposite side of the forest, far from the encumbered liliths.

The race is on.

Now a streaking, transient shade against the darkling sky, she slowed. Her wings came at a cost and she felt it now as she tired. Flying at an easier pace, she aimed for the *Tower of Doom* while attempting to memorise the layout of Jerusalem's devastated ground and, minutes later, she closed on the tower's unoccupied battlements.

Good. The liliths' screeches had failed to raise an

alarm.

The Hell birds paid her no heed. As they lazed in high circles she landed gently on the tower's flat roof. Switching to the *Present Eye* she looked into the chambers below, finding them unchanged. She switched back to *Cloak of Night* and heaved at the trapdoor's gnarled rope, surprised when the door creaked a few centimetres open.

Carefully, she lowered it.

Quietly.

The door of iron-studded hardwood planks was heavy. Adjusting her position, she steeled herself and dragged the trap fully open before hurrying nimbly down the steps. At the table of plenty she shook the bag from her shoulders and stuffed it with hunks of cheese and brown loaves of bread, topping it off with a layer of luscious, ripe fruit. Replacing the bag on her back, she stuffed a little of everything into her mouth and downed a pint of cool, sweet water. Much refreshed, she switched again to the *Present Eye* for one last check on the oppressor sleeping in the room below. She focused through the floor and onto the spot where he slept, only to find an empty floor. A shiver quickened her senses as she searched frantically for him.

Too late!

His upturned face startled her through the floorboards and she dropped the dark sister, letting it swing on its chain around her neck as she stepped back. The lower trap door cracked open as footsteps echoed from the stairs beneath.

He's sensed the dark sister even in his sleep!

Steeped in fury, the oppressor's guttural voice slithered up to her.

"Tyler May..."

Her plan to take the contrap vaporised as Tyler fled the room, dashing up the stairs and unfurling her wings. She ran to the nearest parapet, switched to *Cloak of Night* and threw herself from the edge.

Behind her, the oppressor gripped the battlements, searching for her. He growled orders to the liliths ascending the stairs. Sweeping their wings wide they leapt after Tyler, infuriated by her sudden disappearance.

The oppressor poured venomous words into the atmosphere.

"Death to the Hope Bringer!"

Tyler flew on, weary, disoriented and shaking beneath her camouflage. The Chasm's sun pierced the horizon as she passed ruins and descended to land on a flattened patch of rubble. She scanned around for threats before stepping into a small box of a room, the only one remaining from an otherwise flattened house. Concealed by its fragile roof she switched to the *Brimstone Chasm* to rest the dark sister.

For a while she also rested. She ate a few large, juicy grapes from her bag while keeping watch from a small window. With dawn came an awakening of the Chasm creatures. She felt them stir through vibrations of the floor. Somewhere close by, subs churned the ground and a faint clop of scorp hooves mingled with the pounding of contrapassi feet and the march of the grey coats.

The monsters had risen and the night's respite was over. She knew she would need to be more careful from here on if she was to make it back to the burned house.

Rested and feeling stronger for the food, she took bearings using the tower and the citadel and ventured out into the mist. She found more people bound by the unbreakable chains, beyond help. Their mournful expressions followed her as she passed.

A short way down an incline she paused at a new sound, wincing as inhuman shrieks punctuated a scolding contrapasso voice she recognised. The shrieks grew louder as she walked closer to their smog-veiled source. She switched to *Cloak of Night*. A few steps further through the mist revealed four creatures in a clearing: the contrapassi Scar Face, Poker and their scorp mounts.

While Poker sat astride his mount, Scar Face stood with feet planted apart as he lashed at his scorp with a vicious-looking whip. At each strike the creature screamed in torment.

Crack.

Whine.

"You useless, good-for-nothing slug!"

Crack. Crack.

Wail. Shriek.

Scar Face kicked Boris for good measure, hard in the underbelly. The beast released a sickening groan.

"Serves you right, you filthy roach!"

The whip lashed.

Crack. Crack. Crack.

Howl.

Boris trembled and stamped.

Tyler could not fathom the creature's crime, nor could she abide its torture. Creeping around the clearing so that Poker was between her and Scar Face, she grabbed a lump of rock from the rubble and hurled it. It shot over Poker's head and clapped Scar Face on the shoulder. He turned, first watching the missile as it rolled in the dirt and then eying Poker.

"Was that you?"

Poker scowled into the surrounding mists.

"Naw, course not. There's someone out there. Someone's throwing stones."

"Then *find* them and *kill* them!"

Scar Face growled and resumed work as Boris cowered.

Crack. Crack.

Shriek.

Poker coaxed his scorp to circle the area, returning to the same spot none the wiser. He scowled.

Tyler lobbed a second stone. This one clunked against the side of Scar Face's head. He stopped whipping to snap around and sneer at Poker.

"It *was* you, wasn't it?"

"I swear, it was not me!"

"Then who was it? There's no one else here!"

Tyler waited to time her next launch carefully. Scar Face huffed, uncertainty creasing his brow and twisting his slavering mouth as he searched about. When he dropped his head to glance back at Boris, Tyler cast her third rock, catching him squarely on the back of the skull.

He roared as he spun. In one fluid motion he drew his sword and turned on Poker, skewering his companion through the gut. He withdrew his slick blade as Poker slumped from his mount.

Boris raised his sting, threateningly.

To compound the contrapasso's exasperation Tyler threw another stone. It bounced, *clanging* from his breastplate. His scowl deepened and a low rumble emanated from his throat. With a further swipe, he lopped the sting from Boris' tail.

Relieved of his rider, Poker's mount bolted. Behind Scar Face, Boris' legs folded as he keeled over.

Scar Face narrowed his eyes at the mist around Tyler. With her attention on the contrapassi and the clearing, she had neglected to watch the creeping mist. She realised now as the monster stared that her shadowed outline might be more discernible against the bank of fog, and then she knew.

He had found her.

Scar Face snarled and loped towards her.

The Fallen

Darting sideways, Tyler ran into denser mist. Scar Face knew what to look for now but her camouflage worked. For a few moments she lost him and selected a boulder large enough to inflict serious damage but small enough to heft. She still had her rifle but the sound of that could bring unwanted attention from miles around. A rock would be quieter. She released her wings and launched herself into a staggering flight, straining under the extra weight.

Scar Face was easy to locate. His smell alone would have been enough, but she found his giant form like a tower in cloud and heard his rolling breath, heavy with aggravation. She hovered overhead, released the boulder and heard a satisfying crunch as it impacted his cranium.

With Scar Face felled she flew to Boris, wondering if the ill-treated scorp had already died from his injuries. She landed at his side, switched from *Cloak of Night* and folded her wings to examine his wounds. Deep purple welts streaked the sandy toned plates of his back, and greenish-blue blood dripped from the stump of his tail. He whined softly at her touch.

"Still alive, then."

She took a knife from her belt and cut a strip from her shirt. Bandaging this around the wound she took bread, cheese and fruit from her bag and offered it. Boris took one sniff and recoiled from the food.

"Carnivore, huh?"

A shadow fell across her as Scar Face arose. He roared and brandished his sword, preparing to slice her in two. Tyler's food fell to the ground, forgotten.

Boris lurched, a lightning pre-emptive strike. His sting gone, he snatched with his pincers, catching the unsuspecting contrapasso around the throat as Tyler darted beyond reach. The beasts wrestled, Scar Face lashing with his sword, slicing air. Boris pressed forwards, holding his foe at bay and bearing down. The contrapasso buckled under the scorp's weight, and choking for breath in the pincers' tightening grip, dropped to his knees. A glazed expression seeped over his face.

Boris fed.

Tyler turned away.

*

The battle was long gone. Molly kicked at a mangled piece of contrapassi armour. The corpses of monsters and half-ghosts littered the hilltop plateau, their weapons and belongings scattered across the churned ground. Among the clutter stood ghosts and men as though frozen in time, their chain-entwined bodies rigidly trapped in mid-motion.

As dawn broke, Weaver and his gang had climbed into fog, reached the peak and rested. Nothing had followed them. At least, nothing they knew of. Now Weaver searched the aftermath for signs.

"So many dead," said Yakubu, retrieving a contrapassi sword and testing its balance.

Quintillus scanned the carnage, kneeling to study marks in the ground.

"Thousands fought here."

"But who won?" asked Weaver. "And where are the victors?"

"They can't have gone far." Mr Goodwin crouched to examine footprints.

"It makes no sense," said Weaver. "These wounds on the contrapassi. What made them?"

"Swords, I'd say." Mr Goodwin rose to step closer to the edge of the hilltop.

"But our ghosts don't have swords large enough for these wounds. Not many. Not enough to account for this slaughter."

"Someone else was here, then."

Molly stooped to collect a huge, white feather from the baked mud.

"Master Weaver." Mr Goodwin beckoned.

"Yes?" Weaver joined Mr Goodwin at the edge.

"There. Footprints leaving. The prints of men."

*

Melissa viewed the land from their latest vantage point, a crest in the undulating terrain. As the sun rose to roast the ground, her team left the grey coat speckled slopes behind. Ahead stretched more demolition. Subs roamed unabated and a foul stink carried on the warm wind.

"Soon it will be too hot again." She squinted beneath the sun, hoping for a chance glimpse of Freddy. "How far do you think this goes on?"

"The merged realms? Who knows?" Klaus offered a wry smile. "No Cave of Sorrows. Not here, anyway." He looked at each of his team in turn, every ghost weary and hungry. "We'd better return. Get out of this heat. Perhaps the others have had better luck."

Looking back towards the burned house Melissa saw the jagged ruins they had passed. Further on to her left the citadel sprawled, to her right stood the Tower of Doom. A movement in her peripheral vision drew her attention. A half mile away a black shape darted, cleaving the smog.

"What's that?" She pointed.

"It's not a contrapassi. Wrong shape. Not a scorp or a sub, either."

"A Hell bird?"

Klaus focused his field glasses.

"Perhaps. It's about the right size but the shape's not right. Let's take a closer look, just to be sure."

Melissa wiped perspiration from her brow.

"Me and my big mouth."

They left the crest and re-entered the cover of the mist to steal closer to the darting form.

"It's heading for the tower."

Klaus paused to look again through his field glasses. "It looks like the oppressor."

"It can't be, surely. The oppressor's in the tower. Isn't he?"

"Maybe he went out for groceries," said Zebedee.

Hastening, they descended a slope and negotiated the rubble of more ruined buildings.

"If we're quick we can intercept him."

Racing, they scrambled into a run as the rubble gave way to a plane of fog, their path slowly converging with that of the darting shape. In closer range they paused again while Klaus refocused.

"It's not the oppressor but another of his kind."

"Another fallen angel?" Zebedee wheezed breathlessly.

"Yes. This one's skinny." Klaus led them further on to a low strand of bushes and stunted trees. Creeping through he stopped to peer out from the fringe as the dark angel approached. Klaus ditched his glasses and levelled his rifle. He eased his finger onto the trigger waiting for the optimum shot and, with one smooth motion, squeezed.

Tap, tap.

Out in the mists the fallen angel shrieked and dropped.

"Quickly!" Klaus waved the others on and they ran to search for the body.

The dark angel groaned and hissed at their approach. On his back with a shoulder leaking blue blood, he grabbed for an intricately embellished sword slung at his side, shrieking when Zebedee's foot clamped down to pin the blade to the ground.

"Not so fast."

The dark angel squealed again as Klaus shoved the muzzle of his rifle in his face.

"Don't move."

The dark angel hissed again, measuring his captors.

Part way along a wing, more of the inhuman blood oozed from wounded muscle and blackened, leathery skin where a second bullet had torn a hole.

Melissa rested a hand on Klaus' shoulder.

"There's another over there." She nodded towards the tower where another winged shape soared towards the tower in the sky.

Klaus pressed the gun's muzzle against the dark angel's temple.

"Not a sound or you're history." He turned to his companions. "Get down."

They crouched, allowing the smog to envelope them. The soaring demon glided lower and landed on the tower top.

"We're too vulnerable here. Help me drag him into the bushes."

"Shouldn't we just finish him?" asked Kinga.

"Maybe we should," said Klaus, heaving at a tattered wing.

The demon laughed, his face a contortion of hatred, pain and cynicism.

They dragged him under the sparse cover of the vegetation and the ghosts removed their belts to bind his hands. Kylie tore a strip from her coat to use as a gag.

Klaus leaned close to the dark angel's grimacing face. Skin like burned parchment. An expression twisted with sharp features.

"Can you walk?"

The dark angel shook his head, glowering and releasing a low, muffled growl.

"Good. On your feet. You're coming with us."

Melissa stepped closer.

"We can't take him back with us. He'll give us away."

The fallen angel watched, eyes flashing with intelligent fire to each of those speaking.

"He won't if we kill him," Klaus stated.

"In cold blood? That feels a little too close to murder for my liking."

"He's a demon. He *likes* murder. Murder's his thing."

"I still don't think we should."

"All right. I'll question him here. That all right with you?"

"What, and then release him?" Melissa's eyes widened in horror at the thought.

"Gib mir stärke," muttered Klaus. "What *do* you want me to do with him?"

Melissa shook her head and threw out her hands.

"I don't know! And by the way, you know perfectly well I speak fluent German."

*

Albert and Lucy pressed deeper into the citadel, frequently glancing back. Every so often the sounds of their pursuers echoed from the surrounding battlements.

Lucy stopped and gazed into the long ghostly courtyard behind them.

"What's wrong?" asked Albert. So far Lucy had refused to even pause to catch breath.

"Wait here." She flitted away into the shadows between barracks.

Feeling exposed, Albert flattened himself against a block wall. He noticed the shadows of the buildings around him shifting as though deliberately and glanced at the heavens. They seemed to be moving, too, turning in leisurely unison, pivoting around a patch of crimson cloud. He realised then, the movement was not occurring in the sky but on the ground. The phantom bulwarks, barracks and courtyards of the citadel were all revolving, like a giant wheel.

A sharp tapping turned his head.

Lucy?

He searched the rows of barracks, the courtyard and the stretch of buildings ahead. *Not Lucy.*

Ahead, Morville walked out from between the barracks. The knight watched Albert briefly before bringing his loaded crossbow into line.

"Come now, you should not be surprised. It was inevitable that we would find you."

Albert glanced around for a way out and, finding none, brandished his gallows blade.

Morville laughed.

"I'll make this quick." He targeted Albert's face with the bow.

A gallows blade sliced the air, flashing in from Morville's side to lodge in his throat. Morville toppled and dissolved into dust.

*

Tyler unfolded a lock knife and sliced through the straps of Boris' saddle. It slid and fell away. She grabbed her bag and left the dead contrapassi and the wounded scorp behind.

"Bye, Boris."

Feeling the onset of exhaustion, she wanted to find the burned house quickly so that she could rest or, better, sleep. She walked, wondering how the others were faring and what Chapman was doing.

Probably sipping coffee in his office, watching me suffer and fight via some distant satellite.

She glanced up at the fuming sky.

Anyone there?

I should probably check the phones before returning. Maybe there's a signal out here.

She found a rock to sit on and took out her mobile, catching her reflection without recognition. Who was the person looking back at her from the glossy screen? A girl with a sharp and furious gaze, stress lines marring youthful features, dust-coated and sleep deprived. The bags under her eyes reminded her of a tramp's she had once encountered. Her clothes, too. Her jumpsuit was torn from the clawing branches of the forest, battle-worn, bloodied and soiled. Her cheeks were gaunt. Her hair was windswept and bedraggled.

Nineteen years old? Really?

Her mobile showed no signal and her battery was low. She returned it to an inside pocket and rummaged for the satellite phone in her bag to glance at the screen. Sighing, she threw it back in with her supplies.

Dead. Like Scar Face.

*

The marching of many half-ghost feet reverberated from the citadel's depths. Between the rising flanks of the spoke-like battlements pale crowds roared, their arms reaching up towards the witch's tower. Albert squinted at the tiny distant figure standing at a tall window of the high tower, backlit with ghoulish green. There, Mary Cobbler, Witch Queen of Gravitas, presented herself to her followers. He felt their cheers like a slick of bewilderment in his mind, a rising slurry pool that threatened to overwhelm.

Who in their right mind would abandon all to follow her?

He turned back, fearing more of the hunters and glimpsed Lucy hiding in the shade of the barrack block opposite. She winked and drew a finger to her lips.

His leather boots squelching in the fire-fog, Dagger stepped into the courtyard.

*

Tyler chose her path home with care, rerouting each time she sensed subs and other contrapassi patrols ahead.

During her third such detour she stilled when the trudge of feet reached her through the stinging smog. She crept closer, curious to know who approached as she noticed a metallic clinking sound.

Not the clop of scorps or pounding contrapassi feet. Nor the march of troopers.

Chains.

A line of manacled half-ghosts stumbled through the milky air, poked and prodded with pitiless regularity by their grey coat escorts. A gang chain stretched from each of the captive's necks, swinging to the rhythm of their slog.

She switched once more to *Cloak of Night* but not before a prisoner glimpsed her. Frowning at her disappearance, he looked for her. Knowing better than to speak, the prisoners along the line remained silent and shuffled by.

Tyler fingered the trigger of her rifle counting the grey coats and weighing her odds.

Too many and stationed sporadically on either side. No clear line of fire without taking out prisoners.

Feeling trapped, she watched the cavalcade of forlorn faces advance, their haunting eyes weeping dry tears of despair.

And then they were gone.

As the power of the dark sister waned, her camouflage died and a grey coat re-emerged from the smog to lock eyes, his mouth leering into a crooked grin.

"I told you there was someone there."

Others appeared behind him.

"It's the Hope Bringer!"

Tyler bolted amid a hail of bullets, losing herself in the smog. Without thought to direction she sprinted from them as they chased, shouting after her, their leader barking orders.

"Hold fire. Take her alive. This way. RUN!"

No doubt Tribulantis will want to torture me before inflicting a long, painful death.

If she flew above the vaporous layer she would be an easy target. The grey coats would dispense with their hold fire policy and shoot her. Instead, she ducked low and ran, scrambling over ruins and passing drifts of memory mist dwellings. She slowed to listen.

Have I lost them?

Footfalls betrayed their position on the other side of a ghostly wall.

Not far enough. Not yet.

She darted on but felt an odd sensation and slowed to search the mist. She had felt it before, a gentle numbing of the mind, a softening of her resolve. Questions trickled into her head, small at first, like drips of water.

Why run?

Drip.

Aren't you tired? Aren't you weary of all this?

Drip, drip.

Her jog became a walk. The drips joined to become trickles.

Give up! Give it all up!

Relax. Rest. Let it be over.

Tyler stopped walking and closed her eyes.

Sit down and let them find you.

The trickles grew into rivulets.

What does it matter? Why does anything matter?

The channels merged and swelled into a single stream.

Who cares? Who really cares? What difference does any of this make? Enter. Swim. Release yourself to the waters. They will carry you. The waters will make everything go away. Will make everything al'right.

She silenced the rising voices of her head with a fearful whisper and opened her eyes wide.

"The Shivering Pool."

The grey coats' footsteps and muttered curses grew louder as they, too, showed the signs of the shivering.

"We've lost her. We should give up."

"No. She's here somewhere."

"Where? I can't see her."

"Maybe we *should* give up. What's the point, anyway?"

"Let her go. Who cares?"

Tyler backed away from their words and, feeling the ground rise beneath her feet, glanced around through thinning mist. Before her, the banks of the Shivering Pool edged its crystalline water. The surface quivered in response to her breath, liquid glass in the Chasm light that sensed her presence with pernicious intent.

Enter. Swim. Let the waters bear you. Let the waters wash over you and take your pains. Relinquish fear. Let go anguish and striving. Relax. Bathe in the cool of forget. Deliver yourself to the pool.

Tyler stepped into the shallows, the surface shivering at her touch with a patter like light rain.

She took another step and dipped a hand to feel the

liquid swirl against her skin in gentle eddies.

Deeper and deeper still.

She stepped again and a soft, cool caress rippled over her ankles and licked up her shins, soaking through her boots and the fabric of her clothes.

Her pursuers slowed as they reached the pool, uncertainty marring their faces. They studied the shivering water and, enchanted, watched Tyler wade serenely away from them, the water lapping around her thighs. The first of them climbed the bank and dipped the toe of his boot. His whole foot followed and then his other. He stood, sighing in the shallows, welcoming the numbness that washed over him.

Tyler glanced back and floated a whisper to them.

"Come on in, boys. The water's fine."

Dagger, Dorkins & Dobbs

The grey coats glanced from Tyler to the shivering liquid around her and followed as she let her body fall forwards into the water's embrace. She swam and they waded deeper, water rising to their knees, their waists, their chests.

Tyler neared the opposite bank, fighting the shivering with every ounce of will she could muster. It had already taken the grey coats. She knew it, could see it in their glazed eyes as they succumbed and sank, but she was prepared for its potency. She had fought it before and survived.

Her hand reached the bank and dug into the memory mist. She groped for a hold, heaved her body from the water and dragged her feet clear of its numbing reach. Crawling to distance herself from the edge, she glimpsed bubbles on the surface as the Shivering Pool claimed its prize.

*

The next stretch of land was familiar. Tyler lay in wait, scoping out the last hundred metres to the burned house before making the dash, a track distance she could sprint in under eleven seconds. Kinga opened the door allowing her to dart in, relieved.

Panting in the hall, she slipped her bag from her shoulders.

"Who else made it?"

A shriek sprang from the cellar drowning Kinga's reply.

"What was that?"

Tyler rushed down the cellar steps.

The bound demon glared up, hissing.

Klaus grabbed her arm, turned her and marched her back upstairs.

"I'm glad you're back. Did you get the contrap?"

"*What* are you doing? What *is* that and *why* is it here? Are you mad?"

"He says his name's Odium. He's a fallen angel like the oppressor, or as Odium calls him, Tribulantis."

"You spoke with it?"

"I interrogated him."

Reaching the parlour, Klaus pulled a chair from beneath the map table and gestured for her to sit. Tyler declined.

"Surely we can't trust a word he says."

"I know but some of it I believe. He's not lying about everything."

304

"But you brought him *here?*"

Klaus rubbed at his forehead.

"*This* again."

"Now he knows where we are!"

"So where would *you* have taken him?"

"I don't know. *Anywhere* but here."

"Look, we can't stay here forever, anyway. We have to make a move before too long. Odium says others are coming, others like him. Tribulantis has summoned them and they're gathering. Another one reached the tower as we captured him. We watched it fly in."

"How did you capture Odium?"

"It was easy. He's flightless. Wings too shredded by *the fall*. Not so with the rest, unfortunately. I shot him. He's wounded, but when we threatened to kill him he just laughed."

"They're eternal beings. They can't be killed."

Her mind reeling, Tyler slumped into the chair and planted her face in her hands. She glared at Klaus.

"Okay, tell me everything you know."

"He calls them princes. He's named five others, making seven in all: Impetu, Vindicem, Decepitur and a pair he referred to as the Doom Brothers: Iudicium and Malum."

"They sound nice."

"Don't they? He said a lot of other things – scaremongering and threats mostly – but I think there are probably others. Apparently they have older names but these are the ones they currently go by. What about you? I take it you didn't get the contrap."

"Before I could get close Tribulantis sensed the dark sister and woke. I escaped. I brought some food back, though. I also got a look at the citadel as I flew past."

Tyler grabbed a lump of charcoal from the table and added some details of the citadel to Wulfric's map. She sketched in the area of forest where she'd lost the liliths beyond the citadel and other patches for forest she had observed when flying. Klaus took the charcoal and added the jagged ruins he had reached, the plateau of subs and other ruins where he'd seen the cleansing parties.

"No Cave of Sorrows." Quietly, he set the charcoal down. "Not to the north anyway."

"Any sign of Wulfic and John? Albert and Mojo?"

Klaus shook his head. "Nothing yet but I guess there's still hope."

A glimmer of smile traced her lips as she thought of her wings.

Izabella's legacy. Yes, there's still hope. And hope is my secret weapon.

He took her hand and pulled her into his arms as she hugged him close, relaxing into his embrace.

"Hungry? There're grapes, cheese and bread."

*

Dagger approached Albert as a nearby barracks block dissolved and rebuilt a few paces away.

"Where's your girlfriend, boy?"

Albert planted his feet ready for the attack.

"Dorkins, Dobbs – get over here." Dagger held Albert's gaze as Dorkins and Dobbs sauntered in from the sides.

"The queen's put a price on your head. Did you know? Yeah, you're a wanted ghost, an' we're gonna claim the reward. Take him, fellas!"

Dorkins and Dobbs ran at Albert while Dagger nocked an arrow and drew his bow.

Hurtling from a barrack doorway, Lucy threw a

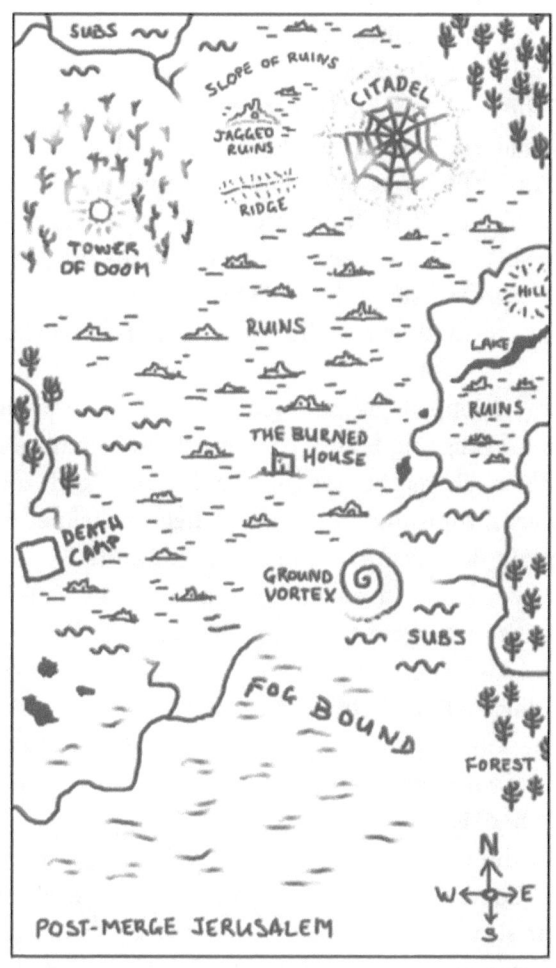

gallows blade. It purred through the air to lodge deep in Dagger's throat. His body twisted as he released his arrow, which thumped into a Dorkins' back, felling him as Dagger dropped and dissolved.

Dobbs – a knight in plate mail wielding a morning star – paused, sensing the doom of his fellows. Turning from Albert he rounded on Lucy, swinging with his mace. Lucy sidestepped the blow and kicked at his arm as the deadly spikes of the mace ploughed into the ground. The knight righted, slid a long dagger from its sheath and readied for another assault. Mace high, he lumbered for Lucy.

Albert looped his rope and released it, lassoing the knight and tugging hard. The rope tightened around the knight's neck as he fought for balance and toppled backwards, thrashing. Albert snatched his helmet free as the knight floundered like an upturned beetle.

Lucy claimed a sword from one of the fallen and pressed its tip against the knight's exposed throat. He released his weapons.

"Where's Ruth Cobbler?"

The knight laughed. "The queen's sister? What do you want with her?"

"Where is she?"

"In the tower, of course. The Witch Queen has her caged. Good luck with–" His words died on Lucy's blade.

She surveyed the corpses and the empty courtyard.

"That was easier than I thought it was going to be."

Albert stared at the armour while Lucy stooped to salvage sections of it.

"It's a little big for either of us."

"Try the other one."

Lucy ripped out the arrow from the other hunter's

back and tugged off his outer clothes.

"They're looking for you, Albert. Here." She tossed him the leathery jerkin. "Wear this. It has a hood that will help hide your face."

Albert slipped the jerkin on, the hide reaching to his shins.

"This'll do me. You can keep the britches."

Lucy pulled on the leather trousers and strapped some of the lose-fitting plate armour in place. She retrieved her gallows blades and stole the sheath for her new sword.

"Should throw them off the scent, at least."

Albert coiled his rope and they hurried on towards the heaving crowds and the high tower. Those at the back of the crowd were less tightly packed. Albert and Lucy slipped easily through as the queen addressed her hordes.

"Come gather now! Bow before me! You are mine. Your souls are mine. Be of stout heart, unite against our foes and triumph!" The crowds cheered and battered the ground with their feet and the butts of their spears while clattering weapons against their shields. The queen raised her hands for quiet. "Our enemies unite, dreams of victory clouding their deluded minds. They would be rid of you. Rise up, say I! Rise up and we shall conquer! A new world awaits you, a world ripe for the plucking!"

"Very rousing," muttered Lucy, threading deeper as the crowds clamoured. Towards the front the assembly clustered more tightly. She and Albert pushed through, jostling against packed bodies. The queen continued.

"What say you, warriors of the citadel? Will you unite in battle?" Again the crowd roared their approval. The queen reached a crescendo. "Prepare! Prepare for

B J MEARS

war against the mortal foe. On the morrow we march!" The mob jeered, applauded and shouted wildly.

"The mortal foe?" Lucy squinted at the queen. "She plans to march against humanity."

Albert studied the guards. From his position near the tower's base he could see two entrances, one grand and one small. Both were guarded by pairs of grey coat ghosts. He leant close to Lucy.

"We don't stand a chance in broad daylight."

Lucy nodded towards a range of ghostly outbuildings adjoining the tower and the radiating crenulated walls where the guards applauded, enrapt by the queen's aura.

"Over there. Quickly, while she has their attention." She grabbed Albert by the jerkin and pulled him with her, pressing through the mass and into the less congested space around the outbuildings. Slipping past the guards and an armoury, they stole through the closest door.

Inside, an eclectic assortment of weapons packed the chamber: swords, spears, guns, canons, clubs, mortars, knives and bows. Lucy appraised the hoard.

"Taken from the ghost prisoners, no doubt."

Albert gave a dry smile.

"Yeah, this'll do nicely. We'll hold up 'ere and wait for night."

*

Shaking Tyler awake, Kinga pressed a finger against her lips. Tyler slid her arm from Klaus as Kinga whispered.

"Shhhush. Follow me. There's something large poking around outside."

310

The Lurker in
the Night

Tyler grabbed her rifle and followed. Darkness had descended while she had slept in Klaus' arms and now moonlight pierced cracks in the boarded windows.

Kinga led her to a spy hole where Tyler peered out at a tumble of fallen blocks, a surviving line of low wall, the ruined arch and windblown smog. Across the wrecked road, the burnt-out carcass of an upturned car harboured countless imagined terrors.

"We have a prowler." Kinga watched from another slit nearby. "To the right, across the road. It's moving."

Beyond the wall, rubble partially obscured a humped shape as large as the car, a form that heaved in the gloom, rising and falling almost unperceivably, shadows of monstrous proportion.

"What is it?"

"I can't tell but it's close enough to constitute a threat. I'm going out."

Tyler took one last look at the monster and knew her assault rifle would not suffice. She descended into the cellar in candle light, edging past Danuta on the steps.

"All quiet?"

"He's sleeping."

In the corner, Odium rested, bound and unmoving, his eyes closed.

Tyler passed him and selected a grenade, stuffing several backups into pockets of her jumpsuit. Returning to Kinga in the hall, she eased open the one-hinged door.

"Alert everyone. We'll be leaving soon."

A bitter chill greeted Tyler. Dropping low to the ground she crept out to the broken wall. From here she could toss the grenade unhampered and shelter safely from the fallout. She edged to a dip in the wall and peered over for a closer look.

The shape jostled and circled like a dog bedding down. She stared at its peak, little more than a silhouette against the lighter fog that shone with moonlight. Clenching the grenade she drew the pin, discarded it and drew back her arm ready to launch.

Ahead on the enigmatic shape, a stumpy scorpion tail twitched into profile.

Tyler paused, mid-swing.

"Boris?"

She glanced at the live grenade in her hand. Swearing profusely, she lobbed it into the unoccupied neighbouring ruin and ducked for cover. The immediate explosion sent a plume of dust into the air, raining debris all around as she buried her head in her arms.

Through the clearing haze Kinga called from the upper level.

"Two contrapassi coming this way! No, four! Ghosts, too, a whole troop of grey coats!"

Tyler scrambled over the wall. Behind her, ghosts peered out from the doorway, the upper floor and the cracks in the boarding.

At least they're all awake, now.

"Everybody out! We're leaving!" She crossed the broken road and stopped in front of Boris as he rose to full height.

He bowed. Confused, she bowed in return expecting the bug to rise but Boris remained stooped, his head hovering inches from the ground.

"You followed me?"

Boris' glassy black eyes watched her. He made a small, bobbing movement.

"What? What does that mean?" She glanced back towards the house at the commotion as the others prepared to leave.

Again Boris bobbed, crouching with the plates of his armoured back rising behind his head like steps.

"You want me to climb on?"

Another bob.

Of course.

Tyler stepped up to mount Boris, finding a spot further back along the plates of his tapering body where her legs could hang at his sides. The saddle was gone but a set of reins remained. Grabbing them, she coaxed Boris towards the house where Klaus, Zebedee and the rest poured out loaded with boxes of weapons and ammunition. She stroked the smooth plates of the scorp's neck and he rolled his head pleasurably in response.

The others gathered around her, gawping.

"No time to explain. Pass up the munitions. Kinga, how long?"

Kinga called down from her vantage point.

"Two, maybe three minutes."

Tyler stacked boxes in front of her on Boris' back. She leant down to speak softly.

"It's just for a little while, okay?"

Boris bobbed.

Okay.

"Where are we going?" asked Zebedee, haggard and sleepy.

"Anywhere but here."

Klaus passed up the last box. "Tyler, what about Odium?"

Tyler coaxed Boris on with a flick of the reins.

"Leave him."   Spearheading the party she steered Boris away from the burned house and into the roving fog. Hoisting her rifle she gave the order. "Move out."

*

"'Ow we gonna get in that tower?"

"I don't know. You're the one who's wise beyond his years. I'm just here to kill monsters."

"Is that really what you fink?"

Lucy locked eyes with Albert.

"It's how I feel, sometimes, yes."

"You're more than that, Lucy Loo. Much more."

In the near-darkness of the weapons store, Lucy shrugged. "Maybe." She thumbed a sword blade, testing its edge, and replaced it with the others. "Any ideas?"

"Not a clue."

"So what now?" She eyed the closed courtyard gates

from the armoury's single window. "We're stuck here. Can't get in, can't get out."

"We wait."

"For what?"

"An idea or an opportunity."

For an hour they waited, watching the guards on the tower doors fight sleep until the sound of marching brought Albert's head up to the window.

Outside, a patrol entered the courtyard gates, two grey coats at their head and two at the rear. Between them, three bedraggled ghost captives staggered on, their hands manacled.

"This is our chance!" whispered Albert.

Reaching the tower doors, the cavalcade stopped as the head trooper addressed the guard.

"Open up. Fresh prisoners for the Witch Queen."

"You wish to disturb the queen at this hour?"

"I have my orders. The queen demands to see all new prisoners. Open the doors."

Wearily, the guards unlocked the doors and swung them open.

"On your head be it!"

The troopers and their captives entered the tower's spiral staircase. The guards closed and locked the doors, returning to their posts.

Lucy exhaled a long breath. "Great. So much for our big chance."

"At least we now know them guards 'ave the keys."

Lucy scrutinised the guards.

"You think you could lure them over here?"

"No problem."

"You get them in. I'll take them down."

*

Weaver saw them first: a gaggle of figures entering the mid-distant woods.

"Grey coats?"

Mr Goodwin stepped to Weaver's side. "I don't know. Molly, your eyes are younger than mine. What do you think?"

From the vantage point of her father's shoulders, Molly squinted at the figures.

"Not grey coats. Ghosts, though."

"I think it's them," said Weaver. "The survivors from Battle Hill." He called back to the rest of the gang. "Wait here and rest. I'm going for a closer look."

The land tilted onto a rolling slope down to the woods. Weaver ran most of the way, slowing as he approached the treeline. Cautiously he ventured in and waited for his eyes to adjust to the shade, acutely aware of every snap of twigs and rustle of leaves beneath his feet.

A hiss pierced the trees.

Weaver turned.

*

Albert launched himself through the door and squeezed behind a collection of spears.

A guard appeared, framed in the doorway and backlit by the high chamber's green hue. He paused, scanning the murky room. Choosing to cleanse the entire chamber rather than search, he levelled his machine gun to fire.

The hiss of Lucy's gallows blade sliced the air. The guard dropped, dissolving as his partner filled the entrance, brandishing a gun and a gallows blade. A second of Lucy's blades zipped to find its mark. The second guard evaporated, his weapons clattering to the ground.

Lucy stepped out from behind a crate of assorted

weapons and stooped to retrieve the guard's fallen keys. She jangled them before Albert as he left his hiding place.

"Next stop, the queen's chamber."

*

Molly watched from the top of the slope. A movement at the forest edge caught her eye.

"Da, it's Weaver."

Along the fringe, others joined him, walking from the shadows. The ghosts of Victorian Londoners, Russians, Roman slaves and soldiers, chimney sweeps and their boys and a vanguard of Saxon warriors.

"An' e's found more of Albert's army!"

Weaver headed out from the trees, a hundred ghosts at his back.

Molly and the others ran down to greet them.

"Not all were chained by the witch," Weaver explained to Mr Goodwin. "There is hope. There's a greater hope: The battle on the hill was won by these ghosts and they had help. The seraphim were there!"

A ripple of awed murmurs arose.

"The seraphim! Then all is not lost!" Gleefully, Mr Goodwin lifted Molly into the air. "Did you hear, Molly? The seraphim!"

Molly chuckled. "I'd like to see an angel."

Weaver grinned, his eyes determined.

"Now we *must* rally to the Hope Bringer. Tyler, where are you?"

*

Lucy unlocked the tower's double doors and heaved them open. She and Albert slipped inside and she closed the doors, leaving them unlocked. Inside they were met with a choice of three arched doorways. They hurried through the central arch, beyond which stone steps curved up to higher levels. They slowed at the next floor to glance through iron bars into the cells either side of a claustrophobic landing.

There, prisoners sat miserably, their wrists and ankles in iron fetters.

Albert grabbed Lucy's sleeve to waylay her.

"We can free them."

"Albert, we can't rescue everyone. Remember our mission: Ruth Cobbler."

Albert followed Lucy up the spiralling stairs. On level six he stopped her again, gripping the bars of a cell door.

"It's Kylie Marsh. We 'ave to 'elp her!"

Lucy backtracked to join him. In the cell, Kylie slumped on the stone floor, bound as the others and asleep.

"Pssssst! Kylie."

"Kylie, wake up!"

Kylie groaned.

Lucy rattled the iron bars. Kylie stirred.

"The witch has power over the memory mist."

"The keys!"

Lucy tested several until one fitted the door. She swung it open and ran in. Unlocking Kylie's manacles, she whispered.

"Take these keys and release every prisoner in the tower."

Albert grinned. "Now ya' talkin'."

Kylie stood. "What are *you* going to do?"

"Find Ruth Cobbler."

"She's caged in the high chamber. The witch lives there, barely ever leaves it. You'll need the key to Ruth's cage."

"Which one is it?"

"It's not here. The witch keeps it on a chain around her neck."

The High Chamber

Lucy stared at her feet.

"Great. I should have taken Tyler up on her offer. Without the dark sister what chance do we have?"

"We'll find a way, Lucy Loo. We always do. Come with us, Kylie. Start at the top and gather everyone on the ground floor."

The three slowed as they climbed nearer to the high chamber, its sickly glow casting long shadows down the twisting stairs. Voices echoed from the walls above.

"Bind these scourges. Let them wane and perish. Now away! Leave me to my rest and disturb me no more!"

A captain mumbled a response and turned from the high chamber to descend the tower.

Lucy pointed to the prison cell below her position on the stairs. Ahead of the troopers and the new captives, she, Kylie and Albert trotted quickly back down to the penultimate level. She unlocked the closest cell door and they hurried inside. She drew the door quietly closed and listened as the troopers and prisoners passed the landing. She sighed as their footsteps distanced.

"What about them?" Albert threw his head towards the retreating captives and their prisoners. "Can't we do something?"

"And risk everything? No." Lucy peered from the bars of the cell. Behind her on the floor sat a pair of exhausted ghost prisoners, a man, bloodied from torture, and a young girl. They watched the newcomers with silent hope, not daring to speak. "They've gone, but we'll have to wait until the witch goes back to sleep. She nearly killed Tyler without touching her or even uttering a word."

"I'll get to work." Kylie unlocked the shackles of the two prisoners, the man wincing at every touch, but nodding gratefully. "The prisoners in this tower have been selected for inquisition by torture, so they're not chained with the Malum chains like the others. Malum chains silence those they bind."

Albert frowned. "Malum chains?"

"That's what the witch calls them."

Lucy guarded the door. "Gather all the prisoners at the bottom of the tower and wait for us there."

Kylie led the two ghosts out to find more.

"Be warned. A lilith sits guard on the tower top." She descended the winding steps.

For half an hour Albert and Lucy waited trying to form a plan. Eventually venturing from the cell they crept up the last of the stairs, pausing at the witch's door.

"I guess she thinks she's so powerful she doesn't need guards," whispered Lucy.

"Her mistake."

Lucy tried the handle and shot a look to Albert.

Locked!

Sliding a gallows blade from her bandolier, she gently worked it into the tiny gap between the door and its frame. She levered up the inner catch, turned the handle and eased the door open. The hinges moaned softly.

From inside, the tall windows dissecting the curving wall appeared dark. At the centre of the chamber, a four poster bed cradled Mary. Above, a large, bright cluster of crystals hung to bathe the sleeping witch in ghoulish light. To one side of the bed, pressed up against the windows at the edge of the room, Ruth huddled in a cage. She twitched at the ghosts' arrival, sensing a chance of rescue.

Lucy drew a finger to her lips and gestured.

Wait.

Gallows blade in hand, she stalked towards Mary's bed while Albert stole closer to the cage.

Mary turned in her sleep.

Lucy froze.

Albert reached Ruth, now roused and wide-eyed.

Mary stirred again and resumed her quiet snore.

Lucy circled the bed to approach from the shelter of the headboard.

Ruth beckoned Albert closer and whispered.

"Her power dwells within her contrap–"

"She has–"

"Shush. Only listen. The contraps dinnae, as a rule, follow their owners into death, but we sisters created them. It was different for us. She did take mine from me." Ruth pointed towards Mary's bed. "And has it placed beneath her pillow. Of the pair, hers be the greater."

Across the chamber, Mary opened her eyes. Lucy ducked behind the headboard as the Witch Queen rose to round on Albert.

"What is this? A trespasser! How come you to my chamber? Guards!" Mary's green hue intensified as she threw out a spellcasting hand towards Albert, creasing him with pain.

Ruth rattled the bars of her cage.

"Cease, dearest sister! Come now. Relent and release me!"

Albert fell to his knees, crippled by agony.

"Is this a blade in your hand? You would damn me and stab at my heart."

Albert dropped his gallows blade as Ruth muttered a spell and aimed a hand at Mary. The witches fought, their minds bending in a potent battle.

Behind Mary, Lucy broke cover to steal up, a blade ready to strike out the witch's spirit.

One.

Two.

Three silent steps and closing, she neared, not daring to breathe.

Ruth shrank back beneath the weight of Mary's wordless retaliation, the power of the Witch Queen's spell unrivalled.

Another step closer and Lucy stared at the blade in her hand, the gallows iron melting into memory mist long before reaching Mary as a defensive charm worked its magic.

In torturous anguish, Albert reeled. His back arched and a white glow blossomed from his translucent essence. Mary's brow knitted at the light, her eyes uncertain. She faltered.

Lucy rushed in from behind and snatched at the witch's neck. Catching a chain, she withdrew with her prize and, finding a ghost contrap where a key should have been, frowned and looked back at Mary.

Mary grasped at her throat and spun to face Lucy. Her face paled and the green light of the chamber diminished.

"NAE!" Mary staggered back as Lucy lifted her trophy. "Nae! T'is mine! This cannae be!"

"Get used to it, Grandma." Lucy took a step closer as, across the room, Albert and Ruth recovered, their curses lifting.

Mary took a further step back.

"Be warned! Do not use it! Desist, desist!"

Lucy pressed nearer, dangling the ghost contrap, taunting.

"It's mine now, you old hag, and there's nothing you can do about it."

"Nae, nae! Return it to me! I command you!"

"I'm not one of your jaded lackeys, hag. Now, hand over the key to the cage."

Mary's frown deepened as she deliberated. Her eyes flicked nervously between the nearest window and the door to her side. Trembling and reduced to nothing more than a shrivelled, bitter old woman, she lifted the key chain from her neck and tossed it reluctantly to Lucy. With the key in mid-flight she dashed for the window and hurled herself through in an explosion of glass.

Lucy and Albert ran to the window. Below, the witch

plummeted towards the sprawling battlements, her
windblown cry rending the night. Around her, falling
shards of glass twinkled like stars. A second cry more
powerful than the first issued from above as the tower
guard sprang from its perch. Wings folded, the lilith
dived after the witch, speeding to her and snatching her
from the air.

Albert dragged Lucy from the window.

"Come on. We 'ave the key!"

"Release me!" Ruth grasped the bars of her cage and
fixed her good eye pleadingly on her rescuers. "Free me
and I shall swear allegiance to you."

Lucy collected the key from the floor and unlocked
the cage. Ruth crawled free and staggered to her feet.

"My gratitude is yours." She bowed and gazed at the
ghost contrap in Lucy's hand.

"Don't get any funny ideas or I'll use this on you,"
warned Lucy.

"Oh, I doubt you could wield Mary's cantrip." Ruth
huffed and rubbed at her back. "T'is a potent device, sure
enough, though years it takes to master."

"I've used one before. Do we need to tie you up or are
you going to be helpful?" Lucy stooped to take Albert's
dropped gallows blade. "Cantrip or not, I can finish you
at will."

Albert fetched Ruth's ghost contrap from beneath
Mary's pillow.

"There are two ghost contraps?" Lucy stared at the
one in Albert's hand.

"And two originals," said Albert. "Because the realms
'ave merged there are now four contraps!"

Ruth raised her hands submissively. "Worry not. I
shall comply. Take me tae the one they call the Hope

Bringer."

*

Tyler passed the last box of ammunition to Klaus and stroked Boris.

"Better now?"

Boris bobbed his head – *Yes, much!*

She found a can of *Vitality*, opened it and shook out the meat and jelly letting it spatter on a dusty, slab of stone.

Boris wolfed it down in seconds and licked the slab clean with his short, black tongue. He bobbed again, clicking his mouthparts contentedly and Tyler had the feeling he would have smacked his lips if he had any.

Their new, temporary home stood crumbling, two ruined streets from the burned house. More broken than the other, its walls rose and fell like a small mountain range. Devoid of a cellar or a second floor, a roof, doors or window glass, its one redeeming feature was a clear, side on view of the burned house they had left behind. Here they posted Kinga to watch, ready to call an alert should any of the others return to their old base.

Contrapassi and grey coat patrols had come and gone, quickly losing interest in the vacant site. Tyler squinted through the murk of darkness and mist.

"Maybe we should return. It looks safe enough now."

Klaus considered. "No. They could be watching it like we are. Why risk it?"

"Okay, but we're almost completely clear of the fog. It would only take one lilith to spot us as it flies over and we'd be toast. We can't stay here for long. It's not safe."

Zebedee thumbed his pipe and watched the skies. "Nowhere's safe. Not until we've dealt with Tribulantis and the contraps. Are you sure there's nothing you've missed in the scrolls?"

Tyler took the scrolls out of their bag and reread them with Zebedee in the light of a small Maglite. Assured she had missed nothing, she switched off the torch.

"Unless we can find a way of reading all the bits that are damaged and illegible, I'm as sure as I can be."

"There must be a forensic technique," said Klaus. "Maybe Mel can do something with them."

"Good idea. If nothing else it'll take her mind off Freddy for a while."

*

Shivering and sombre, Melissa received the scrolls apathetically. Tyler detailed the task, searching for something encouraging to say.

"Listen, Mel. Last time we saw Freddy he was fine and armed to the teeth. Chances are he ran for cover when the dome collapsed and the monsters came. If he has any sense he'll have run a mile. He's probably hiding out somewhere and doing better than the rest of us."

Melissa gazed out with concern at the first hot glimmers of dawn. In the distant clouds a vast fleet of death ships gathered. Turning her head to the side, she pointed.

"Are they moving?"

Tyler peered at the speckled clouds. She set the dark sister to the *Present Eye* and zoomed in.

"They're heading this way and they're moving fast. We don't have long."

Mortal Remains

Albert ran ahead of Lucy, Ruth, Kylie and over thirty freed prisoners. While they loitered by another ruin he crossed the broken road, swung open the one-hinged door, and darted into the burned house. Inside he stopped, turning in the emptiness and sensing Tyler nearby.

"Missy? Mel?"

When Albert failed to reappear, Lucy led the others on, reaching the door and holding it ajar to usher them in. Ghosts filed in to fill the lower rooms.

*

Kinga found Tyler sitting silently against a wall as, surrounded by rubble, Melissa studied the scrolls.

"Albert's back! Come quickly!"

Tyler rose and ran after Kinga, back to a gap in the

wall. Beyond the broken roads, ghosts streamed into the burned house. She glanced back at the approaching death ships and scanned the immediate area. Further down the street a grey coat officer stepped from ruin to wave his patrol on.

"Klaus was right! They were watching!" Tyler shouted. "To arms!"

Her ghosts ran to collect mortars, guns and grenades from their store as she mounted Boris in the open doorway. Clattering to his feet, he clopped out from the ruins as her ranks formed behind. They poured into the wrecked street, marching towards the burned house, a small but heavily armed and determined force.

*

Reaching the house soon after Albert, Kylie immediately clambered up the stairs to spy from the upper floor.

"Patrol at one o'clock!" She fled back down the stairs repeating the warning.

Albert felt Tyler's approach in his essence and spied her in the morning's haze from the boarded windows.

"It's Tyler and the others. Join the ranks! Go!"

He waved the ghosts out of the house to merge with Tyler's force. Her numbers swelled as they shared out weapons and the grey coats advanced. Ghosts on both sides opened fire as Tyler rallied her warriors.

"To me!"

She switched to the *Cloak of Night* and vanished into shadow as one after another the ghosts around her reached for her and so, too, vanished. They sheltered and shot from behind a broken house wall as bullets flew and mortars exploded. The remaining visible ghosts scattered to fight from the ruins either side of the road, setting in for the fight.

The grey coats faulted at the disappearance of the enemy leader, her scorp and the surrounding ghosts. During the lull, Klaus mowed down a dozen bewildered troopers. More followed as the ghosts around him gained confidence. They outnumbered the grey coats and were better armed. The paling enemies' faces reflected as much.

Behind a wall, Melissa trembled. Gripping the scrolls, she closed her eyes and muttered beneath the battle din.

"Please win. Please win. Please win."

The roar of battle lessened to shortening, sporadic blasts of gunfire and the noise ceased. She climbed up a rubble slope to peer over the wall as a cheer arose. Tyler switched from *Cloak of Night*, appearing with a handful of ghosts in the heart of the enemy lines. Grey coats lay dead around them, their bodies scattered. Several of Tyler's ghosts also lay dead, others stumbled around, injured. Tyler gestured towards them.

"Tend the wounded. Gather weapons. Everyone back into the burned house."

Albert ran to Tyler, gawping at the monster beneath her as the other half-ghosts scurried for shelter.

"Albert, Boris. Boris, Albert."

*

Back in the burned house, Tyler gathered everyone in the lower rooms, hidden from the death ships floating overhead. When the ships had retreated, their filth blotting a thick trail in the sky, she organised the ghosts, sending one to watch from the top window and two more to spy from the upper floor. She had ghosts arrange the burned room as a makeshift hospital for the wounded and put Zebedee in charge of collecting and rationing their remaining food. While everyone was busy she searched among the survivors for a spare contrapassi sword before stepping outside with the blade.

A few paces beyond the one-hinged door, Boris loitered low acting as sentry. Tyler spent several minutes binding the contrapassi blade firmly to his truncated tail using strips torn from scavenged rags, giving him a replacement sting.

When it was done, Boris tried his new weapon sweeping it this way and that, and jabbing several test strikes before bobbing in gratitude and crooning a deep, resonant note.

"Well, a sentry must have his arms." Tyler patted his sleek armour. "What's your alarm call if you see anything out there?"

Boris clacked his pincers, an unmistakable sound she would recognise. "That'll do. Keep your eyes peeled, Boris."

Leaving him to guard, Tyler returned to the house, looking for Albert.

"No sign of Weaver or Freddy I suppose?"

Albert shook his head. "But we 'ave 'er," he said, withdrawing from their embrace. "Ruth Cobbler."

Lucy brought Ruth out through the crowd of ghosts in the parlour.

"Here she is. She had a ghost contrap. So did Mary." She passed the half-ghost dark sister for Tyler to examine, a translucent copy of the one around Tyler's neck. Albert passed Ruth's ghost contrap as Melissa, Klaus and Zebedee joined them.

"Do they work?" asked Tyler.

"Oh, yes. Ruth says the contraps followed their creators into death. That one was the source behind the witch's potency. Without it Mary's powers are depleted."

Tyler allowed herself a fleeting half-smile.

"You did great, Lucy. You too, Albert." Tyler passed the ghost contraps back to Lucy. "You keep these. Put them to good use.

"Hello again, Ruth. A lot has happened since we last met."

"Indeed, wee scunner." Ruth's good eye flicked nervously over faces in the crowd. "Yet be warned. Mary willnae admit defeat. Beware! Other paths she will seek. She will draw the symbol to summon a demon and so harness wicked power."

"Can she do that? What symbol?"

"So she has done. So she will again. How else did you think the cantrips were created?"

"You commanded demons?"

"Aye, powerful demons. Each time a symbol is selected, the demon bound within the cantrip is commanded."

Tyler paled.

Ruth continued. "What did you think when spoke you such commands?"

"I thought the contraps were powered by ghosts."

"Ghosts, aye, ghosts of demonic manipulation. We called it the *chain of command*."

"How did you create the contraps?"

"It happened upon a late summer's eve. During those days we lived in a remote highland village, Mary and I, young witches in the making. As the sun set, a man did ride tae the vale upon a pale horse. A painted man, was he, bringing many wonders tae amuse the villagers. His name was Yasine. They did fuss so around him, intrigued by his skin, so darkened as though by a sun far brighter than our own.

"Before long the others left for their beds, yet we three remained in the tavern, Yasine, Mary and me. When our talk turned tae things unnatural, Yasine quickened with interest and, reaching intae his sack, revealed yet another marvel, a tome of spells. It was ancient. That much was clear. We perused this tome. Greedy we were for the knowledge of its yellowed pages, but in a trice the man snapped it shut and, glancing nervously, did tuck it back into his sack.

"Knowing what I now know, I see Yasine was driven by a devilish force of darkness. What was he about, so far from home? Why came he? Surely an unearthly power did guide him to us, to deliver the tome into our hands. I recall his eyes, as darkling as the sister jewels, as devious as a sprite's. Haggled we a price and gleefully he received payment, revealing the tome once more and passing it to us.

"Yasine enquired after board, so rose I tae fetch the taverner, leaving Mary tae paw the pages. Duly, I returned. 'Where is Yasine,' said I. My sister looked up from the tome as though in a trance. 'I didnae see him leave,' said she."

"The book showed you how to create the contraps."

"Amongst other spells and enchantments, aye, though it was nae easy task. Laboured years did we. We purchased silver for the casing and chains, brass for the mechanisms, all as the tome specified. In secret did we employ a jeweller to fashion the devices. A handsome fellow..." Ruth silenced, her good eye darting shiftily.

"Did something happen to the jeweller?"

Ruth sighed.

"Ay, in a manner. On the day of completion a terrible accident befell him."

"Accident?"

"So thought I, yet I wasnae witness. Going to fetch a pail of milk, I left him in the yard, polishing his finished work, whole and hearty. The cantrips were yet to be enchanted, you understand. Later, climbing the hill tae our house, I found him crushed beneath the old birch tree, fallen during my absence. The base of the tree was rotted."

"Mary's work?"

Ruth nodded.

"So I now believe, though I didnae at the time. Her I found in slumber upon her cot, the contrips clasped in her hands. He was one of many she murdered, and I amongst them."

"Why did she kill you?"

"Learned we the intricacies of the cantrips over a course of years. Both proved powerful. Both aided us in fortune, though I now understand they are works of wickedness. I can but assume Mary grew jealous. As long as I possessed a cantrip we would be equals. Yet Mary doesnae consider any her equal. Not then. Not now. Month by month we tracked artefacts that might yield ghosts for empowering, seeking new ways in which to harvest the spirits. Our hunt led us tae many strange haunts: graveyards, battlefields, abandoned homes, shipwrecks." Ruth's good eye locked onto the points of her shoes as she lowered her voice. "Occasionally did we call upon the living to steal their souls.

"In the wee hours of night we did visit a graveyard. One we oft' frequented with some success, though this night we struggled tae raise a phantom. No artefact of ours did work. Nothing we tried yielded a ghost, but greedy for further empowerment, Mary bade us dig the grave, there tae find bones. We dug through the night, stopping at a goodly depth where we found not bone, nor tooth.

"Mary demanded she try my cantrip as hers refused to draw a ghost. Climbing free of the pit, I passed it and stood looking down intae the darkness. I remember thinking *We shall surely give up, now. Venture again a new night. Another's grave.* That's when she struck.

"Phasmatis licentia. The words issued at my back. Turned I tae face the jewel! The cantrip took my soul."

"Murdered by your own sister. How can I destroy the contraps? Can the demons be killed?"

Ruth laughed mirthlessly.

"The demons cannae be killed, yet wound them, you may. Be warned. Look them no' in the eye, or they shall read your soul, learn your every weakness. As for the cantrips, my sister and I gave no heed tae their destruction. Each has a demon confined within, a demon empowered by magical means. By destroying the cantrips you would liberate said demons, entities mightier even than Tribulantis. So now, you must surely understand the implications."

"You mentioned a symbol. A symbol Mary will use."

"The pentacle of course - the five pointed star. T'is the universal symbol. With it will she seek a demon."

"How can we stop her?"

"I'm no' sure we can."

"But you *do* know about the dark sister?" Tyler tugged the blackened contrap free of her shirt and dangled it in Ruth's face. "This contrap?"

"Aye, I know. Behold, Mary's evil creation, its silvered casing scorched by her dark sorcery. This she forged and enchanted as I did mine."

"There are symbols here I don't understand. Will you explain them to me?"

Ruth shrugged, sighed and hung her head.

"I shall aid you as I have so sworn. Yet irked am I tae turn against my own sister. What do you wish tae know?"

"Most of the symbols I know and understand but three remain a mystery: the fylfot, the all-seeing eye and the skeletal hand."

Ruth reached out a bent finger to tap the all-seeing eye.

"Where I chose an ability of knowledge, Mary chose the power tae control the minds of others."

"Mind control? Seriously?"

Ruth nodded.

"Ay, mind control through the *All-Seeing Eye*. Although creating it thus and setting such commands tae work was one matter. Mastering the art proved quite another. Forget this symbol. Mary toiled for many a year before learning the required control. She deemed it worth the wait, for with her cantrip set so, she bended minds tae her will, and poured torture upon her enemies with but a simple thought."

"That explains a lot."

"I fear this symbol grew amongst her favourites. T'is well it lies no more in her possession.

"The fylfot brings the wearer fair fortune, or so t'was meant. Chose this did Mary whilst I, a charm against death."

"The *Safeguarding Skull*."

"Ay, so you name it. Set you the dark cantrip tae the fylfot and, so theory dictates, all shall be well for you. In practise, t'was a thorn in her flesh. She pursued her devious plots believing all would fall in favour and, at the start, so it was. Though the demon bound tae her cantrip be powerful, troublesome and cunning. Time and again it conspired tae corrupt. Heed well my warning. Pursue you no' the fylfot!"

"That leaves only the hand symbol."

"The hand of bones she named *Mortal Remains*. This Mary chose whilst I, the tower."

"*You* created the *Tower of Doom*?"

"Ay, or rather, I so commanded the demon of my cantrip. I bade him raise a strong tower, a refuge should I e'er need tae enter that sulphurous realm. The tower I named Dun Bharraich. I commanded, therein, a high chamber tae be set with a table ceaselessly flowing with fares."

"The *Tower of Doom* and the table of plenty. Did either of you ever enter the realm?"

"Nae, but one other charm we set in place. Fearing we might end up in the Chasm through the demons' treachery, we stipulated a clause. Any living soul who so entered would be gifted wings, indestructible in the realm, wings tae aid us, appearing at times of need, when resolve quickens."

"I have them. Wings of fire."

Ruth's features registered mild surprise.

"So it worked."

"But I seem to be the only one. Why?"

"Did any soul but you enter the realm alive before the merging?"

"Not that I know of."

"Then cease your wonderment. Whence the realms merged, the circumstances did change, though the Chasm recognised your spirit and so wings you have.

"Knowing I would supply our refuge, Mary chose

Mortal Remains and summoned corrupted bodies from the grave. Henceforth an army of bones could she raise tae fight her cause, obedient tae her every whim. She never used it much. T'is a most conspicuous procedure and conjures a loathsome reek..."

Tyler stared at the intricately incised skeletal hand on the dark sister's silver case.

"...a reek that willnae wash oot."

"An army of the dead."

Lucy stepped closer. "With an army of the dead in our ranks we could march on Dun Bharraich."

A fire ignited in Tyler's eyes.

"Prepare for battle."

Pancakes

Throughout the burned house, ghosts clamoured to arms. Tyler drew Ruth aside to find a quieter corner. Several Roman soldiers pressed through the crowd to donate parts of their armour, kneeling to present them.

"The Hope Bringer must be protected," announced legionary Quintillus, bowing his head.

Wulfric removed his battle helm, knelt, and passed it to her.

"Thank you." Tyler accepted the gifts and strapped them in place. Tucking the helmet under her arm, she continued to question Ruth.

"What else do I need to know? Are there secret commands?"

"Set you the cantrip to *Mortal Remains* and utter

these words: Mortuos surgere de terra hac quis iussu meo fecerit."

Fearing she would never remember the command, Tyler scribbled the words phonetically in her notebook as Ruth repeated the phrase more slowly.

"Where so the darkling jewel does point, from yonder land shall the dead arise tae do your bidding. Order them fight and they will fight, run and they will run, be gone and they shall return tae the grave. Yet heed! Fair warning I give. Turn from the symbol and the undead will drop as old sticks!" Ruth closed her eyes and staggered as though faint. They blinked open again, trance-like and unfocused. "Be watchful! A great battle comes!"

Tyler turned to Melissa.

"Any luck with the scrolls?"

"Nothing yet."

Tyler's phone buzzed. She slid it from her pocket and stared at the screen. "One bar of signal. A message from Chapman!" As she read she noticed the feeble signal blip and die along with the remaining battery. "I'm coming for you."

"I guess he's been tracking us. That's good, isn't it?"

"If he's bringing the entire NATO force with him, it could help." Tyler tried to send a reply but the mobile screen turned black. "Dead. Try yours."

"One bar." Melissa hurried to tap out a text and hit send.

Tyler grabbed her arm. "Come with me."

Outside she released Melissa.

"Do you notice anything?" Tyler watched the tower.

"The Hell birds have left the tower."

"Yes. The creatures circling the battlements are

demons summoned by Tribulantis. We can't delay any longer. It's time."

"The reveries?"

"Summon them, as many as possible. I'll summon the *Mortal Remains*. We'll join forces."

"But Tyler, I'm a pacifist. I want no part in physical violence."

"You *want*? Do you think any of this is what *I* want? What any of us want?"

"No, but–"

"Sometimes we have to fight, like it or not. Fight with us. Fight for peace. Fight for me!"

Tyler helped clear a patch of ground a few metres from the house and, shedding her gallows blades, Melissa chalked a rough circle and rattled off the secret names. A few paces away, Tyler switched the dark sister to *Mortal Remains* and read aloud from her notebook.

"Mortuos surgere de terra hac quis iussu meo fecerit." She held the dark sister aloft, circling and repeating the command.

On the horizon lightning flashed and thunder cackled. A green glow birthed in the dark sister's crystal. "Dead of this land arise and rally to me now."

In the following lull the merged realm thrummed, a charged stillness primed with magic. Several ruptured streets across the ruined city, a subterranean broke the surface with a groan. Tyler and Melissa turned, watching for movement in the sweltering heat of the morning. Scattered figures stood, chained, motionless and unreachable, pawns on a war-torn chessboard, among their number Palestinians, Israelis and Westerners. Amid the broiling fire-fog of the mid distance, contrapassi lumbered, the engines of their death ships belching oily fumes overhead.

Through the mist, half-ghost reveries appeared, ambling closer. Between their gawping forms others staggered, dragging their rotting limbs, lurching, limping and crawling. Slowly the reanimated dead gathered, their forms strengthening as they neared the origin of the charm. They burst from the ground around the wrecked car, clawing free of the dirt to join the growing throng of decay as more erupted further down the street. Many clattered forward like stringed puppets, nothing more than dusty, dry bones. Some bore the weapons with which they had been buried, a variety of swords, shields, daggers and spears. Others arrived unarmed. Among the gathering force walked ancient Palestinians, Israelites, Babylonians, Romans and many from other tribes and nations. Decayed and vacuous eyes turned upon the girls in obedience.

Lucy appeared between Melissa and Tyler.

"Zombies! Cool!" She smelled their reek. "Euew."

Tyler shot her a glare and addressed the oncoming dead.

"Our enemies wait in the tower." She pointed to Dun Bharraich as Melissa echoed her words.

Several hundred strong and growing, the baleful army turned in unison, bones clacking. Their empty skull sockets trained with intent upon Dun Bharraich as vacant ghosts gaped. Among the *Mortal Remains*, fully fleshed corpses leaned, their soiled forms oozing with bullet holes, recent victims of the heightened warfare and merging realms.

"March on. To war!"

They scrambled, a field of articulated bones, mouldering flesh and gawping ghosts, to rove over the rubble and squalor of Jerusalem's devastation.

Kinga brought grenades and spare magazines.

"Tyler, we don't have enough ammunition or weapons for a sustained attack."

"Before the realms merged, this place was a war zone. There must be more we can salvage. Organise teams to search as we go."

"Okay."

Across the ruins the rumble of engines quickened. Stashing her ammunition, Tyler turned at the rising drone.

"They've seen us. The death ships are sailing."

She grabbed the dark sister and placed a fingertip on the switch, but caught herself.

No switching while the Mortal Remains *do their work!*

Instead she called for Lucy and, armour clanking, mounted Boris and grasped her rifle. "Lucy, what's happening at the tower?" She squinted at the battlements where dark wings circled.

Lucy switched the half-ghost dark sister to the *Present Eye* and spied, hearing Tribulantis' voice through the viewing glass.

"Call in the ships. All hands. Ready the army of the Black Sun. This shall be our finest hour."

"Tribulantis knows we're moving," Lucy reported. "The witch is with him, the gloves, too. He's giving orders, preparing for battle." She adjusted the contrap to view the base of the tower, its surrounding trees and clearing, where ranks of contrapassi, liliths and grey coats assembled. "His army gathers." She glanced up from the lens to view with her naked eyes. "It's rather large."

A moment of doubt struck Tyler. *The contrapassi are huge and strong. Their death ships will descend on us like a storm. They'll snap us like twigs. The liliths will swoop on us, raining their fire and we'll burn. The army of the Black Sun outnumbers us ten to one. Surely they'll overrun us! The witch will throw everything she can at us, as will the demons and the gloves. Do we really stand even half a chance?*

Around her, armed ghosts spilled from the burned house. Albert pressed through to her, his grime-smeared face creased with concern.

"It'll be al'right, Missy. It'll be al'right. We're bringing freedom. Tribulantis will fall." He turned for the tower, hoisting a sword aloft. "For the Hope Bringer. For the Hallowed Light!"

The surrounding force cheered and took up the chant.

Watching him, this weary, poverty-stricken and barefoot ghost of a sweep's boy, Tyler smiled. His unquenchable spirit never ceased to amaze her. A deep pride swelled in her chest, a pride in Albert, in everything he stood for. She didn't know what the Hallowed Light was, but she didn't much care. It sounded good. And if Albert was ready to fight for it, that was good enough for her. With the chant arose a new hope engulfing her fears, and she knew that if there really was a Hope Bringer, he was it, and she would gladly fight for him.

Fight to her last.

"Mel, you're my advisor. I need you close." She offered a hand and helped Melissa up onto Boris to sit behind her. Straightening, Tyler called the order.

"Move out!"

*

Ahead of Tyler's ghosts, the undead army extended in their thousands. A mile closer to Dun Bharraich a cry rose above the rumble of the march. Ghosts on Tyler's right flank muttered and pointed out towards a ridge stretching from the edges of the citadel. There a second army marched into view, tramping steadily over the rise.

"Who are they?" Tyler asked Lucy.

Marching at Tyler's side, Lucy used the *Present Eye*.

"A mixed bag of ghosts. Must be the witch's army." She wrinkled her nose, straining for details. "No, wait. Weaver's at their head."

"They're ours?"

"Must be."

Weaver's army altered course, bending towards a point ahead between the undead army and Dun Bharraich.

Tyler coaxed Boris into a trot.

*

Tyler halted Boris at Weaver's front line as he stepped forward, marvelling at her mount. Behind her, the undead staggered onwards. Boris clacked his pincers.

"Is he safe?"

"Safe enough. You took your time. What happened?"

Lucy tore past to fling herself into Weaver's arms.

"We were separated when the witch's lot attacked," he explained. "These are the ghosts who escaped her chains, those we found, anyway."

Albert embraced Molly.

"Albert!"

"Al'right, Molly? Da?"

"Right enough, son." Watching the enemy forces massing in the shadow of Dun Bharraich, Mr Goodwin cocked his shotgun to reload. "Looks like we're going to war. We'll teach 'em some manners, eh?"

"There are demons, fallen angels," said Tyler. "Shoot

347

them first if you get the chance. They won't die but they can be wounded. Ground them if you can."

"Wouldn't be the first time I've poached a pheasant," said Mr Goodwin.

"I fear these pheasants are more dangerous than the usual," said Weaver.

"A bird's a bird, Master Weaver." Mr Goodwin snapped his gun shut and rested it against his shoulder. "Bet you two bob I wing one before you."

Weaver grinned. "You're on."

"I can get you close without being seen." Lucy flicked her contrap's switch and shadowed out. She switched again, reappearing. "The *Cloak of Night* will also conceal anyone touching me."

"Kylie, Albert, take over from Weaver. Weaver, select your three best shooters. Find Lucy a descent gun and take out the demons." She addressed the ghosts of the two merging forces, seeing among them women and children – slaves and the free – downtrodden mothers, orphaned daughters and sons.

"Listen to me. I know you have suffered and we've not yet reached the end. I know you've fought and many are lost, but we can't give up. We *must not* give in. Will you fight one last time? Will you fight for justice and for freedom?"

The army erupted with a barrage of shouts and cries.

"We'll fight!"

"We fight for you!"

"Fight for the Hope Bringer!"

"Down with the oppressor!"

"Victory to the Hope Bringer!"

"Down with Tribulantis!"

"Tear down the devils!"

"For the Hope Bringer!"

"Hope Bringer! Hope Bringer! Hope Bringer!"

Tyler waited for their chant to quieten.

"All those who are with me, MARCH!"

With an approving roar, her merged army trooped on.

Nearing the slopes of Dun Bharraich, Tyler scrutinised the foe spreading down from the blackened, twisted trees like a blight on the land. A smatter of contrapassi arrows *plapped* into the ground before her undead ranks. Tyler raised a hand and tugged the reins. Boris halted, clopping restlessly. Behind, her army stopped.

A fleeting memory invaded her mind, a far-flung recollection so alien now that it seemed thoroughly odd.

A child named Tyler. A bright Saturday morning in Watford. Her mother cooking pancakes on the stove. Cartoons blaring on the kitchen TV. The air heavy with hot and heady aromas of melting butter and maple syrup.

Closing her eyes she tried to conjure more detail.

Sunlight from windows splashing her skin, painting her father's face. The fragrant spices of his aftershave. He muttered something witty in the wordless haze and she laughed with him, her mother, too. The laughter shook her, body and soul. She forked blissfully sweet pancake into her mouth. Licked rich butter from her lips.

Boris released a low resonating noise, something close to a growl. In a blink the memory evaporated. She opened her eyes to the hulking ranks of contrapassi, the liliths, the demons and the army of the Black Sun, her tongue dry and bitter.

What happened? How did I end up here?

Boris stamped at the sun-baked ground.

"Easy, boy. Soon." Twisting on his back, she surveyed her troops. Countless faces looked back awaiting her orders, each squinting in the Chasm's merciless glare. At her side, Zebedee pocketed his pipe and discarded his hat. Rolling his sleeves he accepted a sword from a neighbouring ghost.

"A grim day, Miss May, but we're with you. We're with you to the end."

Albert nodded.

"The end is close."

"Just as well. I'm out of tobacco."

"At your command, Missy."

Tyler glanced at her noble friends.

I guess now's as good a time as any.

She donned Wulfric's battle helm. Facing her enemies and hoisting her rifle high, she shouted from the pit of her lungs.

"CHARGE!"

Dun Bharraich

Death ships descended and the charge mounted pace. Below, the ranks of the Black Sun volleyed out as sky mariners slipped ropes from gunnels, descending them to the killing ground. Above, their comrades opened fire with cannon and arrows tipped with blazing pitch. Smoke trails striped the sky.

Below and ahead of Tyler's main army, many of the reanimated dead and the half-ghost reveries crumpled beneath the onslaught. Tyler at once feared a massacre but as she rode in, clattering bullets against the ranks, reveries reached the enemy front line. While they worked their will-deadening effect, the mortal dead climbed the ropes to the ships and, clambering aboard, attacked the crews. Unarmed corpses in the kill zone scavenged weapons and struck at those beyond the reveries' thrall, hacking with axes and swords, and stabbing with spears. Many fell, sliced and battered, their bones scattering as the stench of rot and blood sullied the dust-blown air.

The first of the death ships boomed to ground, its four curving props planting on the dirt. The clinkers of its mighty hull creaked as its engine spewed choking plumes of ashen fumes.

The crew slung a stout gangway in place and a hulking contrapasso wearing a necklace of human skulls, a beast larger and more frightening than any other, clomped down to the fire-fog dirt. Roaring, he sought combat, sweeping a monstrous sword. Ahead of him, ghosts scattered.

"Come to Hakan!" Beneath his bristling fur, thick muscle rippled.

Wulfric stepped out from the reluctant crowd to assume an attack stance, his sword trained on the giant.

A deep, seething laugh rolled from Hakan's throat.

"*You?* You think *you* are a match for Hakan?" He turned to the rest of his enemies. "Is *this* the best you can do?"

Wulfric clapped his pattern welded sword against his circular shield.

"My steel is keen." In a flash, he traced a circle with his blade, bringing it back into line. "My thrust is true." Sword singing, he stormed in to meet Hakan.

*

Contrapassi sky mariners leapt from the galleys to hack in the sweeping shadows of the lateral sails. Their archers picked off nearby ghosts with ease and bodies dropped, burning.

More of the ships beached, shuddering the ground.

Contrapassi threw down their gangways and stomped out to battle. Before Tyler, a dozen swooped down on lines to scythe ghosts, reveries and the undead with curving blades.

"ATTACK!" Tyler spurred Boris into the fight. Arching his spiked tail, he lashed at oncoming contrapassi as she fired in controlled bursts.

A distant order quickened the contrapassi infantry around the tower. Breastplates flashing in the sun, they thundered to battle, swatting ghosts aside in a stampede, slashing, lashing and gunning with bloodlust. Behind them the bestial cavalry observed the bloodshed.

Tribulantis watched from the parapets, a delighted child playing life and death with living pawns. His laughter floated across the battle as liliths screeched their yearnings for the kill.

*

Clinging to Tyler's waist, Melissa continued to utter commands to the reveries in her thrall. From Boris' back she could see over the heads of the army and assess her reveries' progress. She found she achieved the best results when the air between her ring of gallows iron and her gawping reveries was unhindered. Each time she imparted a command, she released her grip on Tyler to raise the hand with the ring high into the air, aiming it as best she could.

"Bank left." The reveries flocked left to meet a spearhead of the enemy force. Grey coats and a handful of the witch's men escaped through gaps. "Close ranks." The reveries bunched into a single, smothering mass.

She hugged Tyler once more and frowned as a troop of enemy reveries ambled out from the demon's ranks.

"Heydrich."

*

Raising his sword for a death blow, Hakan charged in to meet Wulfric. They clashed iron and Wulfric strained behind the beast's considerable momentum. Recovering, he forced Hakan's blade sideways and returned his own. Swifter than the lumbering giant, he caught Hakan with a slice to the forearm that drew blood and clanked against Hakan's breastplate. He darted back, narrowly avoiding Hakan's retaliating swipe that would have felled an elephant.

Towering over Wulfric, Hakan howled in fury. Vengefully, he drew a second sword from his belt and pressed hard into Wulfric with a succession of weighty strikes, left and right, driving him back into a staggered retreat.

Before the onslaught, Wulfric lost his footing and folded. Abandoning his sword to cling to his shield, he sheltered in its shadow and braced himself.

Hakan grinned, revelling in the moment, his victory inevitable. With a defining strike he brought a sword arcing down to splinter the Saxon shield in two.

Through the gap, Wulfric watched Hakan withdraw one pace, preparing for the finishing move.

Wulfric was a man of Wessex, a hardened huscarl of a proud, warrior tribe. Fighting bravely and with honour alongside King Alfred during many battles against the Viking Force, he had gained experience and had engaged many in mortal combat.

The two edged-sword he had abandoned was not his favoured weapon, but a show piece, little more than a badge of military office. He would not miss it.

He waited, weighing the monster's movements, calculating the exact moment to act.

*A little longer. A little longer. One moment more...
Now!*

Releasing the broken shield he rolled aside to tear his langseax from its scabbard.

Hakan lumbered forward, ploughing his blade into the dirt.

Wulfric rose and spun to face his adversary's rear, slicing the first of Hakan's hamstrings. A second cut followed swiftly.

Hakan bellowed and dropped to his knees.

From the edge of the crowd, Quintillus tossed Wulfric a spear to finish the job.

*

Tyler estimated the proximity of the tower and shouted across to Klaus.

"Are we in range yet?"

"A little closer."

They pressed on, Boris dismembering contrapassi with his pincers, stabbing and slicing as Tyler emptied another magazine.

"Now!" shouted Klaus.

"Take down the liliths!" commanded Tyler.

Klaus and Yakubu shouldered rocket launchers, adjusting to target the liliths. The missiles blasted, roaring to the tower. Too late, liliths scrambled to flap clear, two perishing in the explosions as the battlements exploded. The blast sprayed rock and mortar to the force below as the wrecked she-demons fell and a chunk of masonry ripped through a third she-demon in mid-flight.

*

Heydrich' reveries groped out towards Tyler's front line. Melissa lifted and aimed the ring.

"Confront your own kind. Protect our army."

355

Her reveries swayed as one and lumbered towards the oncoming ghouls. Those on both sides slowed as they came face to face and a numbing stalemate ensued where the life sucking half-ghosts occupied a swathe of the killing ground.

*

Hakan's skewered body slammed to the ground like a toppled monolith. A cheer arose from Tyler's army and they streamed forwards to flood the clearing around the body.

Yakubu took a bow from a fallen contrapassi and plucked a burning arrow from the corpse of a fellow warrior. Nocking the shaft, he stretched the bow until it creaked, and released. His blazing missile streaked the sky to lodge in the clinkers of a death ship. The fire spread, licking up the boards of the broad hull.

"FIRE THE SHIPS!"

He snatched a second arrow and launched it as other ghosts around him scavenged bows.

*

Charging in behind the corpse-strewn tide of *Mortal Remains*, Tyler and her ghost army thundered deeper into the melee. Beneath her, Boris galloped valiantly, his makeshift sting poised to strike.

Melissa shouted in Tyler's ear.

"Do you feel that?"

Tyler sensed the vibrations of the battle as they transferred up from the baked earth through Boris' hooves to the armoured plates of his back. Death ships thumped to earth, contrapassi stomped and scorp riders clopped skittishly before galloping out from their lines.

Feeling a new, subtler reverberation she surveyed the ground.

"Subs!" cried Melissa.

Tugging on Boris' reins, Tyler barked orders.

"ALBERT, FALL BACK! KYLIE, FALL BACK! RETREAT! RETREAT!"

Boris slowed and trotted to a skidding halt that sent a cloud of dust and dirt into the air. Either side of Tyler, her captains sensed her agitation. They waved the retreat and bellowed orders as Boris scuttled backwards, his pincers poised to defend. The ghost army responded, disengaging and withdrawing warily while their puzzled opponents pressed eagerly into the breach.

The vibrations intensified until the first subterranean burst open the ground before Tyler. Squealing, it thrashed in search of food and found scorp riders and their mounts, the sky mariners and grey coats. All those in reach fell prey to the pincers of the giant snake as others breached to feed.

The remaining contrapassi rushed in to battle the subs. Bullets and blades ricocheted from the subs' invincible bony pincers and plates. More and more broke from the ground to writhe with deadly force, pockmarking the battleground.

On the tower top, Tribulantis stepped up to the battlements witnessing the slaughter below. Sweeping his clawed hands into the air, he uttered a word.

His eager liliths launched.

*

Weaver and the three sharpshooters flanked the battle, cloaked in night by their grip on Lucy.

She led them clear of the fighting towards the rear of the enemy ranks where the twisted trees grew. One by one, the shooters disengaged from the half-ghost dark sister's power to hide behind the broader trees.

Atop the tower, demons watched from the battlements. As the sharpshooters took aim, Tribulantis spoke another command and the first of the demons launched, bat-like, to swoop to the battle below.

"Now!" said Lucy, hoping to reach the shooters without giving away her position. "Before they all fly!"

A volley of shots rang from the trees. A demon on the battlements hissed as a bullet ricocheted from the stone inches from him.

A second demon took to the air.

Weaver squeezed the trigger of his rifle and the first demon fell, shrieking into the sprawling fight.

*

The battle raged. A scatter of liliths reached the subs to jet their fire. In moments, almost every sub squealed in torment, ablaze. Those that could retreated into the ground and Tyler skirted the flames as Boris loped closer to the tower.

Nearby, Kylie ran.

"The witch's army is among them."

"But where's the witch?" Tyler disengaged an empty clip and snapped a full one into her rifle. "Last mag. I'd hoped to get further by now."

"Don't worry. You still have Boris protecting you."

Boris' pincers shielded his riders from most of the incoming missiles. Bullets ricocheted from his shell and the enemy ahead parted at his approach. A burning arrow thumped into a claw but if he noticed, Tyler could not tell. He continued, thundering into the enemy lines, stabbing and lashing with his steel sting, and chomping with his pincers at any foolish enough to venture into reach.

Ahead, an enemy scorp rider took note and wheeled

his mount from the cavalry line to engage.

His contrapassi commander roared and ordered the entire troop to ride. Several hundred riders plodded out as most of the liliths, their fire spent, returned to their roosts while those remaining over the battle spluttered ineffective flames.

Tyler aimed at the approaching rider and emptied her magazine in one continuous blast.

Unabated, the rider approached.

One Eye

The rider drew a scimitar as bullets rebounded from the glossy armour of his mount's shielding pincers.

"Hold on, Mel!" Tyler checked fruitlessly for more ammunition as Melissa braced herself for the coming clash. Her fingers gripped the handle of Lucy's Glock and she drew it, quickly emptying the chambers. "I'm out!"

The rider speeded into a gallop as, all around, grey coats fell at her army's gunfire. She resisted the temptation to look back and see how many of her own were falling. She could not afford to. Would not allow it.

"Here." Melissa passed her P99.

The rider cantered closer, slowing to weigh his opponent while impatiently drawing his blade in circles. Tyler steadied her aim with a hand on her wrist, feeling the hate from his gaze.

Why do *they hate us so much? Why so cruel?*

She teased the trigger, the gun feeling good, no, *right* in her hand.

Make it count!

Targeting the rider's eyes, she waited for the slight, rhythmic dip of the scorp's pincers and gently squeezed the trigger.

Ten metres.

Tap.

Her shot zipped past the rider's tufted ear. Again she timed her shots with the scorp's gait.

Seven metres.

Tap.

Five.

Tap.

The rider reeled, blood pulsing from a blown eye socket.

Still he came. One-eyed. Hungry for slaughter.

Close now, his stark features glowered. A generous scatter of scars marked his skin, the fur expunged, never to regrow. Clawed fingers were missing from the hand that grasped the reins, and a deep dent pitted the bone over his remaining eye. A bandage supported the elbow of his sword arm. A colossal, battered thug, he bore his wounds like trophies.

The wounded eye was nothing. Little more than a minor irritation to shrug off.

Three metres.

The oncoming scorp raised its sting high.

Two.

One.

The scorps clashed, lunging and snapping, withdrawing to circle, only to skitter in to spar again. Behind the claws, One Eye swung his sword at Boris, hacking at his claws and scarring his armour.

Tap, tap.

Click.

Out of ammo.

"Tyler!" Yakubu appeared at her side and thrust a sword towards her, pommel first. Catch!" He tossed the sword and Tyler snatched it from the air as Boris tired, dropping his guard to retreat.

Through the opening, One Eye stabbed. She parried the blow and readied for the next as One Eye withdrew.

Further into the field, death ships burned. Trailing smoke, one fell from the sky to crash with explosive force, smothering those nearby in flame. Shrill screams rose above the din of battle.

Albert pushed through the crush to Tyler.

"Missy, burn the ships! It's our only chance!"

Around Tyler, blazing arrows stippled the ground and the fallen. Noticing the bow slung at Yakubu's shoulder, she pointed to the scatter of ships hovering over the enemy army.

"Fire those ships!"

Yakubu nodded and ran to claim more arrows.

"Albert, spread the word."

Albert re-entered the throng in search of a bow.

The rider pressed in again and Boris fended away strikes from his opponent's sting. Tyler leaned aside as the sting plunged in through a gap between Boris' claws. Boris snipped at the enemy's tail, clamping it. Melissa shrieked, the sting halting an inch from her nose.

Tyler swung Wulfric's sword, hacking into the trapped tail.

The injured scorp squealed and pulled back, ripping his tail free, the sting hanging limply from an oozing wound.

One Eye lent closer from his saddle and growled.

"I'm not done with you." Turning his mount, he retreated while Tyler caught her breath.

*

"RUN!" screamed Lucy.

Weaver turned.

We've been spotted.

Beyond the treeline, a lilith folded its wings and clawed the ground. It screeched and, sweeping her head, yawned to gush flame across the trees. Weaver and the other shooters fled as the burst of fire rose, leaving behind a dozen burning trees.

They ran deeper into the twisted trees and gathered to fall once more beneath the *Cloak of Night*. Drawing air and shrieking, the lilith stalked after them and let fly a second burst of fire. Bathed in heat, the camouflaged shooters backed further away.

"Weaver, Mr Goodwin–" whispered Lucy.

"One moment." Weaver reloaded while Lucy maintained a connection. On her other side, Mr Goodwin chambered a round.

"Ready."

Weaver gave the okay signal.

The lilith stalked closer and drew breath, preparing for another firing.

"The neck, remember? Now!"

Weaver aimed and sent a bullet into the side of the lilith's neck. Mr Goodwin's shot blew a hole in her throat. She gasped, spluttering fire and swayed briefly before keeling to the ground amid the burning trees.

*

Endlessly jolted and clinging precariously, Melissa studied the battle ahead. A faint bluish hue caught her eye and, squinting, she found others the same, dispersed to the rear and throughout the remaining expanse of grey coats.

"Gloves."

Tyler saw them, too.

"Klaus, your field glasses."

With the last of his bullets, Klaus felled a gang of grey coats who ventured too close, and tossed her the glasses. The sound of gunfire lessened as, from both sides, others ran dry of ammunition. Tyler focused onto the clearing of the tower's slope where Tribulantis had had the twisted trees felled. There the gloves lurked among reserve troops.

"Adolf Eichmann and Reinhard Heydrich."

Again Melissa lifted the ring to command her reveries.

"Divide. Those at the front remain to defend. The rest of you forge a path to Reinhard Heydrich."

Obediently, the rear half of her reveries turned to skirt the others and bore into the enemy line.

Tyler didn't recognise several of the other gloves, but she stared at two half-ghosts standing with them.

"Goebbels and Himmler. All our hard work and they're back again. No doubt Bagshot's with them somewhere."

"Tribulantis has brought them up from the oubliette," said Melissa.

Tyler used the glasses again. "The gloves are commanding the troops. Tribulantis has made them his captains."

"Everyone likes a promotion."

"Where's Yakubu?"

Melissa pointed him out among a tight cluster of fighting men nearby. "He's hemmed in."

Pressed into a close-quarter standoff, Yakubu had been forced to abandon his charge to fire the ships.

"Here." Tyler passed Wulfric's sword.

Melissa took the blade awkwardly and stared at it, dumbfounded.

"What do you expect me to do with this?"

"Boris will look after you. I have a job to do."

Tyler climbed to her feet on Boris' back and, unfurling her wings, launched as Melissa called after her.

"Tyler!"

Tyler drove hard into a steep climb, speeding over the battle towards the ships. From their heights, sky mariners continued to rain arrows upon her troops below. She ascended beyond range before closing on the ships and streaking down to flash between their flanks, making sure to brush every sail with the tips of her flaming wings. The sails roared into flame and soon many of the sky mariners hurried to lower their vessels in a race again the consuming fires.

She rose to assess her handiwork. Flames leapt from sailcloth to rope, from rigging to masts and the decks. Kegs of gunpowder exploded, blowing holes in gunwales and gun decks, pitching ships to the ground. Archers and gunners fell to their deaths, thumping into the ground ranks. A few sky mariners dropped ropes to escape, descending hand over hand. Contrapassi captains ordered archers to shoot, felling the deserters. More orders followed.

"No more fire. Arrows only!"

A little too late for that, don't you think?

Around fifty vessels burned in all, the crews of those still airborne occupied with landing and firefighting.

There were plenty more. She dived again igniting another row. Six more of the ships kindled.

They knew her now, had spotted her fleeting light against the sky and targeted her. Again and again she darted, dodging arrows and tipping sails with embers that grew and swelled. Several untouched ships abandoned the battle as the number of fires mounted. Now, a hundred or so ships blazed as the sky darkened with their ash and smoke.

Yet hundreds remained unreached. She turned in the sky and aimed for them.

The boom of cannons shook the air. The earlier fires reaped a harvest, ships thumping into the crush of enemy ranks. Engines exploded and hulls splintered, engulfing large swathes of the enemy.

She darted faster, tiring but determined to finish the job. Slowly, the fleet of unfired ships depleted. More turned to sail from the battle, hoping to reach a safe distance.

One final dive to finish the job.

Nearing the first in a new line of ships, a searing pain bolted through her side as an arrow lodged between her ribs. Her hope drained. Her wings folded and vanished. Tyler dropped from the sky. She clutched at the gash, her fingers folding around the protruding shaft, slippery with blood.

Beneath her, Adolf Eichmann waited, a malignant smile stretching his lips.

Eichmann

Eichmann traced Tyler's descent and ordered his men to form a circle.

Tyler tumbled through smoke and ash struggling to focus through the pain in her side. As the ground rushed up to meet her and stormtroopers scuttled aside, she knew only one thing that might save her.

Hope.

She hoped. Hoped for wings. Hoped for help. Hoped for victory against brutal odds.

A flutter of flame rekindled between her shoulders, slowing her fall as she slammed to the ground.

*

In disbelief, Melissa watched from afar as Tyler desperately attempted to arrest her descent with the

369

splutter of her failing wings.

"NOOO!"

Tyler vanished into the midst of the grey coats as they cheered. Words drifted to Melissa from across the field.

"It's the Hope Bringer."

"We have her. We have the Hope Bringer!"

"The battle is won."

"Victory. Victory is ours!"

These chants she heard and understood in a variety of languages.

Ships continued to fall, exploding on the ground, but those celebrating paid no heed. Shoving stormtroopers aside, a contrapasso entered the ring. With one hand he grabbed Tyler's shirt, hauled her limp body into the air and roared.

"Victory to Tribulantis!"

The melee before Melissa and Boris parted and One Eye rode out. Beneath him a new scorp mount clopped lithely over the fallen. A few paces from Boris, he paused. One Eye fixed upon Melissa and growled.

"Where is she?"

Swallowing tears and gritting her teeth, Melissa faced him.

"Gone. Somewhere you'll never find her."

One Eye turned his mount to investigate the din from his rejoicing troops. He sneered.

"Already dead." Surprised, yet satisfied. "The Hope Bringer is no more."

Boris lunged. His makeshift sting slipped by the new mount's defences and pierced One Eye, armour, hide and flesh. Clashing pincers with the angered scorp, Boris withdrew as One Eye clutched at his death wound.

*

A change spawned on the killing ground as the army of the Black Sun relinquished war to celebrate. Numerous grey coats retreated with chants of victory, raising high their Black Sun banners. Scorp riders turned back and the Hope Bringer's decimated army paused to survey their wreckage as, across the wavering front line, the battlers quelled. Exchanging wary glances, they parted. Where the reanimated dead remained, the fight continued. Contrapassi swiped at skeletal warriors, dashing bones to shards. Grey coats bled dry their guns and fell beneath the undead tide.

*

"Put her down. *I* shall present her to Tribulantis," Eichmann ordered the contrapasso.

The beast grunted and lowered Tyler to slump at his feet like a rag doll.

Eichmann stepped forward and stooped to examine her as the contrapasso stepped away.

"Not dead. Not yet, at least."

He retrieved the dark sister and immediately switched from *Mortal Remains* to the fylfot and back again. Throughout the field, the waring undead stilled and turned to face him, awaiting his command. Raising the dark sister, Eichmann pointed to his enemies across the battlefield.

"KILL THEM. KILL THEM ALL!"

*

As the army of the Black Sun fell back the undead force charged out, a storm of rattling bones and decaying flesh. Some had lost their heads, others entire limbs. All clambered on.

Klaus had witnessed Tyler's fateful dive and refused to retreat. He rallied those around him as others turned to flee.

"STAND YOUR GROUND! PREPARE TO FIGHT!"

The Hope Bringer's army turned as the undead approached. Those lacking weapons armed themselves with salvaged long bones or the blades of the fallen. Klaus and his phalanx quickened to reform their lines. Behind the undead flood, the Witch Queen's army and the contrapassi fled the field as more of the fired ships landed like bombs.

*

Nearby, Lucy and the sharpshooters watched from the trees.

"Wait here." Camouflaged by the *Cloak of Night,* Lucy left them and stole out into the withdrawing enemy ranks.

*

Eichmann addressed the surrounding grey coats.

"Streifen der rüstung. Tragen sie."

Four stripped Tyler of her armour and hoisted her onto their shoulders. They followed Eichmann towards Dun Bharraich's walls.

Closer to the tower wall the gloves gathered to view their prize. Other prisoners of war, those wanted for questioning and bound for special treatment, were thrown unceremoniously into iron cages. A guard opened the door to one reserved for Tyler. Her bearers lowered her and swung her into the cage. They laughed as she crashed against the bars of the floor and the cage end, her neck crunching.

The gloves applauded, clapping each other on their backs and exchanging congratulations. Grey coats closed in to beat her with the butts of their guns through the bars to spit, jeer and tear her clothes as she lay unmoving.

Eichmann called order as the guard closed and locked the cage door.

"Endlich, comrades, the deed is done! This battle is over and we have won. Tribulantis will receive our trophy and our rewards will be great. When the war is won he will give us lands across the globe, entire continents to rule and we shall live like kings in the New Vision Frontiers. Those insignificant pockets of surviving Jews will be erased from the surface of our planet, along with every other infestation of subhuman. Our children, a perfect breed, shall inherit the Earth."

Again the gloves applauded.

Eichmann quietened them with a smooth gesture.

"Bring sie."

Stormtroopers hefted the corners of the cage and carried Tyler amid a triumphant procession. At Dun Bharraich's portcullis they stopped, lowering the cage to the ground at another gesture from Eichmann. He called to guards in the tower.

"Öfftnen."

*

Lucy dodged between soldiers to reach Tyler's cage.

Heaved by the ropes and pulleys concealed behind the tower's thick masonry, the heavy gate creaked slowly upwards.

While the gloves and grey coats watched the portcullis, Lucy dropped to her knees at the side of the cage. Wincing at the bloodied state of Tyler, she took Ruth's ghost contrap from her shirt and set it to the *Safeguarding Skull*. She slipped the chain around Tyler's neck, and tucked the contrap into Tyler's ragged shirt.

As Lucy crawled away, Tyler felt the contrap pulse, and stirred. She opened her eyes, forcing herself to sit up while rubbing at her aching head and neck. The pain in her side had doubled. The arrow, having driven deeper into her flesh during her landing in the cage, was deeply embedded. Senses reeling, she tested the bars of the cage and glared at her captors.

Beyond her bars the true dark sister hung from Eichmann's neck as he berated the guards beyond the portcullis.

"Schnell! Schnell!"

She scanned the horrors of the battlefield. A central phalanx fought while on each flank the dead pursued her army.

Hopeless. No. Never hopeless. Find hope. Summon hope.

An insect landed on her forearm. She stared at it. Not an insect, a NanoSect spy drone watching her.

Chapman's close!

Tyler felt the weight of the ghost contrap against her skin. She slipped a hand into her shirt, fingers curling to enfold its cool silver casing, and risked a clandestine glance.

Ruth's ghost contrap! But how?

Scanning her captors she found the tell-tale flicker of shadow and light.

Lucy!

She crawled to the cage door and switched to the *Ghost Portal.* Brandishing Ruth's contrap she targeted Eichmann, gasping the command through her renewed pain.

"Phas-matis lic-entia."

Blue plasm shrilled the air. A wordless, surprised sound escaped Eichmann's lips as his eyes widened: *Another contrap! But...?*

The unnatural light flashed, quick and keen. Eichmann's spirit separated from his gloved body and spiralled into the crystal. It returned nearby in a circling flow, skin no longer a shade of iridescent blue but translucent, reduced to a half-ghost form like the other ghosts. Where he had stood, a naked schoolboy now gawped at his surroundings. A moment later the boy vanished.

*

Lucy grabbed Harry McGrath, sharing her camouflage. Dragging him by the elbow, she guided him around the troops to skirt the wall and head for the trees where she thrust him towards Weaver.

"Get him out of here!"

*

Tyler wiped a trickle of blood from her eye.

One down.

Eichmann examined his translucent hand, frowned, and stamped across to open his palm.

"You are trapped, wounded and unarmed, Fräulein. Hand it over."

Tyler backed into the centre of the cage.

"You want it, come and get it. Phasmatis licentia." The blue essence streaked and fizzed. She shouted over a maelstrom as the contrap gorged the air. "What's wrong, Adolf? Not so perfect anymore?"

Eichmann drew his sidearm, aimed at her head and squeezed. The Luger clicked harmlessly. Several of the gloves backed away.

"Out of bullets?" said Tyler. "Me, too."

Eichmann procured a pistol from a nearby subordinate and tried again.

Click.

"That's the problem with guns. Eventually they all run dry." Tyler searched for Heydrich.

Gone, but where?

Blue lightning flew. A second glove sparked into the crystal, only to return a half-ghost version of his former self. In his place, a stunned girl remained, fear darting her eyes.

"Run!" cried Tyler as the contrap tugged at other gloves within reach.

Enraged, Eichmann stamped and pointed. "SHOOT HER!" He threw his gun at her, bellowing furiously when it bounced from the cage bars. "KILL HER NOW!"

In mid-flight, a third glove succumbed as stormtroopers raised their rifles.

A fourth glove released its ghost.

A fifth followed.

Click. Click. Click.

The redeemed youths came to their senses as bewildered soldiers attempted to catch them.

Snatching the keys from the guard, Eichmann hurried to unlock the door as Tyler swept the contrap around, releasing more and more of the gloved youths. As the last of them separated from his host, Eichmann hurled open the door and rushed in, an SS dagger glinting in his hand.

Tyler gritted her teeth, tore the arrow from her wound, and lunged. The unexpected shaft thumped into Eichmann's gut and he folded in the doorway. As he collapsed, she dashed his dagger aside and plucked the dark sister from his throat to sling it around her own.

She darted out of the cage as stormtroopers rushed for her and, buoyed by her success, unfurled her wings. She ascended, blinding those around her with the brightness of her fire, and dipped to collect the last of the redeemed, a girl she guessed was fourteen, hair the colour of damp straw, her skin a sickly hue.

Cradling her, Tyler climbed high as, amid the confusion below, the other naked teens vanished one by one with Lucy's touch. She passed over the retreating enemy ranks and reached the front line where the *Mortal Remains* wavered, their allegiance uncertain.

"What's your name?"

The girl in her arms twisted to look at Tyler before staring at the mesmerising hordes far below on the pockmarked land.

"Jmenuji se Agnesa."

"Agnesa, you're going to be all right. I'm taking you to a friend who's going to look after you."

Soaring over her army she located Melissa astride Boris and set down to release the girl into Melissa's care.

"Tyler, I thought you were..." Melissa's gaze dropped to Tyler's bloodied side. "You're injured. Let me dress the wound."

"No time. Melissa, this is Agnesa. Look after her." Tyler stooped to tear a bloodstained shirt from a fallen half-ghost and tossed it to Agnesa. "Put this on."

Grabbing the dark sister, Tyler held it high and circled.

"Turn again! Your enemies await you in the tower!"

The undead turned back towards Dun Bharraich and with renewed battle cries, charged once more.

Melissa pointed between the armies as the dust settled. A solitary truck rambled over the ruins, kicking up a tail of dirt to cloud the air. In the sky beyond, thunderous clouds lightened to billow brightly. Tyler set Ruth's contrap to the *Present Eye* and focused. Lowering the contrap, she squinted before peering again through the ghostly crystal.

"Mel, you have to see this."

Angel Blood

Melissa accepted the contrap and squinted through the lens at the approaching army truck. She telescoped closer in. In the driver's seat Freddy Carter gripped the wheel and bounced as the tyres bumped over rubble. Dark glasses shaded his eyes from the growing overhead glare.

Shifting view she watched a multitude of seraphim break the cloud to bathe the land in blinding light. Murmurs of awe rippled across Tyler's ground army as observers shielded their eyes. On the slopes of Dun Bharraich, panicked shouts arose and foot soldiers fled in a chaotic stampede.

Tribulantis viewed the oncoming angelic army and cursed from the battlements. He ordered his liliths to fly and called down to his troops.

"Fight, or perish at my hands, you cowards." He summoned his demons. "Princes, to arms!" Steel shrieked as demons across the tower top unsheathed their blades and took flight. Tribulantis paced, trepidation clouding his features. "Show them the might of infernal steel!"

Unperturbed, the contrapassi stood their ground, preparing a keen reception for the newcomers.

Waiting at the fringes, the lingering death ships that had avoided Tyler's fire now belched copious fumes as the sky mariners stoked engines and steered back to war.

As Freddy's truck rumbled in, the seraphim overtook him and divided, some veering down to the field while others flew on to meet the liliths mid-air. Where one or two seraphim flew apart from the rest, their forms could be seen more clearly than the radiant mass. Their wings, an easy match for any lilith's, thundered the air with robust, white feathers and Tyler glimpsed white armour, metallic and reflecting the light that emanated from their skin, hair and eyes. In contrast to the variety of contrapassi weapons, the seraphim wielded only two-edged swords, cast of the same bright metal, the blades flashing with each swing and thrust.

They clashed, bearing down upon the eager contrapassi and timorous half-ghosts as a second wave of battle unfolded.

More vehicles rumbled out of the distant haze. White Jeeps and trucks jostled over boulders and debris while tanks clattered relentlessly on.

Tyler took back Ruth's contrap and studied the vehicles and their black lettering: UN. "Chapman's brought the United Nations." She searched the figures advancing around the vehicles and recognised the white logo on their black hoodies. "And TAAN are here, a whole army of volunteers."

"One of my messages must have got through."

A tank shell drowned Melissa's voice, bursting from the lead tank to annihilate a patch of slope along with a dozen enemy soldiers.

"Mel, take Agnesa and get out of here. I need Boris one last time."

Melissa slid from Boris' back and helped Agnesa down.

Tyler grabbed a fallen spear and mounted up. Ahead, with a stretch of her warriors in between, Klaus led a new charge. Spurring Boris and levelling her spear, lance-like, Tyler rode in to join the fight as more shells erupted to blow holes in the enemy.

Albert pressed through warriors to run at her side, shouting.

"Missy, ya'can't fly off like that! You'll be shot an' killed." He glared at her so ferociously that, even now mid-charge, apprehension shook her. He ran, gasping for breath and clutching a single gallows blade, his only defence. Wondering how he had survived the battle so far, she slowed Boris and released his reins to offer her hand.

"Ride with me, Albert."

Albert's grimace softened. She pulled him up to straddle Boris at her back and felt his arms enfold her waist.

Liliths reached the seraphim horde, screeching fury and breathing their fiery jets. Superior masters of the air, the seraphim divided, spun, circled and dived to avoid the flames, vastly outmanoeuvring the liliths' cumbersome flight. Their purring blades clove limbs from bodies, heads from necks and speared their opponents.

Canon fire boomed from the death ships as contrapassi arrows once more filled the sky. Wounded seraphs darted for safe ground to quench fires, pluck arrows and tend to wounds.

Tanks cranked in from the side and a shell blasted a chunk of the tower wall apart.

Klaus struck the front ranks, slicing into the enemy with a borrowed sword. Tyler and the rest ploughed in to a fight of blades, arrows and spears, driving ever nearer to the tower. Supporting fire from the rambling vehicles smattered into the enemy's flank while seraphim slew abundantly.

Meeting another scorp rider Boris held the pair at bay, scuttling left and right in a strange pincer dance. The rider thrust a spear and Boris retreated squealing as the spear lodged deep in the shell of a claw.

Tyler launched her spear at the contrapasso. It flew fast and straight, puncturing the rider's breastplate and piercing his heart. The contrapasso slumped sideways, dragging on reins and his scorp veered away.

Tyler slid down and with a boot against his shell, tugged the contrapassi spear free. Boris groaned. She saw other damage. Across the front of his pincers an array of wounds bore witness to his bravery. Glancing bullets had dimpled the hard surface of his shell and a dozen had penetrated, the wounds oozing blood like rivulets of treacle. Blades had cut numerous slices amid a pattern of welts and weeping gashes, and a dozen arrows jutted at various angles like pins in a cushion.

"Oh, Boris. Look what they've done to you." Beyond her view, tank shells boomed amid the enemy troops.

Briefly she leant against a pincer and smoothed what

was left of his battered shell.

"Missy! Incoming!" Albert warned her.

Swiping a sword from the ground, she sliced away the protruding arrow shafts and remounted. Winding the reins in her sword hand, she levelled her new, weightier spear and rode back into the enemy lines.

With Klaus and Boris driving in at the centre and the seraphim cutting swathes above and to the sides, a wedge eroded the army of the Black Sun.

Gaining ground, Tyler fixed her sights upon Dun Bharraich's iron gate.

*

Lucy collected the redeemed youths one by one and, leaving the grey coats behind, ushered them between contrapassi warriors, scorp riders and the ragtag remnant of the Witch Queen's soldiers. She gathered the youths in the trees where Weaver, Mr Goodwin and the other sharpshooters picked off any enemies who noticed their presence.

"We have to get these kids to safety," said Weaver, one eye trained on a trooper straying too close to their sheltering trees.

Lucy switched from *Cloak of Night* to briefly appear before him.

"Stick with me." Urgently, she showed the youths the half-ghost dark sister. "This will hide you as long as you're touching me. Stay close and hold tight. Move fast. We've a long way to go."

The silent circle of petrified faces nodded.

"Right, grab hold. Let's go."

Beneath the *Cloak of Night* once more, Lucy headed deeper into the trees before turning parallel to the battlefield. She ran out from cover and bent her path towards the rear of Tyler's army beyond range of bow and cannon, where she found Melissa and Agnesa. Lucy slowed and switched from *Cloak of Night*. Behind her the shooters watched for approaching threats, their rifles primed.

At Lucy's appearance Agnesa stepped back, stumbled and fell. Taking in the naked youths, Melissa helped Agnesa up.

"Mel, you'll have to take'em. I must get back."

"Leave them. Go!"

Lucy turned with the other sharpshooters and flicked the switch once more.

*

Seraphim descended at Tyler's side and an extraordinary voice sang with unearthly tones.

"Here rides the Hope Bringer!"

The sound reverberated with a range of pitches like a tuned chorus, though it came from the mouth of a single seraph.

Others heard and followed.

"We have found the one."

"Rally to the Hope Bringer."

"Protect the Hope Bringer."

Tyler did not feel like the Hope Bringer. All she felt was a nauseating pain from her arrow wound and a general sense of exhaustion. She had lost blood and it continued to flow, taking with it her strength and stamina.

Swooping from the sky the seraphim swarmed down, broadening the wedge as the enemy fell beneath a shock of white steel.

Tyler marvelled. *Angels, but not in the least angelic. More like, butchers of evil, keen enemies of hate.* Beneath the blinding light she glimpsed the flexing of muscle, the draw of formidable wings and the keen flicker of swords.

Yet they fell, wounded. Contrapassi spears dashed from the hordes and scorp riders slashed with swords and axes. They charged in from the back lines, their lances raised, thirsty for angel blood.

A seraph broke away from his fellows and found Tyler. As he neared, she saw blood dripping from a deep gash in his side.

"This will aid you." Dipping fingers in his blood, he smeared it onto the arrow wound at her waist. She felt the muscle and skin ripple and bind and gazed back at his brightness.

"Thank you."

The seraph's severe features softened briefly and with a single sweep of his wings he re-joined the fight.

The battle intensified as the concentrated wedge forced close combat. Scorp riders abandoned their primary weapons for shorter stabbing blades and a crush of bodies surged.

"Missy, we need to get in the tower but you mustn't fly to the top. You'll never make it."

Tyler glanced at the parapets where a vanguard of liliths and demons flew and archers loosed at any enemy who dared to venture within a hundred feet.

Albert's right. The dark sister's set to Mortal Remains and I can't use Cloak of Night without losing the dead army. Even if she tried, she doubted she'd get past the vanguard alive. Tribulantis would sense her approach, liliths would flood the arrow-heavy air with fire and she would be scorched like the blackened trees.

Boris staggered in the heaving crowd, carrying Tyler closer to another warring seraph.

"Get me to the gate!" she shouted, glimpsing the brilliant white light emanating from his eyes and quickly looking away to save her sight.

"To the gate!" The seraph trilled and a new cry chorused with numerous otherworldly voices.

"To the gate! To the gate!"

Tyler progressed steadily through the crush until she forged a place at the tip of the wedge. There, a new target entered her mind. Reinhard Heydrich's blue face flashed from the crowds, his hand raised in command of his reveries.

Tucking the lance under her arm, she fumbled in her pocket for her hard-won artefacts and clamped the little bag of bones to Ruth's contrap. A few more of Boris' tiring steps took her within range and Heydrich locked eyes and jolted towards her. Feeling the contrap's pull, he abandoned his commands to grope for a hold on those around him, slipping ever closer through them. He dropped beneath the mass, reappearing closer still, skidding along the fire-fog and clawing for a grip.

"Phasmatis licentia!"

Heydrich morphed into shining blue essence that twirled into the *Ghost Portal*. A second later he returned, now half-ghost, along with a wide-eyed girl with short blonde hair.

Susan Ellis!

Tyler spurred Boris into a gallop and levelled her lance.

"CHARGE!" She drove her mount harder, speeding to her target.

Her lance spitted Heydrich's half ghost through the chest. As a seraph swooped to seize Susan Ellis, Tyler released the spear, heavy with the ghoul's dead weight.

The portcullis loomed closer, a new problem. Eichmann had partially raised it but with the turning of the *Mortal Remains*, the arrival of the UN army and the pressing threat of the seraphim, the guards in the tower had closed the heavy gate.

Around her, friends and supporters fought. Tyler glimpsed Zebedee hacking at a squat contrapasso, his spidery frame driven back with each bone-jarring parry. With a sweeping stroke, the monster sideswiped Zebedee's sword, shearing the blade in two.

Tyler dealt a killing blow to a trooper and steered Boris around in an attempt to reach Zebedee.

Zebedee pressed in to gut the contrapasso with the remnant of his blade as the beast clubbed him with a fist. He fell as the contrapasso's returning sword strike impaled him.

Reaching out, Tyler screamed.

"ZEBEDEE! NO!"

The contrapasso pinned Zebedee with a clawed foot and withdrew his blade as Zebedee's lifeless eyes rolled skyward. The beast turned for Tyler as Klaus ran in to clash blades.

Boris chomped through a defence of grey coats, the last of those between Tyler and the gate. She searched the arch and portcullis for inspiration but found nothing that could help lift the iron barrier. Boris planted a claw under the lower rung and pushed. The gate jolted and shook. It popped up an inch and he pushed again, forcing his pincer further into the widening gap. He heaved and Tyler felt his entire body strain beneath her. He forced his other claw into another gap and the portcullis rose another few inches. Seraphs reached the archway and shouldered the iron, lifting alongside, and slowly a gap opened.

Clutching her sword, Tyler dismounted and rolled beneath the iron.

Murder Holes

Tyler watched the raging battle outside the gate. A wall of seraphim blocked her from the contrapassi, liliths and demons that hankered for her death.

Albert rolled in behind her and Boris and the seraphs released the gate. Albert scrambled to his feet.

"Albert, you didn't need to come."

"You think I'd be safer out there?" Albert jutted a thumb at the mob thrashing at the seraphim. "If you're goin', I'm goin'. Look out!" He tugged her aside as an arrow zipped from a niche high up in the gatehouse to skitter across the cobbled floor.

Lodged high in the guard chamber on a concealed stair, the archer, one of the Witch Queen's grimy half-ghosts, nocked another shaft.

Tyler and Albert scrambled for the oak door as a clattering on the other side told them they were too late. Together they stamped at the unmoving door.

"Albert, we're stuck."

*

Freddy shot the last of his bullets and veered his truck to edge the battlefield. Across the scatter of bodies and the staggering wounded he glimpsed Melissa shepherding her semi-naked flock away from the fighting. He steered around to head over and cranked on the handbrake as Melissa ran to him.

"Freddy!"

He shouted from his open window. "Get in. I'm taking you out of here."

Throwing open his door, he leapt down to lift the youths into the back of the truck with Melissa's help. Arrows stippled the roof and bonnet like the quills of a porcupine. A hole gaped in the passenger side windscreen where a cannon ball had entered and bullet holes riddled the panelling.

"You're injured." Melissa touched a bloodied rag that was wrapped around his arm. "Is there a first aid kit? That's not even a real bandage."

"It's nothing. A lot of the guys have worse."

With all on board, Melissa climbed into the cab with Freddy and he floored the accelerator.

"What happened to you at the dome?"

Freddy huffed as they bumped along to the sound of canon fire and shell strikes.

"Long story."

*

Tyler had her lock-picking tools but they were useless against the draw bolts and the bar beyond reach. The

390

archer released an awkward shot, his targets sheltered beneath the recessed arch of the door.

"Is there another way in?"

"No. I looked last time I was here. It's this or the roof."

"Look!" Albert glanced at the portcullis as seraphs outside heaved it upwards again. The gate rose a foot and the seraphs released. The gate hammered closed.

Lucy's voice startled Tyler.

"You could have waited."

"Lucy!"

"Yeah."

"Thank God! How did you get through?"

"I had words with a Seraph. They're trying to stop the dark army from using the gate. They're buying us time."

"We must get in."

"Do you have a plan if, by some miracle, we do?"

"Not really. You?"

"No. Make a surprise attack on Tribulantis? Something like that?"

"But he's immortal, I don't see how we can win. Not unless we had a Mordecai chain, which we don't."

A soft clicking sounded and, to one side, Lucy's vanishing camouflage revealed her, a gleaming Mordecai chain draped around her neck.

"You mean like this one?"

"How–"

"The seraphs brought it. Thought it might come in useful."

"Just one?"

"Don't complain. They're not exactly common around here."

"Okay, that's great, but we're still stuck. We have

three contraps between us. There must be something we can do."

"You'd think so." Lucy listened at the door. "Where is everyone?"

"I'm guessing Tribulantis saw the seraphim attack and sent everyone out to fight." Tyler set Ruth's contrap to the *Present Eye* and spied through the closed door. "A few guards and an archer pinning us down from the stairs. Apart from them and the vanguard on the roof, I think we have the place to ourselves."

"We could burn the door."

"It's oak. It would take hours."

"This is ridiculous. The tower was built for the protection of the contrap owners. You'd think it would come with a key or something."

"If there's a spell, Ruth didn't tell us."

Tyler scanned the ceiling, her eyes fixing upon five murder holes set high in the mortared stone vault.

"Albert, I don't suppose those holes are any smaller than your average chimney."

Albert peered up dubiously. "Yeah, I don't 'ave a great record with chimneys, but I'll try."

Tyler passed Ruth's contrap to him and began explaining the intricacies of steering with the *Flight* symbol.

"Al'right, al'right. I seen it done enough times." He took Ruth's contrap and switched to *Flight*.

"Wait." Lucy appeared again and handed the half-ghost dark sister to Albert. "You'll need this or the archer will see you. You'll have to deal with him and the guards on your way down."

Albert put the half-ghost dark sister around his neck, switched it to *Cloak of Night*, and pulled the lever of

Ruth's contrap clockwise to lift off from the floor.

Tyler and Lucy watched the barest trace of his shape flicker up to the central murder hole and a few moments later it vanished altogether.

Tyler leaned out to glimpse the archer's niche.

"The archer's moving." She glanced at a niche on the opposing side of the chamber, one from where they would be arrow fodder. The bowman skulked into place and nocked an arrow. "RUN!"

Lucy and Tyler sprinted to the other side where they flattened themselves against the wall. An arrow splintered against the cobbles at their feet. A cry echoed and the archer tumbled, dissolving into mist before reaching the cobbles. Tyler and Lucy returned to the door and waited. Shouts rose on the other side followed by several screams.

Iron and wood clanked. The door juddered and inched open.

"'elp me, then!" Albert's sooty face and cloth cap appeared in the gap as he heaved. With Tyler and Lucy shoving from the other side the door creaked wide enough for them to file through and they stood in the near darkness of the tower's spiralling stairway.

"Weapons check," whispered Tyler.

"Three gallows blades, a throwing knife and three in the clip." Lucy presented her blades having slung her rifle across her back to shoulder the chain. "You?"

"Just this." Tyler raised her sword.

Albert wiped his blade on his shirtsleeve.

"I still have my trusty gallows blade."

Of all the roughly-forged gallows blades he had encountered, this was one he had kept. It was evenly hammered, and narrower and longer than most others, and in his boyish hands it was like a short, agile sword.

"How do you rate our chances?" Tyler asked.

Lucy pulled a long face. "Three contraps, two ghosts, one Mordecai chain and a girl with flaming wings. Could be worse."

*

Freddy's passengers alighted at a hastily-erected UN checkpoint. Behind them, a line of military vehicles funnelled down the only surviving road for miles around: tanks, armoured personnel carriers, Land Rovers and med units bearing the red cross. Distant sounds drifted in. Gunfire. The chugging of helicopters and the screeches of liliths. A commander talked on a satellite phone while privates stood guard.

"Keep 'em coming. We've barely made a foothold. What's the ETA on air support?" The commander squinted at smoke rising from Dun Bharraich and scanned his surroundings, staring at the chaos. A few trees still clung to the soil but beyond that the landscape was like nothing he'd ever seen. The blasted corpses of jackal-headed giants littered the ground amid dusty ruins and rubble walls and the remains of other unnameable creatures lay scattered. Humans also numbered among the dead, but stranger still were those who remained alive. Seated in crashed cars, standing at random points, lying where they had fallen, people watched, silent and still, bound tightly in ghostly chains. "Yeah, ASAP. Who knows? Affirmative. You know what, Major? You really have to see this place to believe it."

Freddy placed a hand on Melissa's shoulder.

"We've taken back the land beyond this point. You'll be safe here. Find them something to eat. Try the soldiers. I'll come back soon."

"Freddy, you can't leave me again. Not now. I'm begging you. Don't go back."

Freddy glanced at the tower before clasping Melissa by the shoulders. "I can't stay here while Tyler, Klaus and the others risk their lives. I just can't. And these guys need your help." He gestured towards the youths, now kicking around the dirt scavenging for rags to wear. "I'm going for more ammo."

Pentacles

Explosions shook the walls of Dun Bharraich. Albert took a long look at Tyler's healing arrow wound and rubbed his chin.

"We'll 'ave to do somethin' about that before we go any further. Don't want you keeling over on us, do we?"

"Albert, it's fine."

Tentatively, Tyler climbed the stairs, her sword poised as a cloying odour invaded her nostrils.

Who knows what internal defences the demons and the Witch Queen have set in place?

Each carrying a contrap, Tyler, Albert and Lucy approached a shaft of hot light streaming through an arrow-slit. Tyler paused. Chalked on a stone step ahead, a line of pentacles gleamed. In and around them were drawn other strange symbols, unrecognisable numerals and stylised shapes.

"Where's Melissa when you need her?"

Lucy peered over Tyler's shoulder at the chalk.

"That can't be good."

"It's the witch's work." Albert pushed past to scrub with his bare feet, trying to erase them.

"Will that work?" asked Tyler.

"I don't know."

As though in answer, a rattling echoed down to silence them and an emerald light intensified, flickering higher up the staircase. Tyler crept on, craning to see around the curving inner wall. Shadows danced as she ascended and a slow, serpentine voice slithered to them, rebounding from the walls.

"Turn away or meet your doom."

"Don't listen to it," whispered Lucy.

Tyler climbed, hesitating when a phantasm armed with two swords glided into view, its upper half a muscular figure floating amid a wandering, emerald fire, its midriff dissolving into flames. It wore curving plate armour edged by the witch's unearthly light and, within its chest, a ball of the same light hovered; a replacement heart, a gift of the Witch Queen to her unhallowed creation. A tapering, aquiline face set with narrowed, shining eyes, fixed purposely upon the three.

"Retreat or perish," the phantasm uttered through unmoving lips while issuing a strange warning rattle like a cobra's. A forked tongue flickered from its mouth.

Tyler glanced at the symbols on the dark sister.

No help there. Not this time.

Fearful, she whispered to the others.

"At this juncture I'm open to suggestions."

Speechless, Lucy and Albert gawked at the oncoming

wraith.

Lucy grasped her Mordecai chain, preparing to cast it.

"No." Albert shook his head. "Don't waste your energy. "Somethin' tells me that won't work with this'un. Save them bullets, too."

"Who are you?" asked Tyler.

"I am Dread. I am Terror and I will consume you.

"I. AM. FEAR!"

Fear rattled his warning again and readied his twin swords, each lengthy blade broadening to a wide, butchering tip.

Tyler stepped back and raised her sword as Fear closed in.

"No!" Albert joined her. "Do not retreat. Give no ground but stab the 'eart! 'E's all smoke an' mirrors."

Throwing Albert a bewildered look, Tyler climbed another step, her outstretched arm and sword trembling.

Fear laughed, the sound entwining with his rattling. "You choose to die. Very well, I shall take your pretty head as a trophy and present it to the Witch Queen." He swooped to Tyler and lunged. She pressed in, awaiting the bite of searing blades while thrusting her sword upward. They clashed as Fear crossed his blades, sliding them upwards to sweep Tyler's aside. He lunged. Tyler stepped back, parried the blow and hacked at his flank. Fear met her strike with one blade and stabbed with the other. The sword entered her chest. An icy touch shivered through her and she looked down for the wound.

Fear's sword left no mark.

"He's a fake!"

Amazed, she attacked again. Straining forward and targeting a joint between plates where the heart shone brightest, she threaded the armour to pierce the pulsing light. Simultaneously, Fear's sword swept through Tyler's middle as his heart exploded with a subaudible boom that shook the tower's foundations.

Tyler recoiled glancing down in shock. His armour clattered to the steps as his light and upper body dispelled with a final rattle.

"A hoax."

"Illusion," said Albert.

"I wanted to turn back."

"Of course ya' did, Missy. That's how fear works."

"Get ready. There could be other guardians." Lucy speculated.

More of the green light appeared on the walls ahead.

"Here comes number two." Tyler took a defensive stance.

The second phantasm was miniscule compared to her predecessor. She came serenely and unarmed, a beguiling smile dressing her slender face. In the slight form of a child, she stepped lightly down the stairs, a picture of innocence and as palpable as Tyler. The green girl watched the newcomers briefly before sitting on a step.

Tyler approached, the tip of her blade edging towards the girl's shimmering chest where waves of gossamer fabric folded.

"Who are you?" Tyler asked, taking another step but finding an invisible barrier blocking her way, a barrier around the girl that prevented her or her sword from going any nearer.

"The *real* question is who are *you*?" the girl replied in a soft but churlish voice.

"My name is Tyler May. Who are you?"

The girl's smile broadened into a grin and she

laughed.

"But who is Tyler May? Who *is* she, *really*?" She locked eyes with Tyler.

Tyler trembled feeling the glare penetrate as it burned into her, boring deeper still, as though delving into the distant reaches of her soul. It searched her buried secrets and exhumed her innermost thoughts and feelings.

"A girl with an obsessive compulsion for doing the right thing. A girl on an impossible quest. A wasted life. Nothing more. In the end, Tyler May is just a feeble, empty-headed girl, soon to be an empty-headed corpse like so many others who have come before her. What can she truly hope to achieve? What if she fails? What if she backed the wrong side?" With each passing word the girl appeared to grow in stature.

"Don't listen to a word, Missy. You're all right."

"At least I have friends."

"Let's examine them, shall we. Lucy Denby..." The girl rose to her feet, notably taller than before, and aimed her gaze at Lucy. She smiled derisively. "Wait a minute. You lied. You said *friends*. Lucy does not have friends. Lucy does not need friends. Lucy's tough, a friend to no one. At best she's an annoyance, an irritation. Only good for killing. Lucy, the murderer."

"No, you're wrong," said Tyler. "She *is* my friend. Lucy would do anything for me. She would defend me to the last. She would, *did*, die to save me. You can't get a better friend than that. You're the liar. You're a fraud!"

The girl shrank several inches and turned her attention swiftly to Albert.

"Albert Goodwin. So serious, so loyal, so... intense. What a joke! A dead sweep's boy? He's not your friend.

He carries ulterior motives and always has. He's not your friend." She paused and with a hint of fear, tore her gaze from his.

"Don't listen, Missy! I *am* your friend. I swears it!"

"See how he begs for acceptance. He fears a truth I tell. Pathetic. What could such a lowborn ever do against Tribulantis, King of the Chasm?" Again the girl grew in stature, the hidden barrier extending to force Tyler back a step.

Tyler frowned.

"What do you mean he fears a truth? What truth?"

Albert paled.

"Don't listen, Missy. She's tryin' t' poison you against me!"

Once more the green girl laughed, now swelling to the size of an adult. She looked back into Tyler's eyes, delving again.

"His journey, his quest, did you really think he was here to defend you, to look after you, or help you? How foolish! Oh, he has his reasons, but they're nothing to do with you. Ignorant girl."

"What? Albert? What's she talking about?"

"It's lies, Missy. All lies! It's just that..."

"What?"

"It's both, truth be told. I 'as a quest o'sorts, an' part of it's ta' protect you. Don't mean I ain't ya' friend an' all, though. It don't mean I love you any less." Albert shoved past Tyler to approach the girl, an extraordinary light emanating from his essence. The girl retreated shrieking in pain as the light intensified.

Aghast, Tyler turned back to the shrinking girl.

"There. Of course, I have other friends, many of them, but they're not here right now and I'm glad. I hope they never have to meet the likes of you. You're a deceiver. You wouldn't know the truth if it..." Before her words died, the girl shrank to a pinpoint of light and vanished. The screaming ceased, leaving the three in silence.

The white light retreated into Albert and they climbed in near darkness.

"What *was* that?" asked Tyler.

"What?"

"That light."

"Oh, you means the Hallowed Light. Yeah, I'll tell you all about it later."

"Why later?"

"'Cause another of the witch's creations is close. I feels it."

Footsteps pre-empted the third phantasm's arrival as horrors plagued Tyler's mind. *A fearsome warrior of flame. A child sent to riddle us with doubt. What next?*

A slender, shapely figure wound seductively down the steps; an exquisitely formed woman, magnificent in the beauty of youth, face and hands of flawless, bronzed skin, finely patterned silks flowing from her shoulders over which her hair tumbled, a silky tone of copper. Repeating dabs of emerald in her robes matched the intense tone of her eyes. She smiled warmly in greeting and Tyler felt a physical tension dissolve.

"Don't trust a fing she says," whispered Albert at her shoulder.

"I am sent to welcome you." A liquid voice from a silver tongue. "Come in and join with us. The battle is done. You have passed the trials. We are victorious and you no longer need to fear. We will make room for you. Reward you. All you need do is turn from your path.

Turn from this unrealistic, preposterous course."

Tyler stared, listening for signs of the battle outside and hearing none. *Some conjuring trick, perhaps. Unless... Was it really over?* She tried to recall the last time she had heard the boom of the cannons through the walls.

"Your master wishes to strike all of my kind from the earth. Your mistress is a twisted hag who would torture and kill us. Rewarded? With murder, perhaps."

Silver Tongue frowned and the lines of her face deepened, giving her a more mature appearance.

"It is not so. Even now they would forgive. Here I am. Was I not sent to impart the news? Know this. Royalty begets privilege. Monarchs of the Chasm fashion rules at will."

"You're full of bull." Lucy lunged at Silver Tongue with a gallows blade, only to rebound as an emerald glint flickered from an impact with a second force field. Again a veil of age manifested briefly on the woman's features.

"You cannot destroy that which is immortal." The face smoothed back into youthfulness.

"Where there's a will," muttered Tyler.

Silver Tongue's laughter softened into a hum. "Hmmmm. We may find a way to pardon you and your noble companions. Come, kneel before the throne of the Black Sun and beg for mercy."

"I'm not kneeling to them. I'll fight them to my last breath. They're not worthy. We *will* overcome them and their kind."

The woman's skin creased.

"Tribulantis, your queen and their captains are guilty of crimes against humanity," said Lucy. "Their hate will die when we conquer them. And we *shall* conquer."

"But there is no way, no chance. Hark. The war is already won and you have lost. What hope can you now possibly harbour?" Skin tightened once more into youth at the sound of her words.

"Lies! We have the same hope we always had," said Tyler. "The same hope that brought us this far."

"We have the Hope Bringer," said Albert, his voice plummeting to a depth and resonance that Tyler had never before heard. The Hallowed Light arose within him to speak. "And we are but a few steps from our goal. Stand aside! We *shall* pass!"

Tyler stared at him.

Doesn't sound like Albert.

Lucy didn't appear to notice the change but continued the verbal assault on Silver Tongue, who aged by the second and released a scream that grew louder as she wizened. "Liar. Every word that passes your lips is a lie."

"You weren't sent to welcome us but to deceive us," added Tyler.

"Liar, liar, liar!"

Silver Tongue's flesh withered, shrinking onto bone as her beauty and youth drained. Where healthy skin had been, a thinning freckled layer now displayed the underlying veins, knotted sinew and bones. She shrank several inches as her back slumped into an arch.

"Spawn of the deceiver!" the voice of the Hallowed Light thundered.

Silver Tongue staggered backwards.

"You are incapable of speaking the truth."

She twisted bodily with a creaking of old bones and the popping of joints. She hissed, baring teeth that yellowed and cracked.

"You will perish and be gone!"

Silver Tongue's skin and flesh tightened, split and desiccated to dust on her crumbling bones. The hag's powdery remains fell in a heap of tattered rags.

Lucy stepped over the pile.

"Are you two coming or what?"

The Hallowed Light

Tyler and Albert followed the glimmering swing of Lucy's Mordecia chain up the stairs. Tyler paused to survey the battle through a hole blasted in the wall by a tank shell.

"Not *everything* she said was a lie."

Albert and Lucy joined her at the gap.

Fifty metres below, the Black Sun victors plundered the field. The dead lay scattered in and around the burning wrecks of death ships and the living remnant of her army stood frozen, bound by familiar glimmering chains.

Chained seraphim littered the site, their lights much diminished, some heaped where they had fallen from the sky. Bones of the *Mortal Remains* peppered the ground and those retaining their limbs leaned with reveries, silent and still, also trapped by the ghostly chains.

All fighting had ceased.

Tribulantis has played out his war and tired of the effort. Like a bored, spoiled child he has smashed his playthings to the ground with one stroke.

Tyler's stumbling spirits sank into gloom.

"Oh, God, the hag was right. It's all over."

Albert shook her. "It ain't over, Missy. Not by a long way. You said you'd fight to the last. Did ya' mean it, or were that all talk? I do 'ave a mission. Get me to the top."

Tyler glanced back at the carnage of battle before returning to his eyes. Eyes so young, so determined and full of love.

"Do it for me, Missy." He said softly.

"Okay." Taking his hand, she headed into the waiting gloom.

Reaching the first trapdoor Lucy pushed it open to climb through. Tyler and Albert followed her into the chamber where the table of plenty stood laden with fresh fruit, cheese, bread and water.

"Where is everyone?" Tyler walked to the table, her footsteps breaking the uncanny silence. Famished and yet nauseous, she forced down several grapes and a bite from a heel of crusty bread.

My last meal?

Listening intently, she sensed the stillness from the rooftop above.

It's as though the world awaits our arrival. What happens on the other side of that door? A firing squad? A hangman's jury?

"Who's going first?" She gripped her sword and glanced nervously at the upper door.

"Me, of course." Lucy approached the stairs. "You

two are far too valuable."

Tyler gave an ironic smile, emotion cracking her voice. "You're worth a hundred of me, Lucy. We wouldn't have made it without you. Not even *half* the way. This is the end. You get that? Once we're through that door it won't last long."

Lucy's eyes glazed and she stepped close to clasp Tyler tightly.

"Don't give up, Tyler. Don't you dare. You're the Hope Bringer. You hear me? Those ghosts fought and died for you, for your cause. Don't you dare make all that worthless by conceding. Never."

"You're nearly there, Missy. You can't lose hope now."

Tyler straightened and wiped her eyes.

"Promise," demanded Lucy.

Tyler nodded. "I promise."

Lucy brushed hair from Tyler's face. "You look a mess."

"So do you."

"Good, then let's go."

Albert passed Ruth's contrap to Tyler. "'Ere. You take this. You might need it."

"If you're sure." Tyler hung the ghost contrap around her neck and tucked it into her shirt with the dark sister.

Lucy set her contrap to *Cloak of Night* and Tyler did the same with the dark sister. When Tyler regained Albert's hand, all three were hidden and ready.

"We should have a plan," said Lucy.

Tyler twisted her mouth into something resembling a smile.

"Just be yourself. You'll do fine."

Lucy climbed the last few steps and shouldered the

trap. The door swung upwards and, squinting in hot light, the three ascended, climbing onto the rooftop.

Tyler turned around to take in a sea of expectant faces edging the battlements. Among them stood representatives from each of Tribulantis' cohorts: contrapassi, liliths, grey coats, spies of his Black Sun army and several of the witch's men. Among these, a scatter of chained and bloodied captives leaned, frozen in their last free moments of life, grotesque statues. One stretch of the battlements lay shattered from a missile strike, the floor scattered with blasted stone.

Seeking Tribulantis, she found a recently built plinth of stone steps that rose to a throne platform at the centre of the roof. To one side, encompassed by her emerald aura, Mary Cobbler watched, a sneer twisting her wizened face. On the parapets behind, demons observed. Tyler's gaze followed the steps to the summit where a boy of fourteen sat regarding her with amused interest.

Steven Lewis, the lad originally gloved with Josef Mengele, now possessed by the spirit of the oppressor, Tribulantis.

And he knows we've come.

As she watched, the possessed child rose from his throne to survey the tower top, a boy-king surveying the subjects of his newly-won kingdom.

And the almost-invisible intruders.

His lips cracked into a shrewd smile.

Laden with contempt, the oppressor's voice issued from the boy's mouth.

"Welcome, *Hope Bringer*. Welcome to your doom."

The demons on the parapets cackled.

With a flicker, the boy morphed into Mengele's form. "You have arrived safely, Fräulein May. Isn't that nice.

So, all our little games have come to this... this *magnificent* end." He raised his hands, gesturing towards the surrounding chaotic realm. "A fitting close to your days of interference, do you not think?"

Treading carefully, Tyler approached the throne steps.

Mengele whistled Shubert's *Serenade* and paced his platform. "You've been a minor inconvenience though, I must confess, an entertaining one."

She felt his eyes on her, as though she were plainly visible, as though she were utterly exposed before him.

"Are you at last ready to yield and die?"

A lilith descended to deposit a bloodied young woman before Tyler at the foot of the steps. The woman stirred and brushed blood-matted hair from her face as the lilith flew away with lazy wingbeats. Only then did Tyler recognise Melissa.

"NO!"

Breaking free from Albert she ran to Melissa.

Mengele extended an open palm.

"You will yield the dark sister now or witness the prolonged suffering of your friends, before I turn my attentions to you."

A circle of keen faces focused on Albert, now fully revealed. He turned on the spot, his blade outstretched. The demons shrieked. The cohorts laughed and jeered. A voice from the crowd rose above the witch's hiss.

"Stone him!"

They threw lumps of stone from the battlements that struck him, streaking his skin with wounds. The witch raised a hand and muttered a curse that contorted him while the others stopped throwing to watch.

"Albert Goodwin, I presume." Mengele morphed

411

briefly into the winged demon, Tribulantis, before settling into the shape of Hitler. "And one other's presence I sense. Surely it can be no other than Lucy Denby."

Albert vanished as Lucy reached him and grasped his hand. With her free arm she aimed her rifle and shot a valuable bullet into the witch's heart. At the foot of the steps, Mary Cobbler slumped to the floor, a hiss escaping her crumpled body as her green aura dispelled.

On the parapets the demons gabbled with outrage. The watchers gasped. Hitler snarled but stilled his restless cohorts with a calming gesture. Morphing back into demon form, Tribulantis aimed a clawed hand towards Lucy.

"Malum obligo!"

At his command a glimmering chain appeared, hurtling in the air. Lucy's Mordecai chain fell from her shoulders as the Malum chain engulfed her, pinning her arms to her sides, overpowering her contrap's magic and bringing her into clear view, mute and helpless. His camouflage gone, Albert studied his wounds and tried to retreat from the crowd, dragging a battered leg and leaving smears of blood.

Tyler tried a counter spell.

"Malum resolvo."

Lucy's chain remained tightly bound, the command ineffectual.

Tribulantis expelled a deep, reverberant laugh.

"The Malum chains cannot be so easily thwarted, child. They are not like the Mordecai chains that you cast about at one another like petty criticisms and personal gripes. No, these are different. They are true chains of judgement, chains of doom. Let those who are blameless throw off their chains and walk free." With mock apprehension, he watched Lucy, one more statue on display. "No? Oh. How disappointing. Lucy Denby, you must have been a *very* bad girl." He turned to Tyler's shadowed form. "You cannot win. It is time to hand back that which you stole."

Tyler glanced at the Modecia chain on the floor and considered rushing for it.

The cohorts edged closer to Albert.

Albert glared at Tribulantis. "You'll not win. You can never win."

"I have to admire your conviction, boy. Even now, at our crowning glory, our moment of victory, you stand firm. Words fail me. Look around you. What is it you see that *I* do not?"

"I sees hate. It spills from your eyes, pours from your mouth. Hate will never defeat love. It can't. Like I said, there ain't no way the likes of you can win."

Tribulantis smiled and shook his head.

"We'll see." Reaching out a claw, he uttered another command.

"Phasmatis tormentum."

An invisible power ripped Albert's blade from his grasp as he rose involuntarily into the air amid a crackling junction of Chasm lightning.

"ALBERT!" Tyler started towards him but already he had been lifted beyond reach. She spread her wings and flew, only to rebound as lightning struck her. She fell back onto the rooftop alongside Melissa, gasping.

The invisible force stretched Albert's body, throwing his head back and his arms out at his sides. His anguished scream echoed as Tribulantis carried him higher with a controlling claw.

"STOP IT!" Tyler glared from Albert to Tribulantis.

"PLEASE! STOP IT NOW!"

Melissa beckoned. Tyler crawled closer and stooped close as, barely conscious, Melissa muttered.

"I figured it out, the four symbols..." She lifted a trembling hand to point towards the contraps hanging from Tyler's neck, before passing out.

Great.

A hissing ball of yellow light encased Albert mid-air as veins of lightning cracked from the heavens into his tortured body. All around, thunder rolled the darkening clouds and shook the charged air.

Tyler staggered to her feet. She removed the dark sister, set it to the Brimstone Chasm and, fully visible, lowered it to the floor at the foot of the steps.

"Come and get it." She retreated several paces.

As Tribulantis stepped forward, she faced him and aimed Ruth's contrap.

"Phasmatis licentia."

Blue lightning flared into the crystal as the *Ghost Portal* reached for Tribulantis. Unfurling his wings, he flew back to avoid the contrap's draw and set down, morphing into Hitler and drawing his Luger. He waved away the acolytes who rushed forward to his aid.

"No! She's mine." Targeting Tyler with a steady hand, he fired.

The bullet ripped through the air and into Tyler's chest. She felt the searing missile tear through her skin, a rib and her right lung and choked as the lung bubbled air and blood. Falling to her knees she gazed in horror at Albert's frail body as he slowly fractured above her in the sky.

A white brilliance exploded from his core in stark, blinding beams. From high over the tower top it blazed across the land, the shafts wavering and growing as the cracks in his form widened and shredded.

The light struck the prisoners on the roof and their Malum chains began to smoke. Hissing, the ghostly iron links weakened, cracked and crumbled, falling away. The captives peered in wonder at the disintegrating chains that smouldered with fire-fog, broken on the floor. Where the light struck weapons they, too, crumbled. The doors in its path groaned, their locks and bolts melting as they were flung wide.

Tribulantis frowned as his vanguard cowered blindly in the glow.

"This cannot be!"

A cry arose from the freed prisoners as they ran to survey the land from the battlements. Wherever the light reached, the Malum chains decayed and across the battlefield below, free souls gawped.

"Malum obligo." Tribulantis summoned more chains that reeled from his claw but dissolved in the streaming light long before reaching their targets. In vain, he tried again. "Malum obligo. Malum obligo. MALUM OBLIGO!"

Tyler glanced down at the blood spreading and dripping from her shirt.

I'm dying.

She looked at Ruth's contrap in her hand. *The Safeguarding Skull would still save me, but...*

She placed the contrap onto the wound as shock flooded her thoughts.

I am the artefact. Angel's latest victim. Mengele's latest victim. Hitler's latest victim. Shot with a bullet from his own gun.

With ragged breaths she forced out the syllables.

"Phas-ma-tis li-cen-tia."

Her contrap quivered into life as the lightning re-kindled.

Tribulantis fled again, but was caught and dragged nearer, the draw strengthening each moment. As he slid towards the edge of the steps he transformed into his demonic form, hoping to overpower the contrap's draw. Failing, he slipped down the topmost steps, clawing at the polished stone.

The blinding, white light streamed on.

I will *release Steven Lewis.*

"No! The boy is mine!"

The contrap's storm drowned the demon's cry. Flailing, his blackened body melted into blue essence as the *Ghost Portal* sucked him, spiralling and flashing through the air, into the crystal. In his place Steven Lewis stood, a scared boy wearing only the contrap. Tribulantis re-emerged from Tyler's contrap to coalesce before her at the summit of the steps.

Freed from her Malum chain, Lucy retrieved the Mordecai chain and flung it at Tribulantis.

"Mordecai obligo."

The chain sped to Tribulantis and enfolded his body as he formed, clamping his wings and arms. He toppled backwards to land, cocooned on his platform.

Their master fallen, the demons and liliths took flight to escape the pulsing light while Steven Lewis gawped in horror at the bound demon. Tyler beckoned to him and he descended the steps to her. Taking the contrap from his neck, she stared at its circle of symbols and, swooning, staggered to the floor. At the centre, a ten-pointed star surrounded the switch, each point marking the position of an outer symbol.

A ten pointed star? No. Two pentacles, overlaid one

upon the other. Staring me in the face all this time. Two sister contraps, each with two pentacles. The four symbols. Thanks Onuris.

Taking the dark sister in her other hand she brought the sister contraps together, pentacles to pentacles.

Upon the meeting of the four symbols the pacts will reverse and spirit will be released.

They snapped together like magnets and the tower rocked as a pulse issued from the connecting sisters. Around the tower and throughout the land, the earth quaked. The elements of the Chasm distorted in a cosmic shift and a violent wind arose, growing swiftly into a hideous torrent that tore at the shapes of the *Brimstone Chasm*, the *Ghost Portal*, the living and the dead. Out on the battlefield, the reanimated dead collapsed and the ground opened to engulf their bones and mouldering flesh.

Tribulantis screamed a silent scream as piece by piece his domain dissolved. The reveries thinned to a paler translucence before vanishing. The half-ghosts followed, diminishing to mere traces and ebbing away amid the cacophonous lightning storm and a gale that blurred the world.

The distant citadel collapsed amid a rising cloud of fire-fog.

The *Tower of Doom* shifted and began a slow spiralling decline as the ground below devoured its height from the base up.

Tyler let her head rest on the rooftop, feeling the warm flagstones against her cheek and the tower's downward spin. Gasping for air, she glimpsed an enormous black sun that darkened to consume the sky. The orb blinked, shrank and, joined by a second, became a pair of soulless eyes. The demon's distorted face sneered down at the world and distanced until its entire winged form reared into view, rippling in the unearthly torrent.

Another furious orb followed, overshadowing all. This, too, shrank as the second demon of the contraps manifested. Roaring in fury at their five hundred year entrapment, the demons met and locked in a raging battle as the rushing maelstrom ripped apart the realms.

Closing her eyes to the realigning world, Tyler felt the pulse of her heart dwindle. The contraps in her hands crumbled to dust and were blown on the wind.

Sensing an ethereal presence, she felt her heart cease beating.

The Promise

A disembodied voice sounded in her head.

"It's al'right, Missy. It's over now."

Tyler couldn't speak, couldn't even open her eyes, so she listened as a cool numbness flooded her brain. Albert's face appeared in her mind as though he was stooped over her.

"Come on, Missy. It's time to go."

Go where?

"Home, of course. I can tell you now. You're dyin', so you're gonna 'ear it soon anyway when you gets the full knowledge. You're gonna like what comes next. Oh, yeah. You're gonna wake up in the Hallowed Light an' everyfin's gonna be right. We'll be reunited and we'll dine in style. The light will flood the furthest corners of every realm, and we'll feast together. S'gonna make the table o'plenty look like scraps, an' no mistake.

"The poor'll be wealthy. Greed'll be gone. Tears too! There ain't no cryin' where we're goin'. Ain't no suffering at all. No slaves. No cruelty. No hate. No killers. Only love. Everlasting peace and deep joy, friendship, kindness and *love*, whiter than snow. Love, bright as the sun!

"The old passes and the new begins. Ya' see? The Hallowed Light's gonna make everythin' al'right. All them bad fings is gonna go away forever.

"I done what I was sent to do. Now I gotta go. Sleep, Missy. Rest now.

"Gor blimey, they're tryin' t'bring ya' back! For sure! Did ya' feel that? Perhaps it ain't quite your time after all! I'll see you soon, though. Maybe in... seventy years or so?" Albert laughed, a small new sound brimming with lightness and promise. "Make good your days. And never forget, you's the Hope Bringer. Farewell, Missy."

Tyler's soul quickened as, again, an outward force lurched her heart.

Goodbye, Albert!

*

Soldiers and medics collected the wounded and unconscious while, in the back of an army ambulance, paramedics shocked Tyler's heart with the defibrillator and looked on. The monitor displayed an erratic pulse and the paramedics worked with an oxygen mask, tubes, dressings, needles and syringes. Air leaking from her right lung, collecting in a chest cavity, had collapsed the lung. They fought to compensate and correct the pressure and set in place an intravenous drip to get a dose of adrenaline into her blood.

Her heartbeat stabilised and, with a nod, the

paramedics tightened her straps for the long journey.

*

Tyler passed into coma for several days, hospitalised and monitored. On day three she roused, aware of a gentle pressure on her left hand.

Reclining in a bedside chair, Melissa blinked. She released Tyler's hand and pressed a button on the wall to call the nurse.

Tyler clicked her tongue dryly on the roof of her mouth and smelled disinfectant, boiled cabbage, latex, blood and a thousand other dubious scents.

"Water."

"Of course." Melissa poured from a plastic jug on the bedside unit and passed the cup. Tyler shuffled further up onto her pillows to sip.

"Thanks." She tentatively rubbed at her temples, a headache pounding.

"How do you feel?"

"Like I've been shot. Like I've slept for a week."

"Just four days."

Tyler handed back the cup.

The nurse arrived and smiled.

"Good. You're back with us. I'm sure you'll be up and about in no time. I just have to check a few things." The nurse fussed around, taking her pulse, shining a torch into her eyes and asking rudimentary questions.

"Dr Holland will visit shortly. I'll let him know you're awake." The nurse left.

"The others? Klaus, Lucy?" asked Tyler.

"The ghosts have all gone. Lucy, Weaver, every one. Klaus is okay. He took two bullets and will limp for a few months, but apart from that... Just as well he's built like a tank. He's watched over you every night since. He'll be gutted he missed you waking."

Tyler rested a hand on her bandaged chest and thought about Albert.

"I'm going to miss them. The ghosts, I mean. The good ones. Albert."

"Does it hurt?"

"It kind of aches. You were–"

"Injured." Melissa lifted her hair to reveal a dressing that stretched from the centre of her forehead to her right temple. "Just a scratch, courtesy of the lilith that snatched me. Oh, and a twisted ankle. It's nothing. *You* took a bullet to your lung. They tell me that for a few minutes you were clinically dead."

Tyler let her head rest back against the pillows and closed her eyes.

"I'm the risen dead."

"I'm glad you think it's funny. You could have used the *Safeguarding Skull.*"

"It seemed more important to destroy the contraps. They are gone, aren't they? And Tribulantis and his monsters?"

"All gone, along with the contraps and every element of the under realms. I watched it happen whilst slipping in and out of consciousness. The contraps' demons fought and everything changed. When it was over there was nothing left for miles but rubble and a bunch of bewildered survivors."

"How far did it spread?"

"An area sixty kilometres across, radiating from Jerusalem. Chapman and the UN troops were busy forming a perimeter in a failing attempt to halt its progress. It was spreading – would have eventually covered the globe – but you did it, Tyler. You stopped it by destroying the contraps for good."

"No.   *We* stopped it: you, Lucy, Albert, Klaus, Zebedee, Izabella and the others.   Even Onuris played his part."

Epilogue

Klaus lugged another packing box into the lounge and dumped it on top of the others. He prised back the flaps, lifted a stack of folded clothes and dug out a rack of ties.

"At last," he muttered before raising his voice. "You know we really should have waited until we at least settled in. He wouldn't have minded."

Tyler's voice reached him from the master bedroom.

"It was today or wait until July. I told you, the church was booked out on all our days off. Anyway, he'd appreciate the timing, two weeks before Christmas." Her footfalls on the stairs pre-empted her grand entrance. Tyler swirled into the room, demonstrating the float of her embroidered funeral dress. "That was the first time I met him."

Admiring every inch from her glossy stilettoes to the tips of her velveteen gloves, Klaus stepped back to make room as she slowed and stopped.

"No, no! Keep going. Please. You look amazing!" His teeth gleamed through a candid smile.

She narrowed her eyes.

"You don't look so bad yourself." She abandoned her dance in favour of an embrace and planted a firm kiss on his lips. Drawing away, she marvelled at the new brickwork around the fireplace and chimney flue. Fresh yellow paint gave the high-ceilinged room a welcoming warmth. She recalled the name on the tin: Sun Shower. Cream drapes fell from the window sides to match the suite with a simple but satisfying charm.

She glanced back to the chimney breast and sighed.

"Well, it took us a while but we found him."

The house in which Albert had died had a peculiar history. Tyler had dug until she had exhausted the records, but she had found enough to understand. Soon after Albert's demise and abandonment in the chimney, the owners had died. The new owners never lit a fire there. For the following fifty years it was used as a cold store house. No heating required. The premises passed into new hands and the next owners began renovating by knocking down a wall to join the parlour with the dining room. Needing only one fireplace they also bricked up Albert's, unknowingly entombing him for over a century.

"It's over now," said Klaus. "You'll have to move on sooner or later."

"And I will. I promise. After today."

"And then?"

"And then we have the rest of our lives. I feel I've missed out on a piece of my childhood. You'll forgive me if I spend a few years making up for it."

"I'll hold you to that."

"Hurry up. The taxi must be waiting."

Klaus threw his tie around his collar and hand in hand they left the house.

*

Melissa sat on the graveyard wall, absently swinging her legs. The rain had stopped an hour before and the earthy scent of freshly dug soil traced the chilled air.

"It was a good funeral, as funerals go."

At Melissa's side, Tyler sat watching crows fly. "I guess. Thanks for coming."

"Do you think he's happy? I mean where he's gone?

Wherever that is."

"Yeah. He's happy." Tyler smiled a furtive smile. "Show me the ring again. I still can't believe Freddy summoned the nerve to pop the question."

Melissa displayed a gold ring inset with a single gleaming diamond, large enough to catch the eye without being overly garish. On her middle finger the dull ring of gallows iron contrasted, a reminder of things done. She waggled her fingers making the diamond glitter and dance in the morning light.

"Very nice."

Tyler and Melissa viewed Lucy's grave.

"It's going to be strange without her."

"Yeah. She was one of a kind. You brought it, right?"

With a solitary nod Melissa took a cross from her jacket: two rusting gallows blades wired tightly together. "Here. You can do the honours."

Tyler took the cross and hopped down from the wall. She walked to Lucy's grave and stooped to press the base of the cross into the soft turf beneath the headstone. Straightening, she rubbed at her chest wound to ease an ache she feared might never go.

"Goodbye, Lucy. For now."

Books of the Tyler May Series

The Haunting of Tyler May
(book one)

The Thieves of Antiquity
(book two)

The Brimstone Chasm
(book three)

Gallows Iron
(book four)

Ghosts of Redemption
(book five)

Dawn of the Sister
(book six)

Follow the Tyler May series
www.tylermay.co.uk

Acknowledgements

Dawn of the Sister was edited by Edward Field.

Cover artwork and interior formatting by The Dream Loft.